Elite

MERCEDES LACKEY

HYPERION
LOS ANGELES • NEW YORK

Mississippi Mills
Public Library

Copyright © 2016 by Mercedes Lackey

All rights reserved. Published by Hyperion, an imprint of Disney Book Group.
No part of this book may be reproduced or transmitted in any form or by any means,
electronic or mechanical, including photocopying, recording, or by any information
storage and retrieval system, without written permission from the publisher.
For information address Hyperion, 125 West End Avenue,
New York, New York 10023.

Printed in the United States of America
First Hardcover Edition, September 2016
First Paperback Edition, September 2017
FAC-0254381-17202
Printed in the United States of America

This book is set in Adobe Devanagari, Anavio,
Blonde Fraktur/FontSpring; Gill Sans MT Std/Monotype
Designed by Marci Senders

Library of Congress Control Number for Hardcover: 2016010297
ISBN 978-1-4847-4784-1

Visit www.hyperionteens.com

SUSTAINABLE
FORESTRY
INITIATIVE

Certified Chain of Custody
Promoting Sustainable Forestry

www.sfiprogram.org
SFI-01054

The SFI label applies to the text stock

Dedicated to Emily Meehan and Laura Schreiber,
for absolute awesomeness

1

I LOOKED OVER MY shoulder, and fear hit me like a bolt of frozen lightning, because all I could see were teeth.

Hundreds and hundreds of shining white teeth, the smallest of them as long as my hand, the biggest as long as my whole arm, and all of them thin and needle sharp. The mouths holding those teeth were *much* too close.

Dusana and I were running at Dusana's top speed, and it didn't seem anywhere near fast enough. I made myself as small as I could on Dusana's back and tried to tell myself that I didn't actually feel the Drakken's hot, bitter breath on my neck.

Dusana could do more than run away from this horror chasing us; he could *bamph* both of us right out of there, leaving the Drakken frustrated and confused. But we didn't want the Drakken frustrated and confused, because the thing would just turn right back around to the agro-station and take out that frustration on the station and the handful of people inside it. Their power was out because the Drakken had destroyed first the transformer linking the station to the main grid, then the backup solar panels and their wiring. Now the electrocution field that would have protected them was gone, and we were their last hope for getting out of the situation alive. Drakken can and *do* tear entire concrete or reinforced metal buildings apart. All they need is a little seam or crack to get their claws into, and they dig and claw until they pull the toughest wall down.

So we were playing bait. We were a bit of meat on a string, and we were pulling the Drakken toward a trap.

Dusana's run was a lot smoother than a horse, even as he jumped over obstacles in the agri-field we were running through. I looked back over my shoulder again. I'd never been this close to a Drakken before, not even when one had been ravening alongside the train I was in. I hadn't known they had three mouths: the mouth you *see*, then another mouth inside of that coming out on a stalk, then *another* mouth inside of that one coming out on another stalk, the whole thing darting at what it wants to catch like a frog tongue. A tongue that's about half as long as the Drakken. Except instead of being sticky like a frog tongue, the end, the middle, and the beginning are all razor-sharp teeth. No wonder they were top predators among the Othersiders. No wonder they were able to drag victims right out of any shelter they found.

The mouth-tongue darted straight at me just as I looked, and I couldn't help myself, I *meeped* with stark terror and made myself even smaller as the last mouth snapped a few feet behind Dusana's hindquarters. That's not a view anyone wants to see, ever. My insides were so knotted up with panic that I felt sick, and I was shaking like I had a fever. But I was still thinking, still watching, still calculating, and still readying spells; that never goes away. I'm a Hunter: I can be throwing up with fear and still be ready to throw a dazzle spell or put up a Shield. I had both of those ready, just in case.

I *had* to be on Dusana's back, because while the Drakken *might* chase him, it would go over chasms and through buildings to get to *me*. Dusana was just another Othersider, probably something like the thing's normal prey, but Drakken on this side don't want normal prey—they want humans. Humans were the best things on the buffet to Drakken, and a magic wielder like me was a tightly packed, nutrient-dense bomb of manna.

We had to stay close, because if we got too far out ahead of it, the Drakken would start to lose interest and its attention would start to waver. I was only one tasty morsel. There were a dozen yummy bites back in the station. If we couldn't keep its focus on us, it'd remember that and go back for them.

Obviously, there was no way I was going to be able to take on a Drakken alone, not even with a pack of Hounds eleven strong. But I was heading right for some people who could do what I couldn't.

I spotted the markers they'd set out on the tops of two bushes at the same time Dusana did: two bandanas tied to branches. He somehow put on a burst of speed to get out of the smash zone, and I hung on for all I was worth, and just as we got past, right behind us I felt a blast of air shove us forward and heard a *huge*, concussive *thump*.

Dusana skidded to a halt and pivoted on his forelegs at the

same time so we could both see what was happening. The Drakken was frozen in midleap. I averted my eyes and opened up with the light-dazzling spells I'd had ready, hitting the Drakken right in the eyes with the brightest and most powerful ones in my arsenal.

I looked back up as soon as the light show was over. The Drakken, with the front part of it looking strangely thinner and oddly flatter, seemed to be hanging in midair, its forefeet dangling, the claws as long as I was tall just brushing the ground. To people who could see magic, like me, it looked like it'd been flattened in a giant tortilla press, two huge disks of magic slammed together. Then one of the disks evaporated, and it started to slide down on the stationary one, when another disk came out of nowhere and slammed into the first again. I hit it in the front of the head with a hammerblow myself, but what I did was just icing on a devastation cake. This happened three more times, and then the two Elite that were responsible for this phenomena decided the thing was good and dead, and the stationary disk evaporated too.

The Drakken dropped bonelessly down into the blueberry bushes. Bonelessly, because at this point whatever it had that passed for bones had been shattered, at least in the front half.

An avalanche of meat, tons and tons and tons of it, crashed down onto the ground in front of me and Dusana, crushing the bushes underneath it. A shock wave carrying dust and leaves smacked us. Dusana jumped back in reaction, even though we both knew we were too far away for the dead Drakken to hit us. The earth shook, and the sound . . . like the time I'd been way too close when lightning hit a tree near me. It struck Dusana and me with a physical blow that left us both trembling.

And Hammer and Steel came out of the rows of thick blueberry bushes where they'd been lying in wait, and walked over to examine their target.

It oozed greenish liquids from all its orifices. That horrible three-sectioned mouth-tongue lolled on the ground, limp, in two loops of flesh, and the flattened head looked somehow worse than when it had been alive. All those teeth . . . they still looked terrifying. Something inside me was waiting for that tongue thing to suddenly leap to life and lash out at me. It was going to take a while to get my jumpy nerves calmed down.

I'd expected it to stink, but it didn't. It just smelled like hot valerian tea: a bit bitter but not intolerable.

My two partners snagged their bandanas, then leaned on each other, breathing hard. They were sweat drenched and exhausted, as you'd expect, from doing a feat of magic that impressive. Both of them had fumbled out energy squares and were chewing on them, and even the movements of their jaws looked tired.

Hammer and Steel were brothers. Both had perfectly sculpted faces, like amazing statues, and deep-mahogany skin, darker than what I was used to seeing on the Mountain, where people with ancestors from all over had been partnering up ever since the Diseray. At Anston's Well, Safehaven, and the Monastery, we're all sort of tan with brown-to-black hair, and only rarely do you see a blond or ginger. In fact, I was pretty sure that the influx of Mark Knight's people into the area was the biggest concentration of blonds in forever. Both brothers kept their hair at little more than a fuzz on their skulls. Most Hunters either keep their hair very short or get it all tied up and pinned down for Hunting because you don't want to give any Othersider something to grab for. Hammer was a bit shorter than Steel, and a bit broader in the muscular sense. Both of them smiled a lot when they weren't in the middle of a Hunt. They were smiling very broadly now, as they certainly should, for a job well done. As tired as they were, the mere fact of such a tremendous accomplishment was giving them back energy. They were the first two Elite I had ever met, outside of Armorer Kent. That had been back when I first got out of my probation period. They'd come as fast as they could when the "Hunter down" call went out for my friend Karly, though I got there first because Dusana *bamphed* me there, and . . . well, they were just really, really kind and did what they could for me while I was falling apart. Now that I was an Elite and worked with them, I knew that was just how they were: kindhearted, solid, and steady.

Hammer was the implacable force, and Steel was the immovable object, and whatever got between them was going to end up very dead. They only had the one offensive trick, which was a manipulation of their Walls, but really, when you could use that to squash a Drakken, what else did you need?

Their colors were gold and brown, and they were the only Hunters in or out of the Elite who shared colors. Their outfits were exactly the same pattern and cut, but with the colors reversed from Hammer to Steel. Today, for instance, they both wore sleeveless tunics and trousers tucked into boots. Hammer had a brown tunic, gold pants, and brown boots. Steel had a gold tunic, brown pants, and gold boots.

My legs were still feeling too shaky to get down off Dusana, so I asked my Hound to walk up to where they were. Even on Dusana's back, I was just barely as tall as Steel. He looked up from his examination of the dead Drakken, saw us coming, straightened, and grinned. "Well, that worked out just fine. Maybe we oughta make your call sign 'Bait,' Joy." He pulled his brown bandana out of the pocket he'd stuffed it into, and wiped his head and neck down with it.

I shuddered. "This isn't something I really want to get into the habit of doing."

"May not have a choice, kiddo," said his brother gently, mopping his own head with his gold bandana. "You're the only one of us with a Hound you can ride."

I swallowed hard, but I could see his point.

"You said when we were in the chopper that this was a *small* Drakken!" I countered. We'd come up with this idea on the fly, on the helichopper ride in to the site. It was a very, very effective strategy, and unless we did it within sight of one of the Folk, not one that the Drakken would ever learn to avoid.

"It was," Steel replied, his mouth quirking as he tried not to laugh at me. "We've never seen anything smaller than that."

I had no good reply for that, so I got down off Dusana and let him join my pack. The Hounds—my pack of eleven, and the six belonging to Steel and Hammer—all clustered around the dead Drakken. It looked as if all they were doing was breathing hard, but what they were really doing was inhaling manna, which is a sort of magical energy, a force that they live on, and what puts the power behind Hunters' magic. Everything alive has manna, but humans, even non-magic ones, have more of it than anything that comes from Otherside. Mind, something the size of a Drakken has loads and loads and loads, as much as all the Hounds together could "eat."

Hammer was on his Perscom. "Drakken down. Need disposal crew," he was saying.

"Disposal crew dispatched, Elite Team HSJ. ETA fifteen minutes," came over all three of the radios on our Perscoms. He probably hadn't needed to call that in, since the little ubiquitous cameras that hung around every Hunter were hovering discreetly in the background, but it was better to be sure. Something like a Drakken carcass might attract more Othersiders if it didn't get disposed of quickly.

"What are they going to do with that thing?" I asked, a little queasy and a lot curious. Hammer looked at Steel, and they both shrugged, as a breeze blew the oddly mingled scents of crushed blueberries, crushed greenery, and valerian tea over all of us.

"Never asked. Probably goes into the soup for the vat farms, or gets made into fertilizer," said Hammer. "There's a market for things like skin, claws, teeth, horns, and tusks, though. Rich people have books bound in Drakken skin or make boots and shoes out of it. They get decorators to make display pieces out of bones, teeth, claws, and all. Sometimes have artists carve stuff out of them or make composite works."

"I was at a reception at Premier Rayne's palace once," Steel offered. "There was a chair made out of teeth and bones. People were sitting in it and taking selfies."

I shuddered again, this time revulsion mixing with fear. Hammer nodded. "I know, right? Sure, we have the Barriers, but . . . if anything ever comes through the Barriers, I'm thinking you might as well paint targets on all those fancy apartments with dead Othersider knickknacks in them."

Our Hounds began drifting back toward us, now gleaming and

prosperous-looking with all the manna they'd taken in. Hammer and Steel's were pretty typical for Hounds; they looked like over-size mastiffs with heavy coats; Hammer's were ebony and Steel's were chocolate. Mine were a disparate bunch. There were the two that I "inherited" from Karly that looked like wolves, except wolves made out of shadow. That was Hold and Strike. Then there were the two that abandoned their previous Hunter, Ace, when he betrayed *everything* about being a Hunter by trying to murder me during my last Elite Trial. That was Myrrdhin and Gwalchmai. Their heads looked a bit like a cross between a wolf and a big cat, almost exactly like some of the French gargoyles I've seen pictures of. They were an all-over silvery gray.

And then there was my original pack: Bya, Dusana, Begtse, Chenresig, Shinje, Kalachakra, and Hevajra. They were . . . not like any Hounds anyone here at Apex City had ever seen before. In fact, the only other person I know of who had Hounds like mine was my mentor back on the Mountain, Master Kedo Patli.

For one thing, they could choose what they wanted to look like. Right now they were in their "normal" forms, which is to say, like something out of a psychedelic vision. They ranged in size from pack-alpha Bya, whose head was just about at my rib cage, to Dusana, who was big enough to ride on, to Begtse, who was about as big as the shed you'd put Dusana in. They were covered in multiple patterns picked out in multiple eye-watering colors, and sprouted horns, tusks, teeth, spikes, and ridges in ways that made no sense or logic. But when we weren't Hunting, they were generally a pack of black greyhounds with fiery eyes.

Their ability to change form was one big difference between them and the other Hounds around here. For another, they'd accepted other peoples' Hounds into their pack. Nobody had ever heard of that happening before. Normally when a Hunter dies or somehow makes his Hounds desert him, they just go back to Otherside. But these four hadn't, giving me the biggest pack anyone had ever heard of, a pack of eleven. I think that huge pack was why Hammer, Steel, and I had been sent out after a Drakken, instead of a bigger team. My Hounds had been the safeguard; while Dusana and I had been leading the Drakken away, they had been coursing silently alongside, just in case something went wrong. And they had been prepared to jump in and start harrying the Drakken in case Hammer and Steel hadn't been able to kill it right away.

The last difference between my Hounds and every other Hunter's was that they were doing things with me and for me that I'd never even read about Hounds doing before. Like Dusana *bamphing* me along with him.

That would most likely give me an edge over whoever was trying to kill me. Besides Ace, that is. Because although the former Hunter Ace was currently in army custody (and locked up when he wasn't out under guard to use his magic against the Othersiders the army deals with), Ace had been working with someone else, someone who had never been caught.

Steel cocked his head to the side; listening hard, I could hear the heavy *whomp whomp whomp* of a couple of cargo helichoppers. "That's the disposal crew," he said. "We might want to move back to the station and the landing pad."

Since I had no particular wish to watch and maybe get splattered with yuck, I nodded, and we all backtracked along the path between the blueberry bushes I'd taken leading the Drakken away. The guys started helping themselves to berries as we walked, which was all the invitation *I* needed to do the same. Sure, we get whatever we want to eat at HQ, and Hunters get fed really, really well, but working magic makes you hungry.

Fruit off the bush is always the best, anyway. The berries weren't the same as wild blueberries; they didn't have the same intense, slightly tart flavor, but they were bigger and sweeter than the ones back home, and I liked them better than the so-called "blueberry jam" they served at HQ.

The guys were slowly recovering as we walked. The bushes were as tall as Steel's head, and the ground between the rows had some sort of dense, small-leaved ground cover growing over it, to discourage weeds. The stuff was hardy; it didn't really even seem bruised by us walking on it.

"Good Hunt," Steel said, around a mouthful of berries. He was the strategist of the two brothers, as I'd learned on the chopper ride into the drop zone. This was the first time I'd worked with them alone, rather than being in a full six- or eight-man Elite team.

His brother grunt-laughed. "Any Hunt you can walk away from is a good Hunt." He and Steel fist-bumped. The helichoppers must have landed, because there were no more sounds from their blades, but there were other noises behind us now. A breeze carried the sound of chain saws revving up, so the cleanup crew was already at work. Otherwise the only thing you could hear out here was the sound of wind in the bushes and the songs of birds and beneficial insects. That was part of the job of the ag-station—growing bugs that ate other bugs and releasing them at the proper time, and maintaining food stations that attracted bug-eating birds. There's a lot of farming stuff we don't do that they did before the Diseray, and spraying poison all over everything is one of them.

When we got to the station, some of the techs were already outside, fixing the transformer and jury-rigging a link to the wind array, and the rest were looking at the deep scores in the concrete of the building. They kept glancing at us rather shyly, as if they wanted to thank us but were diffident about it. Steel solved that by walking up to them as casually, as if we had not just flattened a Drakken.

"Everyone all right?" he asked. They seemed to take that as the cue that it was okay for them to flock around us and ask for autographs. Crazy, right? But believe it or not, Steel and Hammer both reached into thigh pockets and pulled out little palm-size cards with their pictures on them. Right there, after just having killed a Drakken, they were signing their names, as if they weren't ready to drop, as if they were in a club or a bar. I was hanging back, but Steel beckoned me forward and pulled out *another* set of cards from his other thigh-pocket. This lot had the whole Elite unit on it, including me. I didn't remember posing for that, but I suppose that someone had pasted the picture together from our individual shots. So I signed those. And our Hounds milled around and accepted attention from anyone who'd give it to them. Mine reverted to greyhound shape as soon as they saw the crowd, maybe to keep from scaring anyone, although at this point you'd think all those people who'd watched my channel would know what they looked like.

So weird. So very, very surreal. Back home, Hunters were just not idolized like this. But then, back home, we weren't entertainers. And I swear, even these people, who *should have known better* because they'd nearly become lunch for a Drakken, reverted to being fans as soon as they saw us.

But playing along was part of the job, as I kept being reminded at every turn. "Fan service" it was called, and it was another way to make the Cits believe they were safe, no matter what. So I signed cards and imitated Hammer and Steel. Eventually the supervisor realized they should actually be working, and chased everyone inside except the techs fixing the transformer, and we went over to the landing pad to wait for the helichopper that would pick us up. Hammer and Steel were still keeping up the façade of being indestructible, but I could tell they were fading.

"How long have you been Elite?" I asked, to keep their minds off how tired they were and not trying at all to keep the admiration out of my voice. I hadn't had much chance to talk with them since I joined the Elite ranks. Actually, I hadn't had much chance to talk with anyone. We worked really hard: when we weren't drilling under Armorer Kent's eye, we were either deployed against something big or running patrols in some places in and around Apex that I hadn't even known existed.

"Maybe not as long as you're thinking," Hammer mused, with a raised eyebrow. "Just four years."

"We became Hunters a lot later than you, kiddo," said Steel. "Powers popped at eighteen, full Hunter at eighteen and a half, got sick of the posturing and went for Elite together at twenty-one, and we're twenty-five now." He glanced as his brother as if to suggest he should say something.

"We decided that we had to apply together. My trick doesn't work without my brother," Hammer said modestly. "We did the Trials separately, though. I guess we kind of cheated on the last one."

Steel threw back his head and laughed. "It's not cheating if it works!" he retorted. "Our Walls are so strong, we actually never needed to go on the offensive. It was pretty funny, to tell you the truth. I got Kent; he tapped out and surrendered when he just ran out of energy after beating against my Wall to the point that he couldn't even produce a light-flash."

"I got Archer. I kind of hated to flatten him the way I did—he's such a nice guy, but..." Hammer shrugged. "Playing nice doesn't win the Trials. I just shoved, shoved his own Shield right up against him and squashed him against the big containment Shield. He was at the point of getting the air pushed out of his lungs when he tapped out."

They both laughed. "Joy, you've got to look that up. The look on Archer's face!" Steel chortled. I'd never heard a laugh I could have described as a *chortle* before. It surprised me into laughing too.

"I will," I promised. And that was when the helichopper for our ride back came cruising in just above the berry bushes.

We opened the Way for our Hounds, who went back Otherside, looking sleek and contented. Then we loaded in, with me going last; there was a limited amount of room in the chopper, and the two big guys had to arrange themselves first because I could just squeeze in anywhere. They strapped in, leaned back in their seats, fastened chin straps to keep their heads from lolling about, and closed their eyes as the tough fight caught up with them. They were asleep within a minute; the chopper had just turned around and was starting back for home as they dozed off. They looked weirdly younger when asleep.

It had been a grueling fight for them, no matter how easy it had looked. Doing things with magic isn't effortless—far from it. It takes energy to move magical energy, and that energy has to come from inside the Hunter. Those two had been working like champion weight lifters the entire time they'd been bashing that Drakken. I was amazed they had managed to stay on their feet and look perfectly normal for the station crew.

But that was part of the mythos we were trying to project, I guess. We can never do anything that might make the Cits lose confidence in us or think they were anything less than completely safe.

But although I'd done some to help, I was still at about 90 percent charge. I keyed my Perscom and called up HQ.

"Hunter Joy," I said when I got the handshake.

"Go, Hunter Joy."

"Put me back in rotation. I hardly did anything this run," I said. Because I hadn't, and if we got another callout, it could be that one more Hunter would make the difference between handling it ourselves, and having to call in the army. One thing I'd learned, the Elite hate having to call in the army. Calling in an artillery barrage or some of the attack choppers is one thing, but having to call in troops or army Mages or army Hunters makes everyone feel like they fell down on the job somehow. Right now, I was pretty sure most of us didn't want to get within a mile of an army group that had a Mage with it, because that Mage might be Ace. The army took him, and the army tends to want to use what it takes. So Ace was probably out there somewhere—supervised, sure, but *not* in a prison cell as long as he was "working."

It would be even worse if we had to call in Psimons from PsiCorps, the people with Powers that worked on the mind like telepathy, psychokinesis, mind-control, and that sort of thing. But they never worked outside the Barriers unless they were working with the army. Hunters don't much like Psimons, but then, no one really does. How can you *like* someone who can rummage around inside your head anytime he pleases? Psimons, though, they have this cold arrogance every time they look at Hunters, like they're thinking, *I can do more than you can, and I don't need Hounds to do it.*

"*Roger, Hunter Joy. Noted back in rotation.*" That was another change from being a plain old Hunter and being Elite. HQ assumed you knew your own strength, and if you figured you were good to go back on call, they didn't argue with you. Only the medics could override that, and the medics would know from my vitals that I was just fine.

So I watched the fields roll by about six feet below the skids of the chopper and change from blueberries to tomatoes, to corn, to things I didn't recognize. I thought about Hammer and Steel and their call signs; there was something about that combination of *Hammer* and *Steel* that was hitting a note of familiarity, but not strongly enough that I was getting the connection.

Oh, well. I'll just tuck it in my subconscious, and it'll wake me up in the middle of the night, probably.

We raced toward the huge, conical silver towers that created the Barrier; if I craned my neck, I could see them through the pilot's windshield. The helichoppers, like the trains, have a field around them that cancels out some of the Barrier effects, but I braced myself anyway. Hitting the Barrier feels for a human a lot like breaking the surface of water, except you feel it all through you instead of just at your skin. Of course, most Othersiders would be disintegrated if they tried to pass it.

But now that I knew what I did . . . I had to wonder just how many Othersiders had managed to learn how to pass Barriers somehow. Because an awful lot of them were getting on the city side these days. More than Apex admitted, except to the Hunters, from whom it could not be hidden.

As if in answer to my thoughts, my Perscom beeped. *"Hunter Joy, do you copy?"*

"I copy, HQ," I said instantly.

"You're to bounce when you hit the landing pad. Your old friend White Knight's turned up another Gazer nest. You and Archer are to rendezvous with him."

"Copy that, HQ," I replied. "Out."

I was already so focused on the Gazer nest that the jolts when we passed through the Secondary and Prime Barriers barely registered. I had one hand on my harness release as we came in hot to the landing pad, and the skids weren't even on the ground when I was out and sprinting for the second chopper, where I could see Archer beckoning to me from the door. Then we were in the air, and he and I were neck-deep in strategy as the chopper sped off.

2

SWEAT TRICKLED DOWN THE back of my neck and into my headband. Sweat from working, not fear. I held my magic net down tight on the seething, bobbing flock of Gazers on the other side of the ruined wall we were sheltering behind. Fortunately, they had no idea where I was hiding, because otherwise I would probably have had paste for a brain by now.

The steady *crack, crack, crack* of a high-powered rifle had been punctuating the relative silence for several minutes now, as Mark—that's "White Knight"—picked off the Jackals that were always around as the symbiotic helpers of Gazers. From a distance, they just looked like odd rabbit hounds: white, with red eye patches and ears the color of rust. Up close you saw the vicious red eyes that looked as if they were weeping blood, and the mouth full of needle-teeth. Mark had found himself an excellent perch up in a tree; from there, he could pick them off with his sniper rifle, and they couldn't get to him. And his four Hounds, beautiful things that looked like winged lions, could keep any stray Gazers off him.

I was glad to be doing something other than playing bait. It made me feel as if I was earning my place on the team.

The closest I can come to describing how holding down that net feels is that it's as if I had two giant hands and I was pressing the net down with all my fingers spread around the edge. And it felt like the things in the net were surging against it like a bouncing herd of wild goats. Except, of course, they weren't goats; they were giant eyeballs, each in a nest of greasy hair with fat pink tentacles coming down from the bottom, and if they caught your gaze, they would fry your brain.

"Ready?" asked Archer, squatting next to me and flexing his empty hands.

I nodded. At the signal, he popped up out of hiding, and suddenly there was a glowing bow with an arrow nocked to it in his hands. In a *second* or less, he'd fired off five of those "arrows" and dropped back under cover of the ruined wall we were hiding behind. From the other side came a rapid chain of five sharp explosions. I peeked over the wall to see that the Shields were down on five of the Gazers, and the ugly giant eyeballs now rendered vulnerable were shuddering in shock.

Now! I thought at Bya, and five of my Hounds *bamphed* to the other side of the net, seized the five "naked" Gazers, shook them to death, and *bamphed* out again before the others could get an eye lock on them. They were dead and dissolving so fast they didn't even have time to start that terrible keening cry that dying Gazers gave out.

It had taken me, hitting with my magic like a giant hammer,

and my Hounds and their fire-breath, many minutes to take down the Shield of *one* Gazer. Archer had just shattered five Gazer Shields in seconds.

Archer had his eyes on me now, waiting for me to tell him the Hounds were out again. As soon as Bya gave me the signal, I told Archer, "Clear," and he rose up and fired again.

Archer was one of the older Hunters—short, compact, but strongly muscled, grizzled brown hair and a hint of beard and mustache, a rugged face that always seemed set in an expression of grim determination. That expression was now one of *fierce* determination. I peeked over the wall, saw that once again he'd hit every Gazer he'd aimed at, and gave Bya the word.

The Hounds that didn't *bamph*, like Hold and Strike, were still busy enough with the Jackals that had rallied to the Gazers' defense. The Jackals never uttered a sound, not even when they were wounded. If you didn't know what was going on, you'd be forgiven for thinking that at worst someone was having an easy target practice, punctuated by explosions, because what's a few hand grenades among friends?

The net was getting easier for me to hold as Archer and the Hounds thinned the flock of Gazers. This time when I peeked over the top, I saw I could tighten up the net, so I did. Smaller net, less energy.

Jackals? I asked Bya mentally.

Almost gone. Hold and Strike did well. The Angels are finishing off the ones that Knight wounded. I could hear the snicker in my head when Bya called Mark's Hounds "Angels" because that was what Mark's people back home called them. Mark was a Christer, but he wasn't as tightly wound as some of them I'd met.

The rifle shots stopped. Mark must have run out of targets. *"Knight to Archer,"* came over our Perscoms. *"Jackals down. Jackals down."*

Archer spoke into his comm. "Can you see the nest from where you are?"

"Affirmative. Want to double-tap the ones left?"

"Roger. I'll have Joy hit them with a dazzle." He nodded at me, and I nodded back. Now that I wasn't holding a net full of twenty or thirty struggling Gazers, I could do both. "Dazzle first, then we come up shooting. In three . . . two . . . one!"

I popped up and hit the remaining Gazers with a dazzle spell, basically an enormous flash of light covering as much of the spectrum as I could manage, like I'd used on the Drakken, and once it was off, I dropped down again.

Now that they were blinded, Archer could come up and stay up while he fired arrow after magic arrow into the Shields on the remaining Gazers. Once again, the *crack* of rifle fire split the air, as Mark sent high-powered rounds into the unprotected Gazers. I knew it was over when the shooting stopped.

I let the net vanish and stood up, flexing my cramped hands. Archer just put his back against the wall and slid down it until he was sitting, completely exhausted. I dug into my pack and got him a water bottle and some energy cubes to wolf down. He took both with a faint smile and thanks. Then he and I both ate and drank while we waited for Mark to climb down out of his tree and rejoin us.

"Why arrows?" I asked, finally, something I had been wanting to ask Archer since I'd first seen him in action. "Why not levin bolts? Or fire bolts?"

Mark joined us at that point and squatted down on his haunches, accepting another bottle from me.

Archer shrugged and took a long drink. "Magic works best with what you feel. Less here"—he tapped his head—"more here." He tapped his chest. "Levin bolts never felt powerful enough to me. And a magically manifested gun didn't make sense, didn't feel right. My mentor in Lakeland used to manifest a fire sword, and I thought, why not arrows? I tried it, it worked. So that's why arrows."

"At least you'll never run out of them," Mark said, and grimaced as he checked his ammo pouches. "Wish I could make magic bullets, but I've only got just enough magic to Shield and to cast the Glyphs and open the Way—"

Archer looked at him slantwise. "That's not true," he said flatly.

Mark is a big guy. Tall, strong, blond, he actually *looked* like a fairy-tale knight out of a King Arthur story. Normally he's pretty controlled. But right now he looked as startled as if Archer smacked him in the head.

"You haven't noticed." Archer shook his head. "Unbelievable. Hasn't it ever occurred to you that the only time you failed to make a kill today was when you were shooting to wound so the Hounds could finish off the quarry for the manna?"

Mark looked so stunned I probably could have pushed him over with a finger.

Archer spoke slowly, as if to a child. "You're using magic to guide your bullets," he said. "You've probably been doing it for some time now. I wouldn't be the least bit surprised to discover you can now shoot around corners if you choose to do so."

Mark's mouth worked for a bit before he got anything out. "How—how do you know that?"

"Because I Saw it," Archer replied, giving the word the inflection that meant he'd seen magical energy at work, as we all could. "The only reason you haven't been Seeing it yourself, I suspect, is because you are concentrating on the target, not the bullet. As it should be; your concentration should be on what you want to hit, if you're going to use magic."

"I . . . huh," was all Mark said. Archer gave him a sharp look, and saw what I was seeing, I guess. Mark Knight looking baffled.

"You know what the biggest difference between you and Joy is, aside from pack size?" Archer continued. He didn't wait for an answer. "Joy has always believed there's new ways she can learn to use magic. So she keeps learning, never stops, and keeps getting stronger. That's why Kent had no hesitation in letting her do the Trials even though she was a newcomer. Using magic is like using muscles, White Knight. The more you use it, the stronger it gets, and the more you can do."

"I . . ." Mark shook his head. "I was always told that what I had was all I was going to get."

"Ah. Someone back home told you that?" Archer asked. Mark nodded, while I kept my trap shut. Archer nodded. "Well, now you know. What you do with the knowledge is up to you. Just remember not to force anything. Magic answers to belief, not logic. For now, *believe* you can do this, and do more target practice. Like I said, you could be shooting around corners before too long, and that can come in damned handy."

Then Archer gave me a *look* and a raised eyebrow. "So who told you that it was possible to keep improving?"

"No one had to tell me. It was logical; like you said, if you work muscles you get stronger," I replied. "And stubbornness too,

I guess." I was thinking quickly, trying to remember everything I could about the only Hunter that was *supposed* to be back home, one of the Apex castoffs they sent to us. He's still there, but when he arrived, the first thing he did was square off against one of the feral Folk. That was really stupid and got his brain melted for him, and right now he's playing with his toes while one of the Masters makes up reports and sends them on to Apex for him. "My mentor's not very good, and he's also butt-lazy. He doesn't know the people I grew up with, and I reckon he doesn't really care all that much about them, but I *do*, so I worked as hard as anything to get good fast so I could protect them." I drank a long swallow of water to give myself time to think some more. "If that makes sense?"

"If it makes sense to you, then it makes sense." Archer smiled a very little. "One of the first things you learn as an Elite is that if something works, you leave it be. Nice to work with both of you, by the way. John Shephard." He offered his hand to me, and I shook it. Then he offered it to Mark, who did the same.

"Mark Knight," said White Knight. "And thanks for coming so quickly."

Archer just waved the thanks away. "That's what we do, Mark. Speaking of which, we've lollygagged enough." He turned his wrist and spoke into his Perscom. "Elite team AJ requesting pickup. Gazer nest neutralized."

"Roger, team AJ."

Archer stood up. "You want extraction, Knight? Remember, there's a storm coming."

Mark looked at his Hounds clustered around him. They snorted. It sounded derisive. He laughed and shook his head. "We're good for the rest of our shift, and that storm isn't supposed to come in till after that. There wasn't anything but Goblins until we found that nest."

"It'll make good viewing on your channel," Archer replied, producing something like a grin or as near as I had ever seen him come to one.

Mark shrugged but didn't reply. I was going to say something, but then I heard the sound of chopper blades in the far distance. The chopper that had dropped us must have been parked somewhere safe nearby, waiting for the pickup call. So instead, I just said, "See you back at HQ, Mark," which made him nod and smile, finally.

By that point, the chopper had arrived, and we climbed into it. Mark gave us a wave, then turned and went back on his patrol, his four Hounds spread out in the air ahead of him. As we rose and picked up speed, Archer suddenly frowned and leaned out the open door a little. Before I could ask what was wrong, he'd tapped the pilot on the shoulder and made the circle in the air with his finger that meant "circle around."

Then he turned back to me. "Down there!" he shouted, pointing, as the chopper tilted and began its arc. "It can't be. But I could have sworn I saw..." His voice trailed off in a way that meant that what he'd thought he'd seen wasn't just a monster.

A chill flashed down my backbone, and I leaned forward as far as the harness I was in would let me, and peered down at the ground where he pointed.

And...there *was* something down there! I got a glimpse, hardly more than a second, of flying lavender and mauve that could have been hair or fabric or both; then a flash of light from something highly reflective. Jewelry? And then...

It was gone. There was nothing below us but weeds and bushes. I looked up to meet Archer's baffled eyes.

"Did you see that?" he shouted.

I nodded slowly.

The chopper straightened back up and got back on course, and the pilot called back to us. "Want me to circle around again, Hunter?"

But Archer just gave me a warning look and replied, "No . . . I was just making sure we hadn't left any live Gazers. I thought I saw one, but it was just some tangle of old junk."

I kept my mouth shut. If Archer didn't want to report this, then neither did I. And after all, what had we actually seen? Nothing but a brief glimpse of . . . something. Maybe it was just our tired minds playing tricks on us. After all, we'd just been fighting Gazers, and *they* mess with your head. Then again, so do the Folk.

But . . . that flash of *lavender* . . . the color I associated with that Folk Mage who seemed particularly interested in me . . . I won't lie, just thinking about the possibility made my gut knot up and my whole body go cold with terror. I didn't know why he was interested in me, but when you catch the eye of any of the Folk, much less a Folk Mage, that is generally not a story that ends well.

I nodded soberly at the senior Elite, and he shrugged, grimaced, and made a little twirling motion with his finger next to his ear, the near-universal sign for "brains scrambled." I nodded again. We both sighed and settled back for the trip.

I closed my eyes and wondered if I ought to go back on rotation again. I was snapping back from the exertion of the Gazer Hunt pretty quickly, but then, all I had done was throw dazzles and hold down the net. Archer was pretty drained, but the longer I sat here resting, the more I felt ready to go. By the time we landed, I just wanted something to eat, then to go out again.

But as we left the chopper, Archer grabbed my elbow, and we walked far enough away from the thing so we could talk without shouting. "Come inside; I want to talk with you a minute," he said. "Let's get something to eat."

The Elite had a little kitchen of its own, since we were often too late or too early for the regular meals. There was a freezer full of prepared stuff and a flash-heater, and a cold cupboard with a glass front full of stuff that didn't need to be cooked. Archer got himself three plates' worth of frozen, while I made some tomato sandwiches. We sat down at a little table that could seat about six if you crowded up, and ate.

One of the other Elite, a younger (and really nice-looking) guy call-signed Retro wandered in and grabbed three or four pieces of fruit. He was in his Hunting outfit, as were we—green and gray and silver leather, sleeveless, and . . . quite tight. He turned and saw us there and grinned. At me. I blinked a little.

"Hey, Joy," he said, starting an actual *juggling* routine with the fruit. I blinked again. He had disconcertingly blue eyes, a lantern jaw, and shaggy blond hair—and for some reason, the direct look in his eyes made me flustered.

"Hey yourself," I replied.

"So, when are you and I gonna go out on a date?" he asked as if it was the most logical thing in the world to say.

"I—uh—" I spluttered a little. "I'm kind of seeing someone—"

"Creepy Psimon, right? It exclusive?" He waggled his eyebrows at me, still juggling.

"Uh—" I said cleverly. Of course, I should have known that

people would know about my so-called social life, since until I went Elite it was all over my Hunter channel.

"Not exclusive, then. Think it over! I'm a fun guy!" He grinned even harder.

"You're a mushroom?" Archer deadpanned.

"Yeah, they keep me in the dark and feed me on bullcrap," he quipped right back. Archer rolled his eyes. Retro finished his juggling with a flourish, catching the last apple in his mouth, and strolled out.

I really didn't know what to say after that. Fortunately, Archer didn't miss a beat. "It's three guys to one gal here in the Hunters," he pointed out. "He was going to ask eventually. Knowing Retro . . . I'm surprised it took him this long."

"Uh—okay," I said. "What did *you* want to talk to me about?" *Not a date,* I prayed. I admired Archer a *lot,* and it was obvious I could learn a lot from him, but he was kind of old for someone like me. . . .

"You," Archer said, pointing a potato stick at me, "are not like the other recruits, Joyeaux Charmand. Why is that?"

I bit into the sandwich, buying myself some time to respond.

"Probably where I come from. It started as a commune before the Diseray." Totally true. The Monastery was a sort of commune. I shrugged. "So I guess by your standards I have . . . a different attitude."

He nodded. "Fair enough. So." He finished his potato sticks and started in on some sort of stew. "Tell me, Hunter Joyeaux, what do you want to learn?"

What did I want to learn? Aside from everything? I reined myself in and thought about the question. "I don't know enough to say what I don't know," I replied after a moment. "But whatever anyone is willing to teach me."

He nodded again. "I'll pass that on. And I'll suggest some books. The most important thing I ever learned was what I told White Knight out there. That magic responds better to how you feel about it than how you reason."

That was, more or less, what the Masters had taught me, but I tried to make my expression look as if this had been new to me. But Archer wasn't quite through.

"The other thing is this, because I'm guessing you are not used to thinking like we do," Archer continued, setting the last of his emptied plates aside. "*Everything* in this world is layers and masks. Nothing is ever exactly what it seems to be."

He gave me an unreadable look, and I had the feeling that he meant more than just the Othersiders. I had the feeling he also meant *here*, in Apex City, and I'd already gotten a taste of that.

"Everybody wears a mask," I said finally.

He pointed a finger at me this time. "That," he said with a smile, "is the truest thing you have ever said."

"Well," I told him, feeling more like myself with a meal in me, "the second-truest thing will be that I should probably put myself back in rotation—"

"No need," he countered, interrupting me. Then he pointed behind me, where I knew there was a screen on the wall that usually showed the general-news channel. I turned and looked, and it was a weather-radar image with Apex at the center of it. There was a storm front moving in, *fast,* and it wasn't red and orange like ours usually are. This one was mostly purple, with trailing red. "Storm front," he said casually, confirming what I already knew.

"It's one of the big ones. You haven't been here long enough to see one. *Nothing* moves in one of those, not even a Gog or a Drakken. It wasn't supposed to hit us, but . . ." He shrugged, as if to say, "You can't count on prediction."

And as soon as he said that, both our Perscoms gave a peculiar warbling call, like nothing I had heard since I got here, followed by what sounded like a prerecorded announcement. *"All Hunters. Storm front moving in. All Hunters. Return to base."* I double-tapped mine to acknowledge, and shut the message off, a second before Archer did the same.

"Our big storms are mostly blizzards," I said as Archer looked at something on his Perscom. "They go on for days." And I flashed back for a moment to one of those storms. The Monastery is mostly built into the mountain, so all the Masters do is put the thick wooden storm shutters over the windows, rely on the wind to keep our electrics charged, and move all the practices that we can inside to the big dojos. Down in the villages, though, they spend the early part of the fall making straw-sheltered tunnels between buildings, and by the time a big blizzard hits, it's just another couple of feet of snow on top of what's already there. Once every couple of years, we get an epic thunderstorm, but not more often than that.

"Well, we're locked down for twelve hours, at least, maybe a couple days," Archer replied, and cocked an eyebrow at me. "You know all those storm-sewer tunnels you've patrolled? They're that big for a reason." He stretched as I tried and failed to imagine those tunnels filled with thundering water. "Good thing we got as much Hunting in as we did today. Our Hounds will be fine until the storm is over. But the grumbling in the lounge over the fact that the channels will be on repeat is going to be louder than the thunder." He quirked a corner of his mouth in a sardonic half smile, and I snorted.

"What about if something horrible pops up outside the storm zone?" I asked anxiously, as he stood up to go.

"Hope that doesn't happen," was all he'd say. Then he clapped me on the shoulder. "Look at the map," he pointed out. "Look at the size of the storm zone. It'd take us hours to get to anything that far, even without the storm. There are Hunters in cities outside the storm zone. And there are Hunters with the army."

But they aren't Elite! I wanted to protest, but . . . Hunters and the army and plain old Mages were handling Othersiders before there ever were Elite, or Apex wouldn't even be here. So I nodded, and he went on his way. And I noticed for the first time he had a slight limp when he walked. Well, maybe he only limped when he was tired. I wondered what had caused it.

Curious now, I went out to the entrance to HQ that faced the coming storm, and as soon as I got outside . . . it took my breath away. I'd seen one of the big blizzards approaching back home as I helped put up the shutters. That had been impressive enough. This storm, though—this storm whacked you in the face with how utterly insignificant you were when the planet decided to cut loose around you.

The sky over me was cloudless, but what faced me was blue-black, and there was already a powerful enough wind blowing that I'd had to force the door open. A little bit ago it had been warm, but this wind had ice in its breath and shoved the smell of rain down the throat and into the lungs. And the storm approached on hundreds of bright legs of lightning. The thunder was so continuous, it sounded like a thousand drummers beating the biggest drums in the universe.

This was no place for a mere human being. I dashed right back inside.

HQ didn't have a lot of windows, for the obvious safety reasons, but I knew there was one spot I would *sort of* be able to see the sky, and that was the indoor garden with the little koi pond. So that was where I headed, stopping just long enough to get a portion of fish food, because the fish would neither know nor care that all hell was breaking loose outside their little world, and as Mark would say, it would be wrong to shake their faith.

I sat down on a bench next to the pond, absently tossed the food in, and stared upward through the glass ceiling. It was almost as black as full night up there—except for the lightning. It *never stopped*. The rain hadn't started yet, so I was getting a clear view of the clouds above us, and besides the bolts that were cutting across the sky in an unstoppable barrage, there was lightning illuminating the insides of the clouds as well.

Even through glass that I now knew was a full foot thick, the thunder vibrated everything. I was wrong about the fish. They fled to hide under overhanging rocks or the lily pads. It was just me and the storm, and the foot of glass didn't seem like nearly enough.

Then the rain hit. And I mean *hit*. I actually jumped and nearly fell off my bench. My head knew that hundreds, if not thousands of these storms had struck HQ before this one. My gut, however, was dead certain there was no way that layer of glass between me and the storm was going to hold. My gut, used to the storms of the mountains, was sure the next thing that was coming were hailstones the size of my head. I left, and in a hurry.

But this was no time to go to my room. With something like that raging outside, thunder a constant growl and the very fabric of the building trembling under it, I wanted other people around and I wanted them now. I headed straight for the lounge.

It looked like I wasn't the only one that felt that way, since the lounge was packed. Archer was there, and Armorer Kent, and Hammer and Steel. I saw Dazzle in the middle of one of the big sofas, squashed in between four other Hunters. One of them was another of the Elite, a woman with the call-sign of Scarlet; that might even have been her real name. Scarlet was a totally *stunning* woman, with long red hair, the face and body of an antique goddess, and the poise of a dancer. And on top of all that, she was one of the nicest people I'd met in the Elite. Right now she was being nice to one of the new Hunters, who was clearly shaken up by the storm. The lounge was actually so packed that mostly all I saw were bodies and the backs of heads. I was disappointed not to see Mark, and then concerned; I queried by Perscom and was relieved to see that his status was listed as "in quarters." Well, he didn't much like the lounge get-togethers at the best of times, and as crowded as it was now, he'd probably just put something on his vid that was loud enough to drown out the thunder.

I spotted Retro, and for a minute, I was afraid he was going to work his way over to me and ... I don't know ... press things, I guess. But all he did was raise his eyebrows and grin when he caught me looking at him, wave casually, then go back to the conversation he was in.

You'd think that people that Hunt monsters *every single day* (or night) wouldn't be afraid of a storm. But no matter how much we tried to tell ourselves that we were surely safe behind our thick, clever walls, our guts knew better. The terrible storms of the Diseray were still with us, punishing us for what our ancestors had done.

The big vid-screen wasn't showing Hunt footage for a change. Someone had set it to a loop of a nice, crackling fireplace. It actually made me feel homesick, and I started getting the inevitable horrid feelings of wanting *home* so bad I could taste it.

But before I could leave, Trev spotted me and waved at me enthusiastically, pointing to an empty chair across from him. Regi and Sara looked to see who he was waving at, and started waving their arms around like idiots. I couldn't help it, that put a big old smile on my face, and I wiggled my way through the crowd toward them.

I felt myself being seized around the waist and got lifted over the back of a couch by Hammer and set down on the chair I'd been aiming for. I turned my head to give him a *thanks* grin, and he flashed one back at me, before edging his way toward—well, toward something I couldn't see in the press. Then I collapsed into the chair and turned toward my friends.

My friends . . .

I guess it had never occurred to me that I *wouldn't* have friends here, although the intense competition among the Hunters for rankings had put me off at first. But now that I'd gotten things sorted out, I knew that there was a minority who took that competition way more seriously than our actual job, and then there were the rest of us. And the rest of us were not all that different from the Hunters at home.

"Did you beat the storm in?" Trev asked as Dazzle spotted me, wormed her way over, and plunked herself down next to me on the overstuffed arm of my chair.

"I was out with Archer and Knight, and we left before it showed over the horizon," I said. "I checked: Knight's in."

"Knight was the last one in, stubborn idiot," said Dazzle, shaking her head. She'd let her pink hair out of the bun she usually kept it in, and it fell in untidy waves around her face. "I was just going on shift and got canceled. Good thing too; I was scheduled for the storm sewers. This thing wasn't supposed to blow in until much, much later tonight, and we were only supposed to get the edge of it."

"It got stronger and faster and did a course change a couple of hours ago." That was Regi, a tall, thin guy with a face like a bloodhound. "We're in for a night. Probably longer. Oh, well, you can't always predict what one of the big ones is going to do."

That . . . seemed odd. I'd never seen a storm do that back home. But no one else seemed to think this was out of the ordinary, so I let it slide without questions.

"What about the people in Spillover?" I asked, looking at the others. Regi shrugged—not indifferently, just like *I don't know*.

"That's what Knight was probably doing out so long," Dazzle said finally. After the big Gazer Hunt that had ended so disastrously with the death of Ace's brother, Paules, she'd warmed up to Mark. In fact, a lot of people had. "I bet he was passing on the warning and making sure they could get into some kind of shelter."

"At least when the storm's over, we won't have to worry about sweeping the storm sewers for a while," Trev said as someone brought a tray full of drinks by and we all took one. I looked up at the person as I got mine, and realized with a start that not only did I not know her, but that she was wearing a uniform of a pale green tunic and matching pants. I smiled at her and she smiled back at me, after looking startled, and then took the now-empty tray and vanished into the crowd.

That must have been one of the staff. It was the first time I had seen one of them, outside of encountering them in the Recreation Center. Everywhere else, except the Med Center and the Style Center, they were invisible. But before I could consider this further, more of the staff came sashaying through the crowd bearing huge round metal platters. Three of the platters got put down on the table in the midst of us, and as a delicious aroma wafted around us, I stared at what was on them in disbelief. The only time I had ever seen this food was in pre-Diseray vids. The legendary delicacy—pizza!

Oh, we knew how to make it on the Mountain, but we never had the oven space or the fuel for the kind of hot fire needed to do so, and on top of that we lacked some of the ingredients. The others were not hesitating for a second. They were diving on the metal platters like they were starving, so I went for the one nearest me.

Now, I was used to food down here being just a little disappointing compared to the stuff we ate at home—well, except for the food in the fancy places Josh had been taking me to. But this pizza...

I felt my eyes widening, and then I closed them in pure pleasure. Before I knew it, the slice in my hand was gone, and I went back after another one *immediately*. Dazzle caught my eye as I grabbed that second piece, and grinned.

"Oh. My. God," I said, in answer to the question in her eyes. "This is *amazing!*"

"And it's *so horrible* for you! I think that's what makes it better!"

she agreed enthusiastically. "We only get it on storm nights. I think it's to keep our endorphins up."

Well, my endorphins were probably about to gush out of my ears. I got a piece from a different pie, and it had other stuff on it, which was just as good. By the fourth piece, I was ready to call it quits and just wallow in my chair. But then they brought around more pizzas that had apple slices, raisins, honey, and spices, and it would have been rude not to have some of that.

Everyone else was just as stuffed; the babble of conversation died down, people started finding places to sit, including the floor, and someone tuned the vid-screen to what looked like a club. It was *jammed*. The music was really good, though.

"Is that a recording?" I asked Trev.

He shook his shaggy head. "No, it's a storm party. People who won't have to go to work tomorrow go to their favorite clubs when there's a storm warning up. They'll just stay there, dancing and drinking until the storm's over. That's probably the vid-feed from someone famous."

I nodded. Herd instinct, and weren't we pretty much doing the same here? Something as big as that storm out there . . . made you want to huddle together and do things to forget what's outside.

But that made me think of Mark, and I texted him. *Want some pizza?*

I got back an immediate reply. *I was debating that, but not in the mood for a crowd.*

That decided me. *I'll bring you some.* That was only fair. Mark was one of my best friends here. The least I could do was bring him pizza.

3

I KNOCKED ON MARK Knight's door; my Perscom had led me right to it, of course, even though I had never been to his suite. "Pizza-bot!" I said as I balanced one of the platters with a mix of slices on it, including the sweet stuff. The platter stayed warm somehow, which kept the food warm. When he opened the door, I handed him the platter. "Did you get warning out to the people in Spillover?" I asked.

He looked surprised and pleased that I had asked. "They actually keep better track of the weather than we do," he said. "But, yeah, they got under shelter, the ones I knew how to find. There's more protection out there than you might think—from storms, anyway."

But not from Othersiders . . . Well, by my way of thinking, and by Mark's too, that was why there were Hunters patrolling out there.

But he was standing there looking awkward and I knew why. Knight is a Christer, and engaged to a home girl on top of that. If he didn't invite me in, it would look rude, and if he *did*, well, by his lights he was compromising my virtue (such as it is), possibly being unfaithful to his girl, and possibly endangering both our souls.

"Thanks for looking out for them," I said. "And now that I know you aren't going to waste away, I'm headed back to the lounge."

"If you want a good look at the storm, pull up one of the external feeds on HQ," he said, looking relieved. "I'll just say I'm glad there's a foot of reinforced 'crete on the roof."

I nodded; he succumbed to temptation and started eating. He offered me the tray politely, but I waved it away.

"I should let you enjoy your food. And at least we're going to find the storm sewers clean of Othersiders for a bit after this."

He nodded. "They'll be fishing Othersider bodies out of the reservoirs for a couple of days. I don't envy whoever has *that* job."

Huh. So that's where the storm sewers lead.

"Back home, we saved the storm water too; it's less contaminated than the ground and well water," Mark said, reminding me that his original home had been something not unlike a death trap. Then he smiled. "But now we don't have to, unless we feel like it, thanks to you. I got my first batch of letters today since they moved. My people love it in your mountains...." Then he blinked. "I wonder if you got letters too?"

I didn't mention that I could get letters anytime I wanted them now. Bya had been taking notes for me to my Masters and back. But that was just my Masters.

"Maybe I did. I haven't been back to my rooms yet." Now I

did want to get back there, and not because I was hiding from the storm.

"Don't let me keep you. I was reading mine and I'm only halfway through them." He smiled and ducked his head and blushed a little, which let me know he'd had more than one from his girl.

"Jessie?" I asked. "That's her name, right?"

"It is." Now he looked awkward, like he was a tweener or teener in the throes of a first crush. Which I guess would be normal for his people, since they pick a one-and-only, if they get to pick and not get arranged marriages. So he'd never flirted or experimented the way my people did. It was cute, actually, the way he blushed on and off. He had it really bad for this girl.

"Thanks for letting me know about the letters!" I said, and gave him a little two-fingered salute as I turned to go.

"Thanks for bringing me pizza!" he called after me.

I headed down the halls, which normally were empty but now had the occasional person in them, mostly people in the staff uniforms. Sure enough, when I opened the door to my rooms, there was an open box full of envelopes on the little table next to the sofa.

Now more than ever I was glad I wasn't under that intense camera scrutiny that the non-Elite Hunters were. My reaction to word from home wasn't anyone's business but my own.

There was a big stack of letters from my Masters, using just their names and with the return address being Anston's Well rather than the Monastery. The ones on the top were all from Master Kedo, and I plopped down on the bed and tore open the first one.

The letters were cryptic, but just in how he was coding things about Hunting, as if he and the others were doing it the hard way, the way that Apex *thought* they were Hunting, with guns and traps and explosives, instead of with Hounds and magic. Unlike the messages he sent back with Bya, he also took the time to just catch me up on ordinary things happening at the Monastery and with the other Hunters and Hunters-in-training there.

That was good. Not so good were letters from Lady Rhiannon and Ivor Thorson, a couple of the other Masters, basically advising me that some of the people down in Anston's Well and other villages were . . . not impressed with what I was doing. Apparently, the settlements and villages that had receivers had been getting the four hours of my channel every day by burst-cast—I guess they did that with every Hunter that hadn't come out of Apex: sent their channel stuff back via burst-cast so people could see how their local hero was doing. And there were people who thought I was getting a swelled head and were not shy about saying so.

Ivor and Rhiannon weren't saying that *they* thought I had a big ego. In fact, they said it was a good thing that I was Elite now because there wasn't as much coming back via burst-cast to give people gossip fodder, and when there was something, I was always part of a bigger team. But they did warn me that some folks I'd thought were friends were . . . turning out to be . . . not. That those people were spreading all kinds of gossip about how I was getting above myself.

Honestly, it gave me a real sick feeling in my stomach to read that and the names of people I thought I trusted, because how could I ever counter that? It wasn't as if I could go home and show them that I hadn't changed, that I wasn't wallowing in all that luxury and fame they were seeing, and thinking I was better than them. My eyes stung, thinking about it, and for a minute, I forgot about the storm.

That was when the storm reminded me—all of us in HQ—that the bad old days of the Diseray were not entirely gone.

The entire building shook, rattling everything in my room, and the lights flickered and went out in the middle of the shaking.

I stayed put even though my heart was racing like there was a Drakken after me. The worst thing you can do in a situation like this is move, especially move when your gut wants to panic. The shaking stopped; the lights stayed out. I made a mental map of the room I was in, making sure that if the lights stayed out, I knew how many steps it was to the door to the bedroom, and from there, how many to the closet where my pack from home was. I had a flashlight in there and some chem-lights. And then my Perscom lit up, reminding me that in a pinch I could use *it* as a flashlight.

"Stay calm and stay put, everyone. We got a series of direct lightning hits on and around HQ, and the local grid is down. We'll have stand-alone, emergency power up shortly."

So I stayed where I was, with my ears ringing a little from how *quiet* it was in this room, although the thunder was still a distant presence. Back home, of course, it's always very quiet because we don't have a lot of things running all the time. But here, there was always the hum from electronics and lights, a faint but ubiquitous sound that I had stopped noticing consciously after a while. And there was the sound of the air moving in the ventilation ducts, a different hum from the cool-box when it turned on, a lot of things I had gotten used to, and now were just gone, leaving silence. But not a complete silence—there was still the faint and muted rumbling of the thunder beyond the thick walls, and the distant whine from the wind as well. It made me conscious all over again how the whole building was vibrating from something that was just not adequately described by the word "storm."

I felt the air moving first, then heard the hum as my cool-box came up. Then some of the lights, which were dimmer than usual. My Perscom lit up again. *"Limited electric for now. No vid. Try an old-fashioned book,"* someone announced, dryly. That surprised a laugh out of me. Well, I was certainly well supplied with those. *"Or you can use your Perscoms; wireless is still up."*

I felt Bya tickling the back of my head, not like he was alarmed, but more like, *Would you like me there?* As it happened, between the unhappy-making letters and the threat of being thrown into the dark again, I did. I cast the Glyphs and opened the Way, and he came through in greyhound shape.

I turned off all the lights I didn't need and moved into the bedroom with Bya and my letters. He laid himself alongside me while I read; not only was it very comforting to have him there, but it was very comforting knowing that if some monstrous tornado hit HQ, between his Shields and mine we would survive the second or two it would take him to *bamph* us both out together.

The last ones were a stack from Kei, my best friend from back home. She was absolutely full of cheerful news, ordinary stuff from all the villages on the Mountain and in the valleys, things the Hunters had left out. Like who was paired up, who had broken up, who was doing what new projects. She was now an item with Dutch down in Silverspring—I giggled and hugged Bya over that; it was about time she noticed how crazy he was for her! She described three new outfits she'd made for herself. She'd been watching my vids. She loved what I was wearing as a Hunter, and went into verbal spasms over the dresses I'd worn on my dates with Josh. She thought Josh was adorable. She'd been down with some of the others to meet Mark Knight's people when they arrived to join up with Brother Vincent's "flock." *"Stiff,"* was her estimation. *"But I think they're all right. They seem grateful to be here, and gratitude will take them a long way. They don't know about everything yet"*—by which she meant the Monastery—*"but we figure that'll come when we know how far we can trust them."* I already knew the Masters were thinking of letting them in on the secret soon. Her letters were almost as good as being with her ... and she had all sorts of advice about how I should act around Josh, which I was *really* happy to read. In fact, I read those parts of her letters over a couple of times to cement them into my brain.

There was still no sign of the electrics coming back to normal, so I padded around the rooms making sure everything was turned off that could be turned off, went back to bed, and cuddled Bya. I had a reader from home with a lot of books on it. I chose one at random and started reading. They were mostly pre-Diseray fantasy because we've found we can glean a lot of things about how to use magic from them. This one was written in very florid language, and it made me nod off.

The alarm from the vid-screen in the bedroom woke me up. Bya was still there and the building was still vibrating, but all the electrics were back. I could tell from the hum and the brightness of the reading lamp above my head. "Schedule," I said aloud, and the vid-screen lit up with *Canceled* showing for the whole day. "Weather," I ordered, and studied the screen. That was an ugly storm, and it was *huge*. It seemed to be circling around a center, like a hurricane, but without an actual eye. Was this normal? Up in the mountains, blizzards could last for days, and I *had* seen storms that circled like this, so I didn't know.

Well, no point in lolling around in bed. If I wasn't going Hunting—and now I was very glad I'd put myself back in rotation after the Drakken, so my Hounds didn't need manna—then I should work out, maybe get some target practice in. I got cleaned up and dressed, sent Bya back, and headed for the mess.

It was pretty full, what with everyone having gone to bed early last night and all three shifts canceled. I grabbed food, found some space at a table with Dazzle, Hammer, and a couple people I didn't know, and sat down to eat and listen.

From the chatter, I gathered that the storm parking over us *was* unusual but not unheard of. Hammer at our table and a couple other Hunters within earshot had stories of monster storms that lasted two or more days. "The good news is that there's not one Othersider that will move during a storm like this, not even the Thunderbirds. It's too much even for them. Should finally move off us by nightfall," Hammer finished. "Enjoy the rest while you're getting it."

That sent people off on their plans for the unexpected free day. I stopped listening. I wasn't sure what I was going to do; I just knew I wasn't going to lie around and watch vids all day, or join the people who were planning on marathoning a game they all liked, something where your game avatar wore power armor and was shooting at an invasion of sentient robots. I never could see the point of vid-games, but I guess that might be because I grew up shooting at monsters for real and was not kept safe from them as an Apex Cit.

I thought maybe I'd try to call Josh—not that we were going to be able to meet up or anything, but a nice long call when we were just able to chat about nothing without cameras around would be fun. That was all that was on my mind as I made my way through hallways that actually had people in them for a change.

Well, my day got decided for me as it turned out; when I got back to my room, my vid-screen was flashing with a *Report to armory* on it. "Acknowledged," I said. It went out and I turned right back around, wondering what Kent wanted with me in the middle of a storm.

4

BY THIS TIME, I had figured out that Armorer Kent was the unofficial leader of the Elite. Everyone deferred to him, and although Dispatch in HQ sent the Elite out, he was *certainly* the one in charge of assigning Hunters who weren't Elite to their patrols. And he decided who trained, with whom, and with what. He also chewed us out when we messed up. I was pretty sure I'd done well yesterday, so I was not expecting any kind of rebuke. More like bracing for a very challenging workout or some other sort of session with him.

When I arrived at the armory and opened the door, Kent was waiting for me, wearing his usual asymmetric scarlet-and-yellow Hunt gear. He was the brightest thing in the room, which was filled with every sort of instrument of mayhem I could imagine, and a lot I had no notion how to use. He quirked a finger at me, silently telling me to follow him. Now I was really puzzled, and did so. He led me to his little office, opened the door, and waved me inside, closing the door behind me, with himself outside.

Kent's office was as Spartan as his signature gear was flamboyant: brown carpet, brownish-gray walls, with a couple of beautiful landscape pictures that were clearly taken before the Diseray. There was someone sitting in the high-backed leather chair behind Kent's utilitarian gray metal desk, with the back of the chair facing me. That person spun the chair around as I entered, and—

—it was my uncle! He was in his prefect uniform, which meant he considered himself on duty, regardless of the storm; I've seen him in ordinary civilian clothing, but not often. As always, I was glad to see him. As always, I was very happy to see no hint of being worn down by the threat that I now knew hung over him. Still as erect, fit, and calm as ever. He might be going bald and getting gray, but that's the only sign of age on him.

He chuckled at the dumbfounded look on my face. "How did you get here?" I blurted.

"Armored pod," he replied, waving at a chair. I plopped down into it. "I was going to talk to you soon anyway, but with this storm"—he waved his hand at the ceiling—"nothing is going on; at least, nothing that the police and rescue services can't handle without me, and Kent's office is more secure than mine."

I didn't have to ask him what he meant by that. Uncle might be the prefect of police and, on top of that, in charge of all the Hunters that aren't in the army, but he had political enemies, and one of them was probably behind the attempt to murder me. "What can I do for you, Uncle?" I asked immediately.

"I've discussed this with Kent," he said, leaning forward, which made me lean forward too. "I want someone absolutely trustworthy to run the patrols in the storm sewers under the Hub...the City Center. It's getting too dangerous for my police units."

I nodded. This was something the Cits couldn't *ever* know, or it would send them into a panic. Nasty, dangerous Othersiders *are* getting in past the Barriers, and it's getting worse. If the Cits knew that what they thought were special effects to sex up the Hunts were in fact real, the city might shut down. People would be afraid to go to their jobs, afraid to walk on the streets. They'd know what we Hunters know and what some of the police and Psimons know: that they are *not* safe, and that only the Hunters' vigilance keeps the horrors off their throats.

What Uncle had just told me confirmed what I had suspected. The police couldn't handle what was penetrating into the very heart of the city anymore. That was also probably why he elected to come here to talk with me about it and not risk that his enemies would discover this and use it against him.

"Kent thinks you can do it solo because of the size of your pack," Uncle continued. "The sewers aren't big enough to send down more than a pair of Hunters at a time, at any event."

I thought about that. "I've got a pack big enough for three," I admitted. "If Armorer Kent thinks I can do this, then, yes, Uncle, I will."

There was more than a touch of relief in Uncle's expression. And then he leaned over the desk to speak very softly. "I can't go into details, Joy, but there's something very wrong down there. Something more than Othersiders getting into the sewers, and something I don't want to trust to anyone else. I want you to be extra careful, but also keep your head on a swivel for anything that doesn't look right to you. I'm asking Kent to put you down there as soon as it's feasible. And if you find something you can't put into a report, then exercise your privilege as my niece and ask for a face-to-face with your good old uncle."

I nodded, and he sat back in the chair as if he had never said anything at all.

We chatted for a while about inconsequential things after that. He relaxed, and so did I. I asked him more things about my dad and mom, and whether or not he knew any of my Masters himself. It was *such* a relief to actually be able to talk about home without censoring every word that came out of my mouth!

As it turned out, he knew Lady Rhiannon when they were both kids, before his whole family moved to Apex. And he knew Master Begay and Master Jeffries, who were now senior, senior Masters, as just Hunters.

Just as we were talking about Master Jeffries, another of those gut-clenching barrages of thunder shook the entire building, and the lights dimmed for a moment. I held my breath, afraid they would go out—but they came back up again.

"Storms like this remind me of the time the Thunderbirds came over Anston's Well, and all the Hunters had worked together to create a Shield to protect the entire village from them," he said. "I was only a kid then. Just ten years old."

I'd heard the story from Master Begay, who had only been a Hunter then, but this was a chance to hear it from Uncle! "What was *that* like?" I asked, a little breathlessly.

"I've been thinking about that story a lot lately," he told me as I leaned forward in my chair to listen. "We knew the storm was coming, and we'd need firewood to carry us through because we wouldn't be able to get outside once it started. Everyone who was old enough to carry even a little wood was out by the splitters, gathering up as much as we could hold and running it into the houses. I can't remember how many armloads I'd carried—twenty, forty, maybe more—when Sheila Yazzy screamed and dropped her wood and pointed at the sky. We all looked up and saw them, coming in on the storm front. Black against the clouds, you knew the minute you clapped eyes on them they were something other than eagles. Long necks, long forked tails—they had raptors' beaks and eyes that glowed brilliant red. Even as high as they were, the eyes shone so bright you could see them from the ground."

I'd seen Thunderbirds at a great distance, though never more than two at a time. I could *see* it in my head, the towering, charcoal-colored storm clouds, stark against the blue sky, and black against them, the Thunderbirds. Like cutouts of black paper, because they soared more than they flew, and with that storm wind under their wings, they wouldn't have had to flap at all. You would hardly know they *were* living things, except for the movement at the tips of their wings, their heads shifting as they would look down at their prey, and those fiery red eyes.

"We all stood there, paralyzed, when someone, I don't know who, had the presence of mind to run and blow the alarm horn. That broke the spell on us, and we ran for shelter. The two Hunters of Anston's Well—that would be Shadi Newsom and Yanaba Yellowhorse back then, they put up their Shields to cover the whole village, and just in time, for the first of the Thunderbirds canted over sideways and began a diving run. Have you ever seen them attack?"

I shook my head. There hadn't been Thunderbirds anywhere near the Mountain in all the time I'd lived there—only way, way off in the distance, and they never menaced us. I knew that the story of this attack was the reason why.

"They dove out of the sky, but not like a falcon or an eagle with folded wings. They came down slowly, in a descending spiral, with their wings spread. And as they came, lightning struck from out of their eyes and their mouths."

It was easy to picture; something Drakken-size coming down in a lazy curve; my insides knotted up as I imagined it, because when an Othersider takes its time moving in on you, it's because that monster *knows* it's got you right where it wants you, and you're basically a mouse looking up at the talons of an owl.

"Shadi and Yanaba had gotten the Shields up just in time; if any of those bolts had struck the wooden houses or the wooden palisade around the village, they would have gone up in flames. I ran, then, and got as far as the porch of the community hall, but there I stayed." He shrugged. "I don't know what I thought I could accomplish, but it felt as if I ought to be there. I suppose that's why whoever was blowing the alarm horn stayed at his post too."

"How many Thunderbirds were there?" I asked. In my mind there were ten or so of them, the first one coming down lazily, firing off blinding lightning bolts that were just barely absorbed by the Shield, the rest firing off their lightning from higher above, and the thunder rocking everything like the thunder outside was shaking our building.

"Six, eight, it was hard to tell. At least six, probably no more than ten or a dozen. The storm hit about that time, sleet sheeted down out of the clouds, and there was lightning lashing everywhere, not just the lightning coming from the Thunderbirds. I didn't hear anything like that constant barrage of thunder until we moved to Apex and the whole family was in our first apartment here, in a big storm like the one going on outside." He reached over to the cool-cabinet on the wall, got a bottle of water, and handed me one. I took it wordlessly.

I knew those early winter storms, when it wasn't quite winter but you could still get something as bad or worse than a blizzard. And the Thunderbirds would have been augmenting what would have been a bad sleet storm and turning it into something worse. The only thing that the village had going for it that day had been that the Thunderbirds didn't like the cold any more than any Othersider did, so they had controlled the storm and kept it to rain where they were flying.

But such rain . . . if it was anything like today, here and now, from the community hall where Uncle had been standing, he wouldn't have been able to see the gate to the palisade through the pouring rain.

"Shadi and Yanaba wouldn't have been able to hold out for very long under that punishment, but it wasn't more than fifteen, twenty minutes before the first of the roving Hunters came down from the Monastery. Hunter Begay was the first, but the rest weren't far behind him. I didn't even realize they were there until, all of a sudden, there were four people out there in the clearing in the middle of the village. Then six. Then eight."

They were all there, in my mind, standing in a tight little circle, facing out, hands outstretched as they bolstered the Shield. Master Jeffries and Master Begay must have looked like stone statues, anchoring the rest.

"Between their combined Shields and the relentless lightning from the Thunderbirds, even people like me could see the Shields. It looked like someone had put up a glowing dome of light over the whole of Anston's Well, light that shifted colors the way the colors shift in a soap bubble. By that time, I was riveted. I couldn't have moved if I'd wanted to."

I'd seen that too, seen what happened when more than one Hunter combined their Shields to make one big shield. That was what the Elite had done for the last of my Trials. But this one would have been fluorescing every time a lightning bolt hit it, and—that was where my imagination failed me. It must have been glorious and utterly terrifying at the same time. "Then what happened?" I asked as he stopped to take a drink.

He smiled. "Ah, well, *then* the Masters came down. By that time, some of the Hunters had run out of manna, a couple of them had drained themselves to the point where they were passing out. Shadi was the first; she just dropped where she stood, right down into the rainwater that was ankle-deep at that point. That was when I woke up and ran out there and started dragging or helping people into the shelter of the porch, out of that pouring storm—and people in the community hall came out to my shout and brought them inside into the warm."

I felt a burst of pride for the little boy who became my uncle. At any moment, that Shield could have failed and he'd have been Thunderbird chow. But he'd run right out there to help. No wonder he'd turned into what he was.

"Hon Li was the eldest Master then. He had four huge Hounds that he said were Tibetan mastiffs, sacred temple dogs, and they were the size of your Dusana. He brought them through the Portal, while the rest of the Masters bolstered the Shield. And then at his command, they dropped the Shield, and a bolt of light so bright I couldn't even look at it lanced up from his hands and hit the Thunderbird just overhead square in the chest."

It must have hit the ground like that meat avalanche, the Drakken we'd felled!

"It dropped like a stone, without a sound, and as soon as it hit the ground, those four Hounds were on it. One on the neck, one on each wing, and one in the middle of the back, while the Masters brought the Shield back up before the other Thunderbirds had time to react. The Hounds had that thing broken and dead in moments. And then the lightning stopped."

He paused dramatically. I waited, clutching the bottle of water in my hands.

"Hon Li gestured, and the Masters took the Shield down again. We all looked up. The remaining Thunderbirds were just— hovering. As if they were in shock, totally dumbstruck by the fact that we'd killed one of them. There was even a pause in the storm, as if the storm itself was in shock. It was so quiet . . . so quiet. And then Hon Li bowed to the Thunderbirds."

"He—what?" I said, not sure I had heard him right. Master Begay hadn't told us this part. Then again, by that time Master Begay had been one of the ones passed out.

"He bowed to them," Uncle repeated, "and then he spoke. His voice wasn't loud, but I think somehow it could have carried for miles—it just had that sort of quality about it. *You have lost one of your own today, and now you know what we can do. Of a courtesy,*

I think that you should leave us in peace, he said. Only that. And just like that, the Thunderbirds shot straight up into the clouds, and disappeared."

Master Begay had just said, "We killed one Thunderbird and the rest fled," but then, his version had been pretty bare-bones compared to Uncle's. He sure hadn't told me what Elder Master Hon Li had said. Now, if I hadn't heard that from my uncle, I am not sure I would have believed it.

"Hon Li was a very great man," Uncle said meditatively. "I wish there were more like him."

"Well," I replied after a moment, "I do know that we've never had a Thunderbird attack on the Mountain since. I've seen them at a far distance, generally at the front of a storm, but they go about their business and they've never threatened us."

"Maybe Thunderbirds are the rare Othersiders that can be reasoned with," Uncle mused. "Or maybe they were so shocked by losing one of the flock, they've decided to leave the Mountain alone."

"Maybe both. Maybe some other reason we'll never figure out or understand. And maybe they're just waiting until they're sure Master Hon Li is long dead," I replied.

Uncle laughed. "That would not surprise me in the least." He stood up. "I'll tell Kent what your new assignment is, and he'll take care of the rest. Enjoy your storm days, Joy." He made a little sign that I should come over and be hugged, and I did. Then we left the office together, and he went off with Kent while I went back to my rooms.

As far as I could tell, the storm was still just as bad out there. Someone had put music on in the halls, probably to mask the sound of the thunder, but I could still feel the building vibrating through my feet.

I automatically checked my vid to see if there were any assignments, but of course, there weren't. Well. Now I was on another secret mission from Uncle, or something like that. Of course, it wasn't *exactly* a secret mission, but nobody but he knew what the heck I was supposed to be looking for down in the sewers.

The walls vibrated, and the storm growled, deep in its throat, feral. Not like a cornered beast, but like one that had its prey in sight. It wasn't supposed to have hit us this hard.... Why had it diverted?

I didn't know enough, and I knew too much. I sat down on the sofa and decided to see if I could get a call through to Josh. I wanted to talk to someone, and maybe he already knew about this assignment. He picked up right away, but what I could see of where he was didn't look like either Uncle's office or his own apartment. The lighting was subdued, he was in a corner, and it looked like I was getting the feed from his Perscom camera. He wasn't wearing his black-and-silver Psimon uniform; he was in something that looked comfortable and casual, and his blond hair was mussed.

And it's weird, but seeing him relaxed and completely at ease made me feel better. Maybe subconsciously I was thinking that if *he* was stressed out, that was the signal I should be. "Hey!" he said, sounding as pleased to see me as I was to see him. "Enjoying your storm day?"

"I don't know yet; I just got breakfast," I said. I figured if he knew Uncle had come over here, he'd know what Uncle told me, and if he didn't, it was something I should keep to myself. But ...

I really, really wanted him to know about it because I desperately wanted to be able to talk about it with him. On the other hand, I couldn't just blurt out the questions—channels being monitored and recorded, and all—so I just came up with something to say. "Guess what! They gave us *pizza* last night!"

He laughed. "Then you're eating better than I am. It's military meals for us here." He made a face. I didn't blame him. I'd had MMs a time or two; they were packaged meals that would probably outlast the heat-death of the universe, and while nutritious, they were . . . well . . . utilitarian. So bland they came with hot pepper in a packet on the side, just to make them taste of *something*.

"Where's *here*?" I asked.

"The office. Those of us that didn't get home before the storm hit—and don't get the use of armored pods—have to live here for the duration. Cots, MMs, and a lot of vid and games. We don't even get a spectacular view of the storm; the metal storm shields come up over all the windows." He waved his hand around. "I'm lucky. I get the privacy of the prefect's supply closet to sleep in and the use of his private bathroom, and he lets me keep clothing here so I'm not stuck in my uniform. So there's that."

"What about my uncle?" I asked. "Do you know where he is?"

"He's gone to a meeting in an armored pod; he should be back soon, and I think he's planning on bringing something other than MMs back with him anyway." He raised one eyebrow. "Your uncle might be the most dedicated man I've ever met, but if he went somewhere that has a kitchen, I know damn sure he's going to bring some decent food back with him. 'Dedicated' doesn't mean 'stupid.'"

I laughed at that, as I was supposed to, but that meant Uncle hadn't told Josh where he was going, or why. Dammit. Why didn't he know? Would Uncle tell him later? This *sucked*. I felt a flare of anger, followed by resignation, and I reminded myself it wasn't Josh's fault he didn't know. So I'd keep that to myself unless and until Josh said something indicating he knew that I was doing the sewer prowl under Apex Center.

"Hey, since we're both stuck, you want to play a vid-game?" he asked.

I flushed. "I know this makes me sound like a turnip all over again, but I don't exactly know how," I admitted, feeling exceptionally awkward. "That's not something we do back home." *Because we're too busy farming and making and hunting and Hunting,* I thought, a little resentful now of the leisured lives of city-dwellers.

"Well, how about if I teach you?" he offered. "You'll get the hang of it pretty quickly. I've got a cooperative mystery-puzzle game; I'll send you a link and we'll start it together."

So that was what we did for the rest of the morning, after he moved to the secretary's desk to use her vid-screen instead of his Perscom screen; and I have to admit it was an entirely novel experience, and fun. More fun than I expected. It was a game set in Victorian London, a murder mystery with magic and horror elements. Whoever had plotted it out was really good; it was like being in the middle of a movie, or somehow walking into a really immersive book and becoming one of the characters. Just about when I was thinking I wanted a break for lunch, he froze the scene we were in.

"Time to save and leave it for later," he said before I could ask what was up. "I hear the prefect in the office, so I need to at least see if he needs me."

"More like you want to see what food he's brought," I teased as the game setting on the vid-screen faded away, showing our two avatars frozen and the words *Saving and Exiting* superimposed over them. Josh's face returned to the screen.

He smirked. "Are you *sure* you're not a Psimon?" he teased back. "All right, Joy, I'm sure you're as hungry as I am, and you probably want to go shoot a target anyway, since you're not shooting monsters. I'll catch you later tonight."

"Bet on it!" I replied, and closed the connection so I wouldn't be tempted to stretch out our good-bye to keep him there.

Lunch, a workout, and a session at the indoor range took up most of the afternoon. I did make the experiment of trying to use magic on my bullets the way Knight did, but I had no luck with it. It just didn't feel right. It was a little frustrating, since intellectually it seemed as if I *should* be able to make it work, but I guess my gut didn't agree. Stupid gut.

BY DINNERTIME, PEOPLE HAD gotten over being unnerved by the storm, and things were as back to normal as they were going to get. You'd be insane to go outside, of course, unless you took an armored pod straight out of the garage and to another garage. But people weren't huddling together in a herd in the lounge now. They were doing what I had done: range time, working out, swimming, games.

I hit the mess at the usual time for dinner. *It* was full. I got my tray and looked around for a place to sit. Luckily for me, Hammer and Steel spotted me and waved me over to one of the tiny tables meant for no more than three. I squeezed myself in between them with a nod of thanks.

And that was when—appropriately enough, all things considered—my subconscious hit me with the association of their call-signs. *He picked up a hammer and a little piece of steel*—"All right, I think I got it," I said, by way of conversation, after I'd gotten a few bites in. "Are your real names John and Henry?" I could have looked it up, of course, but this was more fun.

They exchanged a look that was partly startled and partly delighted. "Congratulations, Ms. Sherlock," said Hammer. "You know the song?"

"It took me a while to put it all together," I admitted. "But I remembered the song 'John Henry.'" I sang the first verse quietly—my voice is nothing to brag about. "'Well, John Henry was a little baby, sittin' on his daddy's knee, he picked up a hammer and a little piece of steel, and cried hammer's gonna be the death of me, Lord, Lord, hammer's gonna be the death of me.' We have a lot of amateur musicians back home." Which, of course, we did. It doesn't take electricity to run guitars and other instruments, and winter nights up on the Mountain get pretty long.

"Our mother's a folklorist," said Steel. I nodded; that pretty much meant nothing like what it used to mean back before the Diseray. Now it means someone who's going through all the pre-Diseray records, looking for folktales and myths and cataloging the magic and the monsters found in them. Even pre-Diseray fantasy fiction is fair game because a lot of it was based on obscure myth we haven't found the records for. "And our father's a musician. He collects folk songs for mother, goes out to places like that Anston's Well of yours, when he's not performing. He's brought back some interesting stuff...." He shivered. "I just hope the song he brought back about the Hide-behind isn't true. Makes me glad we don't work the night." I nodded. I knew that song. It was about someone in the remote hills who is walking home one night from meeting his girl and hears something behind him. It's like a Diseray Othersider story before the Diseray. It doesn't end well.

"Well . . . there are those I'd like to see meet one. I wouldn't mind it a bit if *Ace* met up with a Hide-behind," Hammer growled, his brows furrowed into a solid line of anger. "The sooner, the better."

That seemed to come out of nowhere. "Not that I'm arguing with you, but what brought that on?" I asked.

Steel tried to calm his brother down with a gesture, but Hammer wasn't having any. "Word is, he's been spending time outside the lockup. *Too* much, if you ask me."

That made all the hair on my head stand up because I had not for one second forgotten about Ace, and it sounded like the brothers knew things I didn't. Well . . . thanks to the storm, all the Hunters were here in HQ together at once and perfectly able to call up old friends outside HQ and chat, like I'd chatted with Josh. And nothing spreads like gossip. "He's dangerous," I said flatly. "He's still dangerous. Not just to me, either. He's probably decided all the Hunters are against him, and I don't think there's any chance he's suddenly come to understand the error of his ways."

"Well, if he thinks all the Hunters are against him, he's right," Steel agreed. "He's already put up a good front of being all repentant and cooperative. He's probably betting that they'll let him completely off the leash."

So, that just put all my alarms on full. "You know stuff I don't." I said. "Tell!"

"I have friends in the army; I know they've already let him mix with the other Mages," Hammer said flatly. "Ace isn't dumb. He has to make himself real useful to the army, so I bet he's

picking up new tricks as fast as he can cram them into his skull."
The look in Hammer's eyes told me if he ever got a shot at Ace ...
the result would not be pretty. Now, pretty much nobody here
liked Ace anymore, but this sounded kind of personal to me. I
wondered what Ace had done to Hammer. I glanced over at his
brother; Steel was just shaking his head. Steel gave me a sidelong
glance and sort of shrugged, like *I can't do anything with him
when he's like this.*

Finally, Hammer let out his breath in an angry puff, and
seemed to cool off a little.

Steel tapped his finger against his glass thoughtfully. "Here's
the thing, Joy. We've worked with army Mages, and they're not
like the APD Mages your uncle has under him. Being with other
army Mages is only going to give him a bigger ego than he had
before. Army Mages think Hunters are some sort of second-class
magic users. By now they'll have him convinced that having his
Hounds ditch him was a sign he was *destined* for greater things."

"Wait, what?" I replied, bewildered, because while we have
Mages up at the Monastery (quite a few of the Masters are Mages
rather than Hunters, and each one of them has an apprentice), that
didn't sound like the Mages *I* knew.

"The army Mages I've met have egos the size of a planet,"
Hammer told me sourly. "We *used* to have a friend that popped
Powers, turned out to be a Mage, and joined the army. Magically,
they're more powerful than most Hunters, and their notion is they
can do anything that a Hunter can do without needing to depend
on Hounds. The minute Ace is allowed to mix with the Mages ...
If he was a problem before, he's going to be four times the problem.
They're like the Psimons, basically, in that way."

"Except they aren't cold fish like the Psimons are," Steel added. "Other than that, they're two of a kind. Both Psimons and Mages think Apex doesn't need us, and they could do everything we can do in half the time and a quarter of the effort."

I nodded; I could certainly believe that. And sure, the Mages I've seen can do things we Hunters can't. But a single Mage is just one mind and set of powers against the monsters. A single Hunter is *several* minds, bodies, and sets of powers. A Mage can't be everywhere at once. Sometimes we Hunters can, thanks to the Hounds.

So while technically, one-on-one, a Mage might be able to do more than a Hunter, he's just one person. A Hunter, depending on how good his bond is with his Hounds, can be a small army all on his own. The army likes to use Mages more than Hunters, according to my uncle, because the army doesn't really trust Hounds. Hounds are Othersiders too, and the army doesn't really trust *any* Othersiders.

"I've never seen an army Mage that wasn't a colossal—" Steel coughed. "Egomaniac." I knew what he was going to say. . . . My people back home get pretty salty in their language, even if most of us up at the Monastery try to keep it reined in. "They won't give regular army the time of day, and only answer to officers—if then. Ace should fit right in," he added sourly.

"Well, let's hope my uncle managed to drum into their thick skulls that Ace is not to be trusted, and he's only there and not in the deepest, darkest hole he could be stuffed into because Uncle's judgment got overruled," I reminded them. "But you are right. Anytime he shows up around us, we need to keep one eye on him. Or at least, keep a Hound's eye on him."

"Do you think his two might go back to him?" Hammer asked, an expression of worry crossing his face.

I shook my head. "Not a chance. They're disgusted with him. So much so that when they talk about him, I can *feel* how disgusted they are. He's like something nasty they stepped into by accident, and they can't wash him off fast enough."

Hammer's face cleared. He and Steel have really close bonds with their Hounds, almost as close as mine.

"Can you guys ask your friends in the army to keep an eye on him, or at least talk to people who can?" I asked. I tried not to make it sound like I was begging, but I was. Hammer nodded and gave me a pat on my shoulder. "We'll have a chat with them and see what they can find out about Ace, what kind of leash his keepers have him on, and whether or not he's managed to talk his way into loosening up the terms and conditions he's being held under. We'll get back to you."

"I'll see what Uncle can find out too," I told them. *And Josh,* I added silently. Because Josh had means of finding out things only a Psimon has, not the least of which are the things other Psimons have picked up and are talking about.

Hammer changed the subject then, since we seemed to have talked that one dry, and we ended our dinner laughing over stupid jokes. The lounge was crazy-packed, and people were mostly dancing; the cameras for the regular Hunters were crowding the ceiling, and I decided to skip the festivities. I plopped down on my sofa and checked the weather before I tried connecting with Josh. I could scarcely believe the total for the rainfall; those storm sewers I had so blithely patrolled were probably 90 percent full of rushing water that was moving along at the speed of a train. I almost felt sorry for the Othersiders that were caught down there.

Almost.

It looked like the storm was going to clear sometime in midmorning, moving out to sea. Well, the kinds of ships out there were built for that sort of thing. They were few and far between, a small percentage of the traffic that had once moved pre-Diseray, but it was safer to send things to other continents by ship than it was by air. Heck, it was safer to go suborbital than it was to go by air, and our suborbital flights had a habit of augering in so often when Othersiders noticed them that they're operated as drones, and the nickname for them was "Giant Darts."

So about midmorning I could expect to get a callout. But Uncle wanted me down there right away, and I wouldn't be able to do what Uncle wanted and patrol the tunnels under the City Center until . . .

Hmm. "Question. What agency monitors the flow of water in the storm sewers?" I asked aloud.

"*Apex Power and Water, Reclamation Division,*" the room's computer replied. It had a female voice. I'm not sure why.

"Question. Can I access the Apex Power and Water, Reclamation Division flow monitors for the storm sewers?" You had to be careful how you phrased questions, or the computer got confused.

"*Affirmative.*"

"Order. Notify me when the Apex Power and Water, Reclamation Division storm sewer flow monitors beneath Apex Central register zero flow, and/or less than one percent water present. One-time notification."

"*Affirmative. Order logged.*" There. Now I'd know when it was safe to go down there.

As for my getting caught down there if a storm blew up . . . well, that was a possibility. And given that someone had tried to kill me already, I was going to go to Kent and make sure he made it a priority that I *got* storm warnings, even if he had to call me himself.

My alarm went off at the usual time, and my vid-screen popped up with *Report to armory for briefing.* A hand to the wall told me that the building wasn't vibrating anymore; the storm was over, or at least moving off, and it was time to get back to work.

And to reinforce *where* I was going to be this morning, my alert from Power and Water told me that the flow in the sewers was at 3 percent of capacity, and dropping.

I grabbed breakfast with Knight; it was fun hearing about my people through the eyes of his, and he had a lot of questions about the ones where his folk had settled. I was happy enough to answer them, and he left looking pretty contented with his world. I headed for the armory briefing room.

Kent already had the vid-screen up and running, and he waved me to a seat. "This will be short. You'll have the map on your Perscom. There is a maintenance crew that will want your escort today. They are probably the only Cits that know about the danger down there; they're handpicked and hard to rattle."

Well, that was a piece of good news. "Armed?" I asked.

"Some of them," Kent confirmed. "Licensed, obviously, and they get regular range tests."

Also good news. People who can defend themselves are always an asset.

"Pick your kit and get ready to bounce. I'll have a pod to take you to the south entrance."

I didn't get much chance to breathe the storm-washed air as I ran from the building to the waiting pod, but the little I did get I inhaled gratefully. The sky was completely cloudless, everything was a little damp, and the sun seemed especially bright. Too bad I wasn't going to get to appreciate it. I've always loved the hours after a storm passes; it seems as if the world is shining and new.

The pod dropped me off at what looked like a little concrete bunker, a door set in the middle of it with an ID checker beside it. There was also a group of six people in bright yellow coveralls and hard hats—the repair crew that Kent had said might be waiting for me. They looked excited and relieved, all at once, to see me.

"I didn't know we were going to get you, Hunter Joy," said the one in the only bright blue helmet, who must have been the crew chief, as the pod drove off by itself. His face was actually lit up with pleasure. A sturdy girl with short, dark hair dug her elbow into his side before he could say anything more.

"Job first, Kelly. Fan service later," she said with a hint of a smile.

"Let's get this job started, then," I said, and the crew chief presented his Perscom to the ID checker. There was the sound of the door unlocking, but no one made any move to open it.

Smart people, I thought with satisfaction, and cast the Glyphs and opened the Way for the Hounds.

Given we were going to be in a sewer, which meant limited space, all my originals had come in greyhound form. I opened the door, and five of the eleven crowded in, looked down the ladder, and *bamphed*.

The ladder is safe, said Bya in my head, and I went into the little bunker and started climbing down the ladder. At the bottom, I held out my arms, and Hold and Strike jumped down to be caught, one at a time, while Myrrdhin and Gwalchmai *bamphed* down with Kalachakra and Shinje. "All clear!" I called up the ladder, and waited for the maintenance crew to get down while the Hounds and I surveyed the sewer as far as we could see.

All the lights were on, which I was pleased about; I wasn't sure how well protected the lights would have been from the water that must have been pouring through here. There was a thin trickle of water down the center of the floor but nothing more than that. The crew chief, Kelly, was the first down the ladder. "What are we fixing, and how far is it?" I asked.

"Electrical short, about a half a mile north," he said. That would put us just about squarely in the middle of the City Center by my reckoning. "And if it turns out to have been caused by a leak, we're to find and seal that." He coughed self-consciously. "We're hoping it's a leak," he continued. "Because if it's not, it'll be Them."

"We'd prefer our jobs to be routine and boring, but this is what they pay us the big bucks for," said the short-haired woman.

"We get paid?" I said in an incredulous voice, getting a laugh from all of them. "Give me a second to get the troops deployed." I put Hold and Strike with Bya, Dusana, Shinje, and Kalachakra on the front half, Myrrdhin and Gwalchmai and the other three in the rear. I asked Bya to be the front scout, and Myrrdhin to be the lag-behind, and then we set off. They introduced themselves to me; Kelly was the crew chief, Sanders was the woman, and the rest of the crew were Blake, Feineman, Rodrigo, and Lee.

I noticed that Sanders was one of the three packing a handgun, in a well-worn and well-oiled holster, right next to some of her tools on her tool belt. And that gave me some concerns.

I managed to sidle up to Sanders and caught her eye. "What are your loads?" I asked politely, nodding at her sidearm.

"Steel shot," she said without hesitation. "We get special loads from Supplies. Ricochet is nuts down here."

I nodded, relieved, since that was exactly what I was worried about, and why I had a shotgun instead of a sidearm. She chuckled. "You're smart to ask, but anyone they let down here has had the lecture, the demonstration, and the *graphic* demonstration."

I didn't ask what the *graphic* demonstration was. I had the feeling it probably involved a lot of vid of people who had become "cautionary tales."

The sewer was about twenty-four feet wide, and a flat oval, with the lights behind protected slabs of something transparent above us. At about six-foot intervals, there were smaller pipes about a foot in diameter entering the main line about halfway up. The mouths of these pipes were covered in a metal grate; by the rust on the grates, I knew these were cold-forged iron, something most, if not all, Othersiders cannot tolerate. I'd seen the street-level openings of these pipes when I'd gone out running; the openings were not only covered by identical metal grates—they had a fine metal mesh over the top of that. "Hey," I said, "how do you keep the inlets up on the street from getting clogged up by debris during storms?"

"Turtles," said Sanders. "That's what we call them, anyway.

Armored gutter sweepers; they're about twice the size of an armored pod and heavily weighted so floodwaters can't carry them away. They're out as long as the rain's coming down. I used to drive one. It's weird—you obviously can't see anything in the downpour, so there's no windows and it's all drive-by-wire, the same guide wires the driverless pods use. We could send 'em out without a driver, and sometimes we do, but the bosses want a driver on board in case you sweep up a body. Human, I mean, not one of Them."

"There are always at least half a dozen bodies for each storm," said Lee from behind me, before I could ask. "Sometimes more, never less. Accidents, people not paying attention to the warnings, Spillovers that take advantage of the rain to run across the Barriers and don't realize you can't just find a busted-up building to take shelter in once you get over here."

It was the way he said those words that gave me a bit of a chill . . . as if these dead *people* were an inconvenience and of no more importance than a dead rabbit. Less, really—you could eat the rabbit . . . but I managed to keep my thoughts to myself.

"Well," said Kelly, his tone going dark, "I've had my suspicions about some of those bodies for a long time. If you wanted to get rid of someone, it wouldn't be hard to invite 'em over for a storm party, get 'em drunk, then haul 'em outside. The storm would take care of the rest; they'll just drown, probably get washed as much as a mile away from where you left 'em, and no way to trace it back to you."

I made a note to tell that to my uncle. Because Kelly was quite right: that *would* be a good way to get rid of someone. And I made another note to make sure that I was either in my room alone, locked in, or with people I knew I could trust during storms. You know, just in case.

Of course, anyone trying to ambush me would get a big surprise. I can do the emergency summons for my pack in mere seconds now, and if I did that, they'd come over alert and angry.

"Damn, Kelly," said Blake, with an uneasy laugh. "I'm glad you're on our side."

"He watches too many murder mysteries," Sanders replied with a snort. "Last time I was over at his house, that's all that was on the vid. You're gonna raise those kids of yours thinking that every other person they meet wants to kill 'em."

That led to some good-natured bickering about vid shows. I let them chatter. It didn't interfere with my communication with my pack, and it kept them relaxed. They didn't *need* to be vigilant; that was what the pack and I were there for.

Besides, I really wanted them to concentrate on each other and leave me alone. If I had to make conversation with them, that *would* interfere with my communication—and I didn't want this turning into fan service for the same reason.

It was cool, damp, and very, very clean down here—pretty much what you would expect in a concrete tube that had been scoured by rainwater for two solid days. According to my Perscom map, we were approaching an intersection where two smaller sewer pipes joined this one. I sent Bya and Myrrdhin ahead to check both of them out as the sewer crew continued talking, this time about the ranking Hunters. With me and Ace out of the picture, the current top five were changing nearly every time a shift went out to Hunt, and the top ten were all within a few points of one another. Since today would be the first Hunts since the storm started, all of them had opinions about who would come in at the number-one spot after first shift. I didn't really care now that I was Elite, except insofar as Ace's group had pretty much broken up and were being friendlier to everyone, making the competition among the regular Hunters less antagonistic than it had been when I first arrived.

Bya and Myrrdhin went back to their scouting ahead. *No scents at all coming from the side tunnels,* Bya told me.

In addition to sniffing out trouble, some of the Hounds could use senses besides scent; my original seven could tell when there was another Othersider or a Mage or Hunter using magic about. Thanks to the Hounds, we were able to move briskly, passing several more side sewers before ending up at our destination.

Besides the grated pipes leading up to the streets, there had been featureless metal doors painted the same color as the 'crete every fifty feet or so. Our goal was one of those, on the right-hand side of the sewer. As we neared it, the chatter stopped, and the crew got tense. I didn't blame them.

When we stopped opposite our goal, they all looked straight at me.

"How do we open this?" I asked Kelly in as quiet a voice as I could manage, while the Hounds arranged themselves, two pairs facing up or down the sewer tunnel, just to make sure we didn't get ambushed, and the rest in a semicircle around the door.

"Magnetic seal," he said. "I unseal it with this, it pops open and moves to the side, inside." He held out a gizmo, and I nodded.

"All right. I am going to assume there's something in there, and be pleasantly surprised to find out otherwise. So all of you, get in close to me. If you've got weapons, get them out now." I put up my Shield to cover us all; my Hounds each put up their own, and I primed my shotgun. "Kelly, whenever you're ready, pop the door."

He did something to the gizmo. The door made a *thunk* sound, pulled away from us, and slid to the side.

And I was not pleasantly surprised.

THINGS POURED OUT OF the door. Things I'd never seen before: half human-ish with *way* too many arms, and snakes for the bottom half and—they moved *fast*. They came right at us, and I hit them with the first things I could think of, strengthening my Shield around us all while simultaneously making a flash-bang and firing my shotgun, as beside me Sanders opened up with her pistol. The sound was deafening in the confines of the 'crete tunnel, but it still didn't drown out the shrill shrieks of the *things*. My heart was going a zillion beats a minute, and my head was on a swivel, keeping track of them.

Nagas! Bya shouted in my head, which meant nothing to me, and anyway, I was too busy backing the group up so we had the sewer wall at our backs, and opening up again with my shotgun. I got one square in the chest with the combination load of silver shot and blessed salt, and it stopped moving long enough for me to see these things had four arms—they were wielding *swords*, for heaven's sake—and they had mouths full of needle-teeth. *Keep the Cits safe*... That was all I could consciously think of, but lucky for all of us, the crew wasn't panicking, and they were just as concerned about keeping themselves protected as I was about protecting them.

Meanwhile, the Hounds weren't idle. As the unarmed members of the group squeezed in between us armed ones and the wall so they had cover on both sides, the Hounds were attacking whatever parts of the creatures they could get. Gwalchmai managed to get his teeth into the tail of one and tried dragging it away from the others, but the thing was lithe, strong, and smart, and Gwalchmai had to let go and leap out of the way to avoid being diced by four swords. That was the problem all the Hounds were having: these weren't stupid monsters, intent only on their prey.

"Kelly!" I snapped. "The door!" Because I sure did *not* want those things retreating into the smaller tunnel. There was no room to fight in there, no way to use anything more lethal than we already had without ruining what we'd come to fix, and they were better suited to those quarters than humans or Hounds were. I couldn't see Kelly, who was behind me, but he must have triggered his gadget because the door slid shut and sealed again before any of the monsters noticed it was closing.

Now all we had to do was survive a tornado of whiplike snake tails and swords.

My Shield was at least keeping them at bay, and the Hounds had regrouped, rearranged themselves to the left and right of us in a group of five and a group of six, and had changed tactics to defense. They dodged and leapt and stayed in constant motion, always staying just ahead of the whirling blades and the wicked tails, blocking the things from going either direction in the sewer tunnel. And meanwhile those of us with firearms fired round after round of steel or silver shot into them when I briefly dropped the Shield. Their skin was really tough, armored hide maybe, so the shot wasn't flaying them the way it would have something with just skin. But nevertheless it was having an effect. Every time one of them got hit with a load, it lost speed and a little agility, so it looked as if the steel and silver weakened them.

The cacophony of firearms and shrieking monsters was deafening. The monsters might have been slowed, but they never stopped moving. This was a stalemate; even if I pinned them down with a net, I wasn't at all sure how long I could hold it, and they could *still* use those whip-tails and their swords on the Hounds or us.

Was there even a chance they'd be as resistant to fire as they seemed to be to damage from firearms? *Only one way to find out.*

With a shouted cantrip and a quick tracing of Glyphs in the air, I formed up my net and dropped it on them, passing my shotgun to Kelly as I did so because I couldn't hold that net down and shoot at the same time. *Bya! Fire!* I told my Alpha, and in the next moment, my seven *Alebrijes* Hounds breathed inferno on the netted monsters.

The shrieks quadrupled in pitch and volume, and I clapped my hands to my ears, feeling as if someone was sticking red-hot needles into them. Behind me, the crew doubled over, doing the same as we all tried in vain to block out the hideously painful noise.

But the fire was working as nothing else we'd tried. I didn't even need to hold the net on them, which was just as well because with all that excruciating screeching going on, I couldn't.

Thankfully, they had to breathe in order to scream, and when they sucked in air for a fresh shriek, they sucked in fire too, and that ended the noise. The screams cut off before we all dropped over from the pain, and by that point, the monsters were flailing on the concrete, and the few that still had their swords in their clenched hands were utterly unable to use them. The Hounds jumped them then and tore them to bits.

Even though I was blinking away tears of pain, I could still see somewhat, and as I swallowed and tried to clear my ringing ears, I saw something else that was new. These monsters didn't go to goo as the Hounds inhaled their manna, nor did they fade away. Instead, they turned to dust. When the Hounds were finished, the floor of the tunnel was covered in piles of grayish-black powder, with swords scattered about the concrete as if discarded.

We took our sweet time recovering. Before we opened that door a second time, I wanted to make sure we all had at least part of our hearing back.

I passed around headache pills out of my pack, because all of us had *splitting* heads as well as ringing ears. Then for a while we all lined up sitting in a row, with our feet braced and our backs in the curve of the tunnel wall, and waited for our ears to clear and our heads to stop throbbing.

As for the Hounds, well, they were in fine fettle. Those monsters must have been pretty manna-rich, because the sword slashes the Hounds had gotten healed right up in front of our very eyes, and they looked as good as ever they had, long before our heads stopped hurting.

When the pounding in my skull finally eased up, I noticed something else—a scent. Where before there had been nothing in this tunnel but the smell of damp concrete, now there was the smell of snake musk—the bitter odor that some snakes give off when they're handled. I recognized it for what it was because, well, I'm a turnip and I've handled a lot of snakes as a kid. But as the repair crew stopped hurting and started noticing, they clearly didn't know what it was.

"What's that stink?" Lee asked, his nose wrinkling.

"It's from the whatever-they-weres, I guess," Kelly replied.

"Feh. It's nasty," Sanders said. "Reminds me of my ex-husband." By that I knew that they were getting back to normal. I got up first, and although the crew looked at me and sighed, they struggled to their feet as well.

"I have a plan," I said as the last of them got up. "If there are any more of those things in there, they won't have run away when the others died; in my experience, killing Othersiders just makes the rest want your blood more." *Or, except maybe for Thunderbirds . . .*

"Well, aren't you a bundle of good news," Lee said sourly.

"Actually, it is good news because it means they won't be sneaking up on you while you're in there making your repair," I pointed out. "So what we're going to do is: you all are going back up the tunnel, far enough that you're barely in range for that gizmo to open the door again. The Hounds and I will stay here. The second the door's open enough, I'm tossing a gas grenade in, and I want you to shut the door again on it."

"Poison gas?" Kelly wanted to know.

I shook my head. "Just tear gas. You've got nose plugs, right? And goggles." They all nodded; of course they did, that would be standard kit for anyone coming down here to fix things where they might encounter sewage gas. Methane can kill you, and not just by blowing you up. "Right, so we'll leave the door closed for about a minute, then open it up again. If there's any more of those things in there, they'll stampede for the open door and better air, and my Hounds will fry them."

I didn't hear any objections, so I pulled my full-face mask out of my pack and waited while they got their nose plugs in and goggles on. When everyone was ready, we all moved to our respective positions, and Kelly cracked the door.

It went like clockwork and was anticlimactic, because when Kelly opened the door for the second time, nothing came out but gas.

So we waited for the gas to clear some, then the crew went in and did their work while the Hounds and I stood guard. I even had Bya and Dusana in the maintenance tunnel with them to make sure there were no more surprises.

Then I collected some swords and stowed them in my pack, and we all trudged back up to the exit hatch again. Once we got to the ladder, I waited while the others climbed, and sent the Hounds back through their Portal. That was just to avoid putting the ones that couldn't *bamph* through the hassle of getting up the ladder the hard way. They *can* climb, but it's hard for them—they don't like to do it, and I don't blame them.

I was the last one out, and Kelly locked the door. And then they all turned to me. Kelly spoke first. "What in hell were those things?" he asked.

Well, I was already asking my Perscom that particular question. "My Hound Bya called them *Nagas*," I told him, while I looked up the word. "I've never seen anything like them before." My Perscom was no help. So evidently there was no record of those things in any Hunter encounters here in and around Apex, nor in the folklore my Perscom could access. "But look on the bright side," I continued. "We know they burn quite well."

The members of the crew looked at each other as if they weren't sure if I was being serious or not, and then Sanders cracked a smile. "True," she said. "And now we're never going down there without at least one of you Hunters with us."

"That'll be me for a while, anyway," I replied with a little shrug. "The worst part was being caught off guard. That won't happen again. And my pack knows what to do about them now."

None of us talked about the buffalo in the room—how the wretched things had *gotten* down there in the first place. This wasn't a herd of Knockers, who individually are small and have a chance of getting in through some hole in the defenses one at a time, nor Vamps, which sneak in at night. The *Nagas* had been about six feet tall head-to-floor, with another four-to-six feet of additional snake tail.

Then again . . . these people must already have been sworn to secrecy just to be allowed to work down there. This might not be the first time they'd seen something new. Kelly took off his blue safety helmet and scratched his head. He had a baby face, but his hair was going thin on top. "I don't suppose that you've still got the energy to pose for some pictures with us?" he said hopefully.

I am never going to understand this, I thought. Because an hour ago we'd narrowly escaped being turned into cold cuts by snake people. And now they wanted selfies with me.

I reminded myself again that this was part of the job. And I smiled and posed with everyone, and only after their pod had come and taken them off did I call for mine.

Once *in* that pod, though, I called HQ. I cut straight to the heart of things. "HQ, you got the feed from the tunnel cams, so is there any record of anything called a *Naga* in the files, or anything that looked like those snake-men?"

"Negative, Hunter," came the reply. *"Did your Hound give any other clues as to origin?"*

"Negative," I replied. "I think you need a folklorist."

Because of course I was going to get Bya as soon as I had the chance and grill him about it. But I wasn't going to let HQ know that. So far as I am aware, most Hounds, even if they do speak with their Hunters, are just not what you'd call chatty, and very few ever volunteer information.

"Report to debrief as soon as you arrive, Hunter." That was a new voice, and completely expected. I sighed. So much for going back on rotation or hitting another part of that sewer today. Unless a full-team callout came in, I was going to be toasted over a grill for the rest of the day.

This wasn't disciplinary, of course; it was informational, because there's so much that the camera can't pick up, like scent. But once I got back, I was in a little room with three skilled debriefers going over and over every second of the encounter, and pummeling my brain to try and think of something I hadn't remembered the first time. Having a headache the whole time didn't help. I kept drinking water, and eventually the pain faded, but it took a while. Somehow, having a headache that bad is worse than being mauled by a Wyvern.

These were three earnest, focused, and hyperorganized people (two men and a woman who looked so alike they could have been siblings) in a new sort of uniform—like a modified police uniform in dark, dark green instead of black. They sat across the table from me. They had done their level best to make the debriefing room as comfortable as possible: the walls were a nice, soothing pale green, the acoustics were perfect, quiet without being maddeningly so, and my chair was . . . well, as a kid I used to daydream about sitting in clouds, and that was pretty much what it felt like, and it even reclined. They got me headache pills, anything I wanted to drink, and they'd have fed me if I hadn't been nauseous. I couldn't have been annoyed with them if I'd wanted to be; I knew just how important this was. A new Othersider . . . the implications weren't good, and it was vital we get on top of this.

Finally, they indicated they were as satisfied as they were going to get, and let me go. By this time, having skipped lunch, I was more than ready for dinner.

But tonight's meal was going to be different for all of us.

The mess was full of tired people who were not in the least talkative. Hunters and Elite alike had been patrolling or on callouts all damn day. It had been the (expected) "storm" after the storm, as Othersiders who'd been rained into whatever shelter they'd been able to find had been out in force and hungry. It looked to have been a long, hard day for everyone, even those who had patrolled "easy" territories. People were crammed into any seat they could find; I was with two brand-new probationary Hunters who had just come into their packs and Powers and were so exhausted they didn't even notice when I sat down across from them.

Retro passed by, looking for a seat, and heaved an exaggerated sigh when he realized there was no room for him. "You're torturing me, here, Joy!" he said. "I might even start thinking you're deliberately avoiding hanging out with me if this keeps up!"

I'd have taken pity on him, except there really was no room. Then he happened to look over at the exhausted newbs, and smiled and shrugged when they looked up at him and half started to get up.

"Naw, guys, stay put, you look way too beat to move. I'll go drag my wounded ego over to Dazzle." And he winked at me and did just that.

When Kent strode into the place, at first no one took any notice of him, but then he spoke into the near silence, and heads came up all over the room.

"Listen up, Hunters. We have a new Othersider out there."

The four vid-screens up near the ceiling lit up with footage from our encounter with the *Nagas*, about thirty seconds' worth, before it froze on a particularly clear shot of one of the wretched things.

"*Swords?*" howled Tober, a burly, black-haired guy wearing Hunter colors of orange, brown, and black who had once been in Ace's clique. "They use *swords?*"

He was right to be astonished. We were used to Othersiders combating us with natural powers, or magic, but the Redcaps and

Knockers were the only ones I'd ever seen using weapons. The Knockers used crude clubs and flint knives. The Redcaps used slightly more sophisticated bronze knives. I wasn't sure what these swords were made of even though I had brought some in as samples—they certainly weren't bronze or steel. They were exquisitely crafted—even beautiful—blades, slightly curved, and with a wicked single edge.

"These new Othersiders have been identified as *Nagas,* and as you can see, their primary offense is physical. Extreme speed, using the tail as a weapon, and quadridextrous with swords."

Now that I wasn't pummeling my brain, I had time to examine the freeze-frame of the *Naga.* Four arms, all right; the jointing was really strange, as you'd figure from something with four arms. Since there wasn't an obvious set of hips, I wondered if the second set of arms was actually a modified set of legs on a shortened spine and a deformed pelvis. Human-ish torso blending into a snake body and tail. This one had jewelry, a kind of vest made of gold chains, and an engraved gold band binding his long black hair into a topknot. The jewelry hadn't persisted past their deaths, so it was either an illusion or a magical construct. There seemed to be scales on the backs of his arms, and his human skin was a muddy color between brown and green, while the snake part of him was more green. He had his mouth open in a snarl, and he definitely had the pointed teeth I remembered, although I wouldn't call them "fangs"; more as if he had filed all his human teeth to a point.

Kent continued describing everything I'd told the debriefers; I didn't exactly tune him out, but I was studying the freeze-frame more carefully than I was listening to him. The closer I looked, the more it seemed as if what appeared to be a human torso with a very defined set of pectoral muscles wasn't any such thing; it was a human-*shaped* torso covered in thin, flexible plates, perhaps serving the function of light armor. That would account for why the shot didn't do as much damage as it might have otherwise.

Kent started the vid up again; it cut to a freeze-frame of the light damage that had been done by our shot loads as he described what weapons had been used on the *Nagas* at that point.

The vid restarted, this time from when my Hounds unleashed their fire on the things. "As you can see, fire is extremely effective on them," Kent continued. Then the vid panned back to show all of us covering our ears and bending over double in pain. "However, a secondary and perhaps unintentional weapon is their voices. Until we have a better idea of how common these creatures are going to be, or where they are likely to appear, we are going to recommend that if you or your Hounds do not have any form of fire-powers, and that you are not in an area where you can freely use incendiary or armor-piercing munitions, that you retreat and call it in. And we also recommend that you carry hearing protection with you from now on."

The poor new Hunters were staring at the screen in utter horror. I didn't blame them. Here they were, already feeling cowed by the fact that now they were expected to face down monsters ... only to discover there were monsters out there *no one* had ever even seen before. Monsters that had come as a surprise to seasoned Hunters. "Hey," I said in a soft voice, causing both of them to turn suddenly and look at me with eyes the size of my cup. "Don't worry. They won't put you out there without a mentor for a good long time. We need Hunters; the last thing they'll do is stick you guys in training up against things you aren't ready for, know what I mean?"

The one licked his lips; the other swallowed. But they looked as if they had actually *heard* me, and started to get a little less scared.

"Besides," I continued, "I can guarantee that while *you* aren't used to fighting monsters, your *Hounds* are. You can rely on them to keep you safe."

They smiled weakly at that; obviously, being shiny new Hunters so green they still hadn't gotten the tattoos over their Mandalas, they'd already discovered that for themselves.

I might have said something else encouraging to them, but now Kent was venturing into information I didn't know, and I riveted my attention back on him.

"We've had the folklorists researching this, and one of them came through for us. It appears that these 'Nagas' are part of Indo-Asian religious lore." He nodded as that elicited a sharp reaction from the more experienced Hunters. "Exactly. This is the first time we've seen anything that wasn't native to this continent, or Grecian, Roman, or European."

There was absolute silence at that point, as the rest of us contemplated that. If we were going to have to start preparing to face monsters from every single culture on the planet . . . well, that was going to be a long, long list.

"I guess the folklorists are going to start looking for a pay-grade increase now," said someone on the other side of the room, earning a scattering of laughs.

"Just remember," Kent said, replacing the feed of the *Naga* fight with the weather feed. "Every Othersider was new to Hunters at some point. Don't let this rattle you. Just stay alert, and if you're in a position to back out if you encounter something you don't recognize, do so and call it in. And as for those of you who are rankers, remember that novelty is going to make you stand out. If these things pop up in your territory and on your watch..." He left the rest unsaid because he didn't *have* to say it. The competitive among us were already probably working out how to cache a flamethrower somewhere they could get to it easily (those things are infernally heavy, pun intended) or planning incendiary traps they could lure the things into. I will say this much for the Hunters who are focused on the fame and glory and not so much on the "protecting the Cits" part—they are inventive. And they kill just as many monsters as any other Hunter does. The longer I was in Apex City, the more inclined I was to weigh results heavier than motivation.

The new guys—my brain finally connected them with their names, Fox and Levy—were still looking a bit green as Kent left the room, so I did my best to soothe their fears. I don't know how well I did, but at least by the time I left, they had gotten some appetite back. I wondered who their mentors were. I hoped it was someone like Knight or Dazzle, or even Bree. Someone that would take the time to make sure they were okay, and not just breeze through everything and assume they'd be fine.

My vid-screen was blinking with messages when I got back to my room. One was from Kent, with a text rundown of what the folklorist had discovered and an attachment of several pages that I intended to study later. Not that I was sloughing these things off, but I already *knew* how to make them dead; knowing the folklore about them wouldn't help me to make them dead any faster.

The other message was from Josh. *Sky Lounge, Administration building? If yes, meet me there at eight.* That was all it said, but my heart skipped. A date, and this time, given that I was off rotation, unless we got a full-team callout, it was one I wasn't going to have to cut short. There wouldn't be any cameras following us around, just the security ones in the lounge itself. I messaged back *Yes, thank you!* made arrangements for a pod, and began ransacking my wardrobe. I put together a casual outfit that was a little bit dressy, following Kei's recommendations; sadly, the only things in my wardrobe other than what I had brought from home were all in my signature colors, but that couldn't be helped. Instead of putting my hair in a side-tail or putting it up, I let it loose. With any luck, anyone who saw me would think I was just another "Hunter Joy fan."

No cameras were waiting for me outside HQ. The pod that turned up had an older civilian driver, distinctly uninterested in who I was, and un-chatty. Polite, but didn't even play music, unless he was listening to something on earbuds I couldn't see, which was possible. I didn't mind; after all that being talked at this afternoon, the silence was nice. I leaned back in the seat and watched out the window. It was dusk, and with my Psi-shield on, I was pretty sure no one was going to know who was in the pod. When I had time to actually think about it, after so many years of walking or riding a horse and only rarely driving in one of the semi-armored trucks down to the train station, this method of transportation was still more than a little magical. So quiet, so smooth . . . and so much faster than walking.

The driver delivered me to the same entrance that the military drivers had when I came to visit Uncle: down a ramp under the building, ending in closed glass doors, with blast-doors open on either side of the glass ones. I was momentarily unsure what to do as we pulled up to the guarded entrance. Was I supposed to pay him? I assumed I was, but how?

But he turned in his seat and asked me politely for my Perscom. I held out my wrist, and he scanned mine with his. And finally he cracked a smile. "Always a pleasure to pick up you Hunter folk, miss," and popped the door for me.

He drove off as I got out and faced the four uniformed guards at the door. "Hunter Joyeaux to see Psimon Josh, Prefect Charmand's aide, in the Sky Lounge," I said, formally.

"Very good, Hunter," said the one nearest me after he checked his Perscom. "You're expected. Go straight to the elevators."

He held the door open for me, and although I wasn't escorted in this time, I got the distinct sensation of being carefully monitored all the way to the elevators. Which was hardly a surprise, really, after what Ace had done. Even I wasn't above suspicion. It was going to take a long, long time before the reputation of the Hunters recovered from his meltdown in certain quarters— although given the fickle attentions of the public, most people had already dismissed him to the back of their minds, if they even thought of him at all.

The elevator didn't move until after I held my Perscom up to it. Then it shot straight to the top floor without stopping. The elevator door opened right into the Sky Lounge, and Josh was standing there waiting with a big smile on his face. The lights had been dimmed down to almost nothing, making the view of Apex out the windows absolutely spectacular.

The Sky Lounge was practically empty; there were just two people, both guys, sitting at the autobar, but Josh took me over to the west side of the lounge, a section that was divided into private little booths with transparent partitions, each with a fine view of Apex City below us. Once we were seated, the partition around us opaqued, leaving us as private as if we *were* completely alone up here. "Whew," Josh said, punching in something on a screen built into the table. "I think this might be the first time you and I haven't had eyes all over us when we've been together. Even as an Elite, they still seem to have a cam following you."

I couldn't help but wonder, just for a split second, why this should bother someone who routinely scanned through other peoples' thoughts without bothering to tell them. And I wondered if he'd been making tries at mine without my realizing it—I guess Retro, Hammer, and Steel's jabs at PsiCorps had gotten to me a little. Then I shook it off; I told myself, *This is Josh, this isn't some random PsiCorps snoop*, and that I was just letting the other Hunters' distrust of Psimons get to me.

"I think you're right," I agreed, and felt tension just ease out of me. "This . . . is really nice."

A moment later, a platform with iced drinks on it rose up in the center of the table. Josh handed me one. As I raised an eyebrow at him, he laughed. "Mine's alcoholic; yours, however, is not. You do not have tomorrow off, I am well aware that your Perscom could go off at any second, and I would be flayed alive if I was the reason you were even slightly impaired."

I gave him a wry smile and took a sip. Then another, with pleasure. Like so many things, this drink was new to me. Unlike so many things here, it had a very distinct and nuanced taste. This was herbal but not herbal, a sort of green taste with just enough hint of bitter that a touch of sweetness in it made a brilliant contrast.

There was a little lemon, but only enough to enhance the nuanced herbal flavor. "Is this—" I began, not knowing *what* it could be.

"Real green tea, from the authentic tea plant," he told me. "The genuine article. This is from the first commercial harvest. Rare still, but they tell me it will get more common now that we've got places where it can grow and the bushes are maturing."

That's going to make the Masters very happy! I thought as I scooted closer to Josh so that he could put his arm around me. Something in that tea was making the last vestiges of my killer headache fade away. I could not have been happier about that.

"So, you had one heck of a day," Josh said with sympathy. I was surprised for a moment because he hadn't given me any hint that he knew about my special assignment. But I guessed that maybe Uncle had given him access to the restricted feeds from the storm sewers.

Still, it never hurt to be cautious before I went blundering into a situation. "A heck of a day?" I replied.

"I heard you discovered a whole new sort of Othersider. A snake-man?" he answered. "I saw some restricted footage of it. Down in the storm sewers."

So he knew where I had been today, but maybe not why or that I had been under the Hub. I decided to be cautious.

"Nowhere near as bad as tackling that Wyvern solo or playing bait for the Drakken," I told him, leaning against him a little and sipping my drink. "They startled us, is all, and it's never a good thing the first time you run into something brand-new and hostile."

He nodded. "And now we've got something new to worry about."

I thought about that before I spoke. That was the neat thing about Josh: I knew I could talk to him seriously about things and get sensible answers back. "I'm not so much worried about the *Nagas* as I am about what else might be on the horizon," I replied, staring out at the lights and thinking that every one of them represented a cluster of people who were nothing more than items on the menu to the Othersiders. "This isn't a good sign, something we've never seen before cropping up right in the sewers. It was bad enough that things were getting dangerous down there, but it's much worse that something we've never seen before shows up for the first time underground."

"Or," Josh corrected, "we've just been getting a lucky break for a while, and now things are going to correct back to normal, which means a lot more dangerous than we've been used to. That would be my reading of it. In either case, we're much better prepared to face a wave of new Othersiders than we ever have been in history."

"I guess it's not the first time this has happened?" I hazarded.

"Not even the second or the third," he told me. "I looked into this. No matter what we tell the Cits, we've been living on borrowed time. We got a long break, thanks to the Barriers, but the Othersiders aren't stupid, and they can adapt."

"I guess so. . . . Out where I come from, we don't have Barriers to protect us, so we never got the idea in our heads that anything was *safe*," I said. "So . . . back to business as usual. . . ."

"Whoa, wait." He gave my shoulders a little squeeze. "You're not the only Hunter in the village now. It's not all on your back to take care of these things, Joy. It isn't even just on the Hunters. We've got better weapons, we've got Mages, and there's PsiCorps. You haven't even counted us into your equation, and PsiCorps has a lot of tricks up its sleeve. A lot more than anyone knows, actually."

I wasn't entirely sure what PsiCorps could do against attacking Othersiders, since a Psimon can only handle one critter at a time, but it didn't seem very polite to say that, so I kept my mouth shut. I mean, seriously, sure they were fine one-on-one, but what would a Psimon do against a whole gang of things like *Nagas*? And mind-reading wasn't going to help a lot, other than tell the Psimon the Othersider he was facing hated him and wanted to feed on him. Unless... unless all those mind-readers were all mind-*controllers* too, and that was what he meant about "having tricks up their sleeves."

But if all they could do was control one mind at a time... yeah, a mob of Kobolds could take one down. "Well, if their plan is to sneak infiltrators in, so far, it's not working real well. The good thing about going down in the storm sewers is that there's a limit to the size of what can *get* down there," I said. "And I have a pack of eleven."

"There you go," he said approvingly. "Want another drink? Or something to eat?"

"Another drink would be lovely," I said. "Something different?" Because if that tea was as rare as he said, it was probably expensive, and even though I was halfway certain Josh's expenses when he took me out were being covered by either the prefect's office or Hunter HQ, I wasn't completely certain, and the last thing I wanted him to do was impoverish himself just to treat me. I made a mental note to find out for sure and offer to carry my share if he was taking the whole burden. Only fair, right?

"I got a bunch of mail from home before the storm," I said as the table delivered two new drinks, and told him about the letters from Kei and some of my friends—omitting the fact that some of them were Hunters, of course.

Unless he was really good at faking enthusiasm, which I was inclined to doubt, he enjoyed hearing about them. Our way of life probably was as strange to him as living in the city had been to me. He was fascinated by details: how we used solar, wind, and bicycle generators for electricity but relied on highly efficient wood burners for heat. How we used not just wells and rain but snow catchments for water. That we had indoor plumbing, just like here in Apex, using water towers on the roofs for pressure, even though we didn't have a central water-and-sewer system.

And the bigger aspects of living outside the Barriers—like how we ran our Hunting patrols (I was careful, implying that everyone out there was perfectly ordinary), and all the ways we'd found that unmagical people could take out Othersiders.

"It's amazing that you aren't under attack more often," he said after a while, which was something I had been expecting and working out an answer to. Josh was anything but stupid, and sooner or later I had figured he'd wonder just what sort of strange immunity we had that kept us relatively safe.

Now I was nervous. Sure, I had my Psi-shield on, but a Psimon can read body language as well as thoughts. Would he suspect I wasn't telling him the whole truth? And if he ever found out how many Hunters and Mages we had, what would he *do* with the information? I had to hope I could tell enough of the truth to satisfy him, without telling too much.

"We're above the snow line," I told him. "The farms are all

down lower, but where we actually live, the snow never melts. There's not many Othersiders that can tolerate that kind of cold, and even the ones that can aren't able to take it for long. The cold itself is a weapon, but we have something else."

"What would that be?" he asked, intrigued.

"We found exactly the right density for cold-forged iron to mask how many of us there are and repel most of the Othersiders at the same time," I told him truthfully. "So we don't have to have iron fences or anything like them. We have cold-forged iron nails pounded into the wooden palisades around our villages in patterns. So far, the only things that are able to get past that cold-iron pattern are really *big* Othersiders, and they hate the cold just as much as the little ones do."

"With only one Hunter up there, I guess you need to be creative," he said. "I wonder if they'll get someone else to pop Powers with you gone?"

"Maybe." I finally decided that the best way to get him off the track of the Mountain was for *him* to answer some questions. "So since you mentioned popping Powers, when did you find out you were a Psimon?" I asked.

He kind of . . . stopped . . . for a minute. *Uh-oh . . . awkward . . .* "It doesn't actually work that way for us," he said finally, tensing up a bit. "You don't find out. You're born that way."

No hope for it. I'd just have to plow on. But at least it would give him something to think about except the Mountain. "Uh . . . huh," I replied, trying to think through that. "Like, literally? You've got Psi-powers as a baby?"

He relaxed again. "Yeah, which is why we usually get taken away to the Psimon crèche." His tone turned wry. "You can always tell when a baby's a Psimon. They never stop crying. And I mean *never*. Even in their sleep."

"'Cause they can't get away from everyone else's thoughts around them, and they don't know how to shield yet?" I hazarded. He nodded. "But you said *usually*. You weren't?"

"My mom was a Psimon," he said. "I think my dad was too, but I don't know for sure, and no one ever told me. By the time I was born, he was out of Mom's life, and PsiCorps let Mom raise me. She could do what the crèche would have done; she could shield me until I was old enough to learn how to shield myself, and teach me how to use my abilities right along with learning how to walk and talk. When I was old enough for school, I went to school with the Psimon crèche kids, but I got to come home at the end of the school day."

I didn't have to *imagine* how hard that was, having these things you could do that set you apart from people around you at a young age, because obviously that was exactly what had happened to me. At least he'd had a mom. A mom who must have loved him an awful lot to insist that she was going to *keep* him and raise him herself, all alone.

The words came out before I had a chance to think about them. "You must have the best mom in the whole world," I said sincerely.

That made him go quiet for a long time. Finally, he said, "Well, all the times she kept telling me to *use your outside words, Josh*, when it was so much easier to tell her what I wanted to say telepathically made me mad ... but ... yeah."

I wanted to ask more questions, but I decided against it. He kept talking about his mother in the past tense, which suggested that *something* had happened. I figured if he wanted to tell me what that *something* was, he would, and if he didn't, pushing to get it wouldn't be a good idea.

And then I leaned over and kissed him so he wouldn't have to tell me anything.

We've been kissing for a while now, but we'd always had to do it where there weren't cameras watching, our opportunities hadn't been many or long. This time we were completely private, and I was plenty ready to take things a little further.

Not *crazy* further, but . . . yeah, we did some making out, and it was just as exciting as I'd fantasized. I loved the way he made me feel, all tingly and warm and a little euphoric. I loved how his fingers felt on my skin and in my hair, and I was glad I'd left my hair loose tonight for him to run his fingers through. I wasn't *consciously* following the coaching that Kei had given me, but I'd probably read those parts of the letters over so many times it had finally gotten into my subconscious. For *once*, I didn't feel awkward, or like I was making missteps, or nervous.

He was the one to break it off first, with a little sigh of regret. "I need to be careful . . ." he said reluctantly.

"Careful?" From the way he said it, he didn't mean it in the way I would have.

"A Psimon is . . . *discouraged* from getting too physical with someone he's attracted to, because that can form psychic and emotional links that have the potential to get in the way when you least want them. Even through Psi-shields," he said after a moment. "Instead of reaching for the person you're supposed to read, you can end up reaching for the person you *want* to read. Supervisors take a dim view of that," he added, with a grimace.

What? That kind of pissed me off. Back home, I *think* we had people who would have been recruited into the Psimons if they'd been living in one of the big cities, but they tended to join the actual monks, and . . . I wasn't really sure what they did, other than serve as a sort of early-warning service. But they sure weren't *discouraged* from doing normal things like making out!

Okay, okay. It's not Josh's fault. Change the subject.

"So, what's it like to be a kid here?" I asked instead. Awkward again, but . . . what else could I do?

He laughed at that, a little nervously. "Near as I can tell, it's a lot less responsibility," he told me. "All those *chores* you turnips have to do! No wonder you never learned how to play vid-games!"

"Well, duh!" I laughed. "So that's what you do? Play vid-games?"

"They're supposed to be educational!" he protested. "And a lot of them make you actually exercise. I guess I could probably ski for real, if I ever got on a mountain. And snowboard, and I know I ran a lot."

That was when it hit me. Two things hit me, actually. The first was that kids really were not free here, free to be outside—and that was why they did all their playing using vid-games. Whether their parents understood it or not, the people in charge were acutely aware of the fact that it was not safe for them to be outside without one-on-one supervision. To allow them that freedom we kids in Safehaven and Anston's Well had would mean they would have been trained as we were—trained that the world is an incredibly dangerous place, trained in all the things they needed to be able to do to keep themselves from being lured off or carried away. And to give them that training would completely destroy the illusion of safety their parents had.

"Did you ever get to play with other kids?" I asked finally. "Not over a vid-feed. Together."

"Once I was in the Psimon school, yeah," he said. "You don't want a kid with psionics playing with a Norm."

I could see that. Kids lose their tempers; they don't know not to act on their impulses. Depending on what Josh's abilities were, well, a fight with another kid could end with a kid in a coma instead of a kid with a bloody nose or a black eye.

"And we were always supervised, two adults for every six kids," he continued. "Just to make sure we didn't . . . Well, you know, bullies. Psi-gifted kids are valuable, like Hunters and Mages. You don't want to lose anyone with potential to be a Psimon."

"Lose anyone?" I said, not sure I understood what he was saying, or implying.

"Start subconsciously repressing their powers," he said hastily. Maybe too hastily? What kind of "crèche" was this? What kind of school? Then he flipped the subject as if trying to avoid exactly that question. "Kids with minimal powers get weeded out at around nine or ten and go to a different school, where they are taught mostly regular stuff and how to use what little they've got. They're never in PsiCorps at all. That's why they're available to take jobs with the vid-channels, work as gifted assistants, or go into the army."

This was getting way too serious. So I changed the subject entirely and asked him about what other storms had been like— and what he and the others stuck in Uncle's building had done during them. It turned out they did a lot of stupid things that often ended up really funny . . . and resulted in edicts like *Personnel shall no longer engage in racing games using office chairs* and *Personnel shall not use the copying machines for copying any object other than a document.*

At that point, both our Perscoms beeped, letting us know that we weren't *entirely* off the leash on this date, and that we both were on duty in the morning.

"Our masters call," I said wryly. He laughed. "Look, you live, what, a few blocks from here?" I continued. "There's no reason why you should ride back all the way with me only to turn around and ride back by yourself."

"But I like your company," he objected, so I gave in and we ordered a pod and he went with me back to Hunter HQ. Unfortunately, we got a driver-run pod, so we just held hands until the pod delivered me back where I'd started. I wished we'd had another chance to make out a little more. And I kind of wanted to smooth things over after the way he broke off that kiss. I went back inside feeling as if I'd somehow missed something, even though I wasn't sure what it was I could have missed.

THIS TIME I WENT down into the storm sewers from an entrance to the west of the Hub. The pass-box at the door of the little bunker accepted my Perscom just fine, and the Hounds and I made our descent.

The sewer tunnel looked so innocent, and once again smelled of nothing but scoured cement and damp—but after turning up those *Nagas*, even if I hadn't been a Hunter I would have regarded it with suspicion. I looked over the Hounds and decided that since we were alone, I'd let them arrange themselves around me as they saw fit. "Form up how you want," I told them as they all turned their muzzles toward me, waiting for orders. "We're heading to the Hub again."

Bya and Myrrdhin (who seemed to have become Bya's default second-in-command) both nodded. Myrrdhin ranged on ahead of us, Bya put himself right at my side, and the rest packed up loosely around the two of us.

We moved slowly, much more slowly than we usually did in the open. That was partly because I would stop every twenty paces or so, in order that we could all listen and probe with other senses for a few moments. If I'd still had my own channel, our progress would have put my viewers to sleep.

But this wasn't all that different from the way I patrolled in the deep forest. Stop frequently and listen; let the Hounds use all their senses. Use all of mine as well. I wasn't as good at detecting magic and magical creatures as they were, but there were a few times when I'd done so before they had.

On the other hand, I had one thing going for me that they didn't, down here in an all-man-made Hunting ground. I knew machinery. And sometimes I could tell when something wasn't quite right.

As we had made our way down the tunnel, there had been distant sounds getting louder. I already knew from my map what it was: a pumping station, sequestered in one of those side tunnels that contained pipes and cables. The storm runoff didn't need to be pumped, but sewage and potable water sometimes did. And the nearer we got, the more I became aware that there was something "off" in how the pump sounded. As if it was straining, or not functioning quite right. "Contact Apex Power and Water, Reclamation Division, human operator," I said, feeling sure that there must be humans in charge of things there as well as computers. There was. I immediately was put in contact with a bored-looking woman who sat straight up and stared at the screen, flustered, when she saw who was calling her. "Hunter Joyeaux here," I said crisply, before she could stammer out anything. "I'm patrolling sector"—I switched screens and checked my map—"six seventy-one and I'm just on the other side of the wall from what I think is a pumping station."

I'll say this for her, she went straight to business. *"It is, Hunter."* Then she frowned. *"This is odd. That pumping station was just given an inspection and a clean bill of health less than a month ago. But now—"*

"Now there's something wrong with it. I thought so," I said. "Don't send anyone down here yet. I'll keep in touch. Hunter Joyeaux out."

I closed the link before she could say—or worse, ask—anything. I didn't know just who was "allowed" to know that there were Othersiders down here, or rather, how bad the infestations had gotten, so I was erring on the side of caution. Kent had supplied me with one of the dinguses that opened the hatches to the side tunnels, so I was set. Well, as "set" as I could be, knowing that there might be another clot of those *Nagas* in there—or who knew what else.

Still, this time I had come prepared. "There's something messing with the machinery in there. I'm going to gas them," I told the Hounds, who had gathered around me, looking expectant. "So get yourselves ready for gas, then set up for a fire ambush." The good thing about being down here in a cement tunnel was that there just wasn't anything to burn, so they wouldn't have to be careful. I strapped on my gas mask and put in earplugs in case it was *Nagas* again, and arranged my gear. A gas grenade on a very, very short fuse, two more on my belt that I could grab in a hurry, my shotgun slung where I could reach it easily, and the dingus in my off hand.

I didn't have to do any tedious counting down with the Hounds. They *knew* what I was going to do and when I was going to do it. So I got a good, deep breath of air (just in case I hadn't settled the mask quite right and there was a leak), got myself psyched up, triggered the dingus, and threw the grenade in as soon as the door was open enough. The grenade was already hissing gas as it lobbed into the darkness past the door.

But what piled out, shrieking in tiny, high-pitched voices, was *not* a clot of *Nagas.*

This tumble of tiny arms and tiny flailing legs and tiny screaming heads came pouring out. I mean that literally—there were so many they poured out like water. And they sounded like screaming mice. There was a flash of oversize wrenches and screwdrivers in the middle of the horde. Frankly, I didn't know what they were—except that they were armed with what looked like *tools*, and my Hounds immediately began incinerating them.

Tools can also be weapons, and I was taking no chances. I unloaded my shotgun into the mob still pouring out of the doorway in a literal flood, and I didn't stop firing, reloading, and firing until there was nothing left moving but myself and the Hounds. It was a few minutes before I was able to breathe. It had all happened stupidly fast, and my heart was still racing.

By that point, between the fire and the natural circulation in the tunnel, the air had cleared enough I could take off my mask. I walked over to the pile of bodies, but these were sort of evaporating as the Hounds inhaled the manna, and I couldn't get a good sense of what they had looked like. "Hunter Joyeaux to HQ," I said into my Perscom. "Did you get all that? Can you give me a playback and a freeze on one of these things?"

"Roger, Hunter. We did and we can." I waited patiently, but it wasn't more than a minute later that the operator had gotten me a nice clear shot of one of these creatures just before I'd blown it apart.

It was about the same size as a Kobold, but unlike a Kobold, it was clothed, wearing something like a hooded red jumpsuit with black boots and a white harnesslike affair. There were two horns poking through the hood, and it had what looked like a pair of welding goggles over its eyes. It had been carrying a set of wire cutters almost as tall as it was. And I had no idea what the damned thing could be. Once again, this was something I had *never* heard of.

"HQ, any clues as to what these things are?" I asked, baffled.

"Negative, Hunter. Would you have a look at the pumping station?"

"Roger that," I replied, and used the flashlight on my shotgun to illuminate the darkened space beyond the door. Darkened, because, although there were supposed to be lights in here, the little monsters had demolished them. They were lying on the floor of the cubby, pulled out of the ceiling, and bare wires dangling from the hole. And although the pump was supposed to be protected, they'd been doing a number on the casing housing it. Now that I could hear it clearly, it was sounding ragged, as if they'd gotten through to some part of it that made it run unevenly.

"We'll give P and W the go-ahead to come down there and fix that thing. Wait for them, just in case there's something else lurking down there."

"Roger that, HQ," I replied. "While I wait, can you give me a playback from all the angles you have?"

"That would be a whole two angles and one close-up, Hunter," came the dry reply. "And lucky to get that."

"You're disappointing this here turnip," I said, just as dryly. "No twenty-angle shots with zoom good enough to see the hairs on a wart? Here I thought you high-techie city slickers could do anything!" I thought I heard muffled laughter on the other end of the comm, and smiled a little.

Well, I didn't learn much more from the three playbacks I got before the work crew arrived to fix the pump and the lights. Just that the little monsters looked alike, they were all carrying tools of various sorts, and clearly they had no problem with anything ferrous (although the shotgun pellets at close range hadn't done them any good at all). HQ confessed to equal bafflement. Like the *Nagas*, these things were new. Unlike the *Nagas*, these creatures seemed right at home with human tech, at least to the extent of trying to destroy it. From the sound of things, HQ was just as disturbed by this new trend as I was.

This was twice now that the Othersiders had shown the ability to deal with our technology. The first time, when the Folk Mage I had encountered on the train to Apex had dismantled the electrified cage that protected the train far enough ahead of the engine that the cage was safe to meddle with, and now, when these unknown Othersiders had the tools and the know-how to sabotage equipment. It was one thing to be able to pop locks with magic—Othersiders had been doing that for a long time now, and if anything, I suspected that electronic locks were easier for them to deal with than the sort that required a key or a combination. This was different, and I tried not to show that it was making my skin crawl.

By the time the work crew arrived, the Othersiders had vanished, along with their tools, leaving nothing to examine. That wasn't unprecedented; sometimes the objects that Othersiders carried were purely magical constructs that vanished when they died; sometimes they were physical, like the Redcaps' knives or the Kobolds' hammers. The *Nagas* had had both: the swords had been physical, but the jewelry had been constructs. Which was . . . I won't lie . . . kind of sad. Because it had been lovely jewelry, and a shame to have it vanish like that, and I *know* that probably makes me sound like a pirate or something, wanting to loot the bodies, but on the other hand, *they* had wanted to chop our heads off, so a little loot would have been fair payback.

It wasn't the same work crew as last time, but a couple of them were just as starstruck as Kelly had been. Fortunately, their supervisor wasn't, or it could have gotten embarrassing.

We all stood guard while the work crew put things to rights, but nothing else showed up. When the pump was humming away properly again and the lights had been put back together, they went back up, and we went back on patrol.

The Hounds were satisfied, so they didn't mind taking things slowly, but I was glad I was solo down here, because most people would probably have been impatient with how cautious I was being—even some of my fellow Hunters from back home. As we went on—yard after yard of boring concrete tunnel, empty and echoing—all my caution started to feel as if I was overreacting. I had to keep reminding myself that it was stupid to get complacent.

Finally, we got down into an area under the Hub itself. We hadn't gotten this far the last time; now I could see why Uncle was concerned. There were lots and lots of intersecting tunnels here—it wasn't exactly a maze since there were signs inset into the walls telling you exactly where you were and what street you were under, but there were plenty of places for things to hide in ambush, and there were a lot of blind spots and dead ends where there were no cameras or lights. I'm not exactly an architect, so I had no idea how the logical and mathematical storm-sewer tunnels had turned into this warren, but it sure wasn't the ideal situation for work crews afraid of what was getting down here.

My Hounds didn't much care for it either, and they went alert and cautious. One or another would peel off from the pack to check out side tunnels or suspicious sounds every few minutes. I was letting Myrrdhin and Bya handle all that; there was no way, with my limited human senses, that I would be better at deciding what to investigate than they were.

And I was very grateful for the flashlight installed on the top of my shotgun where sights would be on a rifle. There were too many shadows down here; I liked being able to flood where my gun was pointing with light.

I was just about ready to turn everyone around and start making our way back, when Gwalchmai called us. *I believe you should all come here. There is a body,* he said in my mind. *It is freshly dead.*

Well, that left out it being a victim of the flood. *Human, or Othersider?* I asked.

Human, came the reply, making my heart sink.

All the things it could have been ran through my head as the rest of the pack and I caught up with Gwalchmai in a side tunnel, one without a camera and with only one feeble little light in it. I dreaded finding it was a maintenance worker. It would be almost as bad to discover one of the police. Was it possible it could be an ordinary Cit who had managed to get a door open and had gone wandering down here out of curiosity? I had a weird and unsettling wave of all kinds of stuff come over me: anger and grief—mostly grief—and fear, to the point where I had to stop for a moment and put a hand on the wall to steady myself. My throat got tight and my eyes stung, and suddenly, as I choked back a sob, I understood why. The last body I'd found in a sewer tunnel had been Karly's. . . .

But when the beam from my flashlight fell on the body, I saw with a shock by the black-and-silver uniform that it was none of these things.

It was a Psimon. I felt sick and a little scared and jumpy all at the same time.

I was as much puzzled as I was shocked. Why was a Psimon down here in the first place? I hesitated a moment, then decided not to get any closer than I was. Because I'd seen vid-dramas, and I knew enough about police stuff to realize this might just be a murder scene, and anyone who was going to investigate didn't need me trampling all over the evidence. Nor did they need any magical presence other than Gwalchmai near the body. There was such a thing as forensic magic, and if eleven Hounds and I swarmed the vicinity, it would be as bad as sending a herd of kids romping all over the place.

Are there any wounds, or other signs of violence? I asked Gwalchmai.

No, he said shortly.

Well ... that didn't necessarily eliminate murder. It just meant there was no blood, and nothing on the part of the body that Gwalchmai could see. *Come back,* I told him, as the others gathered closely around me. *I need to call this in.*

I was shivering as I did so. It's not that I am a stranger to death; no Hunter is—usually horrible, violent death. I've seen nearly twenty folks dead in my life, a lot more hurt bad, and come way too close to death myself more than I like to think. But this ... this was putting the hair on the back of my neck up. "Hunter Joyeaux," I said. "I'm in sector 832 of the storm tunnels. Psimon down, fatality, cause unknown."

The comm link went very, very quiet. As I stood there in the semidarkness, every movement we made, every click of claw or shuffle of feet echoing strangely out of the tunnels around us, I felt a cold sickness in my gut. This was wrong in ways I couldn't quite quantify but certainly felt.

"Have you approached the body?" came the reply, finally. It wasn't a voice I recognized. Not one of my usual dispatchers.

"No, sir," I said promptly. "One of my Hounds discovered the Psimon and ascertained he was deceased. I kept all the rest away and have not approached myself."

"PsiCorps verifies they will handle it from here. You are to vacate the immediate area and make your way to your exit promptly and without further investigation. HQ out."

All I could think was, *Well, all right, then.* Orders were orders, and I followed them. I wasn't going to go blindly, of course, nor was I going to leave something behind me to ambush me from the rear, so I sent the Hounds around to cover everything that might hold a nasty surprise behind us, and headed back to my exit. They didn't find anything else—more to the point, they didn't find any signs of what could have killed the Psimon. I didn't know whether to be more worried or relieved.

On the other hand, I most certainly *did* want to be away from that spot as fast as I could. I suspected that PsiCorps would send its own to see to this . . . and I didn't want to be there when they came. They would certainly notice I wore a Psi-shield. They might want to know why. They might order me to turn it off, and they would be perfectly within their rights to do so, seeing as I had found a Psimon dead. And I had no idea if my mantra of One White Stone would be sufficient to keep them out of my memories of the Mountain, the Monastery, and the Masters. It worked well enough against the Folk, but . . . high-ranking Psimons were supposed to be better than even the Folk Mages at psionics.

It hadn't been lost on me that most Hunters don't like Psi-Corps. PsiCorps *really* doesn't like Hunters. Most people, not just Hunters, don't trust them, and I don't know why they don't like us, unless they don't like all the attention we get. Worst case, my finding a dead Psimon was going to look very . . . unusual, and no one likes "unusual." And if PsiCorps decided to make an issue out of it, they'd want to know why I was down here and not the regular police, since this was under the Hub and so *supposedly* safe. Then they'd be asking how I found the body "so easily," and might try to imply I knew the Psimon was in trouble and *let* him die.

The only way to completely establish my innocence would be to take off my Psi-shield and let them waltz through my skull, which . . . was not going to happen. The best I could hope for would be that they would leave me alone.

When I emerged from the tunnels, I knew I was not going to get my wish. There was a Psimon waiting for me, standing beside a waiting pod. He was nothing like Josh; his backbone was so straight he could have had a poker instead of a spine, and he literally had *no* expression on his face. He was bald as an egg, and he could have been a statue or a giant doll. He hid his eyes behind a dark visor, and it was clear from the way he turned to watch me lock up the entrance that he had been waiting for me.

"Elite Hunter Joyeaux Charmand," he said, making it a statement, not a question.

I suppressed a shudder at his cold tone, turned, and faced him. "Yes, sir," I replied. "At your service, Senior Psimon."

I'd been down there all afternoon, and the sun was well into the west. It was behind me and glared into his face. He didn't seem to notice.

He didn't beat around the bush at all. "You are to say nothing about the unfortunate victim you found under the Hub," he told me severely. "That is a direct order, Hunter."

Not that he had any right whatsoever to give me orders. The Hunters reported to Uncle and Premier Rayne and no one else. But the last thing I wanted to do was to give him any excuse to look deeper than the surface. So I just dropped my eyes and nodded and said, "Understood, Senior Psimon."

He looked at me coldly for a moment longer, not with any

curiosity, though I guessed he was trying to gauge whether or not I would obey him. So I added, "What do I say to my superiors, Senior Psimon? If they ask?"

"That PsiCorps thanks you for discovering our unfortunate comrade and is undertaking an investigation on its own," he said.

"Thank you, Senior Psimon," I replied, and that seemed to satisfy him. Without another word, he got into the pod, and it whirred off. I waited until he was well out of sight before heaving a sigh of relief and summoning a pod of my own.

When I got back to my room after dinner, my message indicator was flashing. But when I pulled up the message, I got something I had never seen before.

First, the words *State your designation and name* flashed on the screen. Puzzled, I said aloud, "Elite Hunter Joyeaux Charmand," and the screen flashed with *Voice recognition verified.* Then the screen said *State unlock code found on your Perscom.* I checked my Perscom, and sure enough, a text message headed "Unlock Code" had just been sent to it. I opened the message and spoke the words aloud, just some nonsense strung together for a security code. *Unlock code verified* said the screen, and a simple text message appeared.

It pretty much said the same thing that the Psimon had said, but in more detail—you know, the sort of detail you'd go into with a five-year-old who is trying to find a loophole in your orders not to eat the cookies. "But what if I just nibble the edge? But what if I just lick them?" A first, I thought it was insulting, actually, and I started to get angry, when it occurred to me that if they were being this condescending they were hopefully underestimating me.

But then my latent paranoia kicked in, and it stopped being insulting and started being frightening. *Remember that even the Elite are not immune to disciplinary actions if you violate orders,* it continued. *Discipline can include your home community as well as yourself.*

It ended with *need not reply,* which is just as well, since I might have been tempted to say something I shouldn't have. First they send a senior Psimon to loom over me and intimidate me. *Then,* when I think I'm in the clear, they follow it up with a threatening message? They threaten my *home?* Then I got scared all over again at how easily they had manipulated me into being angry. *Psimons know* all *the buttons to push,* I reminded myself. And they must have known damn well that with a turnip like me, threatening my people was absolutely where I was most vulnerable. Well, look how Mark Knight got blackmailed into being sent here! I had let myself get complacent about them, being with Josh so much. But Josh wasn't like the Psimons that my Masters had warned me about, or like the one I had just encountered. That one was much more like the Psimons I had been told to avoid. Even if they didn't get directly into my head, it was clear they knew exactly how to manipulate me so I'd let things slip or let stuff about home get into my surface thoughts where it would more easily be read.

And where there were hidden Hunters, it wouldn't take much for the Psimons to figure out there were probably hidden Psi-talents just waiting to be gathered up. If my people back home tried to resist having their protectors snatched away, they'd probably find themselves facing the army . . . and if they didn't, there'd be nothing between them and the Othersiders but their physical weapons and the snow.

I'd been complacent. I hadn't been thinking. That had to stop, right now.

Just as I came to that conclusion, I got an *incoming call* alert on my vid-screen and accepted it without looking to see who it was first.

"Hunter Joy," said my uncle, with a hint of a sardonic smile. "You've likely heard from the PsiCorps by now."

"Twice," I said sourly. "I've been told in no uncertain terms that I am not to talk about what I found except with my superiors."

Uncle nodded, as if that was exactly what he had expected. "Your conclusion?"

I blinked. "Uh … speculation, sir. This is not the first PsiCorps body that's been found down there." *Which is why you sent me and not someone else.*

"What PsiCorps forgets is that I am the prefect of police," he said, with steel in his voice. "Evidence of a serial murderer beneath my city is more than enough justification for me to order an investigation, regardless of the wishes of PsiCorps, and I have done so. But meanwhile, since you are already assigned to patrol down there, I would like you to keep me informed if—when—you find any more bodies."

"Vid, sir?" I said. I was reasonably sure this exchange was not being recorded and was probably encrypted.

"Definitely. Don't compromise the crime scene, but get as much detail as you can. I want to know what's killing these Psimons." He nodded.

"It could have been those murderous midget tool wielders,"

I said out loud. "There were too many of them for one Psimon to have had any hope of controlling."

"If it's a new Othersider, it's vitally important for us to know that. If it's a criminal, I'll go to Premier Rayne myself to get the PsiCorps to cooperate with the police." Uncle looked absolutely grim at that. I had no idea how often he called in the Rayne card, but I was willing to bet that when he did, he got listened to.

"What...what if it's another Psimon?" I asked. Because the question had to be asked. Things that Josh had said...made me think that all was not peace, joy, and brotherhood in PsiCorps.

"If it's another Psimon...then he's a murderer, and having powers is not going to save him from the law."

"Yes, sir," I said, hoping that he was wrong and that this was the last time I was going to have to deal with a Psimon who wasn't Josh. But really, in the back of my mind, I knew I was too far down the rabbit hole now to be that lucky.

I called Bya. I felt strongly in need of comfort; when he came through, he wrapped himself around me and crooned until I got somewhat more relaxed.

And I spent a long, long time staring into the dark before I finally slept.

I HAD AN UNEVENTFUL patrol of the sewers the next day. Dinner was odd. I went in early, after checking on the rest of the Elite team. Everyone except Hammer and Steel was out on what I had learned was called a "snipe hunt." To make a very long story as short as possible, that meant they were chasing something that was probably long gone, but because it was really dangerous and there had not only been a sighting but a vid capture, they had to check it out, and it had to be with nearly the full roster. I didn't know exactly what they were (supposedly) Hunting, but generally it had to be something as deadly as a Folk Mage.

Hammer and Steel hadn't been along, partly because they'd already spent the morning in an exhausting fight with a Pit Beetle, and partly because their powers weren't well suited to something human-size and extremely agile.

I was curious just what a Pit Beetle was like, because I had heard of them but had never seen one, so I called up the raw vid on my Perscom while I poked at food. Basically it is what it sounds like: a gigantic beetle about the size of a tank that digs a pit with slippery sides, hides in the bottom, and waits for prey to fall in. It wasn't hard for them to target, and they certainly didn't need to ambush it, but it was very tough. It took them a while to squash it, and when they were done, they both looked like they were ready to drop.

I looked up from my Perscom just in time to see both of them come in and get some dinner. They caught sight of me as they turned to look for a spot to sit down, and joined me. I was glad they had. I figured since their mother was a folklorist, she might know something about the murderous midget mechanics I'd seen. I *really* wanted to know what the heck those things were! The mess hall was about half full of regular Hunters, and everyone was jabbering away at once. The vid-screens in the corners of the room were showing an update about Old Yeller, a volcano off to the west and south.

"Looks like you've recovered from bug-squashing," I said, making plenty of room on the tabletop for them.

Hammer made a face. "Better that than a snipe hunt. The team's probably covered twenty square miles today and not one damn thing to show for it." He lowered his voice so that it only carried to me and his brother. I leaned in to listen. "Our buddies got back to us. The ones I figured could put an eye on Ace for us."

Steel nodded as I looked from one brother to the other and back again. "Something tells me you are not happy with what they told you," I said.

"It's crazy, is what it is," Hammer told me while his brother ate. "According to them, he's still on tight lockdown, so they can't tell what kind of conditions he's living in, but when he *is* let out to work, he acts like he's a model prisoner. I can't square that with the Ace we know." His face was stormy, stubborn. He really did *not* believe what he'd been told. Well, neither did I.

"But it's possible," said Steel, giving his brother a chance to eat. "He might have gotten . . . I don't know, maybe therapy."

Hammer snorted, his brows furrowing, as though he would have liked to say something strong, and maybe profane.

"All right, then, maybe he got his head reprogrammed by a Psimon. Or they're drugging him."

"You know that you can't mix drugs and magic," Hammer corrected his brother. "And *nobody* with powers who's ever gotten reprogrammed by a Psimon has been able to use those powers afterward."

"Maybe he actually learned his lesson? Maybe he's sorry about . . ." Steel trailed off. "It's possible."

"Gosh," I said, definitely creeped out now. "I'm not buying it." Hammer gave me a nod to say he agreed with me.

"I've been thinking about this." It was Steel's turn to eat and Hammer's to talk, apparently. "We know he wasn't working alone. And we know he wasn't *that* crazy a few months ago. A camera whore, sure. But not crazy. So I have a theory."

"Which is just a theory," his brother said emphatically. "But . . . I guess it's worth telling her."

I waited. These guys were Elite, after all. Not inclined to make stuff up. Smart and experienced. If they had a theory, it was probably worth considering at least. Mind you, this conversation was just a bit surreal, taking place in the middle of a bunch of people chowing down and discussing fan service.

"What if, for some reason, he really had a personality change after his brother was killed?" Hammer all but whispered, making sure his voice was pitched so low that it was highly unlikely the mics in the room would pick it up in the ambient noise.

"But what would cause . . ." I bit my lip. "What if whoever he was working with had, or was, a Psimon?" That made too much sense, actually. "He was already pretty unbalanced after his brother was killed. How hard would it be for a Psimon to shove him over the cliff?"

"Exactly," Hammer nodded; his brother winced, as if this was far more "conspiracy theory" than he liked. "Not hard to push him straight into psycho, if you ask me," Hammer added. "I don't trust PsiCorps. Never have. The Psimons have always struck me as the kind of people who'd shove their own mothers under the tank treads if they thought it would advance them."

If all I'd known about PsiCorps had been Josh, I might have had second thoughts and certainly voiced some doubts. But after meeting up with that senior Psimon and getting that letter, I was perfectly willing to think there might be Psimons out there willing to aid and abet a murder or two.

Never mind what Steel thought; in my estimation, Hammer was not at all the kind to make up wild conspiracy theories or the kind to believe in conspiracy theories others came up with.

But if his suspicions and mine were correct, then it was more than time to change the subject of conversation. Just in case. And besides, I wanted to ask them about something else anyway. "So,"

I said in my normal tone of voice, "have either of you heard of an Othersider about the size of a Knocker but dressed in a hooded red jumpsuit and black boots and carrying tools?"

They both looked at me, baffled. "What?" Hammer said for both of them. I cued up the raw footage of my little encounter in the storm sewers. They watched, looking even more baffled at the freeze-frames.

"I have *no* idea," Steel said. "Those little guys look more modern than mythic. Are modern myths even possible?"

I started to say something like "I don't know," when suddenly I realized something. "Of course they are," I said. "My Hounds. They're *Alebrijes*, something that never showed up in myth until around 1940, pre-Diseray time."

They both stared at me while I described how Pedro Linares had seen the *Alebrijes* in a fever dream. "Until then, no one, not even the Zapotec shamans, had ever seen or heard of them. And back then, of course, nobody *but* Zapotec would have believed in them. But when I got my first seven Hounds, that was what they were. So I guess you can have modern myths." I didn't mention how my mentor, Master Patli, also had four *Alebrijes* Hounds. More secrets I had to keep, even from people I was starting to trust a lot. It felt bad, actually, but what else could I do? Because what would happen if I confided in someone and PsiCorps came rummaging around in the heads of my friends? The mere idea had me sick with fear.

Hammer rubbed his left hand over his close-cropped scalp. "Oh boy. That opens up an entirely new can of worms, and one I would rather not think about too hard."

"Maybe. Probably? I dunno," his brother replied. "I'm not sure even Ma could answer that one."

"Well, it might give the folklorists someplace to look if they think these things are modern-ish," Hammer replied, still rubbing his head. "I really don't want to think about it too hard. I can really do without having a new sort of Othersider showing up every damn day."

I nodded with sympathy. Here we'd been going on the assumption that there were rules of a sort determining what Othersiders were going to pop up, but now . . . maybe those rules didn't apply after all.

Altogether, it had been a day that was leaving me feeling very shaky. Othersiders that no one recognized—again—and which could be modern. Psimons and PsiCorps taking an "interest" in me. Dead Psimons that could be murder victims. Ace on what seemed to be a pretty long leash, and acting even crazier. And maybe with a Psimon "helping" him along.

◅ ▻

I went straight to bed with my head awash in conspiracy theories. And as soon as I got to the mess hall for breakfast, Mark pounced like he'd been waiting for me.

"Can you spare some time?" he asked, giving me this pleading look. He looked a lot like a giant puppy when he did that. And how could I say no? This was Mark Knight, my best friend here, and if it hadn't been for him and Josh, I might be crippled or dead. Whatever he needed from me, I'd make sure he got.

"Sure, I'm just waiting to see if there's a team callout before I go on patrol," I said, truthfully. "Let me get breakfast. Find a table, and I'll join you."

I went and picked out some food kind of at random and scooted over to the table he'd picked. He was already looking impatient, and Mark *never* looks impatient, which meant whatever he wanted, it was probably something to do with his people back home. So far, the only time I'd ever seen him get emotional was over them. I plopped down in the seat and started eating without looking at what I was doing. "Okay," I said between mouthfuls. "What's got your feathers ruffled?"

I noticed then that he didn't look upset so much as anxious and keyed up. "I want to try out for Elite," he blurted. "I'm gonna need your help, or otherwise I'm never gonna pass and—"

I held up my fork, which made him stop babbling. "Whoa, wait, back it up," I said, not sure whether to be amused or concerned. "Why do you want to go Elite?"

He took a deep breath, and then let it all out again. "Look, Joy, I'm not spectacular enough to rank. We both know that. The only time my numbers go up is when I'm paired with you. The only way I'm gonna get permission to bring Jessie here is if I rank—*or* if I'm Elite. I'll never earn it any other way."

Well, this was a drastic change from the last time I talked to him, so the obvious answer to "why do you suddenly need to bring your girl here?" was something in those letters he'd gotten. And *that* was none of my business. Bottom line, if it was important to him, then it mattered to both of us, because we were friends.

"Okay," I said, nodding and pausing to eat. "You're right. With Ace's old friends on their own and not coasting on his notoriety, trying to fight your way into the top rankers would be like trying to push through a crowd of loggers at the free beer keg. Not gonna happen." That wasn't entirely true, actually, but he had already convinced himself that it was, and I wasn't going to waste time trying to prove otherwise. I did think he had a very good chance of making Elite, now that I'd been in the group for a while. Among other things, those flying Hounds of his would be really useful. "You know what the Trials look like, since you helped me get ready for them, so mostly it's going to be a matter of pushing yourself every time you patrol to get your strength and stamina up. You've got the marksmanship, and if you keep doing what Archer told you to do, you'll fly through everything that requires shooting. You could probably stand to build up your strength and endurance, because the hand-to-hand part is a weakness for you. You already know all of that, so I reckon what you're asking me to do is help you with the magic-combat part."

As I was talking, his normally stoic expression was going through a bunch of changes: relief that I was not going to take any persuading, some surprise that I wasn't trying to talk him out of this, maybe a little confusion too, since I wasn't giving him a cross-examination about his motives, or a lecture about how dangerous being Elite was, or another lecture about how he shouldn't be doing it for such a selfish motive.

What did his motives matter anyway, when the end result was going to be that we'd get another Elite? "That's exactly what I want your help with," Knight said, the expression on his face resolving itself into relief again. I ate. He was about to make as long a speech as he ever did—not long, by speech standards—and that would give me a chance to put my calories away before they got cold. "The things Archer said about you and magic, that made sense. I need your help to get my head shut of the idea that what I have is all I'm gonna get. Once I'm Elite, I can bring Jessie here, maybe get her set up in her own room until we have a chance to find a preacher and get properly married, and then I'll be allowed to have bigger quarters and—" He actually started babbling about his girl and hopes and dreams and all that at that point, and I just tuned him out a little, until he wrapped up with "But I can't figure out how to get something useful for combat-magic; I've tried, and nothing happens."

I was pretty much finished then, so I ate my last bite of buttered toast and pointed my fork at him. "The first thing you do is, you go pull up the vids of other Trials," I told him. "Hammer and Steel— Steel, anyway—have essentially the same thing you do, and they passed the Trials. Shields can be used in combat. I'm sure there are others who've gotten just as creative. You go see what others have done, we'll figure out how to amp up what you can already do, and that will give you the headspace to try new things."

When I said that, he perked right up. "All right!" he exclaimed.

I grinned. "And I want to see you ruin some Hunting outfits, Mark Knight," I said with mock severity. "You're big and strong, but in the hand-to-hand, they'll put you up against someone bigger and stronger. So push yourself. Don't walk when you can trot, don't trot when you can run, don't go around stuff when you can jump it. If you think something's gone to ground, dig it out. Climb those blasted tumbledown buildings to see what's roosting, and don't rely on your Hounds to flush things out for you. The more ground you cover during a patrol, the better." I didn't mention that if he did that and his head count started to soar, he probably wouldn't need to try out for Elite after all.

He nodded, then graced me with a bashful smile. "Thanks for not trying to discourage me, Joy. You're the best."

He took off before I could say anything else. I guess he'd already eaten. I headed for the armory; I'd either need to get a loadout for another prowl through the storm sewers, or get grabbed for a team.

When I got there, the armorer was looking at a vid-screen up near the ceiling. I followed his gaze; it was the report about the volcanic eruption, in more detail. The ash plume was definitely coming our way, which meant most aircraft were going to be grounded for a while, except for the helichoppers specially fitted with ash filters. Those eruptions weren't entirely disastrous; they were the reason we had snowpack up in my home mountains in the first place. If it wasn't for the occasional eruptions darkening the sky and keeping things cooler, the warming caused by all those greenhouse gases pre-Diseray would be *really* bad, like desert or tropical bad. That was the good part. But sunlight-blocking meant solar arrays weren't as efficient, and plants had a harder time growing, and of course breathing in ash isn't good for anything—man, critter, or machine—so good news, bad news, and all that. "This will make the Othersiders bolder," he said, without turning around. "It always does. They know the only close-in air support we'll get during ashfall is the choppers." He brooded a while. "The big storm will have made them hungrier too. We aren't the only ones who have to hole up during a storm that size—they do too. The difference between us is, we get feast and they get famine."

"Double whammy. So should I stay close for a bit and wait on going out to the Hub?" I asked.

He nodded. "If nothing's happened in an hour or so, go out. If something does happen, we'll either need several teams or one really big one. I've got a bad feeling about today."

"Yessir," I replied, and just at that point, the others on dayshift started to trickle into the armory, as if summoned. I guess they were getting a bad feeling about today too. Then again, that was their level of experience telling them what to do; they had way more of it than I did, enough to guess by the reports what might be cooking.

"Mark Knight wants to go Elite," I said to Kent quietly as the others began making weapon selections with one eye on the vid-screen.

"His inclinations and talents are better suited to Elite than solo," Kent observed. "You encouraging him?"

"I'm not *dis*couraging him," I replied. "I told him I'd help him get ready."

Kent just nodded—approvingly, I thought. I slowly put together my usual load-out, then went and sat down on a bench to see what was going to happen.

Now, this was very different from any other morning. This was the first time I'd come in here when every single one of the Elites was here, and lingering. Some of them had taken seats on one of the benches, and some were just standing around with their arms crossed. All of them were watching the vid-screen, which had divided up into stuff I didn't recognize, except that there were some windows of what looked like radar feeds, some scrolling text, some cams, some I had no idea what was being shown. I'm guessing Kent had windowed up the screen, or maybe he'd set it to reflect what they were seeing in Control. They all seemed to be waiting for something, expecting something, and at a guess I'd have to say they had completely forgotten that I didn't know what they were waiting for. But there was a tense feeling about them.

Like home, when we know a big storm is coming. Even Retro was keeping his eyes on the screen and not trying to make me laugh or asking for a date, and that was practically out of character for him.

Then three of the windows lit up bright red. One was a cam feed, one was radar, and the last was a piece of map with a pulsing dot on it. The alert callout sounded not only in the room, but from all our Perscoms, signaling a full-team deployment. "There it is," Kent said, as if this was exactly what he'd expected. "Portal opened up outside Bensonville. Three choppers inbound now to load us up. Joy, you'll be with me, Hammer, Steel, and Archer. The rest of you take your usual fives. Bounce!"

I was loaded for my usual prowl in the storm sewers, so I paused just long enough to swap my shotgun and ammo for an assault rifle and ammo. Then I bounced, following Archer on the run, down the halls to the chopper pads where the first of the three was setting down.

The sky was a slightly odd color, and the sunlight seemed a little dimmer; that would be the effect of the ash plume that had been carried on high-altitude winds as fast as a jet. As I got to the chopper, Archer reached for me without actually looking at me, picked me up, and threw me in the door, then jumped in afterward. That was to clear the way for Hammer, Steel, and the armorer, who were all big men. I knew the layout of the smaller choppers; this one was bigger, and it carried rocket pods on the outside. There was only one door, rather than two. I got myself to the seat next to Archer and strapped in.

Kent was the last one on and banged the side of the chopper as soon as both of his feet were inside the door. The pilot took off immediately, leaving Kent to get to his seat and strap in as best he could while the chopper made a steep bank and a shallow ascent. We would be doing the next thing to ground skimming, I reckoned, to avoid the ash in the upper air. These choppers were *fast*. Faster than the train. Faster than anything I had ever been on before. Once again, I got that weird feeling of *really* not belonging here. How could I, when the fastest thing I knew was a galloping horse? I decided that looking out the open door was a bad idea, since it was making me dizzy, and looked around the interior of the thing instead.

It was *incredibly* noisy. The smaller choppers I'd been in had been loud, but this was unbelievable. No way we were sneaking up on anyone in these things. There were eight seats, so we could have fit everyone into two of them, but I didn't know enough to know why we were taking three birds instead of two. Archer tapped my arm, then tapped his ear. I put in my earbuds and adjusted the little boom mic; I could use both even inside the gas mask if I needed to put it on. The noise level dropped to nothing, and I watched Kent monitoring his Perscom. Finally, he nodded and started speaking.

"*Objective is Bensonville, population twenty-three thousand and some change. Portals formed on the west side and began discharging what looks like a takeover assault. We know of a Gog and a Magog for sure, the usual hordes of foot troops, Harpies, a flock of Wyverns. Given what happened the last couple days, we should expect something new, or maybe some of those Nagas. We'll have support from artillery, some foot troops, and army Mages.*"

I got a sinking feeling when he said that. Was one of those Mages Ace?

"*Our goal is to keep them out of the town. If they get in, we clean them out. Shiloh, your chopper will drop your team in the east, near* the Wyverns, where the army Mages are. My team will work with the artillery. Tank, I want your team to street-sweep; get any Cits in the open to safety, then join up with Shiloh's team. The situation is very fluid, so as usual, we'll be making it up as we go along."

Someone in one of the other two choppers laughed and said, "So what else is new? I assume we leave the big baddaboom to the artillery?"

"That's what they're here for, and our good luck they're in the neighborhood." Kent pointed at me, then at Hammer and Steel, indicating I was to stay with them. I nodded. He mimed pumping a shotgun and raised an eyebrow. I pulled up the AR enough for him to see I'd swapped out my original weapon, and he nodded with satisfaction.

My gut was all clenched up. This wasn't the first full-team deployment I'd been on, but it *was* the first time I'd be going up against an Othersider assault on an entire town, and it was the first time it was so far from Apex. I wanted badly to be on the ground with my Hounds all around me. I was acutely aware that the metal shell that was hurtling toward the enemy was extremely fragile in its own way and was a very big target. The whole chopper vibrated, bucked, and tilted as the pilot ran a random evasive course to keep the Othersiders from targeting us.

Kent suddenly clapped one hand to the side of his head and frowned. Then his voice rang through my ears. *"New deployment. We're facing three Folk Mages. Mei, you stay on the Wyverns. Tank, I want your team with me and Archer on the Folk Mages. Hammer, you and Steel and Joy handle the Gog and Magog with support from the artillery; they'll tear the town apart otherwise. Then you head into town to clean up. Heads up, people, we're about to hit the landing zones. Team HSJ will drop first. Get to the door and get ready."*

Was this normal? I'd never been in on an "Incident" before. Did the Othersiders just open Portals at random and pour minions in without any sort of tactics or planning?

Hammer popped his harness; his brother did the same a second later. I unclipped mine, grabbed the cargo net draping the interior of the chopper, and got in line behind Steel. We were wrenched back and forth for a few seconds, and I hung on for dear life, the rope of the net digging into my fingers, and I dearly wished for Hammer's mass as I got thrown around like a rag doll. Then the chopper slowed and stopped, hovering about three feet off the ground, and we three jumped out and down into a grain field. The chopper banked and sped off as soon as we were clear, blasting us with the backwash of its rotors and making us squint and shade our eyes against debris.

Like the fields nearer Apex, this one was planted in strips of different grains. I was too busy looking for the Gog and Magog to try to identify what was in them; all I could see was waving bands of greens and green-golds spreading out in front of me, the grain stalks rippling in the wind. But once I turned around and looked behind me, there was the town, in the middle of the field; it was a bigger town than back home, with a couple of three-story-tall buildings, a lot of two-story ones, and tons of houses. Wind generators of all sizes were everywhere, and the roofs were covered in solar panels. The railroad went through it, and right on the edge of town, at the railroad tracks, there were the Gog and Magog, side by side, methodically tearing apart grain silos.

I was grateful that was all they were doing; they eat people, and they are always hungry. If I'd had time to think, I'd have been scared. But the situation wasn't giving me any time to think.

They looked fundamentally alike: giants, about three stories tall, with sallow skin that was smeared with filth. They were clothed...sort of...in crude mud-colored tunics with ragged hems. Both were bald. They looked like a chunky caricature of a human, with thick arms, thick legs, and a torso with no discernable waist or chest.

The way to tell the Gog from the Magog is that the Gog has one eye, the Magog has two. Everyone back home assumed that Gogs and Magogs were mated pairs; you certainly never saw one without the other. It seemed about as reasonable an idea as any other you could have about them, and truth to tell, I really just did not want to imagine *how* something like that could mate and give birth. Maybe they didn't. Maybe they just budded off a new little monster whenever they felt like it.

The artillery didn't dare fire on them because they were right on the edge of town. The Bensonville Cits were almost certainly cowering in the cellars of those houses nearby, and the army would need someone close enough to paint the giants with lasers to guarantee every shell and rocket was a direct hit.

I was about to ask Hammer what the plan was when a Portal opened up right in front of us, no more than twenty yards away, and a horde of *Nagas* began pouring out.

Hammer cursed and jumped back, and I shot my Shields up and made a grab for my assault rifle.

But the *Nagas* ignored us completely; instead, they slithered at high speed toward the town, moving low to the ground as the Portal closed behind them. A moment later, they were a hundred yards away and all but invisible in the grain. Hammer made a split-second decision. *"Kent,"* I heard over the radio, *"change of plans. Snake-men heading for town. Joy, get the giants to chase you and get them away from the buildings so the artillery can take them out. We already know the* Nagas *know how to open doors; if we don't stop those snakes from getting into town and into the shelters, there's going to be a slaughter."*

He and Steel called up their Hounds with the emergency summons and pelted after the rapidly vanishing *Nagas,* leaving me . . .

. . . alone . . .

Oh god . . . I summoned my Hounds the same way, ignoring the burning in my hands and the sudden drain of power, in order to bring them in as fast as possible. I knew Hammer was right, totally right: those *Nagas* could open or just plain hack down doors, smash in windows, and go where anything human-size could go. But at the same time, those giants had to be pulled away from the town too—and even if the pack and I could probably have caught up with the *Nagas* and dealt with them on our own, I didn't think that Hammer and Steel could handle both of the giants at once. Sure, they could smash one, but while they were doing that, the other one could squash them like a pair of bugs.

A plan . . . I needed a plan.

As soon as the Hounds were all across, I reached blindly for Dusana and swung myself up on his back as he skidded to a halt beside me. A vague plan sprang up in my head, and I just hoped it was going to work. *Bya, take the rest of the* Alebrijes *pack and give the Magog hot feet. That should get its attention. Get it to chase you to the north. Myrrdhin, you and I will take the rest after the Gog. Go!*

Bya didn't argue with me—he and the others *bamphed*

themselves across the intervening space, and a moment later, I thought I saw a flicker of flame somewhere below the Magog. I *definitely* heard a roar of outrage and pain, and the giant lumbered angrily northward. Gogs and Magogs were hard to damage. Their skin was thick and tough, and bullets generally just bounced off unless they were armor-piercing or specially coated. But the fire of my *Alebrijes* Hounds definitely stung that Magog. It was mad, and it was going after what had hurt it. Its partner didn't seem to have noticed; the Gog was still feeling around inside the silo, its one eye squinched up, and its nasty gray tongue sticking out of the corner of its mouth.

Bamph to the Gog? Dusana asked.

Yes! I said. *Shield and go!* A moment later, there was a gut-writhing flash of disorientation, and then we were standing within thirty feet of the Gog, its ugly butt looming up above us. I didn't want to get any closer. I didn't want to chance seeing what was under that filthy tunic. Myrrdhin and Gwalchmai were with us; Hold and Strike were somewhere behind us, but if my idea worked, we'd be packed up again soon enough.

I'd never been this close to one of the giants before. My gut was all in a knot. And oh *god*, it stank! Like ... concentrated rotted meat and socks someone had worn for a hundred years and the armpits of a nasty, greasy octogenarian mountain man who hadn't bathed since the day he was born. Gagging on the stench, too busy gagging to feel scared, I pulled my assault rifle around and gave it a burst in the back of the knee. I had armor-piercing bullets in there. It was going to feel it, even if it felt like a flea bite. That was okay: flea bites are annoying and they hurt, and that was the point.

It stopped feeling around in the silo, turned, and looked down at me. It couldn't furrow its unibrow, of course, but it managed to look annoyed and puzzled anyway. The head was like a huge boulder, with a smaller blob of a boulder for a nose. The teeth were the only things about it that looked clean. It snarled, showing them.

Now that I had its attention and it was facing me, I fired off the spell I'd been preparing. This was a levin bolt, which I expected to sting it at the very best. I wasn't really trying for much damage; the amount of energy I would have to put into a spell that would hurt it would probably drop me to my knees. But I'd piggybacked the skunk stink on top of the levin bolt, and my target was that little divot in the lip just under his nose.

It hit, square on target, right where I wanted to put it.

First came the sting. Then the stink.

The giant let out a roar of utter outrage, its eyes reddening and watering immediately. You wouldn't think something that smelled that bad would be that severely affected by another stench, but it was pretty clear I'd achieved my objective and then some. I had *all* of its attention, and it wanted me, not just for my manna, but for payback.

The Gog picked up its foot to stomp us flat, then drove the foot down so hard that the ground shook, and the foot left a crater in the dirt.

Of course, we weren't there to be stomped on. Dusana had taken off the second the giant started to bellow, running without any real direction except *away*. I hung on for dear life as Dusana dodged and wove erratically, avoiding the pod-size clods of torn-up earth and pieces of grain silo the Gog started to lob at us.

It continued throwing things at us as we got farther away. Then it started to chase us. Dusana took off in a straight line, due south.

I hung on; Dusana had helpfully sprouted a bunch of spikes I could cling to and brace my legs on.

I managed to get my arm up so I could see my Perscom. "Location," I panted. "Nearest army unit." Lucky. The Perscom was smart enough to figure out what I wanted.

The Perscom obliged, showing that we weren't quite going in the right direction. I corrected Dusana so we were headed straight for them. Hammer wanted me to get the giants placed where the artillery could take them out without endangering the town? Best way to do that was to bring them *to* the artillery. "Contact nearest army unit," I ordered. "Hunter Joyeaux calling command. Come in command."

"Command, roger. Go ahead, Hunter."

"I'm bringing you someone to play with," I said, just barely managing not to squeak it. I didn't look back. The Gog bellowed behind us, and it sounded as close as that Drakken had been days ago.

At least it didn't have a Drakken's triple mouth with all those teeth.

"Roger that, Hunter. Sighting in. Firing when clear."

"*No!*" I yelped. "No, don't wait for us to get clear! Fire when you've got a lock on with all weapons, and give me a three-second countdown!"

They hesitated, probably thinking we were too close for safety. Well, we were, but that didn't matter. Not if our Shields held. *"Roger that, Hunter. Commencing countdown. Three. Two."*

Dusana *bamphed* about fifty feet ahead on *two*, and we both dropped to the ground, hardening up our Shields.

"One."

Just like the moment when the train crew had let loose with the Hellfire missile at the Folk Mage, the world disintegrated around us. For a few seconds, we were literally at ground zero of a little apocalypse. I think they must have had at least one missile launcher of some kind, with something not unlike a Hellfire, because the light was so bright I saw it even through closed eyelids and my face buried in Dusana's neck. I'd hardened my Shield against *everything*, including air. We only needed what was in our lungs, and we surely did not need to get turned into crispy chicken. I felt power being *sucked* out of me as the Shields countered what had hit them.

But our Shields held, and in the next moment, it was dark, and there was . . . stuff . . . pattering down on them. I went to purely physical Shields just to keep ourselves from getting buried in debris.

And in the next moment I knew just what a big mistake *that* was.

I had thought the stench before was appalling. Now . . . it was indescribable. I gagged and covered my nose and mouth with both hands, before I remembered my gas mask, fumbled it out of my backpack, and pulled it on over my face. I was so glad I'd kept the gas mask in my load-out! The next few breaths of blessedly filtered air were such a relief that my eyes watered. Or maybe they were watering from the remains of the Gog . . . there are no words for that smell.

Dusana and I waited until the rain of nasty stopped dropping on our Shields. Then we flexed them violently outward, sending all the chunks of yuck and spills of ooze flying off us.

When we could see past the Shields again, we were on the edge of a brand-new crater in the grain fields. The grain was on fire, but since it was green, the fires were going out by themselves. As the smoke cleared around us, I looked toward the army line and waved. I turned on the mic in my gas mask and said, "Hunter Joyeaux to artillery commander. Ready for round two?"

There was a lot of coughing and gagging on the other end for a moment. Then some cussing. Very creative cussing; I was impressed. *"I thought those things smelled bad on the outside,"* came the reply finally. *"Roger that, Hunter. Ready for round two."*

"See you guys in a bit," I told him.

Bya? I called.

Coming, my Hound replied, sounding amused. *We will meet you halfway there; the creature has already realized what you did to its mate, and it is coming in your direction. You should have no trouble getting it in place.*

With the Gog and Magog disposed of, and me as far upwind from the gross mess as I could get, I called Hammer. After all, Kent had made him the team leader. He replied promptly. *"We're cleaning up in town. There's not just those snake-men; there's Redcaps and Yeth-hounds."*

Yeth-hounds; that was another Othersider I had heard of but never seen up on the Mountain. Possibly because they didn't like mountains; their favored place was flat or gently rolling land, like moors. They were headless hounds, but that didn't stop them from being able to tear you to pieces.

"Join up with us, and we'll work our way toward the others," Hammer continued.

"Roger, Hammer," I said, and we all headed in that direction. Their icons were still moving around on the map.

My last order from Kent had been to stick with Hammer and Steel, and that was what I was going to do. They were in the center of the town, so that was the direction I sent Dusana. The rest packed up around me, with Bya sticking so close to Dusana's side he might as well have been glued there.

Get your mind on your job, I told myself. It didn't matter that all of this was *crazy* compared to the Hunting I'd done at home, because I had the best pack ever, and we'd keep each other safe. "Myrrdhin, take Hevajra and Begtse and quarter to the right. Shinje, take Strike and Kalachakra and quarter to the left. Gwalchmai, range ahead of us with Hold and Chenresig. Stay within a hundred yards of me, take care of anything you find, and if you get into trouble, bring the trouble here to me and Bya and Dusana." That put two fire-breathers and at least one *bampher* to the left and the right and one fire-breather and a *bampher* scouting. I had Dusana and Bya, and we could *bamph* our way out of reach of anything we couldn't handle with just the three of us. "If you don't get into trouble, I want anything that isn't human or a domestic animal on fire and dead. We need this place cleared, the faster, the better."

All the Hounds nodded and arranged themselves as Dusana and Bya and I worked our way through the streets toward Hammer and Steel.

There was no sign of anyone coming to put out the burning buildings, but that wasn't a surprise. Extinguishing fires was a job best left until after the Othersiders were gone, even back home. Hopefully anyone that had been in those buildings was in a place of safety. I couldn't help but contrast Bensonville with Anston's Well; here, everyone seemed to have gone into hardened shelters to wait for the arrival of Hunters and the army—back home, no one would have been waiting around; they'd have grabbed weapons and started a line of defense as soon as the first Portal opened or the first Othersider attacked. I knew why Cits weren't given weapons in Apex, but did that hold in these smaller towns, out here beyond the safety of the Barriers? It must, because as we made our way down the street, past abandoned pods, locked doors, and vacant storefronts, there didn't seem to be a single soul here. And I know the Othersiders couldn't have killed *everyone* in town without leaving a sign of the bloodshed.

The air was thick with smoke, but the fires were not nearly as bad as I would have thought; in fact, it almost looked as if they were starting to go out on their own. Maybe the buildings were built with fire-resistant stuff. That would make sense, if everyone was forced to go into shelter. Still, I was glad I'd kept my gas mask on. The Hounds didn't have any problem with smoke that I could tell, but I'd have been choking without it, and by now my eyes would have been watering and swollen.

Contact, Myrrdhin said briefly. I tensed. *Redcaps.* I relaxed at that. It would have to be a big swarm of 'Caps to give Myrrdhin and my *Alebrijes* more than a moment of trouble. A moment later, Shinje reported the same; he seemed amused. But then, Shinje didn't have any respect at all for Redcaps.

Minotaurs! exclaimed Chenresig, and all amusement vanished from the minds of all the Hounds.

Chenresig, bring them here! The rest of you, mop up and form up on me, I ordered the other two subpacks. *On the double!*

We stopped right where we were, just past a pod that had been abandoned right in the middle of the street. I glanced around, but there was no better place to make a temporary stand. *Plan. I need a plan....*

But first, I needed to know how many Minotaurs there were. Two or three... not a problem with my pack of eleven. But if they matched us one for one, well, we'd be outmatched on paper. They outweighed and outmuscled us, and I needed to be smart.

I put up full Shields, and so did Dusana; Bya saved his in case we needed them later. I could hear the baying of the Hounds and the bellowing of the Minotaurs around a corner ahead as the scouts made their way back to me. A moment later, they came racing back to my side, as Myrrdhin and his two streaked in from the right.

Then the Minotaurs lumbered around the corner and stopped dead at the sight of us.

It looked as though they hadn't been expecting anything like my pack. They peered at us, tossing their horned heads uneasily, and pawing the pavement with their hooved feet.

Not good. We were almost evenly matched. There were nine or ten of them, which was more than we could take on head-to-head. This was the biggest herd I'd ever seen; I'd never seen more than three together before.

Minotaurs don't look exactly like the Grecian ones. They have bull heads and vaguely human, heavily furred bodies, but they have the hind legs and tails of bulls instead of human legs. The ones I'd seen in the forests back home had been naked, which was kind of embarrassing. These weren't; they had heavy leather belts and loincloths. Most of them were dark brown in color; a couple were ebony-black. They stood about eight feet tall and carried enormous double-headed bronze axes, primitive weapons but very effective. But, of course, those axes, and Minotaurs' enormous strength, were not their only weapons. Their horns were deadly, and so were their hooves. And they weren't stupid, not even close, as long as they didn't lose their tempers or get manipulated into herd behavior.

So obviously I was going to have to trigger both.

The last three of my Hounds returned from the left on the run. The Minotaurs snorted angrily at the sight of them and shifted their weight from hoof to hoof. They were bullies by nature and didn't like even odds. If there had only been me and my original pack, there was no doubt they'd be advancing on us, laughing. Right now, I suspected they were psyching themselves up to charge. If they did it while their brains were still engaged, they'd come at us in a V-formation, with heads down, in something like a charging shield-wall. They'd hook us with their horns and trample anything that didn't get out of the way, then reverse, and come at us from behind with the axes.

I didn't give them a chance; a plan had finally come to me. The one thing that would tilt the odds in our favor was to make them so angry they stopped thinking and just reacted without a plan and without coordination.

I sprayed them with my assault rifle, emptying the clip. Normally, I would never use bullets so wastefully, but this was a case where it was justified. Like so many Othersider monsters, Minotaurs have thick hides, with a lot of resistance to weapons grown right into their skin, which was nearly as tough as Kevlar. So I wasn't going to do more than inflict superficial wounds, but that wasn't the point. The point of this otherwise futile exercise was to hurt them enough to anger them, get their bull side dominant over their human side, and get them to chase us without thinking.

It worked. They bellowed as the bullets stung them, and charged chaotically, with no attempt to work together. We turned and fled. That's where we had another advantage. Minotaurs are slower than us, at least initially. They carry a lot of weight, and it takes them a while to get up to speed. We would be able to outdistance them pretty quickly, and unlike Drakken, once you had their attention, you couldn't lose it easily, and they wouldn't lose interest in us just because we were getting away. If anything, that was likely to make them *more* angry.

It wasn't more than a few hundred yards to the edge of town, away from potential victims. We were running on paved roads, and the footing was excellent—all things in our favor. They were coughing in the smoke from the fires. We weren't. Once we were in the clear and we had enough distance on them so I could get a spell ready, we turned and faced the charging herd.

This was a trick I'd pulled so many times I could have cast the spell in my sleep. It was a useful way to stop things, anything from a runaway cart to a herd of angry elk or bison. With an outpouring of manna and an internal *yank*, I created a knee-high barrier, a drastically shortened Wall, right in front of them. I got it up when there was less than a pace between the leaders and it. They couldn't stop in time to avoid hitting it; in fact, I think they didn't even realize it was there until it was too late. The front rank slammed into it and toppled over; there was the *cracking* sound of breaking leg bones, followed by meaty *thuds* as the rest fell over *them*, followed by the frantic cries of cattle in agony. The ones in the front rank had probably broken both their legs. Then they'd probably broken other things as the rank behind ran into and fell on them—ribs most likely, maybe arms. And of course they were carrying those axes, and if they didn't get nasty gashes from the blades, they'd get thwacked by the shafts.

But I wasn't going to waste any pity on them. They'd fully intended to kill and *eat* us; like Gogs and Magogs, Minotaurs ate people. Not just the manna, the meat. One Minotaur could easily down an entire human at a sitting, and if they'd gotten hold of any of the Cits, they probably had already made themselves a meal.

So as soon as they were down, I gave the pack the signal to attack.

And that was when my original Hounds unleashed fire, and I lobbed a half a dozen flash-bang grenades into the pile. Flash-bangs at range disorient; flash-bangs in your face will tear you up, even if you have hide like Kevlar. The bellows coming from the pile were deafening, and I had to keep reminding myself that *they* had been quite ready to tear me apart alive and eat me on the spot. The Hounds without fire dove in, two at a time, and hauled a pair of wounded Minotaurs from the pile and set about dispatching them. The rest continued to belch flames on the pile of struggling bodies, replacing their spent manna as the Minotaurs died, while I lobbed flash-bangs. I regretted now I hadn't grabbed real grenades instead; this would have been a lot cleaner.

I was glad I still had my gas mask on.

Like Goblins, the Minotaurs went to goo when they were dead; eventually there was just a mound of slime oozing into the dirt where they had fallen. Like the *Nagas*, all that was left were their weapons, big bronze axes too heavy for me to lift.

As soon as the Hounds had finished drinking in the manna,

we trotted back into the town as fast as we could. I hadn't heard anything from Hammer, and that didn't bode well. "Range out," I told them, and they scattered.

According to my Perscom, the brothers were just past where we'd encountered the herd of Minotaurs, in what was supposed to be the center of town.

And just as I thought that, I *felt* something like a cold wind whipping through me—the signature of a *lot* of magic being spent right nearby!

I whirled—

And there was a Folk Mage. "My" Mage. The one from the train. He looked as he had then, floating there in midair, his long, long silvery-lavender hair trailing about a foot or so past the soles of his shoes. That hair was ornamented with strings of sparkly beads behind his right ear. He had the same silver headband stretched across his forehead, with a lavender stone in it that matched his lavender eyes. He wore a similar costume to the last time, layers of robes, with an elaborate, embroidered belt, all of soft, shiny silvery-lavender stuff, with floaty sleeves, and every visible bit of it was covered in silver embroidery and more sparkly beads.

My heart practically exploded with fear, and I jumped backward. All my Hounds were ranged out, and it would take them time to get to me, even *bamphing*. I could hear Bya in my head, shouting that he was coming, but that there were *Nagas* between him and me. For at least the next minute, I was on my own.

I snapped up my Shield, but I'd depleted a lot of energy and it wasn't nearly as strong as I needed. Not if I was going to take on a Folk Mage alone.

"Of a courtesy," I squeaked out, "let me pass."

But he was *not* behind his Shield. Behind him was an open Portal.

"Take care, shepherd," he said as my Hounds gathered in tightly around me, vibrating with suppressed aggression. "Take great care, and be wary. Do not let down your guard. Your enemy has friends, still, and they are here. Things are not as they seem."

And then he backed in through the Portal, which closed instantly, leaving me alone with far, far more questions than answers, and a terror that shook me to my bones.

What the hell? What was that supposed to mean?

Then it occurred to me. What if Ace was using this fight as a chance to get his hands on me and throw me to the Folk? Frantic now, I told my Perscom to hunt for combat cams, and after a few seconds, it found me one.

In fact, it found me one that was recording a pitched battle of Hunters and army Mages against two of the three reported Folk Mages. These were the "civilized" kind, although they weren't dressed as elaborately as the one from the train had been; it looked to me as if they'd come dressed for a fight, rather than dressed to intimidate. The Folk Mages were both wearing archaic, elaborate armor, like something out of a vid, complete with crested helmets, and both clutched staffs surmounted by glowing objects.

The Folk Mage on the right wore red-and-gold armor with a fancy cloth thing, like a long vest, belted over it. His helmet had big bird wings on either side of the top, and his staff had a Ketzel embracing a glowing, flame-shaped orange gem. The Folk Mage to the left wore a similar outfit in green and gold, but his helmet was plumed with gold feathers, and atop his staff was a green globe with what looked like a serpent coiled around it.

It was pretty clear that these staves were weapons and not the sort you just hit people with; as I watched, the one in red and gold pointed his staff at one of the army Mages, and the flame-shaped object belched bale-fire at him. The army Mage stumbled back under the onslaught, and his Shield failed spectacularly, fracturing into shards of manna, like broken stained glass. He screamed as the bale-fire set him ablaze; then the Folk Mage turned a little and the bale-fire plumed outward to engulf another army Mage who was coming to the rescue. This one's Shields held, and he ripped off his jacket and beat out the flames on his fellow with it, while a third interposed himself and began firing levin bolts with both hands at the enemy. The levin bolts splattered harmlessly on the Folk Mage's shield. The army Mage kept firing anyway.

I wanted to throw up. I wanted to run. This confrontation was *everything* I had been taught to fear—facing not just one, but *two* full Folk Mages of the civilized sort, and it was clear the army Mages were no match for them. I was paralyzed with terror.

Then the Folk Mage's Shields were hit by something explosive, they flared and cracked, and I recognized Archer's handiwork.

"Get up *here,"* someone snarled into the radio. *"We've got to get Prender out!"* The camera panned in, showing the one who'd come to the rescue of the burning Mage now trying to haul the injured man away by his shoulders, while the third Mage, and Archer, pounded at the Folk Mage with levin bolts and conjured arrows. *Now* I could see what my Masters had told me about: how the Folk Mage kept replacing his Shields from within, so that as the outer layer was destroyed, it was replaced by an inner layer.

"Get him out yourself, I'm busy," replied a voice I recognized. It was Ace.

"Consider yourself reported for insubordination, Sturgis!" the other snapped. I could tell now that the speaker was the Mage who was shooting off levin bolt after levin bolt, his face a mask of rage, as the two Folk Mages backed up, one slow step after another. It appeared that the second one, the one in green and gold, was the one holding Shields over them both.

Ace laughed. It wasn't a normal laugh. It sounded maniacal. *"What are you going to do? Take away my birthday? Do your own dirty work, Kingsley!"*

Ace had something up his sleeve. I *knew* it, right then. I *knew* he knew I would be here, and he had some way of getting to me and he was going to throw me to the Folk.... All I could think of was how to get away, far away, from whatever it was he was going to do to me.

Then all other thoughts were driven right out of my mind as the battlefield frequency erupted with voices, shouting, even screaming. Then the cam just went dead—and a gale-force blast of wind hit the town so hard that the buildings shook as the smoke was driven right out of the streets. My attention was diverted to the sky above the area where the battle was going on—to eyes able to see magic, it was like an artillery barrage or fireworks going off. Lots and lots of magic energy careening off into the air. My heart stopped dead. I had *never* seen that much magical energy all in one place before in my entire life—and this was just the residual leakage from whatever was happening on the battlefield!

Then... it all just *stopped.*

That was when the battlefield comm channel erupted in confused shouts. In all the babble, I could only make out one thing: *"He's gone!"*

I crouched over my Perscom, concentrating on the voices while my confused Hounds gathered around me and people yelled at each other—questions, recriminations, even some accusations. Finally, after about fifteen minutes of this, I figured out *who* it was who had disappeared.

It was Ace.

And I wanted to scream with anger and frustration, and I wanted to beat myself in the head until I was unconscious. Because I had known, I had *just been told* that something was going to happen with Ace, and I had blown it because I hadn't passed the information on *immediately*.

Oh ye gods, what had I done?

OH GODS. THAT WAS all I could think, as the choppers came for us. *Oh gods.* Because what else could I think? I *had* the intel, the information was in my hands, and instead of getting on the comms to Kent, I'd wasted time looking for combat cams. I could have stopped Ace escaping, and I hadn't. Forget how well I'd handled the Gog and Magog; this canceled out every bit of that.

Because my first concern hadn't been for my team, or for the Elite, or the Hunters, or anyone in the whole damn battle but myself. I'd been terrified Ace was coming after me, and that was all I had thought about. I'd let *everyone* down in that instant of selfishness.

Don't tell, snapped Bya in the next instant.

Not even Uncle? I thought back at him.

Bya shook his head. *No one.* Then as my legs gave way and I sort of folded up on the ground, he made his fur all soft and so did the rest, and they all clustered around me until I was encased in a nest of Hounds. I pulled off my gas mask and cried, partly because I was scared, partly because I was exhausted, partly because I was so sick at what I'd done, or rather, hadn't done, but mostly because I just wanted all this to *stop*. I wanted people to stop trying to use me. I wanted people to stop trying to *kill* me. I didn't want to have Folk showing up and delivering cryptic messages. I wanted things to be simple again, where all I needed to do was Hunt Othersiders and do my job well and everything else would take care of itself. I had *thought* everything would be all right, and now it was going all wrong again, and I was running out of ideas and energy.

I am not a pretty crier. My nose got all clogged up, my face got all hot and raw, and my eyes swelled up. There were some rags in my backpack because it's always a good idea to have clean rags no matter where you are, and they were all soggy and nasty by the time the chopper came to pick me up. I sent the Hounds home as it landed. There were two guys who were wounded, but not badly, and a medic in it already. The medic gave me a sharp look when he saw my face as I climbed in.

"Are you hurt, Hunter?" he asked. I shook my head, still not able to talk coherently without bursting into tears.

He gave me a sympathetic look and patted my shoulder. He was an older guy, old enough to have kids my age, actually. "It's been a long, long day, kid, but it's over. Go strap yourself down," he said kindly, and handed me a wad of waste bandage to use in place of my rags. As soon as I was secured, he banged the side of the chopper, and we took off again, me still leaking tears.

The chopper let them off first, then dropped me at HQ. I was the last Elite in, and as I trudged to the debrief office, I was not looking forward to fumbling my way through an interrogation.

But to my surprise, I was just handed a form to sign that detailed most of what I'd done, with a page at the end where I could add what I wanted. So I added the Minotaurs and the rest of the cleanup, signed it, and hurried to my room so I could start the shower and have another good long cry under the hot water. Showers are great places to cry; the noise covers what you're doing, and the water washes away all the mess.

By this point, I was reduced to just one thought: *I want to go home.* I wanted everything to go back to normal, I wanted my friends, I wanted my Masters, I wanted people I could trust around me. Not just people I could depend on. People I could *trust.* People who knew me well enough to know when I might drop the ball and would make sure no one else did so my screwups would be covered. People who were so much smarter than me that they made Kent look like a bottom ranker. People who knew when I was out of my depth. People who I could have told about my moment of selfishness, who would have given me the lecture I deserved, then let me know they could still protect me—protect all of us. And somewhere I could be *safe*, as I could never be safe here, not as long as Ace was alive.

My brain felt like mush, my gut and shoulders and neck were in knots, and I *hurt,* wanting these things so badly. And in that moment, not even having Josh as a boyfriend was incentive enough to make me want to stay, if someone had told me I could leave.

But of course, no one would. I was trapped here. I could never go back. Things would never be "normal" or predictable again. I was so very tired, and there was no prospect of things ever getting better, no chance that anyone *would* ever let me go home again. And that, really, was why I was crying.

I got out of the shower dripping and just wrapped myself up in a thick, soft robe without drying off, and flopped down on the bed. My eyes were sore. My cheeks felt better after the shower, but my nose was raw. I felt Bya tapping anxiously on the back of my mind and sat up long enough to bring him over.

He curled up around me and just let me not think. For once, no one was pestering me (and right at that moment, I would have considered even a call from Josh to be "pestering"), and it slowly dawned on me why that was.

Something far more important was occupying everyone here at HQ, and probably the Prefecture, and definitely at the army HQ. Ace was gone; this was the first time someone had vanished right off the battlefield in front of everybody, and it was a disaster. Above all else, they had to make sure *no one* talked about that outside of the Hunters and the army Mages and those in the conventional forces who had actually seen it happen. And then what would they do? I had no clue and probably neither did they, but they were scrambling.

Let the news come to you naturally. Be as surprised as anyone else. Bya was sharp. And correct. And he was right about another thing, that I shouldn't report that "my" Folk Mage had warned me (although, Cassandra-like, the Folk Mage hadn't exactly been clear about what he was warning me against).

If I'd reported that contact, though, all I'd get out of it would be *more* trouble. They'd just had one former Hunter, now Mage, defect (I was already pretty sure Ace had defected, and I figured it wouldn't take long for everyone else to come to the same conclusion). They knew from the recordings made that day when the Hounds and I saved the train that "my" Folk Mage had made *me* an offer. They'd be right to assume that, if he'd shown up again, it wasn't just to give me some vaguely worded warning, but to repeat the offer; and in their shoes, I'd be looking at me with a lot of suspicion.

I was just glad that there hadn't been a cam around to record his second appearance in my life.

You should eat, Bya chided.

Ugh. I still felt sick to my stomach. Too much running on terror and adrenaline, and too much crying. But there were some liquid meals in my cool-box, and I mustered enough energy to get two and drink them.

I was too tired to sleep, somehow, so I dimmed the lights, then put on some music and just lay there with Bya serving as a source of warmth and comfort and as a pillow. It was rest, kind of.

Every so often I thought about getting up and going to the lounge, but I just couldn't bring myself to move. I had that feeling of heavy exhaustion that comes after you're over the worst of a bad illness but aren't in any shape to get up and do anything.

At least with everyone else running around trying to deal with what Ace had done, probably no one was thinking about me. Except Bya.

Why do you do this? I finally asked Bya. *Hunt with us humans, I mean?*

He took a long time to answer, and I wasn't sure he would, actually. *Me?* he asked. *Or all Hounds?*

All Hounds, I clarified.

He was quiet for a few more minutes. *Partly the same reason why wolves came to hunt with humans and became dogs. Together we are better hunters than either of us alone. And since our prey hunts you humans, it is easier to join you and wait to ambush the prey than it is to chase it down.*

That made perfect sense, of course. But I started to feel disappointment—

But Bya wasn't finished. *But mostly it is because we like you. We are more like dogs than wolves, now. We come to you because we like you, we enjoy Hunting with you, and we enjoy your company. All of us like our Hunters at least a little. Some of us like our Hunters a very great deal.* And he gave me a nudge and a lick. *I would have to like you very, very much to clean your runny nose with my tongue, no?*

I was astonished enough to be jarred right out of my depression. That was one of those things I had always hoped I was right about, but I never thought I'd hear Bya just say it. I put both arms around his neck and hugged. "I love you too," I whispered into his ear.

Good. That is as it should be, he replied, and I sensed his amusement. *Now rest. Learn the wisdom of the Hound. Always rest, eat, and play when you can, because the universe conspires to keep you from doing any of these things nearly as often as you would like.*

Did anyone else have this kind of closeness with their Hounds? Surely *someone* did.... Archer was always curled up in a Hound-ball when he was resting. So was Kent. And I wondered, just before sleep finally hit me between the eyes, if this was something Hunters and Hounds could somehow use against the Othersiders.

We were shorthanded as I came to find out when I signed in. Three of the other Elite had been injured, not critically, but we might be scrambling for a few days.

Between that and Ace's defection—and it was all over Hunter HQ that he *had* defected—no one was paying any attention to me, which was exactly the way I liked it. No messages waiting for me when I woke up, no one calling as soon as my status went green. As I walked into the mess for breakfast, I had planned to be early to continue being left alone . . . but so, it seemed, had everyone else. The mess was packed.

I listened to the gossip over breakfast as I ate off in a far corner. It was pretty lively. There was even some about me . . . some people were wondering what I'd been doing after the Minotaur attack—though in light of Ace's disappearance, people were just shrugging it off with a "Well, looks like Joy's finally had a moment of hitting the wall." Which was humiliating, since some people were snickering when they said it, and it was pretty obvious there were still Hunters here that thought I was getting above myself and needed a little takedown. On the other hand, it wasn't all *that* humiliating, and there were a whole lot worse speculations they could have made.

Even Ace's former friends were making no effort to defend him now. It was one thing when he'd gone after me and another when he'd basically given a big fat "up yours" to every Hunter ever by going over to the Othersiders. Ace's former girlfriend, Cielle, was pretty bitter about it. "'Trust me, baby,' he kept saying," she said to a little group of sympathizers. "'I know what I'm doing, baby, you don't need to know anything.' And sure, I *bet* he knew what he was doing! He was selling out to *Them* the whole time! I bet he even had a deal going with Them so he always had what looked like fantastic Hunts and he'd stay number one! Lousy cheat! I wonder how many of us he planned to hand over to Them?" There was a lot more in that vein. She'd gotten the notion in her head that Ace had been grooming her to present to the Othersiders. She might have been right.

Needless to say, although there were cameras here as always, not a one was broadcasting. So the Hunters could say exactly what they liked, and they were not holding back. If someone didn't have a nasty Ace Sturgis story of his own, there was always the opening to commiserate with someone who did.

Sure, some of this was sour grapes, but all of it was fueled by the deep sense of betrayal shared by everyone in the room. When it had just been Ace trying to murder me, that was terrible, of course, but people told themselves it was just Ace going ape over his brother's death. But this was an outright betrayal of every single one of us. It hit everyone on a personal level. They were angry, outraged, and personally offended.

There was a certain satisfaction in hearing Ace getting smeared by *everyone*. I'll admit it. Sometimes I am not a nice person, and that not-nice person was feeling vindicated right down to her toes. The bad-mouthing also made me feel a little less depressed.

But what really got rid of the depression was that when I was about halfway through my breakfast, a bunch of grapes appeared in front of my eyes. "I thought about an apple, but that's a Christer thing," said Retro from behind me. "I always preferred the Romans. Care for a grape?"

"Sure," I said, taking one off the bunch and popping it in my mouth. He came around with his tray and plopped himself down across from me.

"So. Our Bad Lad has flown the coop." He made a birdlike shape with his hands and flapped it off. "Am I the only one not surprised?"

"I guess . . . I guess the prefect probably isn't," I said after a moment of thought. "He was the one that wanted Ace somewhere they'd have to pump sunshine to him. But other than him and you . . . I guess so."

He picked up a piece of bacon, eyed it critically, and ate it. "I'll admit, it was more dramatic than I pictured. I figured he'd make an illusion doppelganger of himself during a fight and just walk away. Probably go sell his services as a Mage to a warlord somewhere, or one of those bandit paramilitary groups. Or, hell, he wasn't in a position to be picky, to the anti–Premier Rayne bunch of wannabe rebels out there in Spillover." He raised an eyebrow at me. "Mind you, any of those would have been a significant comedown in the world."

"You know who I wouldn't want to be right now?" I said slowly. "The army Mages he must have been palling up to. He royally shafted them, *and* now they're probably being raked over the coals for not keeping a tighter leash on him."

"True, oh wolves," he replied, which actually made me smile briefly because it meant he'd read *The Jungle Books* too. "Have some grapes," he added, offering me the rest of the bunch. I was polite and only took about half.

"Why aren't you angry about this?" I asked—because of everyone in the room, Retro seemed to be the only one that wasn't treating Ace's defection like some *personal* betrayal.

"Waste of my time," he said, and chuckled. "Look, it really is. I got angry at him when he tried to *murder* one of us. After that, so far as I was concerned, he was not getting one second more of my attention, unless and until I was in a position to do something about him. When I'm not Hunting, I want to be having a good time, and being eaten up with anger is *not* having a good time." He cocked his head at me. "So, want to have a good time?"

I was saved from having to answer when *his* Perscom went off. He looked at it, shook his fist at the ceiling, and dashed off.

When I was done, I reported to the armory, which was also packed. Kent came out of his office, looked around, and announced that he had decided to hold an impromptu briefing for us, which was probably smart, since that would short-circuit a lot of speculation. Right now, people were still in the shock phase and venting about Ace. But Hunters are smart; they have to be or they don't survive. I gave it less than forty-eight hours before people started taking the little bits that they knew and blowing them up into full-blown stories.

"This is what we know so far," he said when we'd all settled around the room.

"All the cam footage has been gathered up, and if there was

any doubt before, there's none now. You might as well know the truth, since you're likely to be the ones to butt heads with him. Ace Sturgis definitely defected to the Othersiders. We've got cam footage of him going through one of their Portals of his own free will."

There was some murmuring, but no one sounded surprised. Angry but not surprised.

"The good news was that there were no Cit casualties," he continued. "The bad news is that the analysts have a theory that the entire attack was staged in order to cut Ace loose."

Well, that's going to tilt over the hive, I thought. It might have taken people a while to come up with that theory on their own . . . but on the other hand, maybe it was best to just get it in the open now. Would people speculate less if they thought the authorities were already trying to figure out what that meant and what we could expect?

"They lost an awful lot of minions just to get one human Mage," Archer observed, his voice skeptical. "The Folk Mages are better than ours are. What could they possibly want with Sturgis that they couldn't get easier with one of their own?"

Inside information, I thought immediately. *Details on defenses. Even if Ace doesn't know how the defenses are constructed, or even how they work, he knows where they are and where the controls are. And he knows the Hunters, knows their powers. A lot of them, if not all of them.*

"When have you ever seen the Folk concerned about their foot soldiers?" countered Flashfire, one of the Elites whose pyromancy left me in awe. "I've seen them fling a couple hundred onto the barricades only to wander away when they got tired of the fight and leave the grunts to fend for themselves. We all have. I can easily see them sending in their cannon fodder just to distract us while they hooked Sturgis."

"If all the troops were supposed to be was a distraction, that would account for the lack of tactics. They didn't seem to give them any direction at all," Hammer observed. "They just opened Portals and turned the troops loose."

"And the minions they brought were not the sharpest knives in the drawer," added his brother. "Minotaurs? Harpies? A Gog and Magog? Pretty dim, all of them, when left to themselves. If the Mages had been controlling the underlings, that still could have been a viable attack force—but they weren't. As a distraction, though, they were perfect. They forced us to divide our forces, and that gave them an opening to separate Sturgis from the rest of the army Mages so they could grab him."

Kent held up his hand. "No need to convince me. We were played like fiddles. I don't know *why* the Othersiders wanted Sturgis, but it can't be for any reason that's good for us."

They all discussed this for a while; meanwhile, I had been struck by an entirely different idea, and I wondered how many of them had thought of the thing I'd just thought of.

In order to pull all this off, somehow the Othersiders had been able to communicate with Ace while he was under observation and incarceration.

Kent pointed at Archer, Hammer, and Hawk. "You three are the senior Elite and our best tacticians; you know everyone's strengths and weaknesses and how best they can work together. I want you to brainstorm combinations with me today. The rest of you, take your normal routine. All but you, Joy, I want to see you for five minutes first."

Does he have cam footage of the Folk Mage talking to me after all? I throttled down anxiety. The rest filed out—all but the three he'd indicated and me. "Joy," Kent said soberly. "Sturgis was after your head, and I don't imagine that's changed at all. How are you doing?"

I bit my lip. Tell the truth and make him think I wasn't up to being Elite? Or try to hide it and get caught anyway and prove I wasn't? Either way I could be in trouble. "Better than last night," I said finally, deciding to try and cut down the middle ground. "When it happened, all I could think of was Ace getting his hands on me and throwing me to the Folk. And the same last night. It was a rough night."

Kent nodded in sympathy. "Not a surprise, I'd have been more surprised if you weren't worried. So what are your thoughts?"

"I'm still worried," I admitted. "But I've got a pack of eleven, and two of them used to be his. They should know him better than anyone. I'll put my trust in my Hounds."

He nodded, satisfied. "Just to be on the safe side, I'm going to move your quarters. He *shouldn't* be able to get into the city, and he's a wanted man; every cam system has his face in it. But he's human; he can pass the Barriers without getting fried, and he might get some sort of illusion magic from the Folk that will change his face even for the cams, so I'm taking no chances."

That actually hadn't occurred to me last night, and I think I would have been in hysterics if it had. I resolved to sleep with one of my Hounds from now on.

"It'll be taken care of by the time you're back from your stroll in the underground," Kent continued. "Just check your Perscom."

"Yes, sir," I replied, and took that as a dismissal.

The storm sewers were very uneventful. Just small fry, and very few of them; if I'd had a channel, my viewers would have been very disappointed. By the time I got back, as Kent had promised, all my things had been moved to another part of HQ. I got a slightly better suite of rooms out of it; the shower was amazing, and it did so many things that it came with its own manual. The next time I needed to have a good long cry, I could do so seated under a waterfall of hot water, and finish up by steaming myself in a steam bath or in a one-person hot tub. No more sitting on the bottom of the tub and blubbering—I could recline and weep in style.

I still felt shaken and scared and desperately wanted to go back to the Mountain. I had done a pretty good job of covering that while I was patrolling, but not so much once I was alone. I contemplated having another good cry in my new shower... or maybe, going to the lounge and joining in the snarky critique group, if they'd still have me now that I was Elite. Should I call Josh? I wanted to, I wanted to so badly, but...

Poop. I'm calling him.

"Hey," Josh said as soon as he accepted. "You all right? Need me to come stand guard over you while you sleep? I look awesome with a fire-ax."

That made me laugh for the first time since Ace escaped. And it also let me know that Josh knew about Ace escaping. "No, not really. I think Bya would resent you trying to take over his job."

"Well, all right, then. In that case, how about if we go for a walk in the Hub? It's fun this time of night, and it's not something you've ever seen on foot before." He paused for a moment. "This is one of those 'hide in plain sight' things. Unless cams are specifically looking for you, and they won't be, you'll go unnoticed. Everyone knows that Very Important People only travel by pod. Nobody is going to pay any attention to us if we just dress like normal people. There's street food if we get hungry."

That pretty much decided me. I'd wanted to see the Hub afoot anyway, and I was used to doing a lot of walking. Josh would probably get tired before I did.

"I'd like that," I said. He smiled.

"I'll send a pod," he replied, and before I could reply, he signed off.

On a whim, I dressed in some of my old clothing from home; the oatmeal-colored tunic that Kei had embroidered for me, a wide leather cincher belt, and my doeskin pants. I left my hair loose and didn't put on any makeup at all. Then I went out to the door to wait for the pod. The sun set while I was still en route.

It dropped me off at a corner just on the edge of the Hub, and Josh was waiting under a streetlight for me. As if he had somehow read my mind, he was in some of the casual stuff he'd worn during the storm, and he looked nothing at all like a Psimon. I was positively ambushed by the relief and happiness I felt seeing him like that, waiting for me. I hadn't realized until just now how much better I felt when I was with him.

He grinned to see me. "See now, here we are, just two turnips in the big city, going for a stroll to gawk at the lights and all the things famous people do. Nobody is going to pay the least bit of attention to us."

That actually sounded very appealing. Right now, being completely anonymous was exactly what I needed.

We held hands and wandered in the direction of things that looked interesting. I had not expected it, but I found the lights outside clubs and entertainment places rather lovely. We joined the crowds who were not privileged to go inside and watched the lights change on the façades of places like the Strauss Palais, the Jungle Club, and the House of Tech. I hadn't realized when I'd gone to the Strauss Palais that the lighting went through a cycle; one palace façade faded and was replaced by another, all equally fanciful. And why not? The only thing that these grand "structures" depended on were the whims and talent of the artists who created them.

I also hadn't noticed that there was waltz music playing outside and a rose scent in the air. Was that to make the people out here feel as if they were a small part of the experience?

Most of the people—a lot of them dressed pretty much like we were—didn't seem to be here for the lights, though. They watched every pod going by like kingfishers at a pond hunting minnows, waiting to see if the pod stopped and who it dropped off. Most of the time they were disappointed, as whoever it was that got out was not someone who had a vid channel. But once, it was an actor and actress, and not long after that, it was Dazzle and one of the greenies—Levy, I think it was. That surprised me a bit; I hadn't pictured Dazzle as liking Straussing, but there she was, with her hair all piled on the top of her head, a little crown holding it in place, and wearing one of those "cake dresses," bell-shaped and covered in fluffy lace ruffles. It looked good on her, and she moved naturally in it. I'd have felt utterly stupid in such a getup.

When the people gathered around saw her, they pressed forward, calling her name, while we hung back. Dazzle laughed and pulled pictures out of some hidden pocket in that enormous dress and signed until everyone was happy. Only then did she and the greenie go in.

"Why didn't we get any of that when we came here?" I whispered as we moved on.

"Because when extremely important people—like you—are supposed to arrive, the venues send out security to keep people back," Josh whispered. "When you turn up to something like that"—he waved at the Strauss Palais behind us—"you're there to be seen, not do fan service. Every minute you spend signing pictures is a boring minute on your channel. It's astonishing how much is stage-managed and you won't even know it unless someone tells you."

Well, I was pretty surprised. And resentful and glad all over again that I was Elite. If Josh and I came here again, I'd make sure to do what Dazzle had just done.

When we got thirsty and hungry—well, Josh was hungry, anyway—we stopped at a food truck, which was really a cargo pod with a window set in the middle that served as a food counter. "Street food" is what Josh called it. Pretty basic stuff, very cheap and filling. Falafel and lettuce, peppers, and tomatoes in a pita. It reminded me of home, actually. I was hungrier than I thought after I took the first bite. Maybe my stomach was settling after all the anxiety.

There was a bigger crowd outside the Jungle Club; we didn't bother joining them because I didn't care what notable notable was turning up to dance. But the lights on the club façade were really amazing in a completely different way than the Strauss Palais. It was like we were on a river, passing through deep jungle. Now and then there would be some animal drinking there; sometimes the critter would just pick up its head and stare, other times it would bolt into the deep green underbrush. There was music out here too, mostly drums, and the scent in the air was something heavy and exotic.

"Had enough of being a turnip seeing the sights?" Josh asked me after a while. I nodded, because to be honest, although the real turnips were probably looking at shop windows, admiring the clothing they couldn't afford, or the accessories, or the gadgets, I was paying attention to those broad expanses of glass, and worrying about how vulnerable they'd be if there was an attack.

Josh turned down another street after consulting his Perscom, and I saw something unexpected just a block away.

Trees.

Well-lit trees, mind, but trees, and lots of them. We headed in that direction, and when we reached the end of the block, we were standing across the street from a one-block-square bit of forest.

There was a waterfall at one end that fed into a "stream" that cut the whole area in half. And it was all covered by a wire dome.

"People need nature," Josh said as I stared and blinked. "It's called an 'arboretum.' It's one of the nice things around here that you don't have to pay to get into. The dome keeps most trouble out. Lots of not-obvious protection on the spot, so the very few Othersiders that get in through the wire don't last very long."

Josh held the gate open for me, and we both went inside.

A graveled path led from the gate, meandering away under the trees. And it was so weird to me because it all looked so wrong. After a while, I figured out why. It was all manicured and groomed, until it bore about as much resemblance to wilderness as the version of "me" that had gone Straussing with Josh bore to the real

• 169 •

me. The path was so smooth it looked as if it was someone's entire job to come through here every hour or so and rake the gravel, the way some of the monks at the Monastery did in the Zen garden. The grass was no more than an inch high... *everywhere*... and flowers and (very obviously) ornamental foliage plants gave the impression of being carefully placed, out of the way of trampling feet. Bushes were trimmed so that no errant twigs reached out to snag the unwary, and as for the trees, they were a carefully spaced mixture of deciduous and conifers, arranged so that everything would still be attractive even after the deciduous trees lost their leaves.

We rambled along the path, and I sighed. "This is the first time I've felt ordinary since I got here," I said finally.

"That was the point," Josh told me. By this time we were over by the waterfall, and he gestured at a bench seat near it; it was in an extremely well-lit spot, so none of the other couples had claimed it. I went and sat down, and he sat down next to me.

"So, how are you holding up?" he asked, taking my hand again. "Don't worry about saying anything you shouldn't. The sound of the water will cover up anything we say unless someone goes to the trouble of finding this recording and running background-noise removal on it."

"And if someone does that, they'll be someone entitled to know what we're talking about anyway," I said, giving him a small smile. "I'm... I dunno. Scared. I think as scared as I was when we didn't know who it was that was after me. It's a different sort of scared, though. Then we didn't know anything. Now we know it's someone who knows Apex and Hunter HQ inside and out."

"He still has to get to you," Josh reminded me. "You've got a lot of layers of protection between you and him."

I nodded. "I'm not as scared as I'd be if I was running solo patrols in Spillover, I guess. There were already Wyverns and stuff out there, and Ace wouldn't have any trouble at all setting up an ambush for me. If They let him, that is. That's the thing. We're all groping in the dark about this."

"We've all been given orders to keep watch for him," Josh said somberly. By "we" of course, he meant the Psimons. "Which really just breaks down to *watch for a crazy person*, so it's not much help."

"Even less help if he's wearing the equivalent of a Psi-shield," I pointed out. "The Folk have magic *and* psionics. Given that we've never been able to tell when one of the Folk was about unless we laid eyeballs on him, it's pretty logical to assume that they do have something like a Psi-shield and they might be able to put it on Ace."

I let that sink in for him for a moment. He bit his lip. "So, if Ace has a Psi-shield...and some sort of way to disguise himself..."

"It's possible to cross the Barriers without going through the pylons if you're human," I reminded him. "It hurts like bloody hell if you aren't inside a vehicle, but it can be done."

"It can?" Josh's face got a bit pinched. "I didn't know that."

"There's no reason why he couldn't just get himself down the train line to a settlement and buy a train ticket to Apex either," I continued. "You Apex Cits are used to thinking that no one can buy anything without a bank account tied to your Perscom. But out there"—I waved my hand—"little towns and villages don't have banks, and a lot of people wouldn't trust their income to something that can get fried in an EMP anyway. We deal in physical cash; banks with Apex-issued scrip. If Ace wants to get legitimately inside Apex, all he needs to do is go to some small place with something valuable he can sell, like jewelry, then take the money to a train station and buy a ticket to Apex."

Josh looked at me as if he didn't quite believe what he was hearing. "Yes, but once he's *here*, there's—" Josh stopped. "I was going to start detailing all the security stuff. And none of that matters to a Mage. Does it?"

"Not if all the stories about how Folk Mages have been able to disguise themselves or even turn invisible are true. Especially one like Ace, who knows Apex," I said, glumly. "Heck, the easiest way for him to disguise himself would be as a Psimon. You guys are always Psi-shielded right? So that would be natural. No one ever tries to look a Psimon in the eye—"

"No, I can rule that out right now. We've got ID chips in our collar insignia, and every time a Psimon passes any kind of scanner, it registers. Even a Perscom if you point it at the right place." He nodded as I looked at him skeptically.

"Why?" I asked bluntly.

"Who'd be easier to impersonate than a Psimon?" he pointed out. "So if a scanner registers a Psimon uniform but no ID chip, it sends out an alert."

We sat together, holding hands, but I didn't feel all warm and fluttery inside. I felt sick and scared.

And this conversation didn't seem to be making *him* feel any better either. It was more as if, once we'd gotten obliquely on the topic of the Psimons, he was feeling stressed out. There were probably plenty of things he could be stressed out about, of course. It was pretty clear to me at this point that PsiCorps didn't want people to know much about Psimons. And PsiCorps didn't want Psimons to get too familiar with anyone at all. But I had the feeling there was more to it than that, even though I couldn't put my finger on it. Did it have anything to do with what I was doing for my uncle? Did *he* know about the dead Psimons in the sewer and wasn't telling *me* about it? Why would he hide that from me?

"Sorry I spoiled the night out," I said after a long and increasingly uncomfortable pause.

He sighed. "I'm the one that brought the whole mess up. I'll tell you what, this has got PsiCorps *and* the army *and* the Prefecture stirred up. Your uncle is coming out looking good, since he's the one that wanted Ace in solitary confinement in a maximum security cell, but everyone else is trying to cover their asses. The army is blaming the PsiCorps operatives that were supposed to be keeping Ace under tight observation for not noticing that he was planning this escape. PsiCorps is blaming the army for letting Ace out on such a long leash. There's always been a fair amount of competition in the premier's cabinet, but this incident is bringing the knives out."

We stayed there for a little while longer and I even relaxed a bit, but neither of us went any further than a couple of kisses. I didn't want to "perform for the cameras," and after a while I remembered again that among all the other safeguards in this place, there just might be a Psimon stationed here around the clock. Josh absolutely would not want PsiCorps snooping on him getting romantic. That could get him in a lot of trouble. It was one thing to perform for the cameras, but it was quite another for a Psimon to risk himself getting attached to someone.

So we ended the evening going back to HQ together in a pod;

we might have made out a bit in the pod, but both of us still had Ace in the back of our minds, and something like that isn't going to make you feel in the least bit like fooling around.

And now all I could think of besides Ace was Josh—and not in a good way. In a choice between me and PsiCorps—which one would Josh side with?

THE ROOM WAS PRETTY cavernous by my standards, although it wasn't half the size of the room with the swimming pool in it. I guess what made it seem huge was that it was completely empty, four beige walls and a beige floor covering that was easy and safe to fall on. "So," I asked, "what have you learned?"

Mark Knight shifted his weight from one foot to the other. We were both "out of uniform," so to speak, wearing workout clothing that was loose and easy to move in. "Mostly that Hammer and Steel are the best Hunters to emulate in the Trials."

We were standing together in what was called the "workout room"; normally it was for practicing martial arts, but I didn't see any reason why we couldn't use it to work on Knight's magic, so I had signed us up to use it.

"All righty, then. Did anyone vid what I did to the Minotaurs back at Bensonville?" I asked.

He shook his head.

"Well, this is where you learn that a Wall can be something else. Watch," I said. And I made another one of those short Walls, forming it up slowly so, Glyph by Glyph, he could see what I was doing.

His blond brows creased as he concentrated on the magic. "Okay," he said, slowly. "I see what you're doing. I think. I just don't get wh—"

That was when I brought up my Shield, expanded it rapidly outward, and shoved him over the shortened Wall.

As I had hoped, he tripped and fell over backward. I hadn't shoved him hard enough to break anything, just to get him moving.

"Oh," he said from the ground. "That's why."

"A Wall doesn't have to be a Wall," I pointed out. "Especially not if your opponent doesn't see it. That was what I did to those Minotaurs; they ran right into the barricade and broke their legs on it. I don't advise that you break anyone's legs in the Trials, but demonstrating that you *could* is going to get you style points."

I dissolved the Wall and the Shield and offered him a hand to help him back up to his feet. He took it and got back up again. I was very glad that Mark Knight had both an amazingly even temper and the motivation to take lessons as *lessons* and not as an attempt at humiliation.

"So, let's see you make one. And let's see you make it as unobtrusive as possible," I said.

It didn't take him long; Mark turned out to be a very quick study when he was modifying something he already knew how to invoke. Within an hour, he was making Walls that were only a couple inches high, which was still plenty tall enough to make someone trip and land on their butts.

He was breathing hard and sweating; doing magic in a new way is always exhausting. I was still in pretty good shape. It hadn't been anything but little stuff like a couple of Redcaps and some Goblins in the sewers. "Enough for tonight, or do you want more?" I asked him as I went to the cool-box built into the wall and got him a water bottle.

I handed it to him. He checked his Perscom for the time. "At least another hour," he said firmly. "One trick is not going to help me win the Trials."

I heard a step I recognized at the doorway. "Listen to that boy," said Hammer from the door. "He's learning."

Mark looked up at Hammer. "I'm trying," he replied. "It would help if I could have seen exactly how you and your brother were doing what you did in *your* Trials. For some reason, magic energy and spells don't show up on the vids." He drank the last of the water and put the empty bottle with other empties to be cleaned and refilled later. "Dare I hope that is what you are here for? To demonstrate?"

"He's not as dumb as you said he was," Steel quipped, shoving his brother aside so he could get in the room too. "Of course, what would be best for you is if you could learn the whole of our limited bag of tricks."

"I aim to try," Knight replied doggedly. Steel nodded approval.

I stood back in a corner, leaned against the wall, and let them work. And the truth is, for the first hour, there wasn't much action to see. Hammer and Steel made entirely different Walls and Shields from the sort Knight and I made, so he had to first learn a brand-new way of working.

Needless to say, I was taking plenty of notes too. Different styles of magic, and different teachers, mean even when you think you know everything about how to do something, you really don't. Hammer and Steel's Shields and Walls were much stronger than mine, and now that we weren't facing Othersiders and they could construct them slowly, I could actually see what they were doing. I was getting excited. I loved learning new magic.

After about an hour of practice, they decided Mark should put what he'd practiced into action, and that was when things *really* got interesting.

I just watched for a while. Mark would put his Shields up, and Hammer would form up the version of his Wall that he used as a weapon. It wouldn't take more than two or three hits, and then, *wham*, Knight was flying across the room backward, to slam up against the wall of the room. He just couldn't anchor well enough to hold against those blows.

Finally, I got tired of watching him do that. "Hold up," I said, walking to the center of the room. "Look, guys, all you're doing is repeating the epic fail that gave Hammer his win."

"So?" Hammer replied, raising an eyebrow. "I'm showin' Knight how it's done."

"But what if someone tries it on *him*?" I asked. "He hasn't got a counter for it."

They both thought that over for a moment. "Huh," Hammer said.

"And you've got a counter?" asked Steel skeptically.

"Maybe. I think we ought to see if I do, and then Mark can

learn it." I did a couple stretches to limber up, arms over my head, twisting side to side. "The counter's based on one of the hand-to-hand styles I learned back home. You know, the one that let me plant Ace's face in the dirt when he rushed me?"

"After the Gazer fight when Paules died, yeah." Hammer nodded, and so did Mark. "All right, then, I'll bite. Let's see if you can do this thing."

I was going to see if I couldn't apply the principles of Aki-Do to magic, to deflect an attack rather than try to stand there and absorb it. So when I put up my Shield, I gave it a little counterclockwise spin because I had noticed that Hammer tended to attack with his Wall just a bit to his opponent's left. And as he launched his strike at me, I moved—physically, I mean—and got off the line of attack, same as I would have if I were facing a hand-to-hand attack. At the same time, I was taking my Shield with me, keeping it centered on me.

I felt the hit, but nowhere near as hard as it should have been; most of the force got deflected off to the left, as I had hoped it would.

Hammer narrowed his eyes and launched a second blow at me; this one would have landed squarely if I hadn't gotten a little farther off the line of attack this time. Once again, most of the force went *whiffing* off, leaving my Shield intact and as strong as before.

"All right. That is one *good* trick," Hammer said. Then without warning, launched at me again.

This time I reversed the spin on the Shield and stepped off to the left so his force deflected to the right.

Steel broke into a howl of laughter. Hammer stood there looking chagrined. And Mark had lit up like the façade of a fancy club.

"Let me try!" he said eagerly. I imagine he was more than a little tired of ending up in the wall.

I stepped back to my place in the corner and gave over the center of the room to Mark. It took him about a half a dozen tries before he perfected the move and got the timing right, but after that, Hammer couldn't touch him.

The door beside me opened and closed, and the armorer stood there, watching. His face was impassive, but his green eyes were alight. Finally, he stopped them with a single word.

"Hold," he said, raising his hand at the same time. Both guys instantly dropped what they were doing and turned to face him. He ruffled his hand across the top of his head where his red hair was cut longer than it was on the sides. "Looks like you're coming along, White Knight. Steel, Joy, let's the three of us make a Trial Shield and let them have a real bout."

Well, obviously I had never joined in making a Trial Shield before, but after I watched Kent put up his Shield, then Steel, it was pretty obvious what I was supposed to do; Kent's made the outermost layer, then Steel's, and mine was supposed to go inside that. It was tricky putting a Shield inside two more Shields from outside of all three of them, and it took me a couple tries to get it right, but once everything was set, Kent gave the sign to start.

Then things got downright hilarious, with both men's attacks sailing off to be caught by the Trial Shields, and neither one managing to land a solid blow. Then, suddenly, I saw Mark's eyes narrow, and I knew he was going try something different.

He made a slight movement to his right, as if he was about to launch yet another "Shield Bash," as I was calling those attacks to myself. But I think I was the only one who saw an ankle-high Wall form right at Hammer's feet.

Hammer had the predictable reaction, moving off the line of attack—

—and tripped right over that tiny Wall—

—lost his balance completely out of surprise, and went down like a stunned ox. *His* Shield went down, and Mark was across the intervening space in seconds, ending with his foot on Hammer's chest. "Have a nice trip?" Mark said, deadpan.

Hammer looked at him with the most shocked expression I had ever seen on his face, then burst into laughter. "That was you? Damnation, boy, good for you!" He held up his right hand; Knight took the hint and grabbed it, helping him to his feet. "That deserves a drink!" Hammer continued, slapping Knight on the back, then putting an arm around his shoulder. "What about it, brother, Kent, Joy?"

"I'd say it's a good start," the armorer replied, with a slight smile. "You fellows do know I'm taking you and Joy out of the challenger pool for his Trials, right?"

Steel scoffed. "We'd figured that already, Kent. Even if we hadn't decided to give him a hand, you'd have left us out, because a fight with two Shield specialists would have been boring enough to put everyone to sleep. The first one to die of old age would have been the loser."

"There is that," the armorer agreed. "All right, let's all get that drink."

Now, I had no idea what they were talking about, but I'd assumed that we were going to that little food area where Elite could get meals outside of mess hours. But instead, I followed Kent and the others up to the third floor, to an actual bar. I hadn't even known there *was* such a thing in HQ.

It was windowless, decorated only with framed pictures of Hunters—I assumed as a quick guess, that they were all both Elite and dead, and later found out I was right. It was dark with only a little illumination on the back bar, and furnished mostly with comfortable couches except for a line of barstools at the bar itself. Kent went behind the bar.

"What's your poison, Hunters?" he asked genially.

Everyone chose whiskey but me (even Mark, which actually surprised me, since I expected as a Christer he was a teetotaler). I hesitated.

"Here, Joy, try this," said Kent, pouring something a deep reddish-brown over several cubes of ice. I picked it up and sniffed it. It smelled sweet. I could smell the alcohol, but it didn't seem nearly as strong as the whisky.

Well, just one.

Kent picked up his glass and held it up. "Hunters all," he said, and from the way he said it, the words sounded like something they all knew the meaning of. Maybe this was a toast that was always made here.

"Hunters all," we said, and I cautiously sipped. The others did *not* gulp theirs down; they sipped the liquor appreciatively. Mine was sweet, with a flavor I didn't recognize.

"That," Mark said in what sounded like surprise, "is very fine whiskey."

The armorer snorted. "It should be. We get it from you hill-country folks."

I never did find out what my drink was. I did find out that this bar was exclusively reserved for the use of the Elite and their friends, and that, yes, you didn't get your picture on the wall unless you were both Elite and dead. Kent and Hammer and Steel held forth on the Trials of those people on the wall that they had seen, Mark quizzed them intently, and I kept my mouth shut. This was Mark's chance to learn things—and to become friends with the people he badly wanted to join.

Eventually, as I suspected it would, the talk to turned to a question on Kent's part.

"Everyone has a reason to go for Elite," he said bluntly. "And I'll be honest with you, although you've put in good work as a Hunter, I haven't seen the attitude I expect out of someone heading that direction in you. Joy there... absolutely. I knew she was going Elite from the moment I heard her intake interview."

I took a quick sip to cover my surprise. How had he heard that...?

"But you, no. So what's your reason, Mark Knight?" Kent gave him a long and level look.

Mark hesitated, then shrugged. "I've got a girl. I want to marry her. But you folks aren't going to let me go live with her so we can be married, so I have to have a reason for you to let me bring her here. I'll never be a ranker. Elite's the only way it'll happen."

"Fair enough." Kent poured himself a little more. "And what does she have to say about this?"

"I—" Mark began.

Kent interrupted him. "I know you Christers often don't think that matters, what the woman thinks. A fair lot of you reckon that a girl's under the authority of her old man till she's married, and then under the authority of her husband. But you're gonna be bringing her *here*. She's going to see that it's different for women in Apex. I wonder if you've thought that through."

"I—" Mark said, and stopped. It was pretty clear to me that he hadn't thought about that at all. But then he got a faintly mulish expression on his face. "Maybe that's so for how our parents see it. Her pa promised her to me, and that's all that matters to our people. But that ain't what matters to the two of us. We want to be together no matter what, and Apex ain't gonna change her."

Kent regarded him silently for a long moment, then shrugged. "It's no worse a reason to go Elite than some I've heard. I'll allow it. But if things don't work out between the two of you, for both your sakes, don't let 'em fester. Bring the problem to me. That's an order, White Knight," he continued, his voice hardening. "I won't have my Elite endangered because one of them is having wife problems and is distracted or distraught. Understood?"

I suddenly realized that *this* was Mark Knight's real Trial. The one out in the arena was going to be for show. His answer *now* was going to determine whether Kent allowed him to win that Trial. Oh, if he couldn't admit to Kent's authority over *everything*, including his life outside of Hunting, the Trial would be fair, certainly, except that something in it would be tailor-made to make him fail, and only a miracle would let him pull it off.

But Mark must have been very used to bowing to authority, because his answer was honest and immediate. "Yes, sir," he replied. "That is a promise. My word on it."

Kent relaxed and tilted his glass to Mark, who clinked his own against it. "Good enough. You've still got your Trials to win.

There's no Mrs. Knight here yet, and sufficient unto the day are the troubles thereof."

Mark's jaw dropped. Kent chuckled. "What? Think you Christers are the only ones to read your Book?"

I could tell that Kent went up double in Knight's eyes for that. So could Kent, and he seemed to be amused. "Don't go trying to convert me," he warned. "I read a lot of things. I read about paintings, but that doesn't make me an artist."

"Yessir," Knight said. "No, sir."

I begged off and went off to my room after that, so I don't know what else happened. I was not only tired; the liquor had given me a relaxed, slightly buzzy feeling. Besides it was about time I wrote my Masters about all of this. Or at least wrote it all down in my journal. Somehow putting things on paper makes it easier to think.

So I opened the Way as soon as I got to my room, and Bya popped through. I knew he could go to Master Kedo and be back by dawn because there is a permanent Portal in one of the deep sanctuaries at the Monastery that allows Hounds to come and go as they please. It's something we have to have, since we never know when we'll have to repulse a huge attack, and this way none of the Hunters that live there have to take the time to open separate Ways into Otherside to bring their Hounds over. Sadly, such a permanent Portal is not something you can make easily; it takes at least nine Hunters, Mages, or both together to create one, and it has to be recharged with manna regularly, which is why I didn't have one in my room.

Bya looked at me and gave an amused snort. *Perhaps you should go have a drink more often. You worry too much.*

Hush, you, I replied, but with a little chuckle at myself. *I know Master Kedo would say the same, but the other Masters would not be so amused.*

Some would, he countered, which I also knew, but I ignored him as I dug out my writing materials.

I wrote stuff, by hand, the really, really old-fashioned way, in a bound book of blank pages. I did this almost every night. The stuff I wrote, I really didn't care about someone else seeing, so even if someone came in here and took pics of the pages while I was out on patrol, it wouldn't matter; it was just a sort of diary of what my Hunting that day had been like. But my writing in the book helped me think, and it also helped to cover the messages I was writing to Master Kedo, setting it up so that it wasn't unusual for me to requisition old-fashioned handwriting materials. So, once Bya was across, I took my book and the loose paper I had hidden in it, and went to bed. With the book propped against my knees, I wrote down everything that had been happening, in the order it had happened: the *Nagas*, the dead Psimon, the orders not to talk about it from PsiCorps, right through to Ace's escape. I also wrote in the book, about training with Knight, Hammer, and Steel.

I put the book on my nightstand, ordered the lights out, then, under the cover of the dark and the concealment of the covers, I slipped the message to Bya.

After that I cuddled with him until I fell asleep. I'd been doing that a lot since Ace vanished. I'd been having nightmares on and off. I would leave the Glyphs burning on the floor, and at some point, when Bya was sure I wouldn't have nightmares, he'd slip out of bed and go Otherside, and the Glyphs would vanish. Tonight, he'd just go carrying my message as well.

Knowing that, and knowing that even if they didn't have any answers for me immediately, at least I had been able to consult with the best Hunters and finest magicians I knew of (not to mention the people I trusted most in all the world). For the first time in a couple of days, I fell asleep easily.

◄ ►

I could tell by the look in Bya's eyes when I brought the pack over for the sewer Hunt that he had *some* sort of message for me. There was that *knowing* look he got. The way he looked right at me and held my eyes for a good long moment before nodding slightly.

Urgent? I asked.

No, he replied. He yawned casually, as we all formed up in our usual order. *I will give it to you some place where there is no distant eye.*

By "distant eye," he meant a cam, of course, and it would not be too terribly hard to avoid them down here. Cams were placed farther apart in the storm sewers under the Hub than they were out where the regular Hunters patrolled. Before things started getting weird, this part of the storm sewer network was supposed to be safe, so you wouldn't need full coverage. Hunters hadn't come down here, only Apex police and maintenance workers.

This tunnel was in another section of the storm sewers where we hadn't been before—but it *was* going to end up very near where we'd found that dead Psimon. I wondered if there would be anything at that site left to investigate.

There might be. If magic had had anything to do with the

Psimon's death, there might still be traces of it about. Unless Psi-Corps had brought a magician down here to get rid of such traces. "Stupid," I said aloud, chiding myself. Of course they would. I wasn't thinking. There wouldn't be anything there; I wasn't dealing with feral Folk, or amateurs. PsiCorps was nothing if not thorough. And I had better keep my mind on Hunting and not off on some other tangents that had nothing to do with Hunting, because a Hunter with a wandering mind generally doesn't get a second chance to make that kind of mistake.

There wasn't a trace of moisture down here today, and it wasn't even all that humid. There wasn't a trace of scent either, and the 'crete of the tunnel was so clean it looked scoured. In fact … I noticed as I looked more closely, the 'crete *had* been scoured, most likely by stuff carried down here in the storm. I wondered if we were going to get another day of Hunting for next to nothing.

We don't mind, Myrrdhin told me. *When you get calls to go outside the Great Fences, we eat like kings.*

Now I wondered if Myrrdhin and Gwalchmai had talked as much to Ace as they did to me. "*Great Fences.*" Well, that is as good a way of describing the Barriers as any.

I was glad Myrrdhin had told me that. I worried about my Hounds, worried that so big a pack would never quite get enough manna to eat. I guess I needn't have worried.

"Myrrdhin," I asked as we began our long walk, "did you talk much to Ace?"

He looked back over his shoulder at me. *No,* he replied, and I got the faint hint of … sadness? *No, he gave orders, and we obeyed. There was not much talking.*

"You guys speak up whenever you want, all right?" I said impulsively. "I like hearing you. And I prefer partners to drones."

Thank you. We will. The sadness had lifted. When he looked over his shoulder at me again, his eyes were warm and he was doggy-grinning. So was Bya.

We were thorough, and that was how we always worked. We checked out every side tunnel routinely, so no one would think anything out of the ordinary when we ducked down one out of sight of the cams. I got out my water bottle for a quick drink, and Bya trotted up to me, the note in his mouth.

I took it from him (grateful Hounds have nice, dry mouths) and unrolled it quickly. It was not from Master Kedo, but from Master Jeffries, the actual head of the entire Monastery, the most senior Master. He didn't waste any time on salutations; he cut straight to the chase. *Your information is troubling, and we will need to study the situation and our records before we can give you detailed advice. We do not know what the death of the Psimon you found means, but the mere fact that a senior Psimon gave you such explicit warnings suggests that this was not an accidental death and PsiCorps has a vested interest in hiding it. As for the new monsters appearing, I can tell you that this has happened before. It should be in the Apex records since it is in ours. This has always happened when the Othersiders found a way to counter human defenses, and we here have no reason to think that is not the case now, since you are also finding monsters where none should be. We believe that the defection of Mage Sturgis is a part of this; we will need to consult some very old records to determine if humans lost to the Othersiders have ever appeared again as allies of Otherside. The fact that the*

One you encountered at the train offered you a sort of position suggests this is possible. But as for the high-ranked Othersider who warned you . . . we are baffled. Nowhere, in any records we have, is there such a thing as an Othersider that has taken it upon himself to do such a thing. It may be a deception, although on the face of things, none of us can reckon what such a deception was intended to accomplish.

When we know more from our studies, we will have more for you. In the meantime, trust your Hounds, even when you can trust nothing else.

22

IT TURNED OUT *NOT* to be an uneventful trudge through the storm sewers after all. About halfway into our patrol, we ran into trouble, definitely the sort of trouble a squad of APD would not have been able to handle.

This time it wasn't something new; it was an Ogre and its mate. I'd Hunted Ogres before this; they are not uncommon in the mountains around the Monastery, and unlike Trolls, they can handle sunlight just fine. I did manage to knock the pair into the wall of the tunnel and unconscious, and then the Hounds finished both of them off.

Ogres *do* turn to stone when they die, and then the stone crumbles into gravel, then sand, leaving a pile of sand on the floor of the sewer tunnel to be washed away with the next big rain. Or the next time maintenance sent down a remote-operated cleaner— whichever came first. We were very near the spot where I'd found the dead Psimon, and I wanted to be sharp when I got there, in case (against all odds) there was something subtle left behind that I could pick up on.

I needn't have worried. "Subtle" was not going to be an issue. The Hounds practically ran over the top of another dead Psimon when they turned down the shunt tunnel that linked the one we were patrolling with the one we'd been in before. We all stopped stock-still and stared, and the Hounds all came skittering back to me. For a while, we all clustered together, staring, while I calmed my stomach back down again. Then we backed up in a group, fast, so we'd hopefully avoid muddling evidence too much.

This time, before I called it in, I looked the body and the area over for signs that anyone had been performing magic in the area . . . but there was nothing. Just a pathetic, too-slender corpse in a PsiCorps uniform, lying in a tangle of limbs as if she (it was a woman this time) had just dropped dead right where she stood.

Dropped dead—where she stood.

I suddenly realized that was what was odd about it. The body was not lying in a way that would have made me suspect that someone had murdered her elsewhere and brought her here to hide the body. I might not be a police person, but I have seen far too many dead human beings in my short life. I've seen bodies hauled and left, bodies dropped and left, and bodies deliberately hidden. And this one, like the first, if I hadn't known the Psimon was dead, I'd have thought she'd just passed out cold for some reason. The clothing wasn't disarranged. The hair lay splayed on the 'crete properly. I could go into more boring detail, but I *knew* that Psimon lay just as she had fallen, and just *where* she had fallen.

I stood there after I finished looking for magic traces, just staring, trying to make sense of what I was seeing. Because it didn't make sense, just like the first time. It didn't make sense that a Psimon would be *here* in the first place, given that there was a Hunter, an Elite at that, assigned to check down here. It really didn't make sense that there would be a *second* dead Psimon down here. Sure, the Psimon could have picked up the Ogre's mind and—then done what? Come down here looking for it? *Why?* That was the job of a Hunter. Unless for some reason the Psimon was supposed to try and take control of the Ogre's mind. . . .

But that made no sense either. There's not a lot you could do with a captive Ogre. And the Psimon would have known that the mate was down here too. A Psimon might take control of one mind, but never two. Oh, Psimons who've been particularly bold—and stupid—have tried in the past, but the result has always been fatal for the Psimon, as both "subjects" broke free and objected to being controlled in a very bloody manner.

And no, that was not the case here, because just like the first Psimon, this one hadn't a mark on her. An Ogre would certainly have bashed her about, and then probably ripped a limb or two off for a snack, even if it wasn't particularly hungry.

I studied the body for as long as I thought I could get away with it, and surreptitiously took some vid with my Perscom.

Then I called it in. And *that* was when I belatedly remembered what Josh had told me about how to ID a Psimon. I aimed my Perscom at her, and I *maybe* got a weak signal, but I didn't dare get any closer.

Just as before, I was told to exit the sewer. And just as before, the same stone-faced senior Psimon met me when I came out of the little bunker that sealed off the entrance. I thought he'd given me the stink-eye before, but that was nothing compared to the cold glare he gave me now.

"You touched nothing?" the Psimon asked me sharply.

I shook my head. "My Hounds stumbled over the victim, but I called them back, and I don't think they muddled the scene much."

The Psimon snorted. "I'm not concerned about *Hounds*," he said, inflecting the word in a way that made me think he equated them with dogs. "As long as you didn't meddle with the . . . victim . . . that is satisfactory."

That is satisfactory? *Is that how you talk about a dead—possibly murdered—comrade when you're a Psimon?* I'd thought this guy was creepy-cold before, now I figured he must have ice water for blood, and every single emotion cauterized. And I really, really did not like the way he was looking at me. Like he was looking at someone he considered to be inconvenient . . . or was considering me as a possible scapegoat. I was glad now I hadn't gotten any closer to the body.

And the way he'd hesitated before he said the word "victim" had all my suspicion nerves tingling.

I'd better go to the expected response.

"I'm sorry for your loss. I'm sure the Psimon was a valuable member of your community and will be remembered fondly and missed," I said flatly, and called for a pod. *His* pod was already there, and once again, he didn't bother to offer me a lift. Then again, I would have turned it down if he had. I don't think I could have stood to be confined in the small interior of a pod with this guy.

"Thank you," he replied, just as flatly. "The same conditions apply as last time, Elite Hunter. You will speak to no one about this."

Funny, it didn't seem to have occurred to him that if someone—like my uncle—who ranked above both of us were to order me to talk, then I'd have to talk.

Okay. Maybe he's just making sure I don't gossip. . . . No, he specifically said "no one." Which would mean . . . no one. Not even Uncle. This isn't good. I was getting a very creepy vibe off this Psimon, creepier than normal, that is. It felt as if he had been willing to accept I had discovered *one* dead Psimon by chance, but accepting I'd found two "by chance" was just not going to happen. So now, I was about to come under the magnifying glass.

I picked my single-word reply very, very carefully, just in case my Psi-shield *and* my mantra failed me. "Understood," I said. Which was absolutely true. I *did* understand. I didn't intend to obey him, but I certainly did understand.

He took that at face value and got into his pod and left just as mine arrived. I was actually so relieved to be away from him that all I did in the pod was sit back in the cushions and just not think about anything.

I waited until I was back at HQ, I had made my report, and was sitting in my own rooms to view the vid footage. I thought about putting the footage up on my vid-screen, then thought better of the idea. If, somehow, PsiCorps was having me monitored, anything I threw up on the big screen might be visible to someone else, so I kept it on my Perscom.

From all I could see, it still looked as if the Psimon had simply strolled down there and dropped stone dead. No marks on her. No sign of a struggle. No sign she was *brought* there. No scuff marks on the wall, no drag marks on the bottom of the tunnel. That pose she was in still looked exactly as if her knees had folded up under her and she'd collapsed straight down. Her hair—

Wait a minute—

I zoomed the tiny view on my Perscom in on her head. Okay, this was odd. Her hair was white. And not white-blond, or some sort of bleached white, the way Dazzle's hair was pink. No, this was old-lady white. And what I could make out of her face was wrinkled, with that delicate, fragile look that the skin of old people gets.

She was *old*! And . . . thin. Now that I looked at her closely, her clothing fit a little too loosely on her, and under it, she seemed little more than skin and bones. And sure, someone that old and frail could easily have dropped dead . . . but *how had she gotten down there in the first place* if she was that old and fragile?

I'd never seen an old Psimon. Hunters, if they lived that long, retired to become teachers of Hunters and emergency backup, but what happened to old Psimons? Did they retire? Did they keep working in some lesser capacity? Did their Powers get *stronger* as they got older, rather than weaker, so sending one alone into a sewer tunnel to track something dangerous was actually a reasonable thing to do?

Or . . . what if PsiCorps didn't want old Psimons around? Holy crap, was this what PsiCorps did with its elderly? Dumped them down in the sewers and let them wander till they died?

Had the first victim been old? I couldn't remember. *I'll have to ask Uncle,* I thought. *But he might not know.* Did I have vid of the first body? I couldn't recall taking any, but I couldn't recall *not* taking any. I'd have to search back through the Perscom memory to find it. All this had my guts in knots and the hair on the back of my neck standing up. I could ask Myrrdhin, but he might not remember either; my Hounds had funny memories when it came to people, as if what we looked like on the outside didn't matter all that much to them.

The next thought I had was an odd one. *Should I tell Josh about this?* If someone was murdering Psimons without a trace, he had a right to know. But if someone was just kidnapping elderly Psimons and dumping them in the storm sewers to wander around until they dropped dead . . . well, maybe he still ought to know. Unless he already knew and wasn't telling me about it, and if I told *him*, then this was just turning into one big hot mess.

My Perscom alarm went off, reminding me that I had a training session with Hammer and Steel and Mark. If I didn't want to attract PsiCorps attention, I had better act normally. I drank down a protein drink from my cool-box, changed into workout clothes, and headed for the session.

◄◆ ◆►

"Damn, boy," Hammer said, bent over his knees, and panting as if he had been running for miles. "I think you're ready." He glanced over at the armorer, who was leaning up against the wall with me, both of us in the same, near-identical pose, with our arms crossed over our chests. "Whaddya think, Kent?"

"Ready enough," the armorer said as I did my best not to show my glee. "Ready enough to pass, as long as he doesn't screw up."

Knight looked from Hammer to Kent and back again, as if he thought they were joking. "Really?" he managed at last. "Seriously?"

The armorer shook his head. "Would I have said so if I didn't

• 197 •

think you were? Yes. Really. Seriously. I've had the arena set up and waiting for the last week. Do *you* want more time to prepare, or would you rather get it over with as soon as possible?"

"Get it over with? Tomorrow?" Knight breathed, as if he was still afraid that Kent would say no.

"Certainly." Kent pushed off the wall and walked over to him, slapping him on the back. It was hard enough to stagger most people. Mark didn't move an inch. "I'll get it scheduled. Unless there's a full-team callout, your Trials will be the first thing in the morning."

Mark whooped, and then grabbed the armorer's hand and shook it like a balky pump handle, babbling his thanks. It kind of surprised me, actually. Mark was always so reserved and so rarely showed any emotion at all, that this was . . . astonishing. *I guess he really* does *love that girl of his,* was all I could think.

"I hope she's worth it," Kent observed, with a slight smile, echoing my thoughts.

"Oh, she is, sir, she is. We've known each other since we were kids, and I've never . . ." Mark seemed to realize that he was gushing at that point and reined himself back in, becoming the restrained White Knight I recognized. "I mean, she's a fine young woman, sir. No doubt about that."

Now we'll just have to see how the girl feels about him. Hopefully the same. Hopefully she wasn't some minx who'd enjoy pulling his strings because that was the only sort of power or control a good little Christer girl had. I'd seen things turn out *that* way a time or two among the Christers . . . .

Don't borrow trouble, I reminded myself. Even though I could think of oh, so many ways this could go *horribly* wrong for Knight.

Not that I could claim things didn't go wrong for my own people when it came to romance.

So yeah, I shouldn't judge.

Even though I was probably going to, anyway.

All the while I was thinking these things, though, I was also really happy for Mark and not just because I was pretty certain that while Kent was going to make him work for it, he'd pass the Trials. And I was happy for the rest of us on the Elite team too. He actually was Elite material. He'd have to work real hard to get up to speed with the rest of us, but I already knew he'd do that. It wasn't in him to slack off. I was coming to understand that Elite was more of a state of mind than it was the level of power.

And also that becoming Elite and being thrown into things you thought you couldn't handle tended to make you rise to the occasion, fast. Kent never, ever hung someone out to dry and never left someone to cope with something when they really couldn't.

But he pushes, and pushes, I realized. *Since there're no fans to please, he keeps raising the bar for me, and I bet he does that for everyone, until he finally does find your real limits.* If I'd known he was going to do that, I would have been scared, I think. Since I was just now figuring it out, I was more comfortable with it.

"It's about time, layabout," I said when it was my turn to congratulate him, and I punched him in the arm and we both grinned. "Go get some sleep. And hydrate. And don't forget the prep I did, and do the same. You are going to need every bit of energy you have, plus ten percent more to get through the whole show tomorrow."

"Yes, *ma'am*," he said, and saluted me. I punched him in the arm again.

It was extremely surreal to be on the *other* side of the arena the next morning. Needless to say, although nobody really thought that there would be an assassin lurking in the stands waiting to take down White Knight, nevertheless, under the mercilessly bright stadium lights at dawn, the entire Elite team *and* all our Hounds scoured those stands for anything bigger than a cockroach, and now that Knight was about to make his Trials, we had Apex PD snipers posted all around the top of the stadium, making sure no one else was going to sneak in once the Trials were started.

I was standing next to Retro; he was all done up in his skin-tight green and silver and gray "leather" outfit as usual—I don't think it was real leather because leather doesn't stretch *that* tight. He looked over at me and grinned.

"Hey," he said.

"Hey yourself," I replied cleverly. I'd found out he was the youngest of the Elite except for me, and if I hadn't been dating Josh, well . . . he had an interesting face, with a long jaw, and he smiled a lot. I already knew he could startle a laugh out of me. As if he were reading my mind, he grinned at me.

"So," he said casually, "when are you gonna drop that Psimon and date me?"

Then he grinned, and I thought about what I should say. "Got a good reason why I should?" I responded.

"I'm unpredictable, I'm hilarious, I'm outrageously good-looking, I have a fantastic ass, and you'll never have to worry about me reading your mind." He grinned even wider.

"The answers to those assertions will be: I know, I wouldn't be too sure about that, no, yes you do, and that's true," I said back, not blushing one bit. "Which so far doesn't give me any reason to dump my boyfriend and date you. *Every* Hunter has a fantastic ass. It's not like we sit around eating pizza and playing vid-games all day."

He clutched his chest. "Crushed! You have ripped open my chest and crushed my heart! I'll never love again!"

"That's enough, Retro," said Kent with amusement. "The cams are running."

He mock-pouted, then blew me a kiss and got serious. Or as serious as he ever was, outside of a fight.

Mark wasn't a ranker, so there was no one waiting to interview him beforehand as there had been for me. When we'd finished checking out the stands, the Elite all assembled at the direction of the armorer, down at the Magic Trial area. Mark was still in the dressing room, I supposed. It was now early morning, and the sun was still below the level of the top of the stands, sending rays of light up into the cloudless sky like a special effect. It was pretty chilly, but once the sun got above those ranks of seats, it would warm up quickly enough.

And I still didn't know how Kent managed to get the four Trial areas set up so quickly.

"All right," Kent said when we'd all gathered around in the center of the zone. "I decided we'd get the toughest part for White Knight over with quickly, so the Magic Trial is first. Hammer, Steel, Joy, and myself were exempt from being the challenger, and I was going to draw straws, but Archer stepped up and volunteered before I could."

I wasn't the only one to look surprised. Archer just shrugged.

"Going to try to redeem myself from the face-plant Hammer put me into in his Trial," he said.

Kent shook his head pityingly. "Just remember, buddy, you were the one who asked for this. All right, people, form up. We'll put up the Group Shield after Knight enters the combat zone. Joy, you start off, since you're new at this."

I nodded, feeling a bit relieved. It would be a lot easier to be the first one up and just have to set up and maintain my Shield from outside it than try to build on what the others did. After all, I'd only ever done Group Shields with my Hounds regularly before this, plus when training Mark.

Archer took his place at the far end of the combat zone, opposite the entrance to the tunnel under the stands. The rest of us spaced ourselves at roughly equal intervals around the circle and waited.

I heard the footsteps before I saw him; his Hounds came in ahead of him, flying up and to either side of the zone to land with the rest of ours. He stepped out into the light, and the announcer (whose name I *still* didn't know) said over the speakers: "*Since Hunter White Knight assisted Elite Joyeaux in preparing for her Trial, he already knows the rules. White Knight, are you ready for the Trial of Combat by Magic?*"

"I am," Mark said steadily. He was in his usual Hunting gear, the white-and-gold body armor with a matching white pack on his back. *He's going to look a state when he gets done,* I thought ruefully. *He'll probably have to burn that outfit; it'll never get clean.* He took the pack off now and set it aside, since weapons weren't permitted in the Magic Combat Trial. It looked like he'd opted for his usual Hunting load-out—a rifle, a handgun, and a couple knives. Well, after watching me compete, he already knew that in the Shooting Gallery Trial, he'd be given exactly as many targets to take out as he had bullets, and if he missed any, he'd have to take them out by throwing his knives.

The armorer raised his eyebrows at me, and I took that as the signal to put up my Shield. In short order, the other thirteen had layered their Shields on top of mine. I paid extremely close attention to what they were doing, and they, in their turn, brought their Shields up slowly so I could see exactly how they did it. Next time we had to make a Group Shield, I'd know what to do. When everything was up and good and solid, with no wavering or weaknesses or conflicts, the armorer nodded.

"*Trial One,*" the announcer said. "*Begin.*"

Archer *immediately* started moving and shooting, while Mark put up his Personal Shield and made for him. But not at a run; at a deliberate, if brisk, pace. Archer's arrows kept hitting Knight's Shield and exploding on it with a force that definitely would have killed him if he hadn't been Shielded. Mark just kept his eyes fixed on Archer, quite as if there weren't explosions going off within inches of him, and followed him like some inexorable, unstoppable pursuer in an old horror vid. Meanwhile we had a job on our hands keeping the concussive force of Archer's arrows contained by our Shields.

Archer started to sweat a little, although he didn't stop moving, and his arrows weren't getting any weaker. But I thought I could see Knight's strategy now.

He was going to keep moving, keep his Shield up, and keep Archer on the defensive even though *he* wasn't doing anything offensive yet. He was just going to let Archer wear himself out.

Then he'd make his offensive move. He was playing the long game, unlike what I'd done at my Trial. Although I hadn't had much choice. Ace Sturgis *had* intended to kill me, either with magic or the hand laser he'd palmed.

Frankly, it was a bit like watching grass grow, once the initial shock of Archer's barrage wore off. Bya was lying at my feet, with one of Knight's Hounds beside him, looking bored. *How's Knight doing?* I asked, knowing Bya would know which one of the two was starting to wear out long before I would.

The Archer is beaten, was Bya's opinion. *He just hasn't admitted it yet.*

What Mark was doing had a much lower drain on his endurance than Archer's running and gunning. On the other hand, Archer was putting up a good fight and a good show, and there was always the chance one of his hits would crack Knight's Shield.

If he could get Knight to falter, that is, or somehow miss something he was doing.

Because so far, even when he'd piggybacked a Shield-weakening spell on one of his arrows, Mark had detected it and rather than unraveling it, he had flexed his Shield and actually thrown it off. Disconnected from its job and with no way to anchor back to the Shield it was supposed to gnaw through, the spell curled on itself and died.

I was so proud of Knight for doing that, I wanted to cheer. Because it meant that even though he was *still* only using Shields and Walls, he had figured out something else he could do with them. If he could learn how to do that, who knows what else he could learn?

Definitely Elite material.

Finally, Knight made his move.

He picked up the pace of his pursuit, forcing Archer to run a little faster. I'm not sure if I was the only one of the Elite holding the Group Shield who saw Mark put up a little ankle-high Wall just behind Archer, but I know for a fact that Archer was backpedaling too fast to spot it himself.

He hit it, tripped, flailed his arms wildly, lost his bow. Mark put up a second little Wall behind him, and he tripped over that as well....

And *down* he went. Flat on the turf on his back. Before he could scramble to his feet again, Knight pounced, pinning him to the ground with what I can only think of as a "slow" version of his Shield Bash. Within a minute, Archer was being held to the ground, only his own Shield protecting him enough that he was able to breathe. He sure couldn't get his arms up to fire off his arrows.

Kent gave it about a minute more, just to make sure that Archer couldn't somehow throw Knight off. But after that minute was up, it was pretty clear that Archer wasn't going anywhere, couldn't defend himself from what Knight was doing, and couldn't counterattack.

"Elite Hunter Archer is immobilized," Kent boomed. "The Trial is over."

"Elite Hunter Archer is immobilized," the announcer echoed. *"Trial one: Hunter White Knight passes."*

Mark immediately let up, backed up, and took down his Shield. Archer dropped his own and lay panting on the turf, his expression the very epitome of chagrin. We dropped Shields, and Mark offered his hand to poor Archer to help him up. Archer took it and got to his feet.

"Freaking *hubris*," he said, but not with any tone of rancor. "I could have let someone else try and take you—but no. I volunteered for that. I brought that one on myself."

The group parted to let Mark proceed to the next Trial. He took his time, picking up his pack and settling it carefully on his back, making sure he'd be able to reach everything easily. I happened to know it was the "Shooting Gallery," and his Shields and his own marksmanship were going to let him get through that one absolutely unscathed. He'd probably have the hardest time with the obstacle course, mostly because that was the fourth Trial and at that point he was going to be exhausted and maybe getting clumsy, but I had absolutely no doubt that he was going to pass.

I moved to the area for the third Trial, which was going to be the hand-to-hand segment. I honestly did not know how he'd do in this.

As I expected, he got through the Shooting Gallery in what must have been a record time. There was absolutely nothing in the rules saying that he couldn't use magic to help him shoot, and he must have; I bet every one of his bullets hit the mark square. The Elite that Kent had picked as Knight's hand-to-hand opponent was a guy about equal in size and musculature to Knight, although he was older and presumably more experienced. His name—or call sign, I didn't know him well enough to know which—was Bull. He was the living embodiment of the saying "There are old Hunters, and there are bold Hunters, but there are no old, bold Hunters." Everything he did was planned and executed with deliberation, and with every bit of all that experience behind it. He never got into arguments with anyone. The two of them sized each other up, and the moment the announcer said, *"Trial three: Begin,"* they charged each other like a pair of riled-up mountain goats.

The next ten minutes were shockingly brutal. And I found out what Knight's hand-to-hand "style" was.

Nonexistent.

If there was a polar opposite to the sort of elegant, flowing combat many of my Masters used, it was surely this.

One thing was for sure, nobody was going to fast-forward through this segment, at least for those who could stomach watching this sort of savagery.

In the end, I think it was White Knight's youth and motivation to win that won the fight. Bull was tough and experienced, but Mark recovered faster, and he was pretty desperate to get his girl here. Eventually, he got Bull pinned so that Bull couldn't move and couldn't dislodge him and tapped out. When Knight got to his feet, his pretty white-and-gold outfit was smeared liberally with blood, and he had a bloody nose, a split lip, a black eye, and a lot of bruises. But so did Bull. They shook hands, and Mark passed on to the last Trial.

I ran around the perimeter and up to the stands, where I could see the whole of the obstacle course. And when Mark came out of the tunnel, the announcer greeted him with, *"This is the last of the four Trials that will determine if Hunter White Knight attains Elite Hunter status. Are you ready, Hunter Knight?"*

Mark waved a tired hand, signifying that he was.

"Begin," said the announcer. And Mark . . . lumbered out.

I could tell immediately that he was using all his energy just to keep his Shield up. His progress was absolute agony to watch, and I even wondered if he was going to lose to the timer. But he didn't stop, and he didn't call for an end to the Trial. He pushed himself to and past the limits of his endurance and ended the Trial sprawled facedown on the artificial turf of the "safe zone" at the end of the course with less than a minute to spare.

"Fourth and final Trial is concluded. Hunter Knight passes. Hunter White Knight and pack, welcome as the sixteenth member of Apex Hunter Elite."

We didn't let him lie there, of course. We all piled in on him, not literally of course, but surrounded him.

I'm going to lick him, Bya said, and I kept Mark from getting to his feet.

"Hold still," I ordered, and just as he opened his mouth to ask why, Bya squirmed past the sea of legs around him and began plastering him with licks. The first one went into his mouth.

"Gah!" he spluttered. "Dog tongue!"

The rest of us laughed. "It's cleaner than yours," said Scarlet.

"Just hold still, you big baby," I scolded. "Bya has healing spit, better than anything the medics can do for you."

So he sat there until Bya decided he was satisfied. Then Kent helped him to his feet, while the rest of us stood around congratulating him for a little bit. Even Bull, who by this time had gotten himself bandaged up and had come back out for the end of the Trials.

"You look like five miles of bad road," Mark said when Bull came up to him and shook his hand.

Bull snorted. "Go look in a mirror," he retorted, and about that time, the guys took him off to the dressing room where I presume they stood him under a hot shower while feeding him protein and energy drinks, then took him off to the medics to get himself tended.

The rest of us went back to HQ, where a party had been set up in the lounge. It was a party I never got for myself, since Ace's murder attempt had pretty much derailed any notion of celebrating for all of us.

All the Elite and a good couple dozen of the other Hunters gathered there, which was a nice, comfortable crowd for a shindig. We all settled back with drinks, waiting for the man of the moment to arrive.

When he did, we all stood up to cheer.

He looked around at all of us with surprise; from the look on his face, which was sheer, blank astonishment, he never expected this many of us to show up to congratulate him.

When the cheering died down and he was settled with a steak sandwich and tall mug of beer, someone started shouting for a speech. He held up his hand, the one with the sandwich in it.

"Whoa, I am no good at speeches," he protested. "And it would be a crime to let this fine piece of meat get cold." He looked around then and smiled—something I don't think many people but me had ever seen him do. "But I will say this. Thank you. I reckon that's all that needs to be said."

And he looked straight at me when he said it. Which made me feel pretty darn good.

I HAD NEVER BEEN to a Christer wedding. I'd been to plenty of
ours, which are wildly varied but always end in parties. I guessed
Christer ones were more solemn.

All the lounge furniture had been pushed back, and Mark and
Jessie were standing in front of the main vid-screen. Those of us
who had come were standing behind them, all of us dressed much
more formally than we usually were. Mind you, this was not the
usual sort of wedding by Christer standards either. They both had
been pretty insistent on being married by their own preacher man,
and because there was no way Apex was going to let them leave
to do that, Kent had arranged for a train to stop long enough to
give their preacher the two-way vid link for the ceremony, seeing
that nobody on or near the Mountain had the equipment for a
two-way link that far.

I hadn't actually even seen Jessie before this, since she'd kept much to herself; she was real pretty, though nothing like anything I'd thought. I figured she would be delicate and tiny, but she was almost as tall as Mark and had those lean muscles like Kei had that told *me* she could probably chop wood and haul water with the best of them. I should have expected that, actually—Mark's people had it pretty hard where they lived, and no one was likely to be delicate.

She'd turned down the offer of a wedding dress, and she'd brought her gram's, handed down to her. It was all hand crocheted, which was probably a revelation to our stylists, who likely hadn't seen anything like it before—old enough for the cotton string it had been made from, and the cotton lining, to have turned a creamy color. Long sleeves, floor length, and made with a lot of love by an expert needlewoman. I wondered if it had been her grandmother, or *grandmother's* mother, who had made it. And where she had gotten that much cotton string.

Mark insisted that as many of us as wanted to come should be there. That was about half of the Elite—not that the other half didn't want to be there, but they were out on calls or sleeping after night calls—and some of the friends he'd made in the regular Hunters. We made a pretty respectable showing, and if Jessie was uneasy around us, she had the good manners not to show it.

The ceremony itself wasn't anything surprising, and the preacher man was very mannered. He was quite solemn, and this was close enough to the "traditional" wedding ceremonies I knew—though back home, most of the time the bride and groom write their own. He didn't get enough time to preach a sermon, though, which was probably all for the best. That train could only make up so much time, and it had a schedule to keep.

We could see Mark's people piled up behind the preacher

in what looked like the recreation car. They struck me as being awfully serious for something that was supposed to be joyful, but then ... maybe to them the joyful part didn't come until after the vows were said. I thought I could tell which set of parents belonged to Mark and which to Jessie, but truth to tell, there was strong resemblance among everyone I could see, so it was hard to be sure.

The business was over in about ten minutes. The preacher man said, "I now pronounce you husband and wife; you may kiss the bride," and Mark planted a pretty chaste sort of kiss on her. Then the preacher said, "I present to you, Mr. and Mrs. Mark Knight," and there was a spatter of applause on the train end, and then the screen blanked out as they turned to face the rest of us.

We applauded (a lot more vigorously), which seemed to be the right sort of thing to do. Mark beamed. Jessie smiled nervously. The staff brought in a big, fancy white cake they'd made specially for the two, all covered in sugar flowers, which made Jessie blush and smile a little more genuinely and look as if she was pleasantly surprised by the fact that we were all being nice to them.

Or maybe that was me being mean. She could have been pleasantly surprised by the fact that the wedding hadn't gotten interrupted by a callout.

Anyway, it hadn't escaped my attention that Jessie came from people like the Christers of Hope Harbor and Gilead and Nazarethtown. Like my own people, we were used to making do and using up; the whole "just go to the comp for it" business was hard to get your head wrapped around. And actually *using* the comp? Only the folks at Safehaven, Anston's Well, and the Monastery used comps regularly. Everyone else did their learning and reading out of books, unless you were tech-gifted. So I'd had this notion to make something for Jessie, and every time I thought something mean about her, I'd go and work on it as penance. When it was my turn to come up and congratulate them, I chastely kissed Mark on the cheek, then handed her the book I'd made.

She took it and was clearly puzzled. "We're both turnips," I said as she opened it to glance through. "I know it was brain-twisting for me to figure out how to get stuff and find stuff around here, so that's instructions on, well, *everything.*" I noticed she was sporting a brand-new Perscom on her left wrist. "Perscom and comp terminal," I added. "Remember, Mark's Elite, so you guys can ask for just about anything you need or want." I had no fear she was likely to request gold and diamond tiaras or anything stupid like that. It was far more likely she'd do without rather than be thought greedy.

Her eyes just lit up. "Thankee!" she said, now looking genuinely happy. "I hate to keep askin' Mark, and he's off Huntin' so much...."

I smiled at her. "Well, it's pretty much laid out *for* a turnip *by* a turnip, so you should be able to navigate your way around it all right."

Mark turned up the shine on his smile, so much I almost got blinded. I took my leave of both of them to make way for the armorer, and went and collected a piece of cake and some strawberries.

Eventually, Kent meandered back over to me. Scarlet was complimenting Jessie on her dress, with just enough envy that Jessie would know the compliments were genuine. "You're our resident turnip expert," he said, without preamble. "What do we do with her? I don't want her sitting around with nothing to do all day and—" He shrugged.

"And brooding, or getting hysterical, or watching too much vid feed on the Hunter channels and getting her head who knows how twisted up," I finished for him. "Or worse, doing nothing but reading that Book of theirs, and deciding we're all ungodly. If she's *anything* like the Christers back home, she's been raised to think that doing house stuff and garden or farm stuff is all she's fit for, and there's not that much house stuff to do around here."

Kent let out his breath as if he'd been holding it. "Bloody hell. This's the first married Hunter we've had here since I became senior Elite, and all the ones before that had been Apex Cits. I honestly don't know what to do with her to keep her out of mischief."

"House stuff, garden stuff, cooking stuff," I said truthfully. "That's pretty much all they do, besides religious stuff. All my friends back home would be bringing you lists of what they were good at or plaguing you to put them in some lesson or other, but that's not how Christer girls work. They wait to get told what to do, generally by a man."

Kent cursed under his breath and ruffled his hand through the long hair on the top of his head. Then it looked like something occurred to him. "You know what? I'm going to make her Rik Severn's problem. He's the Personnel man, and *he* can figure out what to do with her."

That sounded sensible to me, so I nodded. I didn't want to stick my nose into this too far. It really wasn't my place, and I didn't want to make things uncomfortable for White Knight the Hunter *or* Mark, the transplanted Christer.

It looked like I'd got off on the right foot with Jessie, but there was no telling how she'd react if Knight and I started partnering up a lot. If *my own friends* back home were capable of thinking I'd gotten a swelled ego because of being a Hunter in Apex, there was no telling what a strange girl stuck in a strange place was likely to make up out of her head because I was working with her husband.

So, just to make sure she didn't start making up things right off, I caught Mark's eye, waved good-bye, and headed back to my room, putting myself on the night-duty roster while I was at it.

◀▷

"Bya," I said, looking down at the third dead Psimon, this one at my feet. "I am getting seriously sick of this."

This time the discovery had come as more of a shock, since I'd literally stumbled over the body. I just hadn't expected a *third* body in practically the same place as the first one had been.

The Hounds had been tracking *Nagas* that we'd flushed out of a side tunnel, and we'd been paying attention to them and not necessarily looking for anything else. This time the body was right at an intersection, and I didn't see it until I had turned the corner.

Nagas first. I'd already "contaminated" the scene, assuming that PsiCorps actually cared about that, so once we tracked the last of the snakes and killed it, this time I could come back and look the body over at close range. *And* vid while I was doing that. And get the ID. This time there was no point in staying so far back I couldn't get a reading.

I have their scent, said Myrrdhin. *Go the other way.*

I left the body and turned down the opposite branch of the intersecting tunnel. We'd managed to intercept the *Nagas* just as they were magicking open the door into the service tunnel, and they'd turned and slithered off instead of fighting. Either they

• 215 •

had just seen the size of my pack and figured fighting was not an option, or we were getting a reputation among Othersiders, since this was the first time, ever, that any Othersider had tried to escape instead of attacking us.

Myrrdhin and Shinje and Hold were the ones who'd found the scent after we'd lost it in a spot where someone, a street cleaner most likely, had dumped a big load of water down one of the sewer grates. That had effectively killed the trail, so we'd had to split up into four subteams. Now all of the others were streaming past me on the run to catch up with Myrrdhin's group. I didn't insult Myrrdhin's intelligence by telling him not to start anything until we got there. I just chambered incendiary rounds as I ran.

And when I finally arrived, with my shotgun loaded and off the safety, Myrrdhin rewarded my assumption by being just on my side of another junction, the rest packed up at his back.

I think they are trying to get into another service tunnel to hide, the Hound said. *I smell magic as well as snake.*

I got my net spell ready. We didn't have much time; if they got into that service tunnel, we'd have the devil's own time getting them out. If they used the service tunnel to try to escape, we'd need the whole Elite team down here to find them and corner them. I thought fast. *Bya, you and my Alebrijes except for Dusana sneak in as close as you can get, then* bamph *to the other side of them. Once you do that, we'll rush from this side. We'll get them caught between us, and I'll net them.*

Bya nodded, and he and the others . . . faded. They didn't go invisible, but they lost their bright colors and turned the exact same color as the 'crete of the tunnel. Then they plastered themselves against the wall. If they moved slowly, there was a good chance they could get close enough to make this work.

We waited, watching as the Hounds crept slowly away, then out of sight around a curve. And waited. I really hated waiting, especially when I couldn't see what was happening.

Now! Bya "shouted," and we all rushed down the tunnel and around the curve.

Only to see that the *Nagas*, instead of retreating, had rushed Bya's half of the pack as they materialized just beyond them.

Dammit! My stomach lurched. And I felt it like a knife in the heart when I heard one of my Hounds yelp in pain. This had just all gone FUBAR. I cast the net anyway, hoping that when the *Nagas* discovered they were trapped, they'd turn their attention to the net instead of the Hounds.

It sort of worked. And being encumbered by the net spell restricted their movement enough that they couldn't put the full force of their muscles behind the blows of their swords. "Go!" I yelled at the other Hounds, and they leapt forward to the defense of their fellows.

It got very chaotic and ugly, and there was more yelping, which hurt almost as much as if *I* was the one getting slashed. It didn't stay ugly long, thanks to my incendiary rounds, which very quickly changed the *Nagas'* minds about attacking, but by the time they were all piles of ash, and I had dropped the net spell, Bya, Shinje, and Kalachakra all had some ugly, deep gashes, going all the way down to the bone.

So we delayed a bit more, while I poured manna into them to heal up their hurts, while the rest stood guard. I was cursing myself the entire time, apologizing to them out loud and crying a little. Nothing makes me feel worse than when I let my Hounds get hurt. Finally, Bya grabbed my wrist in his mouth. *Stop,* he said. *Stop blaming yourself. We are partners. We know what we are doing; you don't force us to do what we wouldn't do on our own.*

"Yes, but—" I said, sniffling, and still feeling guilty as sin.

Stop, he ordered. And so I didn't object. But I still felt horrid.

He licked the tears off my face, and I blew my nose on a rag, and we all got up off the 'crete, put ourselves back in scouting order, and went back to the dead Psimon.

This one was a man. And like the second one, he was *old.* He was bald, but his scalp was covered in age-spots, he was wrinkled, frail-looking, and painfully thin. Now that I was right on top of him, I couldn't see any signs of dragging, hauling, or even signs that anyone had touched his body since he fell here. Nor could I see any signs of damage on him, not even a bruise.

There was also not a trace of magic, and I *looked.*

I sighed and called it in, got vid and the ID off his collar, then began trudging back to my exit, since I knew I was about to be ordered out.

This time the coldly officious Psimon wasn't waiting for me, and I had taken the precaution of ordering a pod before I climbed out. The pod was waiting and I got into it. No one had told me that I had to wait around for the Psimon, and I didn't intend to.

It almost felt like the dead Psimon had been *planted* there for me to find. And that just got altogether too creepy for me. I needed help here, and Kent wasn't going to be able to give it to me. I had not been ordered not to talk about *this* incident, so if anyone found out that I talked to Uncle about it, with his help I might be able to skate on a technicality. I also called my uncle from the pod rather than waiting to get to HQ, where someone might intercept me—feigning that it was a social call. He took it anyway, though I had to wait a little.

"How long has it been since you had a home-cooked meal?" I demanded when he took my call.

He blinked at me in surprise. "Quite some time. I rarely cook for myself. Why?"

"Because I assume you spend time somewhere *other* than your office, and if you can get someone to deliver groceries, I'll meet you there and cook for you, like a dutiful niece should," I said. He raised an eyebrow, and I nodded. We were getting really good at reading each others' nonverbal cues.

"Send me your list, and program your pod for the Arbors. I'll tell the door-comp to send you up." I had no idea where "the Arbors" was, but generally, any building that had a name rather than an address tended to be ... appropriately fancy.

So I sent the grocery list of things I would need for spaghetti and salad, informed HQ I was paying my uncle a personal visit over supper, got the okay, and told the pod "the Arbors," then sat back and watched the city in the sunset.

The sun was just touching the horizon when the pod pulled up at a tall building in the Hub. I got out and walked straight up to the door, holding up my Perscom to the scanner beside it. A vid-plate lit up with a bland male in a suit. "Elite Hunter Joyeaux Charmand, you are expected," said what sounded a bit like a synthesized voice. "Please proceed inside and to the elevators."

The heavy metal doors swished open, and I walked into a lobby: marble floors, marble walls, marble seats, and a lot of plants. There were vid-screens showing news channels on the walls to the right and left, and a bank of elevators at the rear. No need to ask which one I should take, there was one waiting, with the door open.

When the elevator doors opened again, I was in a foyer in the middle of four hallways. Each hallway had two doors on it; each door had a little nameplate outside of it. I found the one that said "Charmand" and presented my Perscom to the scanner; the door opened for me.

And . . . well, the apartment beyond was like something out of a pre-Diseray vid about very rich people. After seeing the lobby, I expected a lot of glass and metal and stone. Instead—

The walls looked exactly like the peeled-log walls of one of our community halls back home, varnished and gleaming a ruddy gold, with a high, log-beamed ceiling. The floor was wood, covered in what *looked* like the hides of buffalo and bears. The furniture appeared to be made of more peeled logs, with comfortable cushions of stuffed leather, and added pillows in warm fabrics. The light came from a chandelier that apparently was constructed of a mass of antlers, and table lamps with square stained-glass shades.

Back home, all this would have still cost a spectacular amount of money. Here? I couldn't even begin to calculate it.

"I'm in the kitchen," my uncle called from somewhere inside.

I followed his voice and found Uncle in a kitchen that matched the rest of the apartment. He was taking food out of a box.

"I'm assuming—" I began.

"Psi-shields second to none, installed by people I personally trust," Uncle said as I took out what I needed from the well-stocked cupboards and began making spaghetti sauce.

"Good," I said with relief. "I have some vid to show you. And I got a couple ID codes too."

"You go clean up. The bathroom is through that door," he said, and nodded to his left. I transferred the vid from my Perscom to his directly, and did so.

Once cleaned up and changed into the loose pants and top I found in the bathroom, I told him everything I knew while he helped me make dinner.

Anyone who was watching us through the panoramic windows would only have seen uncle and niece cooking together, since we kept our backs to the windows the entire time. And I could feel a very faint buzz in the back of my skull that told me Uncle's Psi-shields were strong enough for me to *notice*.

I was pretty sure he knew how to watch a vid on his Perscom without letting anyone spying through the windows see it.

"Well," he said as we made salads while the sauce cooked, "you've done more than I hoped for. Far more. Keep up the good work."

"No one's trying to blame you for these deaths?" I asked. "Or the Hunters?" I gulped. "Or me? Because this last one . . . if I was writing a drama-vid, it would have been a setup to make me look guilty."

He smiled slightly and said, "I wish to draw your attention to 'the curious incident of the dog in the night-time.'"

I don't know how he knew I'd devoured every single Sherlock Holmes story we had in the Monastery archives, but I knew exactly what he was talking about. The dog, in the story, hadn't barked when it should have...and what Uncle was implying was that PsiCorps probably *should* have been looking hard for *someone* to blame the deaths of three Psimons on.

But they weren't. Which was...interesting.

The noodles were ready then, and so was the sauce; we took everything to the dining table. Uncle sat at the end, and I sat at a right angle to him. "You are making sure, not only to keep your Psi-shield on, but to keep up the psionic blocks your Masters taught you?"

"Tighter than a banjo string," I said fervently. "Tighter than the lid on the last jar of jam. Why?"

"Because if the Psimon who has been meeting you thinks you are coming too close to something PsiCorps does not want you to know, he'll alter your memory," Uncle replied grimly. "So be very careful."

Psimons can do that?

And that was when something occurred to me. Actually, when it hit me, I felt absolutely stunned. "Uncle," I said, "can Othersiders alter peoples' memories the way Psimons can?"

It was his turn to blink at me, perplexed. "I suppose they can. They have similar psionic abilities. Why?"

"Because that explains how Ace got away with murdering Karly, and how he put that vamp down in the storm sewers that was intended for me without his Hounds twigging to it and telling on him," I said slowly. "Look, now we know he's obviously been in contact with Othersiders for a while, right?"

"Obviously, given they knew he was in army custody. We know his Hounds had no inkling he was trying to kill another

Hunter. But if he had the memories altered or blocked after every meeting—"

"Then the Hounds would never know," I said. "They'd never get anything from his thoughts; unless we actually *try* to reach them Otherside, they can't pick up on what we're doing when they're off away except for strong emotions. And any Psimons that happened to check on him wouldn't have picked that up either, if it was blocked."

"Or the Psimons who read him after his arrest..." But he sounded uncertain. "On the other hand, while I have never known Psimons to directly lie, sometimes they don't tell the whole truth either."

"They haven't been telling the truth about what's going on in the sewers, have they?" I pointed out.

His mouth went into a thin line. "No," he replied. "They haven't."

I didn't go out on sewer Hunts for the next week, since I was out on teams from dawn to dark; this wasn't *obviously* increased Othersider activity, or at least, not something Kent said anything about, I suppose because Elites got callouts every single day, but it was definitely a workout. Flocks of Wyverns, another small Drakken, an entire tribe of Ogres, just one callout after another, and generally at least two every day. That was because, thanks to my huge pack, not only was I in demand on a small team, I also didn't get worn out as fast as some of the others, so I *could* handle two calls a day.

But by the time I finished stuffing my face each evening—more often than not, long after the mess hall was closed—I was generally so tired (and often bruised up) all I really wanted was to *maybe* mindlessly watch a vid, then sleep, although Retro would always look for me. He was easing off on the asking-for-a-date business; instead, he'd try to make me laugh. I did need those laughs, and I hated to admit it, but he *was* hilarious. Usually he'd tell some outrageous story about what he'd been doing that was *so* over the top I found myself laughing until my sides hurt.

And I dreamed about Karly most nights. Funny dreams, though: all she would do would be to show up, nod decisively once, then fade away. They weren't the sort of dream that left me upset, or crying, or anything like that. Maybe they were just my subconscious telling me I'd solved the mystery of how Ace had done his murdering without giving himself away, and it was time to get on with catching the rat.

As if I could! He was . . . somewhere I couldn't reach, presumably in the hands of the Folk. But of course, the subconscious never pays any attention to logic.

Then, finally, after about a week of this, the Othersiders eased up. I had one callout in the morning, then spent the afternoon waiting, not daring to go down for a sewer Hunt just in case . . . but more calls never happened.

In midafternoon, my Perscom went off, but it wasn't a callout—it was Josh. *"It lives!"* he exclaimed when I answered—because when he'd called before, I'd either been neck-deep in trouble and couldn't answer, or I was too tired to do more than mumble a few apologetic words.

"It does," I agreed. "Don't jinx me!" We got a chance for a

nice long talk about nothing before I started nodding off in mid-sentence. That's when I said good night, but of course . . . he jinxed me.

◄◄ ►►

Before my alarm could go off, the full-team alert shrilled, jolting me out of deepest, darkest sleep. I scrambled into clothing and slammed out my front door, racing down the hall to the armory along with everyone else on my hallway. Kent and a couple staff were already there, making up packs and tossing them to people. Everyone was getting the same thing for basic load-out: assault rifle with steel-jacketed and incendiary ammo, .45 or .50 caliber handguns with the same, knives, and a bag of cold-forged iron caltrops. "Same as Bensonville, people," Kent shouted over the sound of people strapping their gear on. "We've got a multi-mega-beast incident. We've got positive reports of two big Drakken, maybe more, and a lot of small stuff that it's too dark to ID. Town is called Zion; they're fortified with 30 mm Avenger cannon on the walls. Right now, they're holding out, but they won't be able to for much longer. Three choppers, same teams as last time. White Knight, you're with me."

Once we were geared up, we raced out to the pad, where the choppers were already waiting in the predawn darkness, their blades sending up dust we couldn't see, only taste in the air. Me, Hammer, Steel, Archer, Kent, and now Knight. I was first in; as usual, Hammer just picked me up and tossed me in. Knight was next. *What's Jessie going to think of this, I wonder?* I thought as I strapped in next to him. "You going to be all right?" I asked him bluntly. He nodded. He didn't *look* any different, and I didn't get the sense that he was nervous—but then, he was pretty stone-faced, so how would I know? Well . . . it was barely possible Jessie had no idea what the alarm had meant, so she wouldn't even know he was on a full-team callout until someone told her or she asked the comp where he was. Kent got in last, as usual, and banged the side of the chopper to let the pilot know to take off. I tapped my ear to let Knight know that from now on we'd be using the thread mics and earpieces. He nodded.

Kent began our briefing as we vibrated and yawed and rolled across the landscape, the heavy beat of the chopper blades over our heads drowning out everything but Kent's voice in our ears.

"*We're going to be landing in the dark,*" Kent said over the radio. "*Zion will stop firing at that point, to avoid pasting us. Be even sharper than usual, people. Don't shoot unless you know you've got a clear shot and none of us are in front of you. Shields up at all times, just in case someone hasn't seen you. If you have to choose between Shields and attacking, choose Shields until we get some light. Now, sound off, in order of seniority. Kent, yo!*"

And that was how I found out for sure that the armorer was the most senior Elite. Retro was just before me, so after "*Retro here,*" I sounded off with "*Joy, roger,*" and Mark chimed in last with "*White Knight, yo.*"

"*Zion can't give us any intel on what we're facing, so we're playing this one as a full team and by ear. When you can positively ID something, you report it straight to me. If you get into trouble, shout for your subteam lead. Other than that, stay off the comm. Everything we've got so far is streaming to your Perscoms, so eyeball those till we get there, and when we bail out, form up on me. We'll get close air support as soon as we've got light, probably artillery shortly after that."*

Was Knight's girl watching this? We had cams, of course; there were always cams, whether or not the footage got shown to the Cits. If something went right, it was a teaching thing, and if something went wrong . . . it was a teaching thing. Was she worried? Was she scared? That was one position I'd never had to be in—that of the one who watched and waited. It came to me that it must be far harder to do that than to fight.

He was a Hunter at home, before they sent him here. She knew that. You'd think she'd be used to it, right? I couldn't help but think about how Karly had told me the way her wife split up with her, when Karly popped Powers. Karly's wife had grown up with all the Hunter channels, and *still*, when it had come down to the Hunter being *Karly* and not some stranger, the wife couldn't take it. And we were taking on all these huge monsters, things they likely never saw and barely heard of back where she came from. Would it be too much of a shock?

Well, maybe. There was a big difference between the stuff I'd tackled on the Mountain and the stuff I'd faced as a ranker Hunter. And an *enormous* difference between what I faced as a ranker and what I was facing as an Elite. When she finally saw what he was up against—when the light came or one of us managed to light up the field—would she be too terrified to even breathe? Would she be like Karly's wife?

But maybe she bought into that mythology of the always-victorious Elite. Maybe she'd watch it as a Cit would, with the sure and certain knowledge, however false that "knowledge" was, that Knight would come back triumphant.

And maybe I need to stop worrying about Knight's girl and get my head in the game, I scolded myself, and bent over the tiny screen on my Perscom.

It wasn't showing me much that was useful. It looked like the walls of Zion had big artillery guns on them, and spotlights. But the Drakken were moving *fast,* so all you got were glimpses of heads, torsos, the flash of a tail, or an enormous claw. You were supposed to be able to use the laser-sight to lock on to a target on those guns, but not if other things dashed between you and your target, and that was what it looked like was going on. The Drakken, more than two, I was sure, were dodging and weaving around each other, keeping anyone from getting a lock on them, and meanwhile screaming at the tops of their lungs. Some of the gunners were just firing randomly, hoping to hit something. Zion had shot up flares too, but they weren't doing a whole lot of good, other than revealing that there were smaller shapes milling around on the ground.

And then a spotlight dropped just enough that I, and a couple other people, got enough of a good look to be positive. *"Nagas,"* I said, a fraction of a second before Scarlet and Bull.

"Roger that. Nagas *ID'd. We'll use fire for those. Make sure you've got incendiary rounds, or be with someone who does."*

Then my private frequency activated. *"Joy, do you copy?"* Kent said.

"Copy, roger," I replied.

"Think you can pull off one of those Drakken and bring it to the rest of us?"

I swallowed hard. Those were *big* Drakken; probably three or four times the size of the one Hammer, Steel, and I had taken down. But we obviously couldn't wade into that mass of death and take them all on at once. . . .

But then I got a brainstorm. "Can I have Knight? Dusana can carry double; he can layer his Shields on mine and Dusana's, and we'll have better odds of skidding those tongue-strikes off."

That was what I was really worried about. Drakken being magic and all, I thought they would probably have a good chance of cracking my shields with those jaw-tongues of theirs. But with three Shields, even if the outermost one cracked, there'd still be two more between us and it.

"Dusana can carry the weight?"

"Three times that," I replied.

"You've got him." I felt Mark stir beside me and heard his "Copy, roger," as Kent contacted him and told him the plan. He glanced over at me. I offered a fist. He bumped it, and I relaxed a teeny, tiny bit. Good. Mark was on board with this.

Someone else ID'd Ogres, and just before we set down, Minotaurs. We bailed out, and the entire lot of us crouched with our hands in front of our faces because there was no time for anything but the quick, dirty, and painful way of bringing our Hounds across. I felt the searing pain on the backs of my hands, and the sudden drain of manna as the Hounds all burst through. Then the burning of my hands cooled, and I stood up to see myself surrounded by my pack.

And Knight's; Knight was standing right next to me.

I looked at Knight's winged critters. "Can you guys fly as fast as mine can run?" I asked them. They looked at each other, and then at my crazy-colored *Alebrijes*, and I guessed they were quickly comparing notes because all four of the winged ones shook their heads. I already knew they couldn't run as fast as my guys; those wings would catch air and hold them back. "Can you see in the dark?" I continued.

Now their furry faces got a look of excitement, and they nodded. "Good. Get some height, and keep a sharp eye out for Harpies. One of them dropping something in front of Dusana while we're running from a Drakken would be a disaster. Go!"

They went, leaping up and into the sky. Dusana knelt so Mark and I could get on his back, and then he grew a bunch of spines that held us in place, with Mark behind me, and me riding Dusana's shoulders. "Bya, find us a Drakken a little away from the others. When you've got one, Dusana, *bamph* to where it is, and we'll start this thing."

Bya ran off into the dark, past Kent, who was organizing everyone else into the ambush squad.

"Wait, what—" Mark said.

I interrupted. "Mark, your Shield up first; yours is the strongest, I want that innermost. Then mine, then Dusana, put yours up last and outermost."

Mark put up his Shield. I layered mine on top of his, and Dusana put up his. Then we waited for Bya.

We didn't have to wait long. *Got one. He's off by himself. I think he thinks he's found a weak spot in the wall.*

Dusana, go! I ordered, and Dusana *bamphed.*

Either Mark had a stronger stomach than me, or *bamphing* didn't bother him as much. In either case, at least he didn't barf on my back. He was probably wondering just how I was going to attract the attention of something the size of a Drakken, because the odds it would feel any bullet or magic attack I could launch were pretty minimal.

But I wasn't going to do either of those things. "Close your eyes," I said over our shared frequency, and I lit us up like festival fireworks.

That definitely got the Drakken's attention. It had been staring at the city wall; it whipped its head around and stared over its shoulder at us, startled. Before it could move, Dusana launched into his run.

The Drakken screamed, a noise that sounded like tearing metal. I didn't look over my shoulder this time; I was too busy lighting up the ground in front of us so Dusana could see where he was going; a misstep at this stage, or worse, a fall, would put us at the Drakken's nonexistent mercy. Of course this made us more visible to the Drakken, but that was what we wanted. I felt Mark turning his body to look back, though, and I didn't envy him.

Bya, where? I called my Alpha.

Here. Look. And suddenly, ahead of us in the dark, I caught sight of a patch of stripes bobbing along at the same rate of speed that we were going. Dusana snorted with satisfaction, I felt him hunkering down under my legs and putting on more speed. I kept the light going; the ground out here was *bad*, all torn up by the shells from the cannon on the walls. The ground in front of us and the air above us suddenly went red with the light from a flare, but it didn't help at all.

The sound of the Drakken chasing us was something I can't adequately describe. Maybe if you magnified the sound of a galloping horse by a million times—but no, even that wouldn't do it. I couldn't imagine why the monster hadn't caught us, but Dusana was running faster than he'd ever run before. Then the Drakken behind us screeched again. The sound made me cringe, and all my instincts cried out to me to go *hide* somewhere, to go to earth, to dig a hole and pull it in after me and wait for this monstrous thing to pass. All I could realistically do was make myself as small as possible on Dusana's back, light his path in front of him, and feed him manna as he ran.

Then, without warning, Dusana *bamphed.*

We came out again a split second later in darkness; Dusana stopped abruptly by digging all four feet into the dirt, and we lurched against the spines holding us to his back. He whirled, and I saw that the Drakken was stopped, its head flattened oddly against a Wall.

Steel's Wall, reinforced by his brother's.

Behind me, Knight whipped the assault rifle off his back and laid it down on my left shoulder. I understood immediately what he was doing, clapped my hands over my ears, making a protective sound-muffling magical shield over them, and froze. So did Dusana.

There was the muffled *crack* of the rifle right next to my ear, followed by a second shot. The first round must have been steel-jacketed, since nothing obvious happened to the Drakken, but the second was an incendiary round, and the eye nearest us blossomed with flame.

The Drakken tossed its bruised head up, shrieking. The rifle barked twice more, and the Drakken lost his other eye.

Now blinded, all he could do was flail with claws and tail, shaking his head from side to side. And then—he wasn't *shaking* his head; it was being battered, as if by blows from a giant fist.

Hammer, surely—and from the tension in Mark's body behind me, White Knight was getting in his fair share too.

I ran through my bag of tricks in my head, trying to come up with something that would work against this huge creature, because even blinded, it could still kill any of us that got within range of that tail or the claws. And suddenly I had it, and a moment later, I sent a sticky version of my net spinning across the air between us, aiming for the Drakken's right foreleg.

I caught it, then waited until the left came within range, and caught that as well. Catching the first leg hadn't done anything because I hadn't anchored the net. Catching the *second* leg, however . . .

Unable to see what was happening and not able to feel what I had done until it was too late, the blinded Drakken tried to lash out and pulled his own legs out from underneath himself. He toppled over sideways, his head hitting the ground with a *boom*. I netted his head to the ground and held on for dear life, as the rest of the team and all the Hounds descended on the downed Drakken to finish him off with magic and steel, tooth and claw.

And when he finally lay still, Kent said in my ear, *"All right, Joy. Ready to bring us another?"*

13

MORNING CAME, AND WITH it the real fighting, with close-air support and artillery, both from the walls of Zion and the field. At that point, it was clear we'd win this time.

A pack of three Hounds caught the last fleeing Minotaur and brought it down.

A small group of us took down the last Drakken.

And it was over.

I sat down right where I was, in the churned-up dirt and blood and bits of Drakken. I was on the far side of the carcass, alone, since I'd been blinding it with magical fireworks. All I could do was stare stupidly at the gigantic head in front of me. The head looked to be about half the size of a locomotive, though I could have been wrong about that. I could not believe we'd taken down, not just one, but four of these things.

All I could think about at that moment was ... nothing. I was literally too tired to think. I should have been starving, but I was at the point where I was even too tired to be hungry.

And that is when I heard a strange, high-pitched keening sound above and behind me that made every hair on my body stand straight up with terror.

I turned, ever so slowly, looking over my shoulder... and at first, saw nothing except what I took to be a pole or the trunk of a dead tree. Then I looked up... and up...

If it hadn't been towering twenty feet over me, I would have said it was a cellar spider—the kind people call "daddy longlegs." I gaped up at it, a hideous blob-shaped thing with eight shiny eyes looking down at me, slowly clicking its mandibles at me. The blob balanced high in the air on eight legs that would have been spindly—except they were as thick as my arm.

And only all those years of defensive martial arts and good instincts saved me when it struck at me with one of the front legs. I shoulder-rolled out of the way, but that brought me farther underneath it, and to my horror, I saw a spear of white coming right for me. It could spit webbing!

Bya hit me and knocked us both out of the way, and the webbing splatted down into the earth where I had just been. If I'd still been there, it would have enveloped me completely. Bya put up his Shield, and belatedly I put up mine, and the next glob of webbing splatted against the combined Shields, leaving us untouched.

Then the rest of my Hounds appeared. Hold, Strike, Myrrdhin, Gwalchmai, Dusana, Chenresig, Shinje, and Hevajra each swarmed a leg, grabbed it in their jaws, and *pulled*. Bya and I backed up between Dusana and Chenresig as the Hounds immobilized the giant spider and slowly began to pull it down to ground level, splaying it out so it couldn't move. That was when I began pumping bullets into the body, while Bya, Kalachakra, and Begtse hosed it down with fire.

The sound of gunfire brought the other Elite running, or as close to running as they could manage, but by the time they got there, we'd managed to get through the spider's weak Shield and burn it to a crisp.

My Hounds let go, and the legs reflexively curled up toward the body, leaving us gazing at a blackened blob in the middle of a forest of twenty-foot sticks.

And we all stared at the thing.

"What . . . is . . . that?" someone managed as a couple of cams zoomed in from the other side of the dead Drakken and began circling what was left of it, taking pictures.

"A spider?" I said feebly. "I mean, I guess it's a spider."

"Another new Othersider," Kent said in disgust. "First snakemen from hell, and now this." He looked over at Hammer and Steel. "Anything like that in what your ma's studied?"

They shook their heads. I couldn't see their expressions under the masks of caked-on dust and blood and sweat they wore. Disbelief, maybe. Maybe just exhaustion.

"Where the hell did it come from?" someone asked hoarsely. "It wasn't anywhere on this field before, was it?"

They all looked at me. "I dunno," I said. "I was just sitting here, and then I heard this weird sound, and when I turned around, it was rising up behind me."

Kent limped toward the thing, then past it, muttering to himself. Or maybe to his Perscom. He paced about a hundred yards away from us, zigzagging back and forth, looking and muttering.

He got to a spot where there were some scraggly trees, looked around some more, and finally came back to us.

"There's a hollow place back there. It must have been lying in ambush," he said. "Body fitted into the hollow, legs folded up."

"But . . ." Scarlet started to object, then shook her head. "Natural camouflage, maybe a little bit of illusion, and its Shield. And luck, that none of the shells hit it."

"That wasn't luck. That was good shooting on the part of the Zion gunners; they only fired when they knew they could hit something," Retro pointed out, running a filthy hand through his sweaty blond hair. It struck me then, weirdly, out of nowhere, that he looked like a lankier, punkier version of Josh. When you're bone tired, strange thoughts crop up in your head. "About time we had some luck! For an ambush bug, it was pretty ineffective."

"It wouldn't have been, if Joy didn't have such a big pack," said Knight. "That's all that saved her. Well, that and good reflexes."

Retro looked at me and grinned. "You need to keep those reflexes sharp. That's a good reason to dump the creepy Psimon and start dating me!" he whispered at me. I rolled my eyes.

Then I sat down again, hard, shaking once reaction set in. I didn't say anything. Scarlet sat down next to me and buried her head in her hands. She looked like a wreck. We all looked like wrecks. In the time I had been an Elite, I had never seen the team looking this bad after a fight.

Have you ever heard of anything like that spider thing? I asked Bya.

Never. He flopped down next to me and morphed into greyhound. *This is a new thing. I do not like this.*

Was this what that Folk Mage meant? I asked him reluctantly.

Is this why we should be wary? Why nothing is what it seems? Because now they are going to unleash new things on us?

I don't know that either, he replied unhappily. *I do not like not knowing.*

I bet you'd like to go home, I said with sympathy, and opened the Way.

That is, I tried to open the Way. It kind of spluttered and died. I was literally out of every possible sort of energy—magical, physical, and otherwise. I looked up at Kent, as the rest of my Hounds gathered around me. "Uh . . . sir?" I said hesitantly. "I'm . . . gonna need a chopper all to myself. I can't send my Hounds back yet."

He snorted tiredly. "You aren't the only one, kid. Do you mind waiting to be picked up last? You're the best defended of all of us right now."

Because of my pack . . . I nodded. "That's fine, sir. I can wait."

"All right. Let me go organize our rides," he replied, and limped off.

I glanced over at Retro, who was sort of slumped over his knees, his eyes glazing over. "You still okay?" I asked.

He looked at me, and I could tell he had really smacked the wall. "Uh . . . I guess. Why?"

"You're not hitting on me," I replied.

He thought about that for a minute. "Then I guess I must be dead, huh?" And from somewhere, all four of us managed a weak sputter of a laugh.

By the time the choppers came for Retro, Archer, Scarlet, and their Hounds, we were all getting a little bit of a second wind back, but doing anything with magic was right out of the question.

They left me alone then, until the last chopper could come for me and the pack. I did try to open the Way again, but I just couldn't manage it. I managed to stagger away from the carcass of that last Drakken and over to the relatively clear area where the choppers were landing. Then I sat down again, with my back against what remained of a shattered tree. For some reason, no one was coming out of the city to scavenge off the Drakken carcasses.

They have more sense than to bring Drakken pieces into their walls, where they are likely to attract more Othersiders, Bya said dryly. *Unlike those fools in Apex.*

He had flopped down next to me, while the others prowled around me, alert for trouble. I closed my eyes for a moment. I thought I could hear the chopper in the distance. I couldn't wait for it to get here.

That was two big city fights with huge Othersiders within a week of each other. And the second one was bigger than the first. The first had clearly been to snag Ace, but why the second? The only reason we'd been able to handle this "Incident" was because we'd had artillery in the field and on the walls, and close-air support. This had been a much bigger force than Bensonville. So . . . *why?*

And was worse to come?

We'd all staggered into showers, thrown on whatever was at hand, and now were either sleeping in our quarters or trying to muster the energy to eat something. Hounds were flopped down around the lounge, trotted curiously in the hallways, or joined their Hunters in their quarters. *None* of us could dig up what we needed to send them back, and since the Hounds themselves were replete with manna, they were content to remain.

It was the first time *I* had seen Hounds in the halls, but evidently it wasn't anything new to the other Hunters, because no one paid that much attention to them. So it finally dawned on me that although that fight had seemed like the end of the world, here at Apex, maybe it was just the Elite doing what the Elite did.

With a pack the size of mine, there just wasn't enough room in my suite for them all, so although I would have loved to just drink about half a dozen meal-drinks and lie flat on my bed, we were all in the lounge and I was sprawled over a chair. Since they were stuck here until I could muster enough juice to send them home, I wanted to be with them.

Word had gotten around that the Elite had saved Zion but hit the wall doing so, and the other Hunters were keeping out of our way. I think that was the way pretty much every one of us wanted it.

My brain would have ordinarily been buzzing with unanswered questions, but I was so tired it felt like my thoughts were forcing their way through tar.

The only person I felt like talking to was Mark, but Mark was somewhere else. Phooey.

I wasn't alone in the lounge, though. Archer was nursing a beer after inhaling more food than I thought any one person could eat, his Hounds all flopped down around him. Scarlet was pensively eating sliced fruit and petting her pack leader; like the rest of her Hounds, he was a mastiff-size bat-winged dog. She had that expression on her face that told me she and he were "talking," and then she looked up at me and smiled.

"Djinni says he will work with your pack any time we like," she said as her Hound looked over at us and nodded. "He is very pleased with how the coordination went." Bya raised his head and dog-grinned at them both.

"I can't believe we all pulled that off," I admitted. "If I'd had any idea what we'd be doing, I think I might have thrown up."

Scarlet laughed, a deep, throaty sound that made Archer look over at her and smile with appreciation. "That's a silly thing to say. Elite don't throw up until *after* the fight is over."

I put my head back against the back of the chair and stared up at the ceiling. "What just happened out there?" I asked nobody in particular.

"It could be the start of what we call a 'surge,'" Archer said finally. "There was one the year I first went Elite. The Othersiders pick out hard targets and throw so much at them that we're forced to upgrade defenses all around." He sighed. "A few bigger cities that don't have Barriers will have to get them, cities like Zion with walls and 30 mm cannon will have to upgrade to Hellfire missiles, and so on. . . ." He shook his head. "This'll cost a lot of money, which means less money for other things. That puts stress on the entire system, and a lot of it. That's one of the drawbacks to making sure the Cits feel safe; they *don't* feel any urgency to upgrade defenses, not even for themselves. There's going to be complaints, and people here in Apex, and New Detroit, and the other cities with Barriers will be saying that the smaller places ought to pay for their own defenses. It sets the Cits in the big cities against the ones in the smaller ones, and the smallest towns against everyone. Then people in villages and small towns demand to be let into the big cities, even though there isn't room for them."

I said out loud the thing Master Jeffries had suggested. "But what if the Barriers have stopped working?"

"That, my young friend, is something *we* do not need to worry about," Archer replied. "That's for the techs and squints. What we Elite will have to worry about is the callouts until defenses get upgraded. What the rank and file of the Hunters will have to worry about is facing what we are not around to handle. If this is a real surge, that is. It might just be one of those random times when the Othersiders throw a massive attack at us for no reason we can tell."

But I could tell from Archer's expression that he was pretty certain this was one of those "surges." Probably because of all the things that had been getting past the Barriers here in Apex and the fact that we'd just seen two brand-new sorts of Othersiders in less than a month.

What do you think? I asked Bya.

I do not know. And I do not like that I do not know. I am glad we have a big pack; we can keep you safe. He raised his head, and Myrrdhin, who was lying on the sofa across from us, looked back at him and nodded.

I was thinking of other things . . . like home, and making sure *they* were going to be all right. *The Monastery will be safe, now I've warned them. If things get really bad, everyone can retreat up above the snowline to Safehaven. Even Knight's people; I don't think anyone is going to begrudge them shelter just because we haven't had time to break things to them gently.* After all, it wouldn't be the first time the Mountain had taken in people who didn't know the secret.

It may be that this is something else, something new, Bya said, quite unexpectedly.

Like what? I asked, startled.

The Folk Mage said to beware, that things were not what they seemed. Bya looked up at me expectantly.

So? I replied.

What if he did not mean with us? Bya asked. *What if he meant—with Them? What if he meant things are not what they seem with the Folk? What if . . . perhaps even the Folk have their sort of politics, and those politics affect us?*

I don't know either, Bya. I shrugged. *I guess all we can do is hang on for the ride.*

I finally had enough energy back to send the Hounds all home by this point, and it seemed a good time to do so. *You ready to go back?* I asked Bya and Myrrdhin. They nodded, and the others got up from where they were sprawled in various parts of the lounge. We moved out into the hall, and since it was momentarily empty, I went ahead and cast the runes there.

As the last of my Hounds went through, I heard a gasp behind me. I turned, and there was Jessie, although it took me a minute to recognize her. She had her hair pulled back in a tail, and she was wearing the kind of uniform the staff wore.

"Jessie Knight?" I said, bewildered. "What are you doing"— *quick, think of a polite way to say it*—"in a crew uniform?"

She hesitated. "Mistuh Severns said it was all right." She had a thicker accent than Knight did. "I didn't bring much t'wear, an' wearin' it makes me stick out like a sore thumb."

And the stuff Cits wear makes you feel all wrong. I could get that. It made *me* feel very strange when I'd gotten all that Hunter gear, and I'm not normally one for turning down pretty new clothes. Given what I knew about the Christers from home, she probably found everything *but* the staff uniforms to be "immodest."

"Oh, there's nothing wrong with wearing what makes you feel comfortable!" I said quickly. "I was just surprised to see you in the uniform is all. Uh, did I startle you? I'm sorry—"

"I just ain't never seen the Ang—I mean, Hounds put away before," she told me. "Mark never does it in front of me." She seemed a bit defensive to me, but maybe I was just reading something that wasn't there.

I shrugged. "Usually we send the Hounds home before we come back to the base, but we were all too tired to do that, so we brought them back with us. It was a rough fight—"

I stopped because she had gone white. "Is Mark—"

Well, that told me she had no idea what we'd been doing, which was probably just as well. "He's fine; we're just all tired. He and I were on the same subteam for the whole thing. Last I saw he was eating one potato stick at a time, with his Hounds around him," I said. "In the little Elite kitchen."

I could tell she was vibrating between running to make sure he was all right, and staying here and being polite. And there was a flicker of something there too. Anger, maybe, that she hadn't been told this was going on.

"How d'you know that?" she blurted, and there was resentment in those words. Resentment that *I* had known where her husband was, and she didn't. And something else flickered across her face for a moment. Doubt, absolutely, and with it, jealousy.

Oh boy. I should have known. Christer girls that I knew all worried that Outsiders would somehow come and steal their men. They can't seem to grasp the fact that a guy and a female can just be friends.

It probably didn't help that she'd only been married two days and Mark had run off without telling her where he was going, and that it was a callout. And here I was, telling her basically that I had just spent more time with her husband than she had today.

But she still didn't leave . . . still was held by the manners she'd had drilled into her.

And now *I* was torn. What would Mark want? Would he want her falling all over him, fussing at him, when if he was as drained as the rest of us it was all he could do to put one potato stick after another into his mouth? Or would he think she didn't love him anymore if she *didn't* come running to fuss over him?

"Go on, see for yourself he's all right," I said. "The Perscom will show you the way. Just remember he's probably so stupid-tired he won't even be able to remember his own name, much less yours. So don't expect him to make any grand speeches about our magnificent triumph on the battlefield."

That startled a half laugh out of her, at least, as if she was surprised that I'd made a joke, and hadn't expected me to be friendly. "Thankee," she said, then ran off. I plodded back to my room. I was really glad that shower had a seat in it, because I don't think I could have stood upright much longer.

I had another dream about Karly. We were standing in the middle of a big, open space. There was nothing at all around, just flat grass as far as the eye could see. We were looking at the horizon, where there was one of those monster storms boiling up. This time I could see it from the beginning, just the tops of the clouds at first, high and far and anviling out. Then more, the clouds growing darker toward the base, then at last, the whole storm itself, black as night at the base and the land underneath it, lightning lancing through the clouds, lighting them up from inside, like a jar full of lightning bugs. More lightning, a *lot* more, striking the ground over and over again, under the base. And I started to panic because it was coming toward us, there was nowhere to hide, and there was nothing I could do to make it stop. In the dream, it never occurred to me I could Shield—all I felt was this paralysis of fear.

And Karly turned toward me, solemnly, and said, "It's coming."

That was when I woke up.

I tried to think what it might mean—of course, there was the perfectly obvious, which was that I'd taken Archer's warning about a "surge" starting, and translated it into dream terms. Being the most obvious, that was probably what it was.

I didn't have precognitive dreams, although a couple of the monks were supposed to. No one on the Mountain would ever say *who* it was, so the people with the power wouldn't feel pressured to come up with future-telling all the time. So it probably wasn't precognitive. It probably was my subconscious warning me Archer was right.

But I knew that if we were going to be in for something like this "surge" thing, I wouldn't dare send Bya off with messages to my Masters unless I had a good—no, an *overwhelming*—reason to believe we wouldn't have a callout. Which basically meant never, until the surge was over.

Have I mentioned before that being responsible *sucks*? Because it sure did at that moment.

14

I KEPT BROODING ABOUT this all the next day; I'd taken a storm-sewer patrol, but my mind really wasn't on it. It had rained last night, by my standards a huge thunderstorm, but only an orange-and-red blob a bit bigger than three times the size of the city on the radar, and all the tunnels had about two inches of gradually draining water in the center. So far we hadn't had any luck in scaring anything up. I was walking along the side to avoid the water, more because I didn't want to alert potential adversaries to our presence than to avoid getting my boots wet.

Gwalchmai was the lead scout right now, and before I could analyze what was going on in my head anymore, he called to us.

There is another one of those dead humans, he said. *This one is warm. I have sniffed and searched, but I find no magic and nothing but his scent.*

That galvanized me and made me forget about anything else. Warm? *Bloody hell,* I thought, and sprinted down to where Gwalchmai was standing guard, with the rest of the pack loping along beside me. No point in worrying about noise now.

I checked the sewer map on my Perscom, and this was the same general area where we'd found the first three dead Psimons. We all rounded a corner and found Gwalchmai standing over another collapsed Psimon.

The body was down the end of a dead-end tunnel with a big access grate up to street level above us. The first thing I did was to go past the corpse and look up. With Dusana's help, him getting as big as he could and me standing on his back, I managed to get up high enough to poke at it with the tip of my shotgun, but it didn't even rattle. That meant nothing had pried it up because those things were bolted in place, not hinged, so however the dead man had gotten where he was, it wasn't from the street.

I dropped down next to the body, which, like the two I'd paid attention to, looked *old.* Old, frail, and bald. Best to verify what Gwalchmai had told me; I checked it using the infrared scan on my Perscom. Gwalchmai was right; though the Psimon was deader than a stone, he was still faintly warm. The Perscom reckoned time of death to have been about four hours ago, given that he was lying on 'crete. 'Crete would leech heat out of the body, and the ambient temperature down here would add to how fast the corpse cooled, but the Perscom had a calculator for all that. *How far can you trace his footsteps?* I asked Gwalchmai, who had the best nose of the entire pack.

Not far, the Hound replied regretfully. I sighed. I knew why.

The water, of course. The dead Psimon's shoes were still wet, in fact. It looked as if he'd trudged some distance through the water, effectively breaking his trail.

I pointed my Perscom at his collar badge and initiated a data handshake. Sure enough, I got the little green triangle icon of a download for a second, and then there was a new file on the Perscom. I sent it straight to Uncle, along with some vid, and then erased it and the vid from my Perscom. You know, just in case. Four dead Psimons, and I was the one who'd found them all? That was going to make PsiCorps very unhappy with me, and I didn't need them to find anything on my Perscom that wasn't completely innocent.

Here's the thing. Uncle had sent me down here because he thought there was something going on—but he hadn't given me any indication of urgency. I figured that meant there'd been one, maybe two dead Psimons down here before I started patrolling over the course of several months.

Now there were four, plus those two, and those four had turned up within weeks of each other. So *something* had changed, and so far as the Psimons were concerned, not for the better. PsiCorps couldn't just handwave this away. They were going to be looking for someone to blame, and who better than me?

Then I stood up, called it all in, and looked at the pack. "No dinner today," I said, annoyed. "We might as well go back to the surface because—"

Sure enough. My Perscom went off. I got a text from that cold senior Psimon ordering me to meet him at the nearest exit point. I guess he was pissed I hadn't waited for him the last time.

Or else he was pissed that I'd found a body that wasn't cold. Or maybe both.

I ordered a pod, and we began our trek to the exit.

But then...I got an idea, and I put myself back on the duty roster. I might be able to dodge that Psimon after all.

Lucky for my Hounds and lucky for me, just as the Psimon got out of his pod, I got a callout with Scarlet; the location was that dead industrial area of Spillover where Ace's brother had gotten himself killed.

The Psimon looked *very* annoyed when I answered the Perscom instead of immediately talking to him. I tried not to smirk as I replied with, "Roger, HQ. On my way."

"I'm sorry," I said to the Psimon, but not sorry at all. "I have to go; I've got a callout, and callouts don't wait. I need your pod." I turned and practically jumped into his pod, leaving him standing there, mouth gaping with astonishment that I had *dared* to just run off and leave him before being dismissed. And then steal his pod!

I'd won. I didn't have to talk to him and I'd effectively snubbed him, and there wasn't a thing he could do about it.

Best of all? He'd be stranded until the pod I'd called could get there.

I waited until the pod was a good block away before I started laughing.

I needed to clean up before I went to dinner. I'd missed the mess-hall time, but that didn't matter all that much. I'd just gotten out of the shower and into some comfortable clothing when I got a call from Josh. I'd been expecting one after I'd sent Uncle that vid and the ID information from the Psimon, and I wasn't at all surprised when he asked, rather too casually, "Have you eaten yet? Would you like noodles? There's a place where I used to live that's not far from your HQ. It's called Noodles, conveniently enough."

"No, and you're reading my mind. I love noodles, and they don't serve them much in the mess. I thought you Psimons weren't supposed to do that without probable cause!" I replied, smirking.

"I was ready to suggest something else, but I'm always happy to relive my childhood," he replied, just as lightly, although anyone who really knew him would probably be able to tell he was tense. "Meet you there?"

"I might start without you," I replied, pulling on boots. "I'm starving."

"Be my guest," he replied, and hung up.

Well. You weren't really expecting this next meeting to be a date, now, were you? I asked myself. Given what I'd just sent Uncle, Josh's mind was probably on anything but making out.

Needless to say, I made damn sure my Psi-shield was working before I set one foot out of my rooms. Josh wasn't the only Psimon out there. He wasn't even the Psimon I needed to worry about. There was always the possibility—no, probability—that PsiCorps was watching one or both of us, and I wasn't going to make it any easier on them to find out what was going on with me than I had to.

PsiCorps was supposed to be on our side. But someone in high circles in Apex was playing nasty political games with Uncle. And a Psimon *could*, all too easily, have manipulated and controlled Ace into working for them.

When I arrived at Noodles, the little shop on the first floor of the big apartment block where Josh had grown up, I was the only customer, which made me a little suspicious. Then again, it was after the supper hour ... and the staff didn't seem at all nervous, or far too casual, which would have been a tip-off that something was up. But caution never hurt anyone, so I pretended a calm I didn't feel, ordered just exactly as if I was late for my dinner (which I was) and starving (which I was).

The order arrived promptly but not too promptly, and I had already started on my bowl of pho when Josh turned up. He was wearing clothing that looked old, a sweater and pants that had been worn a lot, something I almost never saw anyone doing here in Apex, and something I had never seen *him* do. He was also wearing sunglasses, even though it was dark now, and Noodles wasn't exactly lit up. He slid into the seat across from me, punched something on the menu in the tabletop, and finally pulled off his glasses. His face had a pinched look, and his eyes were clouded with an emotion I couldn't read.

"Did you delete those files after you sent them to Prefect Charmand?" he asked in a whisper. His shoulders were all tensed up, and he hunched over the table, leaning as close to me as he could get. Right now I was really glad we were alone in here. I figured that if there were another Psimon anywhere in the building, he'd know. You can't Psi-scan through a Psi-shield, so in order to scan us, a Psimon would have to drop his own block, whether inherent or mechanical. Any snooping going on would have to have been by someone actually right here in the shop.

I nodded. He relaxed marginally. "Good. Here's the thing, Joy. I *knew* that Psimon."

I blinked. "How?" Then I bit my lip, since that wasn't exactly a tactful response. *Good going, Joy. Nice job.* "I—I'm so sorry, Josh—"

Josh interrupted me. "Not like that. He wasn't a friend or anything; we weren't really encouraged to have friends. But he was in my classes! He was older than me because his Powers popped late, but he can't—I mean couldn't—have been a day over twenty!"

I stared at him. "That's . . . crazy. . . ." I said after a long pause. "That's not possible. If I were making a judgment, I'd have said that body was over ninety!" My spoon was halfway to my mouth, forgotten. I put it back down in the bowl. "How is that even possible?"

Josh shook his head. "I don't know. Maybe it wasn't him? Maybe the guy you saw stole the uniform? That's all I can think. Except that . . . from the vid you sent me, it kind of looked like the guy I used to know, only really, really old."

"Could it have been a relative? His grandfather or something?" Now my mind was racing, thinking up all kinds of crazy theories. "Maybe it was an old relative that wasn't supposed to be in Apex, someone in Spillover maybe, and your guy slipped the uniform to him so he wouldn't get stopped, and he was sneaking into the city by way of the sewers? And then he just fell over dead?"

"And that would be why, exactly? I could see slipping him some decent clothing, but why would he sneak someone in wearing a Psimon uniform? People don't just get randomly stopped in Apex unless they don't have a registered Perscom and don't look like they fit in. It's not that hard to get a registered Perscom. And besides, anyone that a Psimon wants admitted into Apex *gets* admission and Cit status. We don't get all the perks that Hunters get, so that's what they give us." Josh shook his head. "None of this makes any sense."

Talk about coming up with crazy theories, all my watching old vids back at the Monastery gave me about a million of them. Theories were one thing, though; facts were another. We just didn't have any. Because there were three dead Psimons at least before this fourth one.

Josh's noodles came. I finished mine. I am pretty sure we were both scared and confused, although I was probably more scared than confused, and he was probably more confused than scared. He mostly just played with his food; well, that was the difference between Apex-bred Cits and the people where I come from. Where I come from, you never take the presence of food for granted, and you always eat what's set in front of you, unless you are literally sick and can't keep it down.

"What are you thinking?" I asked finally. Because I could kind of tell that what was going through his head was something he figured I wouldn't want to hear, and I was beginning to have a lot of ideas about what that might be. "You might as well tell me because it'll probably come out sooner or later, and I'd rather sooner than later."

He managed a wan smile. "You don't make things easy on anyone, do you?"

There were a lot of responses I could have made, and frankly, I didn't know which one to pick. I settled on a shrug.

"I think..." He gulped. "I think maybe we should break things off between us."

And I just sat there, half of me stunned, a fourth of me just wanting to cry, and a fourth of me nodding in agreement. "You mean," I finally managed, "for good? Or just for now?"

"For now!" he said immediately, which made me feel a teeny, teeny bit better. Not much, but a little. "It's just...I've got a lot of reasons, but none of them have anything to do with *you*."

"Well..." I looked at his hand, not at his face. The tabletop was smooth, reflective glass, now that we were done ordering and the screen under it was off. His face was reflected in it, like the face of someone drowned, deep underwater.

So was mine.

Right now I was all knotted up. He said none of his reasons had anything to do with me, but that wasn't how it felt. It felt like he'd been keeping secrets from me all this time. It felt like, down underneath, I'd actually known that and was trying to push that knowledge away. Maybe they'd been pressuring him to get inside my head already....

Yeah. My "creepy Psimon boyfriend"...I guess Retro was right about that.

"This sucks," I said. He nodded.

The silence was so deep we could hear the staff in the kitchen talking to each other, and people out in the shopping area. My hand was the same temperature as the tabletop—cold.

"If...when all this is sorted out...would you..." he began. "I mean, I shouldn't even ask you. You might hook up with someone else who'd..."

"Or I might be digesting inside a Drakken," I said. Cruel, I know, but I wasn't feeling as generous as I might have been. "Let's not make any promises, okay? I really like you a lot too, Josh. But you don't even know *if* this is going to get sorted out, much less when. And I don't know what tomorrow is going to shove in front of me. I don't even know if I'm going to go back to my rooms or back to a callout. You go on doing your best for Uncle. I'll go on doing my best for this city. And let's just leave it that way for now."

I got up and walked out, calling a pod from my Perscom before I'd gotten as far as the shop door. I didn't look back. And I could tell you that I'd done it that way so if anyone was watching, he'd look appropriately devastated, or I would, or both of us would. But the real reason was because—since there was going to be breaking up, I wanted to be the one to do it. I didn't want to be the one sitting there and trying to figure out ways to make it work after all, even though I knew all my frantic planning was utterly futile. I wanted to be the one walking out, not the one left behind.

Maybe I *am* mean. And maybe I'm a coward. I don't know. I just knew I didn't want to prolong the pain, pretending that there was some way to salvage this when we both knew there wasn't.

YOU KNOW HOW WHEN the universe decides to crap on you, it never just craps on *one* thing?

I didn't even get as far as the sidewalk before I got a call from Uncle's office. I stopped just outside the outer door and took it.

Maybe it was just a secretary with a message. Did Uncle work this late?

The face on my Perscom was Uncle, but—

The background was the prefect's seal. Every button was fastened. "Hunter Elite Joyeaux, I know it's late, but I require your presence here in my office. There are some matters we need to clear up." He couldn't have been more formal and official if he'd been making a public announcement.

Uh-oh.

"On my way, sir," I replied just as formally, and got in the pod and gave it my destination. He'd already closed the connection a nanosecond after I said "sir," so I put a quick call in to Kent.

"Senior Elite Armorer," I said as soon as he answered it, signaling him this was serious business. "I've been ordered to report to the prefect's office. I don't know how long this will take."

He looked startled. So that meant *he* hadn't been alerted to this, which meant I wasn't being called on the carpet for anything on the record. *So what am I being called in for that would make Uncle go official?* "There's nothing on your schedule from this end, Elite Joyeaux. I'll make a note of it. Check in as soon as you go officially back on duty." It was a given that Elite were *always* on duty, so unless I was going to be arrested for something, I could get called right out of this meeting. And if we *were* in a "surge"... well, the last attack had happened at oh-dark-thirty, right?

"Will do, sir," I replied, and shut the connection down. The lighted buildings of Apex glided soundlessly past my window, and I pushed all my brokenhearted feelings down in a box in my head, slammed the lid down, and sat on it. Metaphorically speaking. I could sort through them later and maybe come to some kind of terms with them. Maybe. When the pod dropped me off at Uncle's building, at least I wasn't ready to burst into tears right that second.

Rather than talking, though, because I wasn't sure I could yet, I presented my Perscom to the guards, who checked theirs and waved me through. There was one elevator in the lobby with the door standing invitingly—or threateningly—open. I took it, the scanner read my Perscom, and up I went.

A secretary/receptionist was on duty at the front desk; a new one, so I guess Uncle *did* work late enough to require more than one secretary. "Please go in, Hunter," she said as soon as I opened the office door. "They're waiting for you."

They? I just knew this couldn't be good.

It wasn't.

When I walked in the door, the very first thing I saw, even before Uncle Charmand, was the rigid back of someone in a Psimon uniform. A very, very, very high-ranking Psimon, judging from the epaulets and the shoulder jewelry. She had swept-back white-blond hair, and that was all I could see of her. She was standing, facing Uncle, who was sitting behind his desk.

I stopped in the middle of the room and saluted. "Elite Hunter Joyeaux Charmand reporting as ordered, sir," I said, staying in the salute.

The Psimon whirled, and I caught a momentary look of shock and surprise on her face. Well, of course, she wasn't used to people "sneaking up on her"; she hadn't sensed me arriving, since Hunters walk very softly, and I had my Psi-shield on. The look of utter hatred she had on her face before her expression smoothed out into a cold mask felt like a slap. I don't often take an instant dislike to anyone, but this Psimon had a face like a ferret, and she carried herself as if she was trying to project with body language just how superior to everything and everyone around her she considered herself to be.

"You—" she said. "You're the one that allegedly found four PsiCorps members dead."

Allegedly? That's an odd choice of words. I certainly found them. Unless she thinks I did something more than just find them...

Since that wasn't a question, I didn't say anything. In fact, I made up my mind that anything she got out of me, she'd have to pull out. I wasn't going to volunteer a word.

She waited for me to say something. I let my salute down, but I continued to say nothing.

It was Uncle who broke the silence. "This is Senior Psimon Abigail Drift, Hunter Charmand. The chief officer and head of PsiCorps."

Oh, great. I was pretty sure I knew exactly what she wanted. One Psimon dead was awkward. Two dead, and it was going to get hard to keep the word about it secret. Three dead, and the secret had certainly gotten out. Four, and you needed someone to blame. A scapegoat, someone to accuse of murdering Psimons. I had "history" with Ace Sturgis. She could concoct some wild story about me wanting revenge on PsiCorps because they'd let him escape. I'd do, for someone to point a finger at anyway.

"She's here to ask you some questions," Uncle continued.

No, she's here to conduct an inquisition.

The Psimon prowled around me with her hands behind her back, while I stayed where I was and attempted to be as stone-faced as she was. She didn't order me to remove my Psi-shield, which probably meant—what?

She knows Uncle is recording all this. That was a possible explanation for why she didn't demand the shield come off, but I sensed it was a partial one. *She knows that if she demands I take off the shield, it will be on record she did so, and then anything I say would be invalid because she could make me say* whatever she wanted. That was the most likely. There were plenty of people who didn't trust Psimons and PsiCorps because no one really likes the idea of mind-readers. Compared to Hunters, they were distinctly unglamorous, and there was a substantial percentage of the population who suspected they went waltzing through any unprotected Cit's head whenever they pleased, laws or no laws.

"Just how is it that *you* came to be on the scene every time one of my Psimons turns up dead?" she snapped at me, trying to catch me by surprise.

"I am the only Hunter, Elite or otherwise, patrolling that part of the storm-sewer system, ma'am," I said with stiff politeness. "I am the only one who *could* have found them. If I had not, they'd simply have lain there until the next storm washed them into the reservoir."

Chew on that for a while.

"That was at my request," Uncle put in, as if it was an afterthought. "There had been attacks on maintenance crews that the conventional police squads could no longer handle without arms that would do considerable damage to the sewers themselves. Since Elite Joyeaux has a pack of eleven, I deemed it possible for her to patrol solo there. She is also my relative, and I knew I could absolutely count on her being discreet and not spreading rumors about what she found there."

"Yes, yes, we know all about your *special* niece," Drift replied. Her expression didn't vary, nor did her tone, but the hatred behind her eyes drove every other thought out of my mind but this: she wanted blood. And mine would do. She spat another question at me. "Did you kill them?"

That was so unexpected, I was shocked, almost into a panic. I hadn't expected an actual accusation; I'd been prepared for an elaborate dance of innuendo but not this. "No, ma'am," I said, and stopped myself quickly before I said anything more. The first rule of being interrogated is to never volunteer anything. The second is, never elaborate a simple answer.

"According to the readings we got from the recordings made at the time of the discoveries," Uncle said as if he were speaking to a child, "the other Psimons all died six to twelve hours before they were found. I'm sure if you were to check the *many, many* records available, you will discover that Elite Joyeaux was elsewhere during those times, often with multiple witnesses."

Of course I was. I should have thought of that.

"There are ways of falsifying those records," the Psimon snapped.

"Really? There are?" Uncle replied, in tones of deep interest. "I would be fascinated to hear about them. I would also be fascinated to know how you came to hear about them. Security holes *are* my department, after all. Are you withholding information from my office? That's a very serious breach of protocol, if not the law itself."

The Psimon just stared a hole in him, or tried, anyway.

"We could also come to the question of motive, although as any good detective will tell you, you need to find the *means* first, then the opportunity, all bolstered by evidence, and then you will have the motive without needing to look for it. You don't immediately go about accusing every random person who has motive to kill someone." He chuckled. "If you did that, you'd be arresting a great many innocent people. Still! Where's the Hunter's motive? She didn't know these Psimons. She has no grudge against Psi-Corps. She certainly isn't inclined to slip away from Hunter HQ and slaughter random strangers for fun. If she wants to kill something, there are plenty of Othersiders out there." He spread his hands wide. "Drift, you're grasping at straws. If you are really looking for a murderer, and not something else, you'd be better off to hand over the bodies and what evidence you collected to me and let my detectives do the job they're paid to do. So far the only cause of death we were able to determine before you confiscated everything was that your Psimons died of simple old age and multiple system failures."

The Psimon's attention was completely off me now. If I had wanted to know who might be playing deadly political games with my uncle, well . . . I had one answer now, anyway. The only question in my mind was this: Just how far was Psimon Abigail Drift willing to take this game?

"She might have no motive," Drift growled. "But *you* certainly do!"

I half expected a spirited rebuttal. But Uncle just snorted with contempt. "Drift, first of all, if you know of a way to murder someone with old age, it will come as news to me. Secondly, if I wanted to undermine PsiCorps, there are a great many things I *might* do, but randomly murdering Psimons is not one of them. I'm the last person you need to worry about in this case. If you want to know who's behind this, look to your *own* ranks. Your position in PsiCorps is just as vulnerable to ruthless ladder-climbers as any other CO's is."

Uncle was outwardly calm, but I could read him. He was *too deliberately* relaxed. He'd lived on the Mountain; he must have learned relaxation techniques so his body language didn't give him away. I knew at that moment he was balancing on the edge of a sword, and if Drift called his bluff. . .

The Psimon glared at Uncle, then abruptly turned on her heel and left. But not before shooting *me* one last, venomous look. She bought it. At least for now.

When the door had shut behind him, Uncle motioned me to a chair. I took it, because my knees felt shaky. "Are you all right?" he asked.

"Do I look that bad?" I replied.

He shook his head and shut down the electronics in his desk, then sat down himself. And he let down *his* mask. He looked very shaken. So . . . like I thought, at least half of what he'd said was bluff. "You look very unhappy, Joy." He grimaced. "Josh called me and told me you'd broken up, so I would be warned that PsiCorps might make an immediate move. It seems he was right. That must be what just precipitated this little visit. The timing is too exact to be a coincidence."

"It is?" I said. I was too tired and stressed to be clever.

"Drift will use anything and anyone she can get leverage on." Uncle shrugged. "I take chances having Josh here in the office, and I trust him—to a point, but not beyond that. I need him, or to be more exact, I do need a Psimon—and better the devil you know. Your breakup was in public. And Josh's call to me was probably monitored. Any chance they could pressure him to get inside your head was gone, so Drift gambled she could rattle one or both of us." He changed the subject quickly. "I have the feeling Drift is not going to release any more than I already have, and certainly not the IDs of the previous victims before I put you down in the sewers."

"Wait, you had remains of other victims?" I replied. "How many other dead Psimons have there been before this?"

"Just some bones and pieces of torn uniforms, without the

collar IDs," Uncle replied, steepling his fingers together. "Which PsiCorps confiscated. It could have been one or several dead Psi-mons. Drift never did give me a straight story about why we found the remains in the sieves at the head of the reservoir, so I decided someone needed to start going down there, not just to clear out the Othersiders, but to see if more dead Psimons were going to turn up."

"What happened to the ones—the earlier ones?" I asked.

"From the marks on the bones, Ogres ate them, probably the pair you eliminated. But given what you found, it's very clear that the Ogres didn't actually kill them."

"I'm just a Hunter," I said faintly. "*I* don't have any idea why they died!"

Uncle smiled reassuringly. "I know, Joy. I'm not expecting you to solve this particular mystery, especially since it seems pretty clear Drift doesn't *want* it solved." He chewed a little on his lower lip as he thought. "Well, I don't have Josh to use as a contact con-duit for you, but Kent's perfectly safe; if you need to send some-thing to me or say something to me that can't go through official channels, and can't be handwaved off as my niece wanting some family time, go to Kent."

"I'll do that, Uncle," I replied, and stood up to go. He got up himself.

"We'll go down together, shall we?" he said. Actually, I was kind of glad of that, and nodded. As we left his office, the lights went out behind us, and he paused for just a moment at his sec-retary's desk. "Go on home, Grace," he said. "And call two pods for us, will you?"

We went down in the elevator together, and there were two

pods already waiting for us when we got to the external door. Uncle's was manned by a driver who probably served as a bodyguard as well; mine was driverless. We said good night, and Uncle being formal again, we shook hands and I saluted. Then we got in our pods and went our separate ways.

As soon as the pod got to the street, I called to put myself back on duty. I had only just done that, when Armorer Kent called. "Private, encrypted channel," he said. "Rank hath its privileges. What's going on, Joy?"

I told him everything because he needed to know everything, and that Uncle wanted me to use *him* as an indirect connection to the prefect's office from now on. All the time, I was wondering—how much had PsiCorps been pressuring Josh to get inside my head? Lots? None? Did he think that *now*, with four dead Psimons to account for, they were going to start? Was *that* why he had broken up with me? Or had he broken up with me because he knew he'd never be able to get anything out of me and didn't want to get in trouble?

Had it been to save me, or to save himself?

Kent signed off, and I put my aching head back against the pod cushions and contemplated the wreck my life had turned into over the course of a few hours. At least there was nothing else that could go wrong.

◄ ►

I did not expect to have a message waiting for me from Mark when I got back. I certainly didn't expect the contents. *Meet me at the fishpond at 22:00*, it read. *Don't reply to this.*

My first response was exasperation. *Now what?* I could only think of one reason why he'd tell me not to reply; he didn't want his Perscom to go off and have Jessie ask him who it was. And that, all by itself, boded nothing good.

But it was Knight. I couldn't say no, now, could I? So instead of curling up in my room around Bya and a hot mug of Chocolike, and having a good cry, I dutifully made my way to the atrium, the garden, and the pond full of colorful fish.

There were lights there, but he hadn't turned them on, so there was only the faint illumination coming up from the water of the pond from the three underwater lamps. He sat at on the side of the pond, throwing food to the fish, and his posture told me everything I didn't want to know.

"So," I said, sitting down facing him. "Let me just fill in the blanks, here. Jessie doesn't like it here. She doesn't fit in, and she wants to go home—or back to her folks, anyway. She wants you to come with her. And she's jealous of me."

I'd have laughed at the look of astonishment on his face, if I hadn't felt so miserable myself. "How did you—"

I shrugged. Oh, I could have explained how I'd seen this coming because I knew the Christers back home. Christer girls plainly could not fathom how any girl could be just friends with a guy. And given they were raised in a flock, like a bunch of hens, they pined for the familiarity of the flock if you took them out of it. "Jessie probably had some vision in her head of how things were going to be when you got married, and it looked a lot like the lives of her friends. But now she's found out that you can be gone at any time, without warning and without telling her where you're going. She's discovered that you're hobnobbing with women she secretly thinks are more glamorous than she is, because they're Hunters and have all the fancy Hunt suits and photo shoots and all that. And she's figured out there's not a lot for her to do, because there aren't any other Hunter wives; any Christer women she could meet up with are a scary pod ride away all alone, and you don't need her to mend and make, work the garden, or farm the bigger plots. She's probably used to sewing circles, quilting bees, community suppers, and canning gathers, and all that sort of thing, and here, she can't even cook you a meal. So she wants to go back, and she obviously can't go back without you. That would mark her as a failure in the eyes of her people, that she can't keep her man at her side."

I didn't go into all the religious crap she was probably churning over in her head. And maybe regurgitating at him. That was kind of inevitable, and it was *nothing* I could argue with, unless I wanted to alienate Mark.

"I can't go back," he said miserably. "I could have, maybe, if I hadn't gone Elite, but now—"

"I dunno, you might be able to," I said, which I hadn't wanted to say, but I owed him the truth. "There's only one other Hunter out *there*"—I darted him a *look*, and he nodded; I was pretty sure that Jessie had told him there *were* other Hunters back home, though she wouldn't know about the Mountain and the Monastery and Safehaven yet—"and if something were to happen to him, the folks there could petition for an Elite to be assigned there, and they'd be within their rights."

And all that would take would be for me to send a message via Bya that my "mentor" needed to have a tragic Hunting accident, and that they needed a new Hunter, an Elite by preference, because they were getting bigger and badder nasties. HQ would probably be so relieved that an Elite was *all* my people were asking for, they'd send whoever volunteered without a second thought.

Knight nodded again, slowly and deliberately. "I can see where having an Elite out there to replace all the good you were doing would be something they could ask for." And he gave me a little nod and a ghost of a smile, which was the one good thing that had happened this evening. Then he patted my shoulder, to reinforce that he completely understood *why* we had hidden the fact there were other Hunters up there. Heck, I bet his people would have hidden *his* existence if they could have gotten away with it. For that moment, it was us turnips against Apex . . . and us turnips had to stick together to protect our people.

"You know good and well that no one is going to want to go there but you," I continued. "There isn't even a single Apex Hunter that will want to go back there. I'd have precedence over you, if I volunteered, because it was my home first, but I won't bump you if they say someone can go. I won't lie to you, I think something's building and we're going to need every Hunter Apex has, Elite or not; if nothing else, this is probably the start of something Archer told me about called a 'surge.' You can ask him about it. But you're going to be no good to anyone if you're getting torn up over this, and the armorer isn't an idiot—he probably knows what's going on with you already."

He sighed heavily. "Don't tell Jessie this—" he began.

I snorted. "She wouldn't believe it if I did. If she's jealous enough of me to make you meet me here in secret, she won't believe a word that comes out of my mouth. But if things get to that point where you're too stressed to Hunt properly, then I think maybe it can be arranged." I sighed. "Remember, this is why Kent warned you to come to him if you and Jessie started to have problems. You all stressed out means we have half a Hunter out there when we need to have you at your sharpest."

I had been going to tell him about me and Josh...but now, why should I put another weight on his shoulders? It wasn't fair, and friends don't do that to friends.

"My pa would tell me I'm a fool for not keeping my woman in line," he said unhappily.

"Your pa is an idiot," I said, not feeling at all charitable toward *anyone* that was contributing to this mess. "Unless he means you should beat her, in which case he's a sadistic bastard, and if I ever meet him, I'll break his jaw."

Knight stared at me, openmouthed, for a long time. "You know, I think you actually might," he said after a long silence.

"Damn right I would." I threw food to the fish. "Then I'd ask him how he likes *being done by as he did*."

Actually...right at that moment, I really would have liked to have a target like that in front of me.

"Well...he doesn't beat Ma..." Knight said uncertainly. "It's—"

"Never mind. I know, it's a godliness thing," I replied, cutting him off because I didn't want to get into an argument with him over "godliness" and how woman was decreed by scripture to obedience and all that rot. And I didn't want to get into an argument that if his Jessie'd had an upbringing that didn't keep shoving her in that role, she might have had the gumption to try and fit in here.

Because those were arguments I would never win, and anyway, Karly hadn't fared any better with her wife when she popped Powers, and they had both been Apex born and raised.

I wished devoutly for a callout at that moment because the only thing that was going to make me feel *any* better was to kill something. But, of course, given the turn my luck had taken, there was nothing.

"I don't know what else to tell you," I said finally. "I really don't."

"I thought once I got her here, everything would be grand," he mourned. "The hard part would be over, and we could be happy."

Yeah, I can relate.

"You could try flirting with Scarlet," I said. "Then at least she'd stop being jealous of *me*."

He gave me a long, long look. "You are devious, Joy."

"Never pretended to be otherwise," I pointed out. "I've been forced to be devious since I got here." Then I softened. "Look, the Personnel guy, Rik Severn, was supposed to find something for her to do. Tell Kent to build a fire under him and find her something that will really occupy her right now. Maybe she can see something else that can be done with the inedible parts of what we farm, or improve the critters who supply the cores for the cloned meat. Maybe she can work with the kitchen to build us some new recipes; heck, maybe she can figure out a way to make the basic ration biscuits taste a little less like wooden slats. And that'd be helping out the downtrodden, or at least, as downtrodden as a Cit gets around here, so that would be godly." I let out my breath in a puff. After my initial annoyance, I was beginning to feel a little sorry for her. Only a little, but . . . yeah. All this had to be hard on her. Maybe all it would take would be finding some-thing useful for her to do. Something to make her more than just "Mark's wife."

He shook his head and dusted off the last of the fish-food crumbs on his hands into the pond. I did the same, and we both stood up.

"Good luck," we said at the same time. I laughed weakly.

Then we said a clumsy good night. I left first because I just couldn't take any more awkwardness.

When I got back to my room, I opened the Way and Bya stepped through. He looked up at me soberly. *It has been a very bad day,* he observed.

"Not the worst, but . . . yeah." I made that cup of Chocolike that I'd promised myself, and turned the vid-screen into a "fireplace" so I could stare at the flames while I cuddled up on the couch with Bya.

I wished this were yesterday. I wished I could rewind all of it. I wished I'd known about Abigail Drift weeks ago, because there might have been something I would have done differently if I had.

I wished I was a Psimon and I could read *everyone's* mind to find out what the *hell* they were all up to, even if I couldn't actually do anything about any of it.

You do not wish to be a Psimon, Bya said vehemently, although he didn't say why. *No matter what, you still have your pack.*

So I do, I replied, and put my head down on his soft back. *So I do.*

IN FAIRY TALES AND folktales that involve wishes, there's always the underlying theme of "be careful what you ask for."

Too bad I didn't remember that. I had wanted a callout because I needed something to take my hurt and anger out on. And I got my wish.

I was awakened out of the dreamless part of sleep by the alert Klaxon. That harsh *ahWOOgah, ahWOOgah* was enough to shatter the peace of the dead, which is probably why everyone uses that particular horn. I'd never heard that in Apex in all the time I had been here. It shocked me awake with my heart racing, I literally jumped out of bed on automatic, and as soon as I did, my vid-screen in the bedroom lit up with yellow text on flashing red.

Attack on Apex. Report to armory.

My brain couldn't make sense of that, Attack on *Apex*? How was that even possible?

But my body was smarter than my brain and knew that nothing mattered except that fact that an attack was happening at right this very minute. I scrambled into Hunting gear, wadded my hair into a messy knot, and hit the door running.

I squeezed in the door with two more Hunters who got there at the same time, with more pounding toward us. The armory was packed—not just with Elite, but with every Hunter in the building, no matter what shift they were on. Assistants were running weapons, ammo belts, and packs up to the counter. Anyone who hadn't armed up was wiggling his or her way there and picking up what best suited them. The armory assistants were making sure everyone took a pack and a belt before picking up any other equipment. I took my place at the counter, snatching up an assault rifle, ammo, and grenades before going back to the group and working my way up to the front.

Kent was looking down at some gadget in his hand; it was sort of clipboard shaped, so I guessed it was an electronic version of a noteboard or something like an oversize Perscom. The vid-screen behind him was blank, and here in the armory, the Klaxon still sounding out in the halls came through the walls as a mere hint. People were talking, but in a sort of nervous mutter.

Finally, as I heard the door behind me open and close again—letting in the *aWOOgah* one more time—he looked up and whistled shrilly. Anxious conversation stopped dead. The only noise in the room now was the sound of weapons hitting the counter or being snatched up and the whisper of the Klaxon.

Now the vid-screen lit up—to display a scene that drew a gasp from every single one of us.

There was an army—a literal army—of Othersiders, spotlighted by huge lamps on the Barrier pylons that I didn't even know existed. But I knew that spot, on the west side of Apex, where the big farm fields began.

Bad enough that there were more Othersiders than I could ever have thought possible, but they were at the Prime Barrier! Gogs, Magogs, Wyverns, Drakken, Trolls, an ever-moving sea of smaller Othersiders surging around their ankles—all I could do was stare in horror. This was like a scene from the Diseray, when the Othersiders first broke through and swarmed the cities, waves of destruction as powerful and primal as tornadoes or earthquakes.

"About an hour ago, Portals opened up in the area between the Second and Prime Barriers," Armorer Kent said into the shocked silence. "Despite heroic efforts by the army Mages to close them down, they remained open, and Othersider troops under Folk command emerged and formed up. Fifteen minutes ago, they commenced an attack on the Prime Barrier."

The vid-screen switched to another cam; this one showed Gogs and Magogs using enormous battering rams against one of the Barrier pylons. A chopper gunship flew by, strafing them, but they paid very little notice as bullets stitched across their tough, magic-hardened hides, and as we watched, a levin bolt lanced upward from the mass of Othersiders at their feet, narrowly missing the chopper's motor. The chopper veered off and up, out of reach, and the attack on the pylon continued,

"We've got troopships on the helipad," Kent said. "You'll work in teams of eight. Your assignments are on your Perscoms. Scramble for the choppers; your Perscom will flash red if you're trying to get on the one that isn't assigned to your team. We have to hold them back until the missile launchers can get into position. Go!"

Well, most of us couldn't go—there wasn't enough room at the door for us to all surge through. Those of us stuck for the moment took the chance to look at our Perscoms. I was afraid that Kent might have put me in charge of a group of Hunters, since I was Elite now, but to my relief, I was listed along with Hammer and Steel and a group of five, one of which was Dazzle, with Steel designated as the leader. I clicked my acknowledgment. Then the door cleared enough for me to squeeze through, and I sprinted as fast as the crowd would allow to get to the landing pads.

As I burst through the outside door, I spotted Steel sprinting for one of the farther choppers. I followed, then caught up with him. We both jumped in the open door of the chopper at about the same time, and after a quick glance at my Perscom to make sure I had the right chopper, I strapped down into a seat. Dazzle strapped down next to me in the next minute. Then the rest came on in a rush, and I checked my Perscom again. *Headset and mic, front left pouch,* it was saying, so I fished mine out and stuffed the little earpieces into my ears and adjusted the threadlike mic. The chopper took off with a jolt and a sideways tilt as the others were putting on their gear.

"Sound off," Steel's voice said in my ears.

"Hammer," said his brother, followed by *"Dazzle."* "Joy," I said, and the other four signed on in succession.

"All right, listen up," said Steel. *"This is a shitstorm of epic proportions. Nobody's got a strategy. I have no idea where we're gonna*

get put down. *So here's what we'll do. We'll all bring our Hounds over, and my brother and I will Shield the whole group. Then we'll keep the Shields up while we work our way toward the group attacking the pylon. Dazzle, if the Gogs and Magogs are in your range, I want you to concentrate on blinding them; if they aren't, hold back and save your energy until they* are *in range. The rest of you eat away at anything standing between us and the pylon gang. To give you a chance to rest magic, we'll drop the Shields at intervals so you can hose the enemy down with conventional fire. We'll give you a countdown when we're about do that. Clear?"*

We all answered in the affirmative.

"Folk are commanding here, we assume using psi to issue orders. So Folk are priority targets. Folk Mages, doubly so. Joy, if we spot any Folk, I want you to sic your entire pack on them."

"Yessir," I responded immediately.

"The rest of you, keep your Hounds close. Getting cut off from the rest of the group is going to be fatal." There was a pause. *"All right, we're coming in hot. The pilot's not landing, and it'll be about a three-foot jump. Get out the door, ready weapons, summon your Hounds, and wait for the Shields. If you've got grenades, use 'em once the chopper's away."*

We all felt the chopper slow down and stop. Then we were bailing out the door into the chaos and the darkness, a darkness split from time to time by the flash of magic. I rolled out the door instead of jumping, dropping about four feet, landing in a crouch with the others around me.

I felt the prop wash as the chopper sped away, and clapped my hands over my eyes and did the emergency summons. I've never had my Hounds come through so fast before; there was a kind of tearing in my chest as a sort of Portal formed in front of me; I couldn't see the Portal because my hands were over my eyes—and yet I could see it, or sense it anyway. The backs of my hands still felt as if they were on fire as the last of my Hounds joined the others, and I took my hands down, just in time to see the Portal fade into nothing.

We'd been set down at some distance from the enemy forces, and they didn't seem to have taken any notice of us yet. I guessed maybe the army Mages had put some sort of stealth-spell on the choppers. That "invisibility" wouldn't last now that we were away from our transport. But at least it gave us a few minutes to organize and for Hammer and Steel to put their stacked Shields on us.

The noise was unbelievable. The Othersiders shrieked, roared, howled, and screamed in a hundred different cries and tones. Helichopper gunships did fast flybys, door guns chattering. Ahead of us, grenades exploded irregularly. I couldn't see where the Othersider Portals were, but I guessed they were somewhere in that mass of Othersiders ahead of us, continuing to feed fighters into the fray. Occasionally, the sizzle of a levin bolt or the splash of a fire bolt lit the mob from within, but mostly the only illumination came from the spotlights on the pylons themselves.

And under all that noise came the steady, inexorable *boom, boom, boom*, as the ram hit the pylon.

I was sandwiched between Dazzle and Hammer; our Hounds were all packed up in front of us. There was no way to shoot without the risk of hitting a Hound, and I wasn't willing to take that risk. I could give them immunity from my offensive spells just by willing it so, but I had no way of protecting them from our conventional weapons. I wished I had Mark's trick of curving bullets; it would come in really useful about now.

Just at that moment, the brothers got their Shields up; strong enough to be visible even by ordinary people, they shimmered dimly in the darkness, covering us. *"All right, time to move out; take it slow and steady. When we hit their back lines, let them have it. Have the Hounds protect our backs."*

I relayed that to my pack, they ran around behind us, and we began to move forward.

Dazzle got within her effective range a lot sooner than the rest of us did; suddenly the heads of the Gogs and Magogs blossomed with blinding flashes of light. I was glad I wasn't looking straight at them at the time; even catching an indirect glance left spots in my vision. I couldn't see anything of the ground beneath the enemy's feet, so I couldn't put up trip Walls. All I could do was to find single targets I actually *could* see, and fire off levin bolts at them.

"Close your eyes!" yelled one of the Hunters I didn't know. *"Night-vision spell!"*

I'd never heard of this, but I obediently closed my eyes, felt a kind of electric tingle in my eyeballs that made me yelp with surprise, and my eyes flew open again. And I could *see!* It wasn't like night-vision goggles at all. It was more as if everything around me emitted its own inner light; the world painted in black and white, everything, down to single blades of grass, with its own little glowing outline,

And oh, dear little gods and great, I really wished I hadn't been able to see. Because while they were just an amorphous mass, it had been possible to think that there might not be as many Othersiders as there seemed to be.

Now, however, it was all too obvious that there were more than I had guessed. They were *jammed* together, crowded up too closely for anything but the couple of ranks on the outside to effectively fight, but that just meant that no matter how many you cut down, there would be dozens, hundreds, to replace the fallen.

Immediately in front of us, and turning, as they became aware that we were behind them, was a herd of Minotaurs. On their right was a group of Trolls. On their left, a bunch of skeletal-looking Wendigos. All three groups were at least three deep, and I couldn't make out what was behind them. But before I could do more than feel the first surge of terror, Steel shouted in my ears.

"Grenades out!" Automatically, I obeyed. *"Shields coming down in three! Two! One!"*

The shimmering bowl of the Shields vanished.

"Grenades! Three! Two! One!"

I put as much arm-power and magic-power as I could behind my throw; the grenades fell among the Othersiders who were only now turning to attack us. The Shields came back up as the first of the grenades exploded, and the world erupted in sound and light. Explosions, howls, screams, the sound hit us with almost the same impact as the blast wave.

It looked as if we had a mix of flash, incendiary, and explosive grenades, and I had no idea which I had thrown. None of these grenades threw shrapnel; at these close quarters, shrapnel could hit us as easily as the enemy if the Shields faltered for that critical second. By chance, one that fell among the Minotaurs was incendiary, and as closely packed as they were, facing us, there was no way for them to escape it. Several of them caught fire at once and began thrashing and kicking, trying to escape or put the flames out, creating chaos and panic in their ranks. There was the terrible stink of burning hair, followed by the disconcerting smell of cooking beef, as I backed up the incendiary grenades with fire bolts.

The flash-grenades disoriented, making their victims easier targets. The explosives all landed deeper into the mob; I couldn't see what they had done. Besides, I was too busy trying to keep the things that were already on fire burning hotter, and setting everything else around them ablaze.

The chaos caused by our grenades was enough to halt the enemy advance for a moment. *"Weapons out!"* Steel ordered. Everyone but Dazzle pulled their assault rifles to the ready position. Dazzle already had her orders: keep the Gogs and Magogs from battering the pylon. To do that, she had to concentrate on nothing else. *"Shields down in three! Two! One! Fire!"*

We all braced and fired. As densely packed as the Othersiders were, it was impossible *not* to hit something. The ranks nearest us reacted to the hail of bullets, which seemed to have been divided equally between incendiary and the steel-jacketed, iron-cored "Othersider" rounds. I'd never seen rounds like that until I got here, and they were effective even against Othersiders with tough hides like the Minotaurs, or with Shields or magical resistance to ordinary bullets, like the Wendigo. These were *big* monsters, and bullets didn't kill them, but bullets sure *hurt* them, interfered with their own magic, and slowed them, down a lot. And they reacted to the impacts with bellows of rage. Even better, you could cripple them with bullets in the right place; it would take more than one to shatter a knee, but we were all good marksmen.

We fired until the barrels of our guns were hot. Then the Shields came back up and we went back to spellcasting.

Inside, I was petrified. Nothing I had experienced in my entire life had prepared me for this. All the time I was firing off spells, shooting, or lobbing grenades, I was crying out of pure terror, and I had to keep shaking my head to clear the tears away. And I wasn't even thinking, not really; I was operating on pure reflex and a drive to stay alive just short of panic.

Because no matter how many Othersiders we cut down, there were always more behind them. It seemed as if there was no end to them.

I was vaguely aware of the greater impact of Hellfire missiles hitting deeper inside the mobs, but no one dared fire them at the Gogs and Magogs trying to batter the pylon down, for fear of hitting the pylon rather than them and doing their work of destroying the Barrier for them.

That was when Dazzle passed out, completely drained. I felt her fall against me and half caught her before she hit the ground. My brain woke up from terror for just a little bit at that point, and I turned to look behind us, spotting my Hounds defending our rear. *Dusana!* I called silently, and before I could blink, he was there. He must have seen what I wanted in my mind, because he knelt so I could drape Dazzle over his back. *Find the medics—*

I didn't get a chance to say anything else. He *bamphed* out, and I turned back to face the Nightmares. Literally. The Minotaurs were gone, and in their place were Nightmares: utterly impossible, vaguely horse-shaped black monsters with glowing red eyes in a skull head, fangs and claws as long as my hand, and fire for manes and tails. They attacked us with claws and teeth, with storm wind and terror, howling like the damned things they were. Their high-pitched howls carried even over the cacophony of explosions, screams, bellows, and the *boom, boom, boom* of the resumed attack on the pylon. I'd seen pictures, but I'd never fought them before. My insides shook, and I had to lock my knees to keep from falling.

We were running out of energy. We were running out of bullets. And there was no end to these creatures. There was only the screaming night, the orders in my ears, and cutting down one monster only to have three replace the one I'd killed.

The Nightmares were joined by Goblins in their natural forms, and the vicious little buggers were *everywhere*. The Othersiders were forcing us back and to the right just by sheer force of numbers, until we found ourselves mixed in with three army Mages and their troop, right up against the Barrier on our right. The enemy was pushing us back, and we were losing, and from the sound of things on the comm, it wasn't just us, it was everyone. The Gogs and Magogs were about to take down the pylon; without Dazzle, they had gone back to pounding on it. When it went down, so would two sections of the Barrier, and this army was going to pour over the gap, and there was nothing we could do about it. Every Hunter in the entire city was here! There *were* no reserves!

And just when I thought things couldn't get any worse, they did.

The ground underneath us *erupted*.

One second, I was shoulder to shoulder with Steel and Retro. The next second, I was tossed into the air like a ball, literally ten feet up and twice that backward. The double Shield of Hammer and Steel vanished; every particle of thought was knocked right out of my head by the shock, and if my Hounds hadn't gathered beneath me to catch me in their massed Shields, I probably would have broken my neck or back. As it was, the wind got knocked out of me, the comms went ominously silent, and suddenly I was alone except for my Hounds and way too many Othersiders.

They surrounded me; I scrambled to my feet and looked wildly around, but all I could see were monsters, too many monsters—hundreds of them and only twelve of us, and no other Hunters or even army anywhere in sight

The monsters seemed as surprised by our sudden appearance in their midst as I was getting thrown there.

I clutched my rifle and tried to look confident. I don't think I succeeded.

The Othersiders eyed me. Some of them were actually laughing, others merely licking their chops.

We backed up to the Barrier, the Hounds in a semicircle around me, and braced for the onslaught.

Then, before they could charge us, I heard the welcome beat of helichoppers overhead! Close enough that even the monsters looked up.

The choppers descended in a phalanx from the sky on the other side of the Barrier, disgorging Psimons. Dozens, hundreds, of Psimons. They tumbled out of the choppers and formed up in orderly ranks on their side of the Barrier.

What?

The Othersiders froze, for a moment caught completely off guard at this new development.

Eerily, as if they were all linked together, the Psimons bent their heads at the same time—

And the Othersiders went insane.

Literally insane.

I stood there with my mouth falling open as all the monsters within sight freaked the heck out and completely forgot about me. Some of them dropped to the ground, clutching their heads with hands, paws, or claws. Some clawed at their own bodies, shredding their own flesh until they fell down, senseless or dead. Some, like the Gogs and Magogs that had been attacking the pylon, turned on their fellows, and attacked their own allies with their massive weapons.

All of them forgot about us.

The Psimons... It had to have been the Psimons! Somehow they were getting inside the heads of these monsters and driving them crazy, so crazy they were turning on each other! *Ohmigods,* I thought, dazed. *We're saved!*

I shook my head to clear it, and we waded back into the fray. A flare went up to my left, and I heard Kent shout over the comm, *"Hunters! Form up on me!"* and took that as an order to cut my way through the chaos of the crazed and witless Othersiders until I could get to him. I had run out of bullets, so I used my rifle as a club, and the monsters were paying absolutely no attention to us. All we needed to do was clear a path. When one of them got past the Hounds, I'd knock it down, and one of the Hounds would finish it off. My arms felt like wood, my legs as if I were wading through sticky mud up to my thighs, and every particle of me ached and burned with exhaustion, but I was only halfway to where Kent was sending up another flare. My focus narrowed to the next enemy in my path, the next six inches of ground to cover.

A glowing figure appeared directly in my path, his Shields knocking my Hounds aside. He dropped the Shields for a moment, seized my shoulders before I could raise my rifle butt to club him, and he shook me, hard. I stared into his lavender eyes without comprehension as he shouted at me.

It was *that* Folk Mage . . . .

"Do not just *look,* shepherd! *See!* See what *we* are doing! See how we work together and power flows! Power always comes from *somewhere!*" he cried, and then he *bamphed* away before I had time to react.

His face was still an afterimage in my head when Steel hacked his way to my side. Somewhere, maybe from one of the Trolls, he'd picked up a battle-ax, and although it wasn't Cold Iron, he was doing a good job of cleaving his way through the opposition using it.

"What the hell was that about?" he shouted over the comms. I shook my head.

"Doesn't matter!" I yelled back. "We need to get to Kent!"

I was still so dazed, so shaken by the encounter that I wasn't paying attention to what was around us, nor adding my Shields to Steel's. And I should have been, *especially* the Shielding part, because that was when a levin bolt hit Steel square in the chest, or at least, in his Shield at about the level of his chest.

My heart stopped.

Steel went flying backward and disappeared beneath a wave of Othersider monsters. Still blank with shock, I turned sluggishly to face in the direction the blow had come from.

And found myself staring at Ace.

But this was an Ace transformed. He had strings of beads and feathers tucked behind both ears, and what looked like a crest made of bright red horsehair attached to the top of his head. He was bare armed and bare chested, with a floor-length vest in scarlet leather, and skintight pants to match that left *nothing* to the imagination tucked into scarlet leather boots. There were wide gold armbands on both his biceps, and a huge gold torque around his throat.

And the hate in his eyes as he stared at me made me drop back a pace.

Ace was not alone. There was a Folk Mage with him, one of the feral ones, all dreadlocks and beads and ragged leather clothing, bearing a staff that appeared to be made entirely of crystal. The staff glowed a sickly green, and Ace's eyes glowed the same color.

I managed to get my Shields up just in time for Ace to hit me with another levin bolt. I'd put a spin on my Shields, so instead of knocking me back into the mob, the power was deflected off to the side and it blasted down a half dozen of his allies.

He didn't seem to care. His face twisted into a mask of hate as he sent blast after blast at me, each one glancing off my Shield and atomizing a few more Othersiders. My Hounds quickly added their Shields to mine while I lobbed a return salvo of fire bolts, which fizzled out on *his* Shield.

The Folk Mage did absolutely nothing except stand at Ace's back, but it didn't matter. Ace was overclocked, somehow; he was doing things he *never* could before. I was totally on the defensive now, literally fighting for my life. My vision began to get gray around the edges, and the only thing that was saving me was the effort of my Hounds. *I* was running on fumes, but they were at more than full strength; every Othersider that died nearby just added to their stores of manna. Ace pounded away at me, and we united our Shields and kept them spinning, kept unraveling the passengers he had riding on every levin bolt, every fire whip.

But I knew I couldn't keep this up for very much longer. My knees were starting to give way, and I sagged up against Dusana's side, holding on to him to keep upright through sheer force of will, panting as if I had been running a marathon. I saw Ace suddenly grin as he sensed I didn't have anything more in me. I watched him spinning up something... terrible....

Then he paused, hands glowing with power, and glared at Myrrdhin and Gwalchmai. "You!" he barked arrogantly. "Come *here*!"

There was a long, long pause. The two Hounds that had once belonged to Ace turned their heads and looked at each other, then back at Ace.

Then, to my dismay, Myrrdhin and Gwalchmai suddenly *bamphed* away from my side and reappeared next to Ace and the Folk Mage.

My heart twisted at the sudden desertion—

Ace laughed and held out his hand to Myrrdhin. Feeling sick and betrayed, all I could do was watch.

Which was when Myrrdhin lunged for Ace's hand and arm and viciously savaged it, while Gwalchmai sank his fangs into the Folk Mage's legs. Both of them shook their victims like terriers shaking a rat.

The Mage shrieked, a strangely girlish sound, and struck at Gwalchmai with his staff, and Ace just stood there with his mouth open in a silent scream of agony as blood dripped from Myrrdhin's jaws. Then they came back, *bamphing* back to my side, as the spell Ace had been about to cast at me unraveled and sputtered away in a shower of sparks.

Gasping with pain, the Folk Mage seized Ace by one shoulder, and then they were gone, *bamphed* away, out of range of my Hounds.

I slid to the ground and stayed there, one arm around Bya and one around Myrrdhin, until someone found us.

The choppers were full of the wounded. Those of us who could still walk were told to make our way to the pylon (dented, but still functioning) and go back through the Barrier by means of the door at its base, then wait for pods on the other side. I wasn't about to take the chance on something rising up out of the piles of disintegrating corpses to attack us, so I kept the Hounds with me and let them through the Barrier a few at a time, starting with Bya and Gwalchmai.

Dusana and I were the last ones through, and when we got to the other side, I finally mustered up just enough energy to open the Way and send them all back. Bya paused before crossing the threshold and looked back at me. He didn't need to say anything; I knew what he meant by that look: that if I needed him, all I needed to do was bring him back.

Then he crossed, and the Portal closed behind him.

It was all industrial buildings on this side, long windowless oblongs of 'crete that didn't even have doors in them, just underground tunnels to the barracks-like quarters of the prisoners that worked in them. Not for the first time, I shivered, thinking what a horrible existence that must be, never seeing the sun, never getting a breath of fresh air.

Speaking of the sun, it was just now false dawn, the sky in

the east lightening to gray. The Barrier didn't allow a clear view of the other side, but it looked as if the only things moving were rescue squads from the army, looking for more wounded. *Or... the dead.* I had no doubt there were dead. I dreaded to find out who they were.

Here and there some of the big Othersiders that didn't disintegrate when they died created odd, dark mounds that looked out of place in the flat field.

I slumped down into the grass at the side of the road, and wondered, dully, how bad the toll was. It had to be bad. *I* had barely survived, and I had a pack of eleven. How well could someone with two or three Hounds hope to fare? Or an army Mage with no Hounds at all?

I thought bitterly of the Psimons, standing in safety on the other side of the Barrier to do their work—then immediately felt bad about thinking poorly of them. *They* weren't trained to handle weapons the way we were. *They* had no way of defending themselves, once they'd mentally locked into a target and began messing with its mind. And since they were the only ones of us whose only powers worked across the Barrier, of course they needed to stay behind it.

And I shouldn't think of them as a bunch of cowards because they had.

Besides, they'd probably been under orders.

And besides that—face it, they'd saved our sorry asses. If it hadn't been for them turning up when they did, we'd have gotten overwhelmed. As it was, we'd only just *barely* beaten the Othersiders back.

If it hadn't been for them ... the Prime Barrier would be down right this minute, and Othersiders would be pouring into Apex.

I was vaguely aware of someone trudging up to stand next to me. I looked up; it was the armorer, and my relief at seeing him made me feel dizzy for a moment. "Joy," said Kent, sounding relieved and just as exhausted as I felt. Then I felt panic because his head was bandaged, his arm was in a sling, and there was a huge bandage covering his right thigh. This was Kent! Kent never got hurt!

"Who's hurt?" I asked, seeing what was in his eyes. "Who's—"

"Everyone's injured. Archer, Flashfire, and Scarlet were evac'd to the hospital. Archer's still unconscious. Retro's dead, and Bull. Steel . . ." He shook his head. "Missing, but . . . there's no ping from his Perscom, and his comm's dead." He took a deep breath, as my throat closed and my eyes burned. I knew what that meant. Now I felt guilt just pour over me. I should have been paying attention! Ace had slammed him out into the mob, and it was my fault! I should have gone after him! I began to cry; Kent was so exhausted he didn't even notice—or maybe he noticed, but what could he do? "That's just in the Elite. We've lost twenty-three of the ranked Hunters, and half the ones left need serious recovery time. I've never seen anything like this. It's like—like the Breakthrough and the Diseray, all over again. This is more than a surge. They've escalated this into all-out war." The exhaustion in his voice came as a shock, on top of everything else. I had never heard the armorer sound like this. Ever. "If it hadn't been for PsiCorps, they'd have hammered us into the ground." I could tell how much he hated admitting that. "Can you wait a while for transport?"

"I'll be all right," I lied. "You see to the people worse off than me. I'm just worn-out." The truth was, I was so exhausted I was slurring my words. But then, so was Kent.

"Thanks, Joy," he said, and stumbled off, I supposed to check on people who had actual injuries.

I lay back in the grass and stared up at the sky, which got brighter and blue, while my eyes streamed tears. Steel was probably dead. Retro *was* dead. The guy who'd gone out of his way to make me laugh, regardless of how he was feeling, was gone. And what had I ever done for him? I was too tired to think. Which was just as well because I didn't want to think about Steel, or about Hammer, his brother. How could I face Hammer now? At least Mark wasn't missing or badly hurt.

Finally, someone in an army uniform came and shook me enough out of my daze to get up and load into a transport vehicle with a bunch of other Hunters. This wasn't a pod: it was more like a goods transporter, and we all sat on the floor with our backs braced against the wall. I didn't recognize any of the others; I only knew they were Hunters by the tattoos on the backs of their hands and their Hunting colors. Nobody said a word the whole way back; two of the seven actually fell asleep, curled up on the hard metal floor.

Good gods, what are we going to do if the Othersiders attack again? I suddenly thought, and felt a moment of sheer panic at the idea of having to turn around and go back to the Barrier, because I had nothing left to fight with.

But that was when we pulled up at HQ, and we all more or less tumbled out of the transporter. We staggered into the building, and I headed for my room since there didn't seem to be anyone wanting to debrief me. I sat down on the couch, just for a minute—

The minute lasted twelve hours, according to the clock on my vid-screen when I woke up.

WHEN I CAME TO—IT wasn't exactly "waking up," since the entire twelve-hour period had passed in something like a dead stupor—the vid-screen displayed a single message, dated from about two hours ago.

Report to the armory. It took me a couple of minutes to grasp what it said, actually—I still felt stupid with exhaustion. I shoved myself into a sitting position with arms that still felt as clumsy as if they were made of wood, and everything that had happened all came rushing back, and I burst into tears and cried myself into throwing up.

Oh, Steel, I am so sorry—

It was my fault. We were on the same team, and if he hadn't been with me, Ace would never have attacked him. If I had been paying attention, if I'd had *my* Shield up or even just the Shields of my Hounds, he wouldn't have gotten knocked away.

I didn't want to report to the armory. I didn't want to have to face Hammer. Steel had been *with me* when he'd been blasted by Ace. I was probably the last person to see him alive. I didn't want to have to tell Hammer that. I didn't want to tell him I hadn't gone to Steel's rescue. Even though there was no way I *could* have gone to his rescue, since Ace was monofocused on turning me into component atoms. Yet, at the same time, I knew I had failed Steel, failed all my fellow Elite. I was the Hunter with a pack of eleven. I was supposed to be able to do the impossible, right? What could I possibly say to him?

I wasn't hungry. In fact, after throwing up, my stomach was all twisted in knots, but I downed a couple of meal-drinks. Then I went and stood in the shower for five minutes and changed before I left for the armory, still trying to figure out what to say to Hammer. The walk there seemed both too short and took forever, at the same time. What was I going to say, not just to Hammer, but to everyone? How were we ever going to repulse another attack like that? Some of us were dead, all of us were exhausted, and the Psimons were in no better shape than we were. How could we ever save the city?

And Ace . . . we were lucky he'd just been so focused on me that he ignored everything else. If he'd actually turned his attention to getting through the Barrier, he *would* have. He could have cut his way through the defenses like they were made of paper, and once he'd gotten inside the pylon, he could have destroyed the workings from the inside and taken down the Barrier.

At that moment, as my hand touched the doorknob, all I could think of was Ace, with that Folk Mage behind him, doing impossible things, as if he'd gotten some sort of super-serum boost like in a pre-Diseray story, or had tapped into a whole new power source—

And out of nowhere, that was when I remembered what "my" Folk Mage had said when he'd grabbed me and had shook me so hard for a moment that my teeth had rattled.

"Do not just look, shepherd. See! Power always comes from somewhere!"

I froze with my hand still on the knob. Because at that moment, things started falling together. What if I ignored that this was a member of the Folk, who had always been our deadly enemies? What if I forgot his weird behavior?

The Folk almost never said anything directly. "Power comes from *somewhere*" was about as close as one of them was ever going to get in telling me how they—specifically, how *Ace*—had gotten overclocked. Besides, he would have known that, as a member of the enemy, I would never trust anything he just told me until I saw it for myself.

So, I should not let myself get distracted by the source of the warning, and concentrate on what I was supposed to figure out. The first, that things were not what they seemed, had been something I already knew. But he had also told me that there was something right in front of me that I wasn't seeing.

Right in front of me. And right after he'd yelled that at me, Ace had shown up.

Ace. Doing things he shouldn't have been able to do, more powerful than anyone I'd ever seen, even the Masters. And the Folk Mage, standing behind him, who instead of joining Ace in attacking me, had apparently been doing *nothing*—or at least, had been passive until the moment came when they had to escape or be savaged to death by Myrrdhin and Gwalchmai.

Except that if "my" Mage was right, I'd been wrong about all of that. I had looked, but I had not seen. Now…what if the Folk Mage *had* been doing something? It just hadn't been obvious.

What if he had been acting as Ace's power source?

It was one of those things the Masters were always saying: *As soon as you realize the candle is a flame, your meal is cooked.* Once you know something can be done, you're halfway to doing it yourself. It had never occurred to me—or anyone else, I guess—that it might be possible to share magic. But magic was just another form of manna….

It wasn't that crazy an idea. I already knew that some Hunters could supply manna directly to their Hounds. I could do that, for instance. What if that feral Mage, acting as a sort of power supply, was the reason why Ace had been doing impossible things, things he never could have done on his own with only his own magic energy to fuel his spells?

If that was true, it meant that not just manna, but magic itself could be stolen, donated, or shared. And that information could change everything. *Would* change everything. If that was true, I knew where us Hunters could get "power supplies."

All that flashed through my mind in the time it took me to open the door to the armory. Suddenly, I felt something I hadn't for the last twenty-four hours.

Hope.

Someone had hauled in chairs for everyone to sit on, and it was obvious from the slumped shoulders and postures of exhaustion that everyone was just as drained and dispirited as I had been. And that didn't even take into account all the bandages and bruises and other signs of injury. Even Armorer Kent was sitting, one wrist and the opposite ankle strapped into elastic supports, his eye blackened, a big bandage on his head, and the bulge of another on his right thigh under his clothing. I couldn't remember the last time I'd seen him sitting down except when we were on a chopper. He looked toward the door as I opened it, and nodded at me.

"Here's the last of us," he said, and waved me toward a chair. I felt horribly conspicuous as I edged between two rows of seated Elite to get to it. I didn't look for Hammer; I was just as glad I didn't immediately spot him. I still didn't know what to say to him.

Kent looked past me. "Go on, Siren. You were saying?"

"Well, PsiCorps has been all over the news feeds," said a woman behind me—I didn't recognize her voice. "Taking credit for saving the city, and pledging they'll do it again."

"They can't, not unless the Othersiders hold off any more attacks for a couple of weeks at least," Kent replied. "The Psimons are as depleted as we are. Half of them were collapsed on the ground at the Barrier, unconscious, if not dead, the last I saw."

There were uneasy murmurs at that. "We're in no better shape," Elite Mei protested from two chairs over. "There's not a single one of us who isn't hurt or exhausted or both. We aren't ready to face another attack like that."

Kent's jaw tightened, but a shadow passed over his face. "No, we aren't. I—"

"Sir?" I said, putting my hand up. "I—sir, I maybe have an idea—"

Now all eyes actually *were* on me, and I squirmed a little in discomfort and began to doubt my sudden inspiration. What if I was wrong? But Kent nodded. "Go ahead, Joy."

So, into the silence, I explained about facing Ace and the Folk Mage. Described how the Mage had acted. I kind of decided *not* to mention "my" Folk Mage because I was pretty sure that if I did that, everyone would think my mind had been melted a bit by him. Heck, I'd have thought the same, except that I had eleven checks on my behavior, and none of my Hounds were treating me any differently.

"... so I couldn't figure it out, how Ace could be doing all that spellwork without dropping over, unless he was getting magic power from somewhere else. It's been stewing in the back of my mind until I got to the door of the armory. And that's when it hit me—that what if that Folk Mage hadn't just been acting as his minder, what if he'd been acting as Ace's battery bank?" I concluded. "And if he could do that, maybe we could too. That would mean we wouldn't be limited anymore, if *we* could find another source of magic energy." I didn't add that we wouldn't need PsiCorps next time, though I was pretty sure that thought had occurred to just about everyone here. "Think of what each of us could do, magically, if we had twice, three times the magic power available to us!"

"Well ... what sort of *battery bank* were you thinking about?" the armorer asked skeptically. "And how were you thinking of verifying this notion in the first place?"

"Same answer for both questions, sir," I said. "I figured I'd ask the Hounds."

Well, that caused a stir. People began looking at each other, then back to me, then started muttering to each other. Did they think I was crazy? I wouldn't blame them if they did. But I had to get everything I'd figured out in front of them before they made up their minds I was insane. So I continued right on, over the murmuring. "See, Hounds are magic, and they eat manna. I thought, maybe they could turn manna into magic. I know some of us can share our manna with them so they can heal up. Maybe they can share magic back with us."

"That's a lot of maybes," remarked Elite Flashfire from my right. *He* looked like death warmed over, his head completely wrapped up in bandages and one arm in a sling. I didn't blame him for feeling skeptical. But at least I had a source for the answers, and if the reply was no, well, we were no worse off than when I'd walked in.

"But it's easy enough to find out," I pointed out. "I just bring over one of my Hounds and ask him. I haven't had a chance to do that yet—the idea just hit me as I started to open the door here."

Kent made an impatient little gesture that more or less said "then get on with it," and I got up, went to the front of the room, and pulled up magic inside myself. For the first time in a *long* time, it ached to do that, a dull, unpleasant throb deep in my chest followed by an all-over tenderness, like after you've overused your muscles and then try and do something before they've gotten a chance to recover. But it didn't matter that it hurt, what mattered was that after that twelve-hour coma there was magic enough in me now to bring one Hound over, and I cast the Glyphs and opened the Way.

Bya leapt through and stood there in his greyhound shape, looking from me to Kent and back again, waiting for me to say something.

"Bya," I said, "you know we're in trouble; you know we can't possibly face the Othersiders right now, not without help. So I need to know, can Hounds share magic with their Hunters? And if you can, will you?"

Bya put his head to one side and thought about this for a moment, while all the Elite in the room held their breaths and stared at him. Finally, he nodded slowly, and there was a kind of collective sigh of relief. *Tell them all what I tell you, exactly as I say it,* he ordered.

"He wants me to tell you exactly what he tells me," I said. I heard some murmurs at that, as if some of my fellow Elite were not used to being spoken to by their Hounds as if we were all equals. Well, that didn't matter, because we *are*, and if they hadn't figured that out by now, it was time they learned it.

In the course of ordinary Hunting, this would not be possible, Bya continued. *In the course of ordinary Hunting, there is only enough manna released in a kill to allow us to feed and prosper. But we do not face ordinary Hunting now. We face war.*

Obediently, I repeated that word for word. A few of my fellow Elite looked shocked, not at what had been said, but at the fact that my Hound was smart enough to figure it out and say it.

"He's right," Kent said flatly. "We're into a whole new phase of hostility now. What we faced out there was all-out war." There were murmurs of agreement, but also a sense of fear.

You saw what happened when you faced so many of the enemy back there. You are depleted by what you do, but we have so much manna flowing to us that we cannot use more than a tenth of what is available. There is no reason to hoard it, since we cannot store that much manna, no matter how much we would like to. And it is foolish to let it go to waste. We can change it to the energies of magic, and, yes, we can give it in that form back to you. And I do not think that any Hound will refuse to do so. But do not take my word for this, Bya added. *Ask your Hounds.*

I repeated all that, and needless to say, the reaction was pretty electric and was followed *immediately* by everyone in the room, Kent included, casting their own particular Glyphs, opening the Way, and bringing through their pack alphas, until the room was full of all the wild and weirdly varied kinds of Hounds we all had. Each alpha turned his attention to his Hunter. But I saw something new in the eyes of some of my fellow Elite—a realization that their Hounds were not just smart, magical *animals,* but something much more.

And whether the query and reply was by thought or by word, the answer was the same as Bya had given me. *Yes.* They *could* turn surplus manna into magic, and they would, and they would feed us with it.

We weren't fighting against overwhelming odds anymore. We might not have more Hunters, but we Hunters had just been given a whole new weapon to fight with.

The mood in the room, which had been somber, quietly frightened, and deep in despair, was transformed in that moment.

The room had turned from a gathering of Hunters to a sea of Hunter-Hound pairs as each Hunter went into deeper and more involved conversation with his or her alpha. For some, I sensed, it was the first time actual "conversation" had *ever* taken place. But Kent glanced down at his Perscom and looked stunned.

Then, without a word, he grabbed me by my elbow and dragged me out into the hall. Even limping hard, he was still a big, strong man, and I wasn't exactly resisting. "Medbay," he said as the door closed on the buzz of conversation. "On the double. I'll catch up."

Even though I hadn't a clue what was going on, I blindly followed the order, racing down the corridors at the direction of my Perscom to the medbay, which combined the infirmary, where minor injuries were tended, with the surgery and hospital. I still didn't know *why* I was being sent here—but no sooner had I burst through the doors when Jessie grabbed my elbow and started shoving me toward the Hospital ward. "Wha—" I said.

"Hurry up. He's askin' for ye, an Kent, I reckon Kent's a-comin'." Jessie was a big girl and muscled, and she wouldn't have had any trouble frog-marching me anywhere she chose, but I didn't see any reason to resist her. My only question was, who, exactly, was *he*?

I winced to see that all the beds were occupied, but Jessie steered me toward one in particular.

One that Hammer was standing beside.

One that held—

I gasped, but before I could say anything, Jessie had me parked on the other side of the bed from Hammer and laid a gentle hand on his unbandaged shoulder. "Mistuh Steel," she said. "Got Joy here, an' Kent's a-comin'." And only now did I realize that Jessie was still in a staff uniform—but it was medic white, and she had a little red cross over her left breast with an embroidered name, *Jessie Knight*.

Steel looked like someone had been beating him with clubs. His face was so bruised it was blue-black, and his eyes were swollen shut. There was a stitched-up gash across his forehead and the top of his head, and he had his left arm in a cast. Frankly, he looked like everything in the world had used him for a punching bag.

"Wait for Kent," he croaked. His voice sounded as if he had been screaming for about ten hours. Maybe he had been.

"They brought him in a couple hours ago," said Hammer, which explained why he hadn't been at the meeting. "He's concussed, and the Othersiders had a grand old time dancing on him. His Hounds grabbed themselves a search party and practically dragged the rescuers to him. Once they got him here, I sent his Hounds home and positively ID'd him. He wasn't in any shape to do anything more than mumble, so he was only marginally more incoherent than normal." I knew by that little dig that Steel really *was* going to be all right.

"Ears work fine, moron," Steel croaked.

That was when Kent got there. Jessie had left us to wait by the door, and towed him over so Steel could tell us what we needed to know.

He told his story in little bits, resting between each sentence, his words slurring together a little. "Last *I* saw of that rat Ace, he'd slammed me in the chest with a massive levin bolt and I was flying backward. I ended up landing soft, so I didn't break every single bone in my body." His paused for a breath, and Jessie stuck a straw leading to a glass of ice water in between his swollen lips. He took a couple sips, then continued. "Unfortunately, I landed soft on a bunch of Goblins, and they weren't exactly in a forgiving mood." He winced a little as he took a breath. "I managed to get something like a Shield up after they'd pounded on me with clubs for a while, but my Hounds couldn't get to me, I knew I couldn't keep the Shield going for very long, and I figured I was a goner."

He paused for a lot longer, Jessie hovering like a protective bird. "Then, all of a sudden, they stopped beating on me and parted like the Red Sea, and this Folk Mage just strolled through them. Not the one that was helping Ace—this one was different."

"How do you mean?" Kent asked when Steel paused again.

"Fancy," Steel replied. "For starters, he wasn't feral. For another thing, I think he must have been pretty high ranking, given how he looked. I've seen rich people out Straussing that weren't dressed as fancy as he was."

"You're sure about that?" demanded the armorer as my mouth went dry. "You're sure he was a civilized Folk Mage?"

Steel made a tiny little motion of his head that could have been a nod. "Mind, none of us have seen many Folk Mages, but this one would have stood out in any crowd."

"Is this important?" Jessie demanded sharply.

"Yes," Kent told her, so she backed off.

"All purples and lavenders, hair most women would kill to have, fancy robes, pretty face...You'd think he was going to a party, or out of some fantasy vid, not walking around on a battlefield."

Kent thought about that. "That's...Something about that is familiar, but I can't put my finger on it."

I kept my mouth shut.

Kent shook his head. "Never mind. Go on, Steel."

Steel managed to crack his eyes a very little; I could see the glitter of them between his swollen lids. "Anyway, I figured he was going to monologue for a few minutes, then finish me off. But he didn't. In fact, he didn't say a damn thing. He just stood over me, but the fact that he was there kept all the other monsters off me."

There was a murmur of astonishment at that, and who could blame us? I was the only one that I'd ever heard of who'd had a nonfatal encounter with a Folk Mage.

"I tried saying something to him," Steel continued, "but he didn't answer. I didn't know what to think, and my head had been beaten on enough that I wasn't all that good at thinking anyway."

"And that's all he did?" Kent prodded.

Steel nodded again. "Eventually I just passed out, with him still standing over me, and when I woke up again, he was gone, the fighting was over, it was about noon, and it was all quiet. My Hounds were standing guard on me at that point."

"That would be after PsiCorps showed up and we beat them back," Kent told him. "I wouldn't call it 'winning,' but we're all right for now. Joy's got us something I'll explain when you're feeling better."

"I could barely think when I came to. My Perscom was trashed, my comm set was gone the second Ace hit me, and if it hadn't been for my Hounds, I never would have gotten the attention of the folks looking for survivors or human bodies. That's it. Now, Jess promised me the *good* drugs."

"And you'll get 'em, Mistuh Steel, now we got yer brain swellin' down." Jessie made shooing motions, and we moved away as she went and got one of the docs and towed him back to Steel's bed.

But I was thinking about that description; there was no way there could have been two identical Folk Mages like that on the battlefield. What Steel had been describing was *my* Mage. All right, so that Folk Mage had been, for whatever weird Folk reasons, trying to give me warnings. That was bizarre enough. But now there was *this*! Why had he protected Steel? Why had he helped both of us? Who in the history of the world since the Diseray had ever heard of one of the Folk helping us? I had more questions, and no answers at all.

But my questions had to be put aside for the moment. We needed to tell the rest about our new power sources—and, as it turned out, Kent wanted *me* to be the one to tell them.

Kent sent out orders for the Hunters all to gather in the only room big enough to hold them all at once: the chopper hangar. I hadn't even known HQ *had* a hangar, although it should have been obvious that we did, in retrospect. Our pilots weren't army, and neither were our helichoppers, and they had to be kept somewhere near HQ when they weren't in use.

"Why *me*?" I asked, extremely uncomfortable with being put in this position. "I'm not—"

"You're Elite," Kent replied, giving me a stern look. "If Elite were allowed to trend, you'd still be trending and in the top spot. You're Elite Joyeaux, with the pack of eleven. Half the younger set have you as wallpaper on their vid-screens."

Wait—what? I wanted to say.

But . . .

I already knew people idolized me. And if any of the other

Hunters had thought I was getting a swelled head, that idea got killed dead when I went for Elite, because if I'd been a glory-hound like Ace, that was the last thing I would have done.

Right now they'd listen to me. And since I had done things with Hounds no one else had, they'd believe me, which was the important part. Archer had said it: what was important in magic was not so much what you thought, but what you *believed*.

"And you have the Elite to organize," I said, more thinking aloud than anything else.

"Not just the Elite. I'm going to have to go pretend-humble to PsiCorps as our rep. That's going to take a lot of time, about three times more than I want it to, and about six times more than I can stomach." His mouth twisted up in distaste, and I could scarcely blame him. "So what are *you* going to tell the Hunters?"

"I'm going to tell them something true that they desperately want and need to hear—that Hunters are going to be able to stop the Othersiders, and I know how," I said. "Then have them bring their alphas over and ask them. That'll clinch it."

He nodded. "Good. And the next time you need to tell them something, they'll listen to you because you were correct *now*." Once again, he gave me that look that reminded me of the Masters when they told me it was time to try something new and harder. "Like it or not, you're about to become a leader. You lead a pack of eleven, and they listen to you. This is the next step. No argument. Go."

And he literally pushed me out the door of the armory. Bya followed. When I looked down at my Hound, he was . . . grinning. Grinning like this was something he'd expected all along.

"Shut up, you," I said. Because I hate attention, and I hate fuss, and all this *leader* business was nothing but attention and fuss. But if Kent was right, and he rarely was wrong, at least I was the right person to stand up in front of the ranking Hunters right now and give them some good news after all the bad. I'd worry about the rest of it—Kent trying to make me into some sort of permanent leader—later.

The hangar was empty—they'd moved all the choppers outside. It was a big, plain room with huge metal doors at one end, a 'crete floor, and 'crete walls, all painted a sort of beige. There were bulletin boards and posters and suchlike on the walls, and equipment and tool racks shoved out of the way. Sounds echoed off the 'crete floor and walls. The Hunters—like the Elite, all of them more or less injured—milled in a group, some looking hopeful, most looking desperate. The air of *doom* hung over everything, and I got the feeling that they had all expected this meeting was because someone was going to tell them that the next time the Othersiders showed up, we needed to have an evacuation plan in place because we were going to need it. Before I could say anything, Dazzle (oh, how relieved I was to see *her*!) spotted me.

"Joy!" she squealed, which got everyone looking in my direction. I cleared my throat, and just as I did that, a cam-drone zoomed over to me, and suddenly the sound of me clearing my throat came at me from speakers all over the hangar. I winced a little, then straightened my spine, telling myself that *I* didn't matter, but what I had to say did.

"I'm Hunter Elite Joyeaux," I said formally. "Senior Elite Armorer Kent gathered you here because I've got some important stuff to tell you." I paused. "But the most important thing you need to know is this: Something happened out there, which is what I am going to tell you about. And because of that, now we know how to win."

It went a lot faster this time; not only was there no initial skepticism, but Kent had been right. Just because of what I was, and my reputation, deserved or not, the rankers were willing to believe me from the get-go. Then, as Hunter after Hunter called up alphas and got confirmation, things got positively euphoric.

"Don't get cocky!" I shouted, forgetting that the cam-drone was taking my voice and amplifying it. *"DON'T GET COCKY!"* boomed out of all the speakers, and we all covered our ears in reaction. But at least it put a damper on things a bit. "We're not out of the woods yet," I warned. "We can only win this if we fight *smart.* Senior Elite Kent and a team are putting together strategy. The good news is that as far as anyone can tell, the Othersiders use exactly zero strategy. Anyway, the first op is for everybody to get as rested and healed as you can, and the second, if we're given that long before the next attack, is for all of you to practice your spell-casting and get it accurate. I don't need to tell you what a cluster things are going to turn into if your spells are both overclocked and inaccurate."

I got nods for that. Good. "Right, then. Get fed and rested, and practice, and anything new in the way of orders will come in on your Perscoms," I said. "Good Hunting."

Since I couldn't think of anything more to say, and I didn't want to get buttonholed for zillions of questions when my stomach was telling me that meal-drinks were not going to cut it, I got out of there and headed for food.

Eat, Bya ordered. *Everything else can wait.*

I got food out of that little kitchen the Elite used because the mess hall was mobbed. So was the kitchen but not so badly that I couldn't just grab a tray, fill it with stuff grabbed randomly, and take it to my room. Bya sprawled next to me on the bed. While I gulped down food without really tasting it, I was scrolling through all the permanent cams on all the pylons of the Prime Barrier. I didn't think the Othersiders would try for the same pylon twice, though I was fairly certain that they *would* try what they'd failed at the last time. It was just too logical; to get into Apex proper, they had to attempt to take down a pylon, and with it, a section of the Barrier. Given all the stepped-up patrols I saw as I paged through cam-screens, I was by far and away not the only person who had thought of that either. Which was comforting because it meant there were lots of people putting their brains to work on this, and I not only didn't *have* to try and think of everything, I'd probably already done my share.

I was too restless to sleep, even though I still felt as if I could sleep for a week, so when I finished eating, Bya and I went to the one place in the entire building that I was pretty certain no one else would go to. I wanted to get away from everyone else, what with most of HQ looking like an anthill someone had just stuck a stick into. The quietest spot would likely be the atrium garden and the koi pond.

My head felt . . . not achy, but overfull. Too much had happened in too short a time. I just needed to go somewhere that wasn't my room, where I could pace or sit or whatever and not have people around me, because I didn't want to rehash everything I'd told people a million more times. It's human nature to ask the same questions over and over; we're wired to repeat things so we get them right. But since that cam had been there while I told people everything we had figured out, I knew for a fact every muscle twitch and word had been recorded. That meant if people *really* wanted to listen to what I said over and over again, they could refer to the recording and not keep barraging me with questions.

But when Bya and I got to the garden, I discovered I had been mistaken about finding it empty. There was someone there already. And as I entered, the tall, white-clad figure straightened.

"Oh—" I said uncertainly. "I didn't mean to disturb you, Mark."

"You didn't," Knight replied, standing up. "I figured you'd be here sooner or later. I've been waiting on you." He looked down at my alpha. "Hello, Bya. Glad you're keeping an eye on Joy."

"You've been waiting for me?" I shifted my weight from my right to my left foot, taken off guard. "Uh—I—" What on earth did he want? Surely he knew better than to ask me to rehash everything . . . unless, maybe he wanted Bya to interpret for his Hounds?

"I just wanted to tell you, I'd made up my mind about leaving," he said, standing over me. "Looming" was what I would have said, except it wasn't intimidating. Just . . . he was awfully tall.

"This is—" *This isn't exactly a good time,* I was thinking, and was planning on saying. Why now? Was he here to tell me he wanted me to put that word in with the Masters? Unless he wanted to get himself and Jessie out before the next attack. I could see that. The Mountain would be a lot safer than here, and she was probably babbling with terror at this point.

"I'm not," he continued, interrupting me and short-circuiting my thoughts and what I was about to reply. "Leaving, that is. It's pretty obvious this is the worst possible time even to consider it, but even if that wasn't the case, well . . ." He paused, and then said, "Jess, you might's well come out and say your own piece."

From the back of the garden, Jessie came out of the shadows; I hadn't seen her because she was wearing a dark tunic and pants. "You go first, hon," she said, sidling up to him and taking his arm, with a little bit of a defiant glance, maybe a touch of jealousy in it still. Or maybe it was just warning that she wasn't going to stand around and let some heathen hussy grab her man. Okay, I could live with that.

Mark shrugged. "I'm a Hunter, and that's a risky job and it isn't gonna change. Jessie needs to understand that, needs to get her head wrapped around the fact that I am always going to be in danger, one way or another."

Jessie shivered a little, but nodded. "It's . . . I cain't say I like it here. There ain't anyone to talk to like I do back home, an' till I got talkin' with that Mistuh Severn, an' he found out that while Mark was gone I turned into Doc Bellow's assistant, I didn't have anythin' t'do. At least now I got somethin' other than bein' *Pa's girl* or *Mark's wife.*"

Mark chuckled. "She won't brag on herself, but I will. They tell me she's a crackerjack nurse, and if she's willing, they'll put her in field-medic training."

She shivered again. But she didn't say no. *Huh. Hope for her yet.*

Mark half turned toward her. "Now look here, Jess. You got to figure out that just because I have a friend that's a gal, it doesn't mean that friend is anything more than a friend."

Jessie nodded dubiously.

I decided to ham things up a little. "Sorry, Mark. You're a nice guy but—forgive me. Yuck. I'd rather date Bya."

That surprised a snort and choking laughter out of Mark. Jessie looked at both of us as if we were crazy. "Bya's her alpha Hound," Mark explained. And then she just looked at *me* as if I was crazy, which was an improvement from looking at me as if I was the enemy.

There was an awful lot more I could have said and, actually, wanted to say, but it would have been insulting to their religion. It sounded like he'd already come to the conclusion that some of his peoples' religious customs were things that needed changing all by himself, anyway, and he could very likely bring Jessie around to his way of thinking.

I dug up a smile from somewhere. "Mark, I'm glad to hear that you aren't leaving. But, Jessie . . . the Mountain might be safer for you, and I sure wouldn't blame anyone who wanted to get out of Apex right now—"

"That may be so," she said stoutly. "But my place's here, now."

"I am not going to argue with a decision that gets us another nurse," I replied. "Just . . . Jessie, the option's open. You can always come back when it's safer."

"Not unless Mark goes too," she replied.

Mark didn't exactly *beam*, but he looked a lot happier than he had the last time we talked about this. "I reckon that's all that needs be said. Now I'm gonna get some shut-eye, while I still can. I got the feeling the Othersiders aren't gonna let us get much breathing room."

"I get the feeling you're right," I replied. He and Jessie edged past me, and he patted my shoulder in passing. "'Night, Mark."

"'Night, Joy," he replied, and disappeared into the hallway. For a big guy, he sure could move quietly. All I heard were Jessie's footsteps.

I got some food for the fish and fed them, listening to the trickle of the water, slowly breathing in the damp air full of the scent of earth and green things. The soft dark was as soothing to my eyes as the gentle sound of the water was to my ears.

For a moment, I totally sympathized with Jessie. People I knew were *dead*, and while that wasn't a new thing for me, it never eased the hit when it happened. I let that part hit me and had a bit of a cry for Retro. I longed for the option to just run away from all this, run far, back home, back to the Monastery. Because, sure, we'd just come up with a way to even the odds against us in what had gone from simple defense to a repeat of the Diseray, but that didn't mean we'd win. It didn't mean we'd come out slightly ahead or even achieve a draw. And even if we *did* win this time . . . there would be a next time. How many more "next times" would there be?

Kent was right. Something had changed.

Now we were at war.

18

"THAT'S . . . ODD." I LOOKED UP at the sound of Kent's voice, to see what he was looking at. I was in the armory, which, for the past three days, was where I *always* was if I wasn't eating or sleeping. Practicing, mostly—not with the Hounds but just to make sure that my targeting was at the peak of perfection and I could get off my spells without needing to think, automatically and without hesitation. Every tiny bit of magical energy we used had to count, so I was practicing everything I knew to make sure it was going to hit what I needed it to hit and do what I needed it to do. The only break had been when we'd hung the pictures on the wall of the bar and toasted the dead and I'd gone to my room to have another, longer, more heartfelt cry. Seeing Retro's grinning face in that picture had hit me in ways I hadn't anticipated.

The others had their own way of dealing with the waiting; I felt better if I was practicing. For me, doing something was better than pretending everything was fine or trying to lose myself in a vid or a game, or . . . well, whatever else people were doing in the privacy of their rooms. No one got drunk, though, or left HQ, because we all knew that when the call came, we couldn't afford to waste minutes getting to the attack site. Whatever else we were, we were still Hunters. I heard that the army had dug up a couple of their Healing Mages to work on Steel, which was a good thing, if true. They could compress a couple weeks of healing into a couple days.

Did the Cits realize the danger they were in? Since I hadn't watched any of the vid channels, I didn't know. *Some* people certainly did; high-ranking officials, surely, and I was pretty sure they had sent their families out on fast trains, maybe had gone themselves. Premier Rayne had left the Premier's Mansion. Officially, he was vacationing, but we all knew that he'd deserted the City, and there was unvoiced contempt for his cowardice.

Not Uncle, though. *"I'm not leaving while there's a single Cit or building left to defend,"* he'd said in a little speech he'd made in the hangar for all of us. I didn't even bother to argue with him; truth to tell, that pronouncement had won over a lot of Hunters, who up until then had just taken him for another bureaucrat.

I'd been cleaning the weapons I'd been using at my last practice session when Kent had spoken out loud. So now I looked up to see what had caught the armorer's attention. "That's . . . very odd." He was looking at the vid-screen, which had been tuned to the weather radar. I felt my eyes widen. Because what was on there was not "odd"; it was right off the scale for "shouldn't be there." A storm was heading for us, moving stupidly fast, arrowhead shaped, and increasing in size with every passing second. A storm that had not been there ten minutes ago.

And I knew what that was. I'd heard about this from the Masters back home.

"Kent! That's the attack!" I said urgently, pointing at the storm. "*They've brought in Thunderbirds!* They're coming in under the cover of the storm, and they're going to use Thunderbirds to short out a pylon!"

Kent cursed and slammed his hand down on the alert button he now wore strapped to his wrist beside his Perscom. I went over the counter into the armory proper and began grabbing my chosen weapons and ammo, too impatient to wait for the assistants. When I had what I needed, I rolled back over the counter and grabbed a headset from the wall, sprinted out the door, and made for the landing pad. All the choppers were being kept out there, to minimize delays in deploying—including a couple old models we didn't use much anymore. I dove into one of those older choppers at the same time the pilot reached it, throwing myself into the seat farthest from the door and strapping down even as the motor whined and the blades over my head started to move. This was an oddball ten-seater with no door gunner, so that would be the size of our team. The minute my butt hit the seat, I was registered on that chopper and no other; the same would go for everyone else piling in. *One-Nine-Alpha.*

The first Hunter bar me threw himself into the chopper and strapped down next to me. I didn't know him, but I did know the next two, Tobor and Trev. And the next three, Cielle, Hammer, and Steel; Steel had lightweight casts on his leg and arm, but otherwise he looked about a hundred times better than the last time I'd seen him. Then came three more I didn't know, and the chopper lifted off, angling sharply into the east. I concentrated on the orders that the armorer was rattling off, assigning leaders to teams depending on who had piled into a particular chopper together. Finally he got to us. *"Chopper One-Niner-Alpha. I see your crew as Hammer, Steel, Cielle, Tobor, Trev, Denali, Trooper, Hudson, Souxie, and Joy."*

"I've seen Thunderbirds, sir. I can go lead on this." I almost didn't believe the words I was saying, but...it was true. No one else on that chopper had the experience I did.

"Roger that, confirming team lead and assignment on the Thunderbirds; Joy's right, she's seen them before and should be the one dealing with them. I want to be having drumsticks and wings for dinner when this is over. Do you copy?"

"Roger, Armorer. Copy," I said, my throat tight. Hammer gave me a thumbs-up, and Steel a wink.

"Brief your team, Elite Joy." Then Kent was on to the next chopper. All eyes were on me. I took a shuddering breath and held up three fingers, then two, to signify what channel we'd be on. I was pretty sure no one had grabbed thirty-two yet, and when we all tuned in to it, it showed green. I locked it to our team.

I remembered what I'd seen—but mostly, I remembered Uncle's story. "Thunderbirds are about the size of a fighter jet," I said. "According to everything I know, they're generating the storm. Their weapon is electrical in nature, pretty much identical to lightning. They come down slowly, in a descending spiral, with their wings spread. And as they come, lightning will strike from out of their eyes and their mouths. I'm pretty sure that they are the ones that are going to be going for a pylon. The Othersiders tried brute force last time, and it didn't work; what they'll probably aim to do is short out the innards of the pylon rather than taking it down."

"*Plus this time their offense will be in the air, less vulnerable to attack,*" Tobor pointed out. I nodded.

"So who has offensive distance spells besides me?" I asked. "Once the storm hits, the choppers won't be able to stay in the air, so it's all going to be us and anything the army or Psimons can bring to back us up. Sound off clockwise, starting with Tobor."

My team began calling out what they were bringing to the party. Everyone but Hammer and Steel had *something* that worked at a distance. Cielle had something like a fire bolt, but ice instead of fire. And that gave me an idea.

"All right, this is the basic strat," I said. "Hammer and Steel, you'll shield us, same as last time. I'll need you to drop the shield three times so we can cut down some ranks and generate manna for the Hounds. Once the Hounds are ready to feed us, you keep that shield up, and Tobor, Trev, and Denali, you concentrate fire on the ranks around us to keep that manna coming. The rest of us will work on the Thunderbirds. You guys on the birds, hit them as hard as you can. I'm going to work with Cielle to try and ice their wings and tails."

Cielle got it first. I could see from the sudden widening of her eyes. "*Oh! You're going to try and bring them down! Like an airplane in an ice storm!*"

"Exactly," I replied. "Once we get one down and finished, hold your fire. I'm going to try something else. It worked once for my people. It might work again, and if it does, the Othersiders are going to lose the cover of the storm *and* their Thunderbirds."

"*And if it doesn't?*" asked Steel.

"Then we go back to the original strat," I told them. "Using Thunderbirds was a good idea. The storm they generate is going to limit our backup to ground support. The Psimons might not be able to get a lock on their heads. And they're pure murder in the air. But their fundamental weakness is that if you bring them down, they're helpless."

"Let's bring 'em down, then," said Hudson, with a feral grin. *"You heard the boss. He wants drumsticks and wings."*

I'd never heard from *anyone* that Thunderbirds had Shields of any sort, and why should they? Normally they flew out of the range of most weapons, conventional or magical. The thing about lightning as a weapon was that once you got it started toward your target, the target itself, especially if it was metal, like the pylons, would generate a current that would "reach" for the bolt and connect the circuit for you. Obviously the pylons were built to withstand a few lightning strikes. But this wouldn't be a "few" lightning strikes. This would be a barrage of lightning calculated to melt the lightning rods that protected them, overwhelm surge protectors, and fuse every component in the pylon. And the Thunderbirds would just circle the pylon, plastering it with lightning until eventually it failed, using the rain to cover their movements and staying high enough that they'd be harder to hit.

We just had to make sure that didn't happen.

The chopper bucked and yawed, and we all clutched at our seats and safety harnesses; that would be us hitting the winds generated by the storm. I just hoped that we could all get over the Barrier and in place before the *real* storm hit, because trying to channel our teams through one or two doors in the bases of pylons would be fatal.

Just as I thought that, the chopper pitched over sideways and began a rapid descent. When it stopped moving, we popped the buckles on our harnesses and piled out into what looked like acres and acres of grazing field or maybe hay. It was all long grass, anyway. The chopper fled, and I didn't blame the pilot at all because the tempest that was speeding toward us was seven kinds of ugly.

It wasn't as big or as bad as the storm that had locked everyone in Apex inside their buildings for three days, but it was bad enough. I didn't know enough to know whether the Thunderbirds had caused that first storm, but now that I knew they were in the picture, I would be willing to bet they'd steered it away from its natural course and straight for the city. The attack on Bensonville hadn't been timed that way because the Othersiders had been hungry; it had been timed that way because it had followed the first blow of the new offensive, meant to soften us up. We just hadn't known that.

Black clouds raced toward us, covering most of the eastern horizon with a phalanx of black dots in the front, riding on the wind. There was lightning, but it was minimal. The Thunderbirds wouldn't want to waste a single electron that could go toward breaking the pylon. "Stay down," I cautioned. The pilot had set us down near the base of the pylon they seemed to be making for, but I didn't want the Thunderbirds to spot us and change their target. *At least Steel isn't going to have to move on that leg.* "Get your Hounds here, but stay low—"

"I've got something for that," Souxie said with a feral grin. "Let's get the doggies here, and you'll see."

We overlapped Glyphs; experimentation had proved that we could do that to minimize the amount of space we took up, and Hounds could come through just fine. In moments, the area around us was full of Hounds. "Put up those Shields, boys," said Souxie, screwing up her face and beginning to trace Glyphs in the air with both hands. "We're about to give them a surprise."

She finished with a showy handclap . . . and I didn't see anything. But then I did a check on our position with one of the cams on the pylon, and even though I zoomed in on us, there was *nothing* where we were supposed to be. "Nice trick!" I said with admiration.

Souxie shrugged but looked pleased. "Light bending, instead of illusion. That way it fools everything, from monsters that can see through illusion to cams. If you look really hard, you can tell there's something here, but I figure the big chickens aren't going to be looking all that hard when there's so much else to worry about." Souxie was right about the "so much else" part, for sure; the chopper pilots were coming in hot all around us and dropping their teams, concentrating on the three likeliest pylons to be attacked. "Kent, tell the pilots to back off my pylon a little, but not too much," I said into the comm on Kent's frequency. "If they back off too much, it'll look like a trap. I just want it to look attractively weak."

"*Roger that,*" the armorer replied.

Now the winds before the storm came in at ground level; we hunkered down as we were buffeted by heavy, cold gusts and blasted with kicked-up dirt and debris. "Goggles," I said as I pulled mine out. "It's gonna be raining pitchforks in a few minutes." The rain line was visible now, in fact, as a silvery curtain that reached from the cloud base to the ground, obscuring everything behind it.

"*All Hunter teams on the ground,*" Kent said on the common frequency. "*Army moving in, pincher formation, but you'll have to hold your own until they get here.*"

"*Psimons?*" someone asked hesitantly. Kent's only reply was a snort.

Now it was possible to make out that the shapes riding the storm front were ebony birds, birds easily the size of a small jet, riding the winds like a hawk or a vulture rides an updraft, wings scarcely moving except at the tips. But they were nothing at all like a hawk; they had long forked tails, long necks, and their wings were long and pointed, like a swallow's, not blunt like an eagle or a hawk's. They did have raptors' beaks, but the thing that put chills up my spine were their eyes, eyes that glowed brilliant red. In a way, they were beautiful—but I remembered the other stories about them, how they snatched up humans and carried them off to eat, decimating entire small villages. And most of all I remembered how they had attacked *my* people and would have destroyed them, and I hardened my heart.

They were definitely making for the pylon we crouched beneath, and Bya and Myrrdhin trembled under my hands with tension.

Just before they got in range to start pasting the pylon, they swooped down, neatly skimming the earth, and little dark figures leapt off their backs at the bottom of their arc. Moments later, Portals opened up all over the place as the Thunderbirds rowed their wings to gain the altitude they'd lost and get into formation to make *their* attack.

"They dropped off Folk Mages to open Portals. Hold steady," I murmured into my mic. Hordes of monsters were pouring out of Portals and engaging with the other teams. Some were converging on our pylon, unopposed for the moment. "Remember, we're not supposed to be here." It was hard to crouch in place as the sounds of battle erupted all over the field; I could feel my Hounds burning to get out and attack. But we needed them nearer, near enough that our Hounds could absorb their manna.

Without the need to fight their way to the base of our pylon, the troops of Othersiders coming our way were trotting along with grins on their faces. I was extremely happy to see that most of them were creatures that were vulnerable to plain old bullets. Goblins, Kobolds, Redcaps, a gaggle of Hags. What Shields they had were rudimentary and wouldn't stand up to much physical punishment. It looked to me as if they had been told to set up a little distance away from the pylon and defend the Thunderbirds from attack from the ground. The really heavy rain hadn't reached us yet, but it was bad enough, coming at us slantwise, hitting the Shields and sliding down them in sheets, deforming our view.

I waited until the monsters were so close that it was a dead certainty that every bullet and shotgun pellet we fired would hit something. *"Now!"* I ordered, and Souxie dropped the camouflaging spell, and the rest of us let loose with blasts of magic intended to shatter their Shields. The Othersiders were caught so completely by surprise that they froze for a moment, mouths agape. Their Shields broke like so much glass, leaving them vulnerable.

"Shields down in three, two, one!" called Steel, repeating the tactic that had worked so well the last time. And while the Othersider Shields were still down, we unloaded with everything we had, as the rain, no longer kept away by the Shields, pounded down on us, plastering our hair to our heads in seconds.

The front ranks and part of the second were mowed down like so much hay. The Hounds leapt out of the circle of protection to finish off any creature that had survived the volley and to take down a few uninjured ones just for good measure. Then they raced back in among us, and Hammer and Steel put up their Shields, giving us shelter from everything the Othersiders could throw at us. And from the rain.

Three times we repeated this because the response by Othersiders to being attacked was to charge in a rage. We could have been synced up like a bunch of Psimons, our coordination was so perfect—first, a magic blast to take down the Othersider Shields, followed by a hail of bullets and iron shot. I was keeping an eye overhead, just in case the Thunderbirds decided to take a hand, but they were circling high above the pylon, black against the charcoal of the clouds, occasionally discharging lightning into the top of it. So far, they hadn't even melted the lightning rod on the top—but it didn't look to me as if they'd ramped up to full power yet, and I knew it was only a matter of time before they did. And when they did, they would melt through or short out all the pylon's protections. And then one good concentrated burst of lightning from all of them together would take down the pylon and with it, two sections of the Barrier.

Just wait, I kept telling myself. *Wait. Wait until the Hounds are sated. It can't be long now.* And then, as the third wave of Othersiders fell, I felt it—the rush of magical energy into me from my Hounds.

I was not expecting this. And I don't think anyone else was either.

It was as if I had been asleep and suddenly came completely awake; my vision sharpened to a point that I can't even describe, every sound struck my ear as separate, clear and completely distinguishable, and every nerve ending on my body politely informed my brain of what it was feeling. I was immersed in sensation, but not overwhelmed by it. And as for my brain—I was thinking at light speed, processing all that information as quickly and coolly as a computer, and I was aware of *everything*, but especially of magic. Sensing magic wasn't something I had to concentrate on now; it just happened and came more easily than breathing. Last of all, I had the uncanny impression, not that my perceptions and reactions had sped up, but that the entire world had slowed to a crawl.

I glanced up and immediately identified the lowest-flying Thunderbird, and I almost laughed at the unsuspecting monster, circling slowly, building up both electricity and magic from the clouds and the storm. Fatigue was gone. Sheeting icy rain meant nothing. I activated the ice spell with a mere flick of my fingers. The spell lanced up into the sky, struck, and stuck. In moments, it had pulled rain out of the sky onto the monster's wing and tail feathers, then sucked all the warmth out of the air around it. And since that heat had to go somewhere, as a nice little side effect, I brought the heat down to us, creating a cozy pocket around us. My team and I stopped shivering, even though we were still being pounded by the storm.

The Thunderbird noticed what I was doing immediately, of course; it broke off its attack on the pylon and frantically pumped its wings for altitude, trying to get out of my reach. But more and more magic came pouring into me, and the bird would have had to get above the clouds and out of my sight before it would have been able to do that, and I felt Cielle's spell working with mine, her ice bolts layering on top of what my spell had laid down. It couldn't shake itself to break off the ice; birds can't shake unless they're perched. It could flap hard enough to clear its wings—but not its tail. That long forked tail that worked so well as a kind of anchor to allow it to turn quickly now worked against it as more and more ice built up on the feathers. Layer by layer, I added the ice; the bird's wing beats became more labored as it tried to overcome the added weight. And Cielle turned her attention to icing the wings while I concentrated on the bird's tail and back.

Then it wasn't gaining height; it was *losing* it. It wasn't thinking now; in the battle to stay aloft, its world had narrowed to the fight to escape the pull of gravity. Desperation overcame it, and all it could do was call out frantically to its fellow Thunderbirds as it fell, slowly, to earth.

In the last few yards, it gave up the fight altogether—or maybe it just ran out of strength. It crashed to the ground with a piercing cry of mingled fear and despair.

"Don't shoot it!" I yelled into my mic as Dusana and Hevajra *bamphed* to its shoulders, pinning its wings to the earth without breaking any of the delicate wing bones. *"Cover us!"* I added as I sprinted to the front of the fallen creature. Like most birds, now that it was pinned breast-down on the ground, it couldn't raise its head very far and certainly couldn't strike at me. The deadly talons were extended beneath and behind it, and it couldn't lever itself up enough to stand and rake me with them.

The rain poured down on both of us as we took the measure of each other.

"What are you doing, Joy?" Kent shouted in my ears.

I didn't answer. He'd put this in my hands. I hoped he'd continue to trust that I knew what I was doing.

I hoped I knew what I was doing. Now that I was here, in front of the thing, I was galvanized by something that was not quite fear but was not far from it.

I stared into its eyes—still red, but no longer glowing. I've never had much to do with birds. That was Master Pepperberg's specialty. I didn't think I was misreading what I saw there, though; behind the flattened feathers and staring eyes, it was terrified of me. *Good.* I wanted it terrified. This would only work if it was afraid of me, and the original plan of picking the Thunderbirds off one at a time while more mobs of monsters attacked us was not an optimal strategy.

"What I have done to you, I can do to every one of your flock," I said. The eyes flared fiery red for a moment, and then the light subsided again, leaving only the fear. "And you know that. You know what we can do. But I think you have been misled, and I am willing to allow you to correct that mistake." Now I bowed a little to it, remembering what Master Hon Li had done so long ago. "Of a courtesy, I think that you should abandon your allies, who did not warn you of this, and leave us in peace."

This was what I was gambling on; after that encounter my uncle had described, the Mountain had never again been troubled by Thunderbirds. That made me think they might be very different from the Othersiders we usually fought. That they could be something we could negotiate with.

The circle of my reality narrowed to the Thunderbird and myself. I stared into those glowing, alien eyes and tried to project confidence, even though I was probably as terrified as the Thunderbird was. The bird's eyes blazed. Finally, the great hooked beak opened, and a strange metallic voice emerged from it.

"What surety do you give us that you will not pursue us?" it said in perfectly good English. I nearly jumped, I was so startled. But I managed to cover my surprise by turning that into a shrug. *Does it understand a shrug? Never mind. . . .*

Overhead, the other Thunderbirds circled, their attack on the pylon aborted as they stared down at us. This was what I had hoped for—that the Thunderbirds would remember or had heard of the encounter with Master Hon Li and be willing to listen. They'd shown they could be talked out of attacking once, so why not a second time?

"The surety that we have more than enough to deal with without pursuing you," I replied, forcing a laugh. "Your allies have done you no favors; they lured you here with promises they could not keep, and they lied to you about our strength. Escape with your lives, and stop your ears to them in the future." Bya came up beside me, and we put a double Shield over ourselves. *Get off his wings,* I told Dusana and Hevajra, taking the chance that even if the Thunderbird struck at me, the Shield would deflect it and the rest of my team would cut it down with their weapons before it could get in a second attack.

The two Hounds *bamphed* off it. Then the rest of them gathered up beside me, still feeding me magic, and the huge bird got clumsily to its feet and gave itself a tremendous shake, finally breaking the ice on its tail and sending shards everywhere. Now that it was free, it was threatening enough to bring my heart up into my mouth. It was taller than Dusana and loomed over us all, staring down at us with its neck curved so it could stare at us directly, strange and indecipherable thoughts passing behind its eyes.

It looked from me, to its fellows, and back again. Was it talking to them? It looked as if it was.

Then it spoke for the last time. *"I do not understand why you would do this, but we say yes,"* it replied shortly. It raised its head skyward and uttered a deafening, piercing cry. The others answered it, and it spread its wings. Warned by that, the Hounds and I scrambled backward, and it shoved itself up into the air with powerful thrusts of its legs and wings. We were buffeted by the blast from those wing beats, nearly knocked off our feet, in fact. Or at least, I was. I had to hang on to Dusana and Shinje to keep my footing.

It gained height rapidly now that it was no longer weighed down by the ice. When it reached the same altitude as the rest of the Thunderbirds, they circled the pylon three times before shooting up into the clouds, heading westward, and abandoning their attack.

An unnatural silence fell on this part of the battlefield; for a moment, the rain slackened off, and I turned to see that the rest of the monsters that had been attacking us were staring, dumbfounded, at their retreating allies. Before they could break out of their shock, I pulled my rifle around from my back and stitched their front line with bullets. A second or so later, so did the rest of my team. My Hounds and I sprinted back to the group, and Hammer and Steel raised their Shields again. The rest of my team cheered, while they continued to hammer at the Shields of the latest lot of monsters.

I became aware of someone sputtering at me on the comm.

It was the armorer.

"What in—Joy!—how did you—what—"

"Elite Joyeaux here, Armorer," I said between levin bolts.

"What did you just do?" He finally managed something like coherent speech.

"I convinced them to go away," I replied. "Can you send us some help? I don't think the rest of the Othersiders appreciate my negotiation skills."

Kent's response was definitely colorful, mostly unprintable, and in the affirmative. Which was good, because now we were really getting hammered.

With this pylon no longer in immediate danger, Kent's plan was to work all of us toward the Barrier. Eventually, we formed a ragged line with the pylon at our rear center and the Barrier at our backs. That took us out of the army's line of fire, in theory at least.

In practice, not so much; shells fell and rockets exploded much too close to our line for comfort.

The Thunderbirds had not taken the storm with them either. The last encounter at the Barrier had been in the pitch dark of predawn; this one was in a tempest.

The skies opened up. If we had been getting pounded before, now it felt as if we were standing under a waterfall. Once the Thunderbirds were gone, nothing was exercising any control over this storm. Lightning arced across the sky, and the barrage of thunder was indistinguishable from the artillery barrage.

The Hounds continued to pour magical energy into us, and we continued to work just short of miracles, but it takes physical strength and endurance to use magical energies. That strength and endurance are the same resources anyone uses to run marathons, chop wood, or lift weights. Eventually, they run out, and no amount of magic will replace them.

And to make matters worse, what had been a hayfield was now a muddy morass, only getting deeper and stickier with every passing moment. We were mired up to our knees in water over thick, sucking mud. Just moving took herculean effort, and we were moving *and* fighting.

We were starting to flag. PsiCorps was nowhere to be seen. Although, to be fair, by the time *they* would have gotten into choppers, the rain was coming down so hard I'm not sure choppers could have flown in it.

The only thing we had going for us was that the Othersiders were just as handicapped by the muck and mud as we were. More, some of them. The *Nagas* were not doing well; you'd have thought that snakes would have no problem slithering through mud, but their weight played against them. If they went erect, and they had to in order to fight, they were getting just as stuck as anything with two legs. Only the giant monsters were unaffected; to them, the mud was barely halfway to their ankles, and for the Gogs and Magogs, it barely covered their insteps.

I wasn't bothering to move, and when my Hounds did, they *bamphed* instead of trying to wade through the mud. Fire bolts were all but useless; they fizzled out halfway to the target. The good news: because their own forces were slogging just as much as we were and stood between them and the pylons, the Gogs and Magogs couldn't get close enough to the pylons to attack them without squashing their own allies. And that was about the only good news that there was.

You couldn't see more than twenty or thirty feet, but that was more than enough, when that twenty or thirty feet was full of things that wanted to kill you.

I wasn't just wet; I was sodden. I was stuck, and where I was standing, the water and mud were just over my calves. Every muscle ached, and there was a metallic taste of fatigue in my mouth.

Can they just keep throwing cannon fodder at us until they wear us down?

"Huddle up and form layered Shields!" Kent suddenly ordered. *"Artillery incoming! Right flank launching Hellfires."*

I looked in Hammer's direction; most of my team was with him, but the Hounds and I had gotten too far away.

"Joy!" Steel shouted. *"You—"*

"Don't worry!" I called back. "Not my first Hellfire rodeo!" And at the same time, I was calling all my Hounds in. Hold and Strike, who couldn't *bamph,* had never left my side, but the rest started popping up next to me like gophers.

Just in time. *"Hellfires in five, four—"*

Shields up! I told them all, and put up my own.

"—three, two—"

We were covered in a lovely, multicolored dome, which had the added relief of keeping off the rain, at least for a moment.

"—one!"

The middle distance, beyond the curtain of rain and the waterfall effect of the downpour streaming down the Shields, bloomed with red and yellow. The concussive force that followed a fraction of a second later actually made the Shields bow in toward us, and I felt it in my gut as magic got sucked away from me to compensate.

Then came a wave of welcome heat.

"Hellfires, incoming, left flank in five, four, three—"

The left flank of the army support must have been farther away than I'd thought—I hadn't had a second to look at a battle map on my Perscom—because this blast was a bit more distant, though it had almost the same impact on us.

The effect on the monsters around us depended on the monsters themselves. Some, with little or no protection against the concussive blast, were knocked unconscious. Sadly, there were not as many of those as I would have liked. The rest were shocked, at least, and that gave most of us a little breathing room.

Most of us.

But not me. Because striding through the morass straight toward me, walking *on top* of the water, with the rain sheeting over their Shields...

... were Ace and his pet Folk Mage.

29

"HAMMER!" I SHOUTED ON our team freq. "I've got company.
Ace and his buddy. Take over the team." Before he could reply, I
switched to the general freq. "Kent, Hammer is now lead," I said,
and transferred all my attention to Ace.

Behind him, that feral Mage just stood there, knees flexed,
eyes unfocused. Ace must have heard what I said; he wasn't that
far away from me, and I don't think even all the battlefield noise or
the roar of the rain drowned my shout out. He glared at me, then
opened his mouth. . . .

I had the sudden and absolute conviction that he was about
to do something that would give him more than an edge; it would
give him the win without even trying for it. Like calling in some
big favor from the Folk—more than just getting his Folk Mage
battery. Or if not that—what if he'd been given the spells to calling up Portals? He could bring a *flood* of Othersiders, right here

to the base of the pylon, and with his help, they could get inside it and destroy it from within.

So before he could get a single syllable out, I let him have it. Powered to the teeth by all that magic my Hounds were pouring into me, I delivered a tremendous hammerblow right on the top of his Shields.

It didn't break his Shields, but it bowed them the way the distant blast of the Hellfires had bowed mine, and more to the point, the blow shook him physically, actually made him stagger for a split second and enraged him that I'd gotten a salvo off first.

That was what I wanted: to get his attention centered on *me* and make him forget what he'd been sent to do.

And that worked. The Folk Mage put a hand on his shoulder, and Ace shook it off—and if he'd been able to shoot lasers out of his eyes, I would have looked like a piece of lace. Whatever mission he'd been on, it was forgotten now.

And *he* didn't know I had my own eleven-Hound battery system.

Before he could recover, I followed the hammerblow up with cold; with all that rain pouring down his Shield, casing him in a dome of ice was going to be a *lot* faster than it had been when we'd dueled in the arena. I sucked the heat out of the area around him so fast it looked as if I was flash-freezing him. In fact, the ice was an inch thick before he reacted and flexed his Shields to shatter the frozen shell.

Dammit. If that had only worked, I could have cut off his air and knocked him out. . . .

He tried fire bolts . . . which fizzled out in the downpour before they even reached me, something the rest of us out here had already figured out. The rain was just coming down so hard and fast, fire bolts didn't have a chance. *I guess he wasn't paying attention.* While he was launching fire bolts, I hit him with another hammerblow and followed that up with a blinding light-flash, learned from Dazzle.

"Joy! What's going on?" Kent called as Ace switched to levin bolts, which were not unlike Archer's explosive "magic arrows."

"Got company," I said shortly, bolstering my own Shields against the barrage of levin bolts. "Ace and his pet."

At least this time he doesn't have access to a laser. One thing we did know, the Folk had absolutely no use for our tech and either abandoned it or left it melted and useless when they found it.

Both of them were standing higher than me, right at the level of the mud or a little above. Ace and his pet Mage must have created some sort of solid surface out of the water; I'd have given an awful lot to know how they'd done that. Or maybe the Folk Mage was floating them both; we knew the Folk could float in midair and seemed to prefer floating to standing. There were rumors they could fly too, but no one had ever actually seen one doing so. Then again, why fly when you can *bamph*?

Then, suddenly, the attack stopped.

It took a moment or two before the Shields washed clear of mud again. And when we could see, my heart stopped too.

Ace stood there, grinning, looking just as lively as before. The Folk Mage with him didn't look particularly tired either. And standing to either side of his Shield bubble were Drakken. Huge, golden-eyed, *hungry*-looking Drakken.

My mind went absolutely blank.

"Like my new Hounds?" Ace called with a sneer in his voice.

"I think they're a definite upgrade on the old ones. You might as well keep my mutts, ungrateful whelps that they are. I like the new ones better."

I'd thought I was afraid before. That fear was not even close to what I was feeling now. This was way out of my league. It was too late to run, there was nowhere to hide, and I couldn't handle a single small-size Drakken alone—Ace had two, two of the biggest Drakken I'd ever seen.

Bya whimpered, staring up at the two monsters as they stared down at us. I would have whimpered, if I could have gotten my paralyzed throat to produce a sound.

How tall were they? All I knew was that they seemed to fill half the sky. I felt like a bug. Rain sheeted down the Drakken's heads, creating waterfalls that cascaded over their scales and down their shoulders. Their golden eyes were like searchlights, pinning us where we stood in the mud. They didn't move; they just stood there, breathing, biding their time before they turned us into snacks. The only reason I could tell they were alive and not some illusion was the perfection of those streams of water tumbling down their scales, as if they were mountains in a Japanese wall scroll. When people make illusions, they usually forget details like that.

And then, they moved. Not much. They just arched their necks and brought their heads down a little farther. Just enough so that it was completely obvious that they were lazily deciding how they would attack us.

"So how should we do this, do you think?" Ace continued, an evil glee in his voice. "Should I let them pick off your Hounds first? Should I give your Hounds the option to desert *you?* Should—"

There was no warning. One moment, those monstrous heads were looming over us. Then in the time it took me to blink—

—in no more than a second, maybe less, everything changed.

Because something invisible *slammed* their heads together, just like those pre-Diseray 'toons, where one anthropomorphic animal would put a paw on either side of the heads of two others and slam their heads together to teach them a lesson.

They hung above me for a moment like that, mirror-image Drakken heads slightly deformed, flattened, against a space between their heads, invisible except for the fact that their heads were pancaked against it; it was poised right between them.

A moment later, whatever had just hit them let them go again, leaving the two Drakken reeling and swaying like a pair of drunks. If Drakken could be concussed, these surely were.

And before I could take another breath, I got a glimpse of something distorting the rain in the air between their heads, something like an invisible disk set edgewise toward me, made visible only by the way the rain didn't fall through it. Then the Drakken's heads *slammed* together again, impacting that disk.

This time I snapped out of my paralysis and reacted. I gathered all the magic energy I could and fired off two of the most powerful levin bolts I'd ever produced at their distorted faces.

That force—no, *forces*—let them go again, as my levin bolts connected and blasted holes right in the centers of the Drakken's foreheads.

And over the comm I heard Steel saying *"You're welcome,"* while Hammer and Knight whooped in the background.

I started thinking instead of reacting, and I realized I had just seen Hammer *and* Steel *and* White Knight pull off the biggest Shield Slam that anyone had ever seen, with Steel's rock-hard Wall between the two Drakken making sure Hammer and Mark got the maximum benefit off their head slam.

"Thank you," I whispered over the comm. Whispered, because I could scarcely believe what had just happened. It was like one of Knight's Christer miracles.

The Drakken, now quite, quite dead, toppled over like a pair of trees. They fell over sideways rather than squashing the Hounds and me; I think that was with a little help from Steel and Mark. When they hit the ground, it shook everything, and they sent up a huge splash of mud and water over us. And once again, we were inundated, and I had to wait for the rain to clear the mud off our Shields before I could see.

When the mud sluiced away, there were Ace and his Mage, staring at us, paralyzed with shock, as if they could not believe what had just happened to turn the tables on them.

But not for long. Now it was *my* turn.

The deaths of those behemoths had sent a huge surge of manna to our Hounds, and they filled me with so much magic I felt as if every hair on my body was standing on end. In quick succession, I sent off a levin bolt with a rider, a spell to turn Ace's Shield brittle, and followed it up with a series of flash-bangs designed to leave him blinded and deafened. I followed *that* with Shield-pushes, concussive shoves like weaker versions of what Hammer could do, to test whether Ace had anchored his Shield to the ground or not, and give him a rude awakening in either case.

The answer was, he had not. He was "floating" his Shield, and that was a major mistake on his part. It meant that I could hit him with his own Shield, shove it right into him, hard, and I did just that.

The first push knocked him and the Mage over, slamming him with his own Shield as I shoved it back about ten feet. The second push sent them both tumbling into the mud as they lost control over what was keeping them out of the muck. And the third just added insult to injury, bouncing them around within the skittering Shield-sphere, like a couple of pebbles rattling around inside a gourd.

Then I landed a concussive blow on the top of the Shield, and it shattered, leaving them utterly unprotected—and clean, since the drenching downpour washed them both free of all the mud they'd collected on their trip.

That was when the Folk Mage decided he'd had enough. But instead of opening a Portal and pulling Ace with him as he'd done the last time, he *bamphed* out, leaving Ace standing there, with no Shield, no "battery," and no backup.

Ace had been abandoned by his allies.

Guess Ace wore out his welcome. Or they decided he wasn't worth the trouble of defending anymore.

With a look of utter panic on his face, he turned away from me and tried to run. But as I already knew, running in calf-deep mud in an epic downpour is an exercise in futility. I swung up on Dusana, and we pursued—but not before Myrrdhin and Gwalchmai, who didn't need to wait for me to get on Dusana's back, *bamphed* ahead of us and leapt on Ace, knocking him down into the mire until the rest of us could catch up.

Since Ace was already cut off, I took a little time getting Hold and Strike up out of the mud and onto Dusana with me. Meanwhile, Myrrdhin and Gwalchmai were between Ace and his escape path, teeth bared and growling. At least, I thought they were growling. I could see them vibrating, though I couldn't hear anything over the pouring rain and the distant sounds of battle.

Finally we *bamphed* to where he was sprawled, and I looked down on him, on his hands and knees in mud so deep it was all he could do to keep his head above it, and I will not lie, I considered murdering him right then and there. It would have been easy: knock him unconscious, let him fall facedown in the mud and rain, and let him drown in it. Not one person would have blamed me. A horrible death but no less horrible than the one he had surely left Karly to, or the one he'd contemplated for me, as a chew toy between two Drakken.

It wasn't pity that kept me from doing it because I hadn't one drop of pity to spare for him. To my mind, craziness was not an excuse for what he'd done. The fact was, he'd started down that path before he went crazy, and "crazy" just came along for the ride. It was partly the feeling that although he deserved a wretched death, I shouldn't be the one that delivered it. I wasn't judge, jury, and executioner; I was only *one* of the long line of people he'd wronged. And it was mostly the fact that I wanted answers, and I wasn't going to get them out of a dead man.

So I had Dusana clamp his teeth into the back of Ace's jacket and haul him erect by his fancy collar. Then I had Shinje go all tentacles and wrap him up like a mummy, pinning his arms and hands to his sides and covering his mouth so there was no way he would be able to manage so much as a hint of a spell. Then, finally, I was able to consult my Perscom as to where on the field everyone was, and slog back through the mud to meet up with my team, the wrapped-up Ace in tow.

Not exactly a triumphal procession, but I've never exactly gone in for triumphal processions anyway. They were just another kind of fuss, and I'd had more than enough fuss in my life so far to make me wish for invisibility.

I'm not sure I have ever seen anything more welcome than that dome of Shield, rain sluicing off it, with everyone on my team packed together underneath it. They dropped it long enough for us to join them, then brought it up again, but at this point, it was less for protection against Othersiders and more to keep off the rain and keep *in* the blessed warmth that Hudson was generating. Oh, warmth at last! It was like Heaven. I was finally able to stop clenching my jaw to keep my teeth from chattering. Hold and Strike slid off Dusana's back.

I wonder what he's pulling the heat from. Somewhere out there, I bet there's an ice rink forming.

The magic Hudson had invoked wasn't doing anything about the mud, but once the Shield was up, our clothes started steaming and I, at least, stopped shivering. Not "dry" but at least a little drier.

"Handing team back to you, Elite Joyeaux," Hammer said formally as everyone eyed Ace, who looked like nothing so much as a skein of muddy, multicolored rope with four sets of eyes and a pair of mud-caked legs. "Welcome back."

"Very, very, very glad to be back," I said fervently. "Excellent save, guys."

White Knight—who was nothing like "white" at this point, since he was as mud covered as the rest of us—must obviously have joined my team at some point after I handed them off to Hammer. I raised an eyebrow at him. He grinned and shrugged.

He seemed to be smiling more and more these days. The great stone monolith was cracking, and so far as I was concerned, that was a good thing.

"And what brought you to our part of the battleground?" I asked.

He shrugged. "My Hounds got smacked out of the sky, then got driven into the mud, and the team had to go on without me. By the time I got them free of it, they were drenched, and their wings were too heavy to fly in this deluge, so once we got moving again, we hooked up with what was nearest. Happened to be your team."

I looked at his Hounds; poor things, they looked utterly miserable, their legs sunk in the muck, their beautiful white coats caked with mud, their graceful white wings clamped tight to their backs, sodden and useless. I slid down off Dusana's back, and with Mark's help and Dusana's agreement, we boosted them up onto Dusana's back in my place. Dusana obligingly sprouted some new spikes to hold them in place. They looked much happier.

"My good luck that you did," I said. "Seeing those Drakken heads splat together might be the most beautiful thing I've ever had the pleasure of beholding."

Knight, Hammer, and Steel grinned at each other and engaged in a three-way fist bump. I could foresee a very fruitful partnership there. I could also foresee me playing bait a lot. . . . Oh, well. Steel was pretty mired too, and I didn't envy him getting those casts cleaned out, even if they were hardened-resin bandage.

Maybe when he got back, they'd just stand him in a shower until he stopped shedding mud.

"What are our current orders?" I continued, looking over at Hammer and not wanting to joggle the armorer's elbow if I could get the information I needed without interrupting him.

"Protect the pylon," Hammer said. "PsiCorps turned up, about a quarter of the strength of the last time, but they're turning some of the bigger monsters, and that's helping. We're winning. Kent doesn't know what's happened since Ace made his appearance here—"

"So I'd better report in." I toggled the general frequency. "Elite Joyeaux, status report."

While I waited for an answer, occasional bands of demoralized Othersiders blundered into our sphere of influence. By the time they realized that they were in danger, we'd cut them down, adding to the overflowing manna and magic energy. There was *so* much, in fact, that we did something we'd never done in the middle of a battle; we started using it to heal up any injuries we or the Hounds had taken. Somewhat to my surprise, it was dour Tobor and saturnine Denali who had actual healing magic spells in their arsenals. Hunters with healing magic are pretty rare; we're better at taking things apart than putting them together again.

"Status report, Elite Joyeaux."

"Hammer has passed back team command. Encountered and recaptured renegade Ace. Folk Mage backing him deserted him. Currently experiencing only light opposition." I figured that summed things up pretty well.

"Hold your position. Defend the pylon. Sending a pickup team for your prisoner. They'll be coming from the other side of the

Barrier; until further notice, anything that approaches you from this side is not a friendly, so attack at will and with lethal force."

Well, that was clear enough. And it suggested that some of the enemy might have tried using illusions to pass as Hunters or army. Hags, probably, they were the best at illusions. So we held position and took out opposition until no more opposition was turning up.

I was frankly expecting an army squad to come fetch Ace, but what eventually came sloshing toward us out of the storm from the direction of the pylon was a special Apex PD unit. There were a half a dozen APD in body armor, armed to the teeth, and a medic. They even had two rocket-propelled grenade launchers with them, and I wished strongly I'd had *those* around when I'd first seen Ace's Drakken. We dropped the Shield to allow them to join us.

They appeared very grateful for the heat, once we got it back up. "We're here for the prisoner," said the one with sergeant's markings. "Special orders from Prefect Charmand."

Oho. So Uncle is not going to let Ace slip out of his hands a second time. No more chances for the army to lose him. No more chances for the army to stall off an interrogation. That cheered me up immensely. "Here he is," I said as someone shoved the Shinje-wrapped renegade toward the newcomers. "Are you going to need to take my Hound with you?"

They all eyed the Shinje-and-Ace bundle with varying degrees of startlement and bewilderment. "That's—a Hound?" the sergeant finally asked.

"Anything that looks like rainbow rope is, yes," I confirmed. "The rest is the prisoner."

They looked the situation, and Ace, up and down for a while, trying to decide how to proceed, because the mud and the rain were certainly going to complicate getting him back to a secure pod on the other side of the Barrier. Ace's eyes were dilated. I couldn't tell if it was from fear, insanity, or rage. Maybe all three. Shinje seemed highly amused. Myrrdhin and Gwalchmai were on the alert for the faintest hint of trouble from their former master. I got the distinct feeling they'd have been perfectly pleased to murder him themselves. Or at least, sink their teeth into him and shake until I ordered them to let him go.

Oh, that was tempting....

"Well, I have an idea. Can you get your Hound to give me a way to his neck?" the medic asked finally. Shinje obligingly moved tentacles and bared Ace's neck on the left side; the medic murmured his thanks and went in with a hypospray. In a couple of minutes, Ace's eyes lost focus, and his legs started to buckle until Shinje reconfigured himself to add some support. "That's a powerful hypnotic; it's safe to let him go at this point," the medic said. "He couldn't spellcast his way out of a wet paper bag now, but we'll still be able to get him to the other side under his own power."

Shinje gingerly unwrapped Ace, who appeared to be utterly unaware of his surroundings now. He swayed where he stood, as two APD supported him on either side. He let the APD put him into a straitjacket and strap his arms down, demonstrating nothing but complete docility.

"Are you sure you're going to be able to get him back all right?" I asked worriedly. After all, he'd escaped once—

"There's a secure pod waiting for us on the other side of the Barrier," the sergeant assured me. "And once we get him there, the medic has enough tranqs and hypnotics to sedate a Drakken. But you're right: we should take every possible precaution with him.

Give us an escort to the pylon door, keep your eyes peeled for Othersiders making a last-minute try for him, and once we have him on the other side of the Barrier, we'll get him out of your hair."

Well, that was just fine with us; we did exactly that, keeping our Shield up, most of the Hounds outside it, running scout. Dusana stayed in the Shield with all four of Knight's Hounds keeping eyes on Ace at all times, until we reached the base of the pylon and the door in it. There, the APD squad stuffed Ace through and loaded him straight into the secure pod. Their sergeant came back and took his leave of us, and we went back to mopping up whatever small fry came our way.

There was no definitive "end" to this fight; eventually the field commanders decided that there were no more open Portals, that every Othersider of any note was either dead or disappeared, and whatever creatures were left could be dealt with when the storm was over if they were stupid enough to stick around. There was no way choppers were going to be able to fly, and the storm didn't look as if it was going to end for another eight to twelve hours, so we all trudged back across the Barrier using the doors in the pylons. By "we," I mean the Hunters. The Psimons were still on the "safe" side of the Barrier, just as they had been the last time—although they looked pretty unhappy about it. They might not have been knee-deep in mud, but there wasn't anything keeping the rain off them. The army had brought in troop carriers from the combat side of the Barrier to bring their people here, and they would use the same means to take them back to the base.

As for us, we lucked out; by virtue of the fact that we were closest to our pylon, we got to exit first. "My god," said Souxie while we filed out of the door onto grass instead of mud and saw the transport pods lined up on the road, waiting to take us home. "It's over. We lived!"

"We did," Hammer agreed as Glyphs hit the grass and the Hounds leapt gratefully through the Way to get back to whatever it was *they* called home. I hoped there was something like hot baths and soft beds waiting for them over there. "And I don't think the Othersiders are going to try that again."

"So may it be," I murmured, and followed the others at a tired trot for the pods.

20

ACE SAT IN A chair in an otherwise bare gray interrogation room, behind one-way mirror. There were a couple of medics in the room with him. They were very good at their jobs. Even better was the Psimon that was behind the one-way mirror, standing next to Uncle.

That Psimon was, of course, Abigail Drift, the Psimon in charge of all of PsiCorps.

I stood on the other side of *another* pane of one-way mirror, watching and listening to both of them. Their voices came through a speaker in the wall, tinny but clear enough. I was wearing the strongest Psi-shield ever made, turned on to a level so high that I actually felt it, as if someone had wrapped my brain inside a dozen layers of wool batting. If Abigail Drift knew I was here, she had to be superhuman. If she was sensitive enough and paying attention to what was behind her, she might realize there was *someone* here, just by the interference pattern the Psi-shield was making, but she would never be able to tell it was me. I was here at Uncle's invitation and without anyone else's knowledge. So far as anyone else was concerned, I was waiting for Uncle in his inner office, scheduled to have lunch with him in the Sky Lounge.

One of the medics kept Ace pumped full of hypnotics; the other read him questions off a touch pad. Abigail Drift had a matching touch pad; I assume she was the one supplying the questions. Ace's voice came through a speaker in the wall too, but it didn't matter what he said. The hypnotics guaranteed he could not keep *his* thoughts blocked, and Abigail Drift was here to read them for herself.

They'd been spending the last half hour establishing the correct level of drugs in his system and asking a lot of questions we already knew the answers to, in order to give Drift a sort of baseline to work from. I tensed because now we were going to get to the questions that I was most interested in. The medic cleared his throat and began. "Were you responsible for the presence of the vampire within the storm sewer tunnels that ambushed and killed Hunter Karly?"

Ace just laughed at him. Drift frowned.

"Well?" Uncle demanded. "Did he—"

"It's complicated," Drift interrupted irritably. "Give me a moment."

I frowned too. "It's complicated" was not an answer I had expected. How could it be "complicated"? Either he had gotten that fang-face into the tunnel, intending it to attack *me,* or he hadn't.

The medic tried again. "Did you arrange for the vampire to be in that section of tunnels?"

Ace mumbled something that didn't quite make it through two sets of speakers, but Drift gave an abrupt nod. "As I said, it's complicated," she repeated. "Ace did not personally plant the monster in the tunnels, nor did he smuggle it past the Prime Barrier. He *did* know that *something* unpleasant would be planted there because he transmitted Hunter Joyeaux's scheduling information to someone."

"Transmitted *how*?" Uncle asked sharply. "Every frequency transmitting into and out of Hunter HQ is closely monitored! And outside of the HQ, every moment of a Hunter's activities is recorded!"

"Who were you working with when you attempted to murder Hunter Joyeaux at her Trials?" the medic continued.

"Yes, well... if you find a way to monitor psychic transmissions, I would very much like to hear about it," Drift replied dryly. "Because, according to what is in his memory, he 'transmitted' it by thinking about it, while he was patrolling."

Uncle's face was unreadable. Drift's was more than unreadable; she looked like a wax sculpture.

"Now, if you would be so kind, *shut up,* Charmand," Drift continued. "I'm following memory traces and I don't need any distraction."

I held as still as ever I had while stalking my prey on the Mountain. If Drift could be trusted to tell us the truth—if Ace's partner had been a Psimon, she probably would never tell us—

But there's the problem. It might have been a Psimon, but it might not have been, I could not help thinking. Because Folk had psionic powers too. And we didn't know how strong they were. Could they read thoughts from outside the Barriers? Maybe.

Hadn't I been perfectly prepared to believe they could pick up mere thoughts about them from the playgoers watching *A Midsummer Night's Dream*?

"It seems," Drift said, her voice curiously uninflected, "that his first contact with this … unknown … occurred while he was taking a little excursion to a private party outside the Prime Barrier, shortly after your niece arrived and began making such a splash. The excursion was authorized, a 'fan service' visit to one of his admirers who possessed a highly protected and fortified villa and vineyard out there. Ostensibly, this was a simple meet and greet, but there was psionic contact with an unknown person that Ace obviously did not bother to report. There was a suggestion that if Ace's position as number one in the rankings was seriously challenged, the contactor was prepared to help him reestablish himself. Ace assumed the contact was either from one of the guests who had hidden Psi-talents, or from a Psimon in the employ of one of the guests. Knowing what we know now, however …"

Uncle nodded. "It could have been a human with Psi-talents. Or it could have been one of the Folk."

Drift made some notes on the pad. The medics continued to question Ace. Drift concentrated on following Ace's thoughts, which were surely wandering at this point. "Ace was subject to several more attempts at contact, all of them when he was away from your HQ, and all of them when he was Hunting solo or visiting wealthy or otherwise important fans. He ignored them, although he did not report them; my sense is that he was waiting for a …" She paused. "A 'better offer.' I am not sure what a 'better offer' would be, and I'm not sure he had anything concrete in mind. However, once his brother died, he answered the next attempt that was made at contact. That was when he transmitted Hunter Joyeaux's schedule."

Uncle nodded. "I think we can deduce the rest, although I would like you to confirm the deduction, Drift."

"That when the initial attempt failed, and Joyeaux elected to attempt the Elite Trials, Ace transmitted this as well, and instructions were given him as to how to proceed at the Trials themselves." Drift's mouth thinned into a hard, angry line. "I do see him acquiring the laser himself, however, though he was told where it would be and how to conceal it on his person. So there was never a point of physical contact between himself and his associate."

"Convenient," Uncle said dryly.

Convenient for Ace? Or convenient for Drift? Would one of the Folk even know what a laser was? We tended not to use them against Othersiders, since they healed up too fast from any injury that wasn't caused by iron or steel.

"Then, once he was imprisoned, the contacts continued," Drift went on, ignoring, at least outwardly, any implications in Uncle's comment. "And before you ask, he was unable to tell if this was the same person over and over, or two or more people. The memory he has is of a mental voice with no suggestion of gender, and no images at all. That was how his escape was arranged. And at that point, the Folk he was with spoke to him directly. So he was never able to tell which one of them—if any—was his patron."

It didn't have to be a Psimon or *a Folk Mage,* I thought to myself. *There's no reason why it couldn't have been both. Working together.* But I had no proof, other than the fact that I really disliked Abigail Drift in particular and Psimons in general.

Uncle gave me a little hand signal that told me I should go back to his office and wait for him there. Although I was really curious to hear what else was forthcoming, I obeyed, using the private elevator, a couple of barely used corridors, and a secret back door to get from the interrogation rooms to the office without encountering anyone. So when he returned—without Drift, I was happy to see—I was where I was "supposed" to be.

He was rubbing the back of his neck as he entered. "I sometimes think I wear a Psi-shield around Drift as much to irritate her as to keep her out of my head." He chuckled, motioning for me to remain seated. "She really, truly hates being around people she can't read. Here." He handed me a memory stick. "The recording of the session with Ace and the recording of Drift and myself are both on there. If you catch anything I didn't, let me know through Kent. Otherwise, erase it when you're sure you have everything you want to know."

"Then I'd never erase it," I pointed out. "Because what I want to know is probably not on there. I'll erase it when I've memorized it."

Uncle sat down at his desk and took care of a few things while I fast-forwarded to where he'd sent me away, but I didn't learn anything. Drift was angry and evasive and gave away nothing. Ace rambled like someone talking in his sleep. I sighed and pulled the stick out of my Perscom and tucked it into a pocket sewn—by me, and by hand—into the inside of my tunic.

"One other thing, Joy," Uncle said, without looking up from his keyboard. "During the first attempt by the Othersiders to destroy a pylon, you recall when PsiCorps came riding in like the cavalry to save the day?"

I made a face. "I'm not likely to forget."

"And you may recall that a great many of those Psimons collapsed before it was all over."

I nodded. He swiveled one of his monitors to face me. "Not all of them recovered. This is what the dead ones looked like."

I found myself staring at vid of a dead Psimon being collected by PsiCorps med techs. An apparently *ancient* dead Psimon, who looked almost exactly like the ones I had found in the storm sewers under the Hub. My jaw dropped, and Uncle swiveled his monitor back around. "And thanks to all the vid taken at the Barrier, we know, for a fact, that before they collapsed, those elderly Psimons were quite young and healthy Psimons. That's why they could only field a quarter of their numbers the second time."

"But what does that *mean*?" I asked, bewildered.

"Probably that Drift is exposing some, if not all, of her Psimons to some experimental procedure, which has unintended consequences, a procedure she doesn't want the rest of us to know about." Uncle shrugged. "The reason is obvious. Drift will stop at nothing to have PsiCorps supplant the Hunters as the primary guardians of Apex and the territories. I suspect that she intended to paint PsiCorps as the real saviors of Apex, and not the Hunters, but she assumed that the one attempt at breaching the Barrier was the only one there would be. And I don't think she realized that what she'd done to her Psimons would be fatal in so high a percentage."

I had very mixed feelings. On the one hand, I was begrudgingly grateful to PsiCorps because the appearance of the Psimons at the Barrier really *had* pulled our fat out of the fire at a point where we were seriously outgunned. And I could not in good conscience feel anything but horrible that it had cost so many of them their lives.

On the other hand—I was really, *really*, angry at Drift. First of all, that she'd done this to her own people; second, that she'd tried to pin the initial deaths on *me*; and third, that she hadn't done the smart thing and worked with the Hunters on this. If she hadn't thought of herself and her power games first and foremost, we'd probably have a lot fewer dead Psimons—

Uncle was watching my face closely and nodded as I looked up at him, making no effort to hide my anger. "Drift is a fool, but she's a ruthless fool," he said. "And she is not someone I care to turn my back on. My hope is that she'll go hunting through the Psimons still left alive for whoever was working with Ace, if only to get some kind of advantage out of the information. I personally don't believe she'll find anything. But . . ."

"But?" I prompted him.

"It's possible she's playing an even deeper game than I thought," Uncle admitted, looking very troubled indeed. Then he shook it off. "But it's equally possible that she *will* find a renegade or at least the traces of one. Sufficient unto the day are the troubles thereof." He got up and gestured for me to join him. "Now I have starved you long enough. Let's go up to lunch."

We passed Josh coming into the office just as we were leaving it. My heart felt like it was being squeezed by a giant hand, but I nodded to him in a cool but cordial fashion. He nodded back to me, though his eyes had a hurt look to them as he opened the door for us.

As I could have predicted, we were just about to order dessert when my Perscom went off. I looked at it and sighed. "Drakken at a coastal weather station," I said apologetically. "I have to go."

"There's a helipad on the roof," Uncle said immediately, doing something with *his* Perscom. "The elevator—"

But I was already running for the elevator, which opened at my approach and went up a floor instead of down. I emerged on the windy rooftop, and within five minutes, a chopper came in hot, with Hammer beckoning to me from its open door. I groaned a little as I ran for it, and took his hand so he could pull me in. *Playing bait again.*

They'd brought my load-out with them, and as I kitted up and the chopper banked sharply to head toward the coast, I got a good long look at the side of the building that held Uncle's office. You couldn't *see* anything, of course, except for the blank wall. Nobody had the sort of glass-wall buildings anymore that they'd had before the Diseray. It was all armor plating, from first floor to last. Even the Sky Lounge didn't have actual windows, just vidscreens repeating what cameras placed on the outside of the building saw. But I knew where his office was, and that only served to remind me that I was playing bait for more than just Drakken. In fact, I'd been playing bait from the moment I arrived here; just now, I was aware of the fact.

And I thought I might know what it was Uncle had thought of but had not said. If Abigail Drift was ruthless enough, it was entirely possible that "deep game" she was playing involved her—and the Folk. Because she'd had to have gotten this dangerous new technique of boosting the power of her Psimons from somewhere, and the Folk knew more about psionics than we did.

That, however, was above my pay grade. There were Drakken that needed slaying.

And a City, and Cits to defend.

And I am a Hunter.

TURN THE PAGE FOR A SNEAK PEEK

#1 *NEW YORK TIMES* BEST-SELLING AUTHOR
MERCEDES LACKEY

APEX

A HUNTER NOVEL

2

A YEAR AGO—

A year ago, I was a different person, just one of the Hunters at the Monastery on the Mountain. A Hunter who kept our area free of monsters, under the tutelage and direction of my Masters. A Hunter who'd lived in a place so different from Apex and the other big cities it might just as well have been on another planet.

A year ago, I'd never given a thought to Apex, except once in a great while when I'd watched some important news vid, or someone decided to play something that had been sent out to us turnips by the mail-car that came once a week on the supply train. I'd never thought I would leave the Monastery, and never wanted to.

A year ago, the Elite had been an untouchable legend to me, mysterious heroes I wasn't entirely sure were real.

A year ago, I had never faced a Folk Mage on my own.

My Masters always told me that a lot can change in a year. Well, now I was in Apex, I was one of the Elite, and it didn't look as if I was ever going to go home again. I didn't even recognize the person I saw in the mirror anymore.

A mere two months ago I hadn't been sure Apex was going to survive. I'd been even less sure that *I* was going to. Because two months ago, the Othersiders had hit us at the Prime Barrier around Apex with everything they had, and they very nearly ran over the top of us. It would have been the Diseray all over again, at least as far as the capitol city had been concerned.

We'd won in the end, but the two Battles of the Barrier had nearly flattened the Elite. I still could scarcely believe we'd not only survived it but had driven them back.

Of course it would have been too much to ask that the Battles of the Barrier had finished the Othersiders. Far from it. We got a month of respite, and then they were at our throats again. Except now the Othersiders were concentrating on targets away from Apex; smaller cities, towns, even villages, but by chopper, all within a couple hours of Apex at most.

So far as the Cits of Apex were concerned, everything was back to normal. The Hunters and the Psimons had driven the monsters away, and there had never been the slightest danger that their safe and ordered lives were about to come crashing down around them.

If I thought about it at all, it would make me crazy. On the Mountain, we all lived our lives with a healthy sense of paranoia and self-preservation. Here . . . the Cits were oblivious.

Be that as it may, the army and the Elite were still getting hammered. Callouts every day and every night, never less than two in twenty-four hours, sometimes six, even eight on the horrible days. The Elite were split into a day and a night shift, twelve hours on, twelve off—except any of us could get called out even when we were asleep, if things were bad enough. No one had died—yet. But now I remembered fondly the days when I was "just" a Hunter of Apex and got a day off if I had two strenuous Hunts in a row. And the days when I'd been a Hunter on the Mountain—when we had all the resources of each other *and* the Masters at the Monastery— seemed a far-off dream.

Today the callout was a town fifteen minutes by chopper from the Prime Barrier, not even a fortified one. At this point, I didn't even remember the names of the towns we were defending any-more. This was a grain-farming center, that much I knew. They'd had walls and heavy defenses at one point, but they must have figured they were safe, that the Elite could handle anything that got close to them, because those walls and defenses had been taken down years ago.

Anyone who'd been raised on the Mountain and in the com-munities we protected could have told them that removing defenses was a bad move. But there it was again; they were close enough to Apex that some of the complacency had bled over.

The army had gotten there before us; they were based on the west side of Apex, a lot closer to this spot than we were. I was in the last chopper the Elite sent out, riding solo. I'd been the last one *in* from the previous fight, and I'd literally jumped from a chopper running low on fuel to one waiting for me at HQ.

"*Joy,*" Kent said over my comm channel, as the new chopper

slowed to let me drop off. *"Some of the Othersiders have penetrated the town."*

I swore to myself; Kent continued. *"We're to the west. Most of the Othersiders are facing off with the army. There's supposed to be three Folk Mages here."*

Of course. Since the Battles, we'd never seen Othersiders without at least one Folk Mage with them.

The chopper hovered, and I bailed, hitting the ground and rolling, then to my feet again. "I'm on the ground, east side of town, Kent," I replied.

"Hammer and Steel were in the chopper before you. I sent them into town. You follow and hook up with them."

"Roger," I replied. I did the fast-and-dirty summons, bringing the Hounds over by opening the Way purely on magic energy, will, and the Mandalas on the backs of my hands. I'd been doing this so much lately that I didn't even notice the Mandalas burning as I brought the Hounds over. I ran in on foot, with Hounds in front of me acting as scouts, Hounds behind me guarding our backs, and Bya and Myrrdhin right beside me. My original seven were in their *Alebrije* forms, appearing as weird animals with crazy patterns and colors, the better to be seen at a distance. Hold and Strike, ahead of me, were a pair of wolves, if wolves were made of shadow. They had been Karly's before she was murdered. Myrrdhin and Gwalchmai, both dark-silver gargoyles with silver eyes, had been Ace's before he betrayed us all by trying to murder me. I could speak telepathically with all of them except Hold and Strike, but the others would tell them what they needed to know.

We passed the wrecked grain silos, following the paved main road into town. Probably held several thousand people. About half the buildings were "old-style," built defensively, solid blocks of 'crete with very narrow windows, if they had any windows at all. Unfortunately, the other half of the buildings were wooden and brick structures, and while I am sure they were pleasant to live in, they were . . . flammable. And dead easy to break into. I just hoped that the Cits here had had the sense to make for the old-style buildings when the attack came.

Because a lot of those other buildings were burning.

In moments, I was deep into the town, and by now the air was thick enough to cut. I could tell by the noise that the army was pounding away at the Othersiders outside the town limits. I was wearing my gas mask and goggles as protection against the smoke, or I wouldn't have been able to see or breathe. And I was keyed up and alert, with a nice edge of fear. *The Hunter that isn't afraid is soon to be a dead Hunter,* as my Masters said. The trick was making your fear into something you could use, rather than letting it use you.

The Hounds and I went in deeper and passed more buildings on fire—most likely the work of some sort of incendiary Othersiders like Ketzels. I kept Dusana with me and sent the others ranging along to either side, including Bya and Myrrdhin. As pack alphas and pack seconds, they would keep the others coordinated.

There was no sign of Cits, but there *were* drifts of that gray ash the *Nagas*—four-armed Othersiders that were snake on the bottom and something vaguely human on top—turned into when they were killed, with discarded swords in or near the ash. Hammer and Steel must have caught up with the Othersiders inside the town limits. Fortunately it looked as if the *Nagas* hadn't gotten as far as breaking into houses to go after the people sheltered there. And clearly the guys hadn't had as much trouble with the snakemen as I'd had when I'd first encountered them.

I stopped Dusana for a moment and tried contacting Kent. "Looks like the guys hit *Nagas* and cleared them out. They're somewhere ahead of me."

"Roger, carry on," he replied. Static flooded the channel as a plume of magical energy erupted to the northeast, visible as a dense tower of sparkling glitter over the roofs of the buildings nearest me. *"I know it looks bad, but I need your eyes and talents and most of all, your pack, right where you are. These bastards could be using their Folk Mages as a distraction from something else there in town, and if they are, I want you there to deal with it."* He cursed, then continued. *"Two of the Folk Mages are here, fancies, not ferals. The third disappeared just before we got here. Keep your head on a swivel looking for him. They're using bale-fire."* I shuddered. Balefire was kind of like napalm and just as hard to put out. Just as he said that, I heard a distant shriek over his freq and more plumes of magic appeared over the rooftops. I hoped the team could get a handle on the situation.

The smoke was thicker, billowing down the street in dense gray clouds mingled with streaks of black. I tried not to think about people who were going to come out of hiding to find everything they owned had burned up. Hopefully *they* weren't burned up. "Yes, sir," I replied. "Out."

We rounded the last corner and came out at one edge of an open space with a watch-tower in the middle. It was *really* hard to see, but I thought I spotted two moving figures on the other side of the watchtower. I urged the Pack toward them. A sudden gust cleared the smoke between us; it was Hammer and Steel. Hammer was farther away from us, shooting at something on a rooftop with a shotgun loaded with slugs instead of shot. Steel was closer, and his Hounds were packed up with Hammer's. I started to shout at him.

And that was when a flash of blue and copper suddenly appeared next to him.

Fear blazed up inside me. It was the third Folk Mage. This one didn't have a staff; he just thrust out both his hands, and Steel *flew* across the road, hit the wall of a building, and slid down it. The Folk Mage raised one hand with a fireball in it. It flamed a hideous green. Bale-fire.

"Bya!" I screamed; I couldn't pull up a spell fast enough to save him. Bya *bamphed* away from me, appearing beside Steel, and threw up his Shield, just as the Folk Mage hurled the fireball. It splattered against the Shield. The Folk Mage turned to face me. I expected him to be furious. It was a lot more unnerving to see that his face was absolutely expressionless.

I Shielded; my Hounds were already moving, rushing him. I saw a brief moment of surprise in his eyes, then he was gone. Not through a Portal; he *bamph*ed. I had no idea the Folk could *bamph*. My Hounds plunged through the empty air where he had been.

I ran to Bya and Steel. Steel was just coming around; he raised his head and rubbed the back of it. I helped him sit up, and a moment later his brother was beside us. *You are the best Hound ever*, I thought at Bya. He lolled out his tongue and grinned smugly at me.

"Give me your flashlight," Hammer said. I got it off my belt and slapped it into his outstretched hand. He half-supported Steel with one hand while he flicked the flashlight at his brother's eyes, then grunted in satisfaction. "I knew that hard head of yours would come in handy some day," he said. "Breathe deep." Steel did so. "Any stabbing pains?"

His brother shook his head slowly, then coughed. "Just got the wind knocked out of me," he said. "Where in *hell* did that come from?"

"The third Folk Mage *bamphed* in next to you," I said. "He knocked you across the square."

"Damn smoke. I didn't see anything," Hammer muttered.

"It was awful fast and your back was to him," I replied. "I wouldn't have seen him if I hadn't been looking right at you."

Hammer reached out and patted Bya. "If it hadn't been for this guy…"

Bya grinned even bigger. Which, in *Alebrije* form, was kind of unnerving. He has a *lot* of teeth. *Tell him he's welcome*, Bya said into my head. *And he owes me a Goblin at the least.*

I repeated Bya's message faithfully. Steel managed a laugh and slowly got to his feet, just in time for all three of our Perscoms to light up with a message from the armorer.

"Team HSJ, come in."

"Roger, Kent," Hammer said, speaking for all of us.

"We're getting our asses kicked out here. We're already down one army Mage. If you two think you've got the worst of it taken care of, leave Joy to clean out the small fry in town and you two rendezvous with me."

They both looked at me. I nodded, and Hammer replied, "Roger that. On our way."

Hammer hauled his brother to his feet; their Hounds packed up around them, and they lit out at the trot, disappearing into the smoke. I looked at my Hounds. "All right. Same groups as before, same tactics. Let's go."

We split up. I kept expecting more big surprises, but everything else we encountered was relatively small. Clots of Redcaps with their wicked, two-foot-long knives, a single Ogre (which looked like a shrunken version of the two-eyed giant called a Magog and carried a big wooden club for a weapon). I finally found out what it was Hammer had been shooting at: Harpies. I *really* wished that Knight and his winged Hounds were with us; I couldn't even see the Harpies, much less shoot at them.

I listened to them calling and screeching at each other up on the rooftops, veiled in smoke, and cursed. "I wish I was any good at casting illusions," I said to Dusana. "I could make the image of something small and helpless out in the street and—"

You don't need an illusion, Dusana interrupted.

Bya snorted. *Of course you don't,* he concurred. *Give me a moment.*

I'd seen him change from *Alebrije* form to greyhound before, but as he shimmered and glowed for a moment, I didn't know what to expect. When the glow faded, I was astonished to see a human toddler in Bya's place.

Is this convincing enough? he said anxiously. *I've never had the chance to practice this form.*

I got over my surprise and looked him up and down critically. "It wouldn't convince another human, but I think you'll fool the Harpies," I told him. The shape he had taken was a little crude; the face was blobby, the hair too coarse for a small child, and the limbs were too stubby. But the Harpies weren't going to notice any of that. My astonishment was more that he could actually shape-shift into human form at all. It was one more thing my Hounds could do that I had never heard of anyone else's doing.

As long as those stupid birdbrains are fooled, he replied with a snort. Then he waddled out into the middle of the street, plopped down in the dust, and started to cry.

Needless to say, he got the Harpies' attention immediately.

I might not have been able to see them through the smoke, but I could certainly hear them. Not only were they noisy fliers, but they kept screaming at each other. Dusana and I pressed ourselves back into the shadow of a doorway and waited as Bya sobbed convincingly. His imitation of a child crying was really excellent. My heart was pounding, more with excitement than anything else. This took me right back to my days on the Mountain when I used to shoot down Harpies all the time.

The Harpies couldn't resist Bya's performance, and it wasn't long before they swooped down into the street to nab him. There were three of them, practically colliding with one another in their eagerness to snatch up the tasty morsel.

That was when he turned the tables on them.

Quick as a shot, Bya morphed into *Alebrije* form, snatching the legs of two of them with tentacle-like arms and chomping down on the tail of the third. They screeched and flapped, beating him over the head with their wings. He probably couldn't have held them for very long, but he didn't have to; I got three shots off within a minute, and nailed all of them. Unlike Minotaurs, they had no resistance to bullets. Dusana jumped into the street quickly enough to suck the manna off the last of them.

About that time, the other three sets of Hounds came back to us. *We have not sniffed in every doorway and under every bush,* Myrrdhin said for all of them, *but we are certain there are no more enemies here to Hunt, unless someone opens a Portal.*

Bya regarded his second-in-command thoughtfully. *If they do that, they will do so in the middle of town,* he said. *I think that is what that Mage intended to do, and he was not expecting us to be there.*

I licked my lips, aware of how dry they were. "That would account for why he didn't just kill Steel on the spot," I said. I got my canteen out of my pack, pulled off my gas mask, and took a long drink. "He was expecting the place to be clear of us, and he reacted without thinking." I quickly put the mask back on; just the whiff of smoke I got while I was drinking was enough to make me cough.

Then we should go back to the middle of town and hide, Bya said, nodding. *Just in case.*

We made our way back to that watchtower and found doorways and overhangs to give ourselves some concealment. I crouched down behind a 'crete barrier intended to keep something from running straight at the door behind me and breaking it down. We did things like that all the time back home. Of course, it wouldn't stop a Gog, but then, there wasn't a lot that would.

I was about to feel guilty about being able to sit there and rest, when Gwalchmai alerted and a wave of *Nagas* poured through the streets straight toward us. It got . . . very busy.

By the time we were done with them, I was soaking wet with sweat, and the only thing keeping me standing was the wall at my back.

"Kent to Joy."

"Joy, copy," I replied. "We're clear here for the moment."

"Good. If you can still stand, and the town is still clear, we need you out here."

"Roger that," I said, finding another reserve of energy and pushing myself off the wall. Too bad the Hounds couldn't feed me physical strength along with the magic they fed me.

Then again, I should be counting my blessings that we'd discovered the Hounds *could* feed their Hunters magic. Without that boost, we'd have gone under months ago, at the second Barrier fight.

We made our way to the side of town where the fight was still raging. Twisty, maze-like streets such as these were another defense; only *Nagas* could "charge" through the sharp bends every twenty feet or so. But the narrow streets had trapped the smoke, which was coming from somewhere behind us now. I wondered if something had set the grain elevators on fire. If the Othersiders had settled on a war of attrition with us, taking out some of our food supplies would be a logical thing to do.

Between the streets and the smoke, I couldn't tell that we'd come to the edge of town until we were just past it. Suddenly a gust of wind blew the smoke away and I found myself looking at the back of another Folk Mage.

There weren't *three* Folk Mages, there were *four!* And not just *any* Folk Mage—this one was floating about three feet in the air, encased in his Shield bubble, a Shield so damn good and tight that it was keeping the smoke out while still letting him breathe. This was one of their big guns, someone with as much power as any three ordinary Folk Mages put together.

But this wasn't "my" Folk Mage, the one that had taken an inexplicable interest in me, although his outfit was just as elaborate as the one in lavender wore. His blond hair was shorter than the lavender one's hair—it barely came below his shoulder blades, and it was fastened into several tails by gold bands. From the back it looked to me as if he was wearing a combination of fanciful armor and ankle-length robes of various shades of gold. The armor was engraved with elaborate designs and inlaid with gemstones. The robes were heavily embroidered with gold bullion and gemstone beads.

My nerves rang with fear, like guitar strings, and my Hounds suddenly clustered themselves around me, adding their Shields to mine. Then he turned.

Like "my" Mage, he was so handsome he was somehow . . . *too* attractive. In the uncanny valley where inhuman perfection lives.

But his gold eyes lit up with an expression I did not like at all, and his smile mirrored what was in his eyes.

"Well, well, well," he said in a voice like icy velvet, if such a thing were possible. "The famous shepherd. Save your sheep, shepherd—if you can."

And before I could react to that, he conjured a Portal, stepped through it, and was gone.

Great, was all I could think, as I reeled from the shock of being recognized. *I'm famous among the Folk. This can't possibly end well.*